POWERLESS

POWERLESS

A NOVEL BY

JEFF O'HANDLEY

Published by Breaking Night Press in 2022.

Breaking Night Press
52 W. 3rd Street, Box 26551
Collegeville, PA 19426
breakingnightpress.com

ISBN-13: 978-1-735-7253-2-1

This is a work of fiction. Names, characters, places, and incidents either are the product of the author's imagination or are used fictitiously, and any resemblance to actual persons, living or dead, businesses, companies, events, or locales is entirely coincidental.

Cover art by Laura Duffy
Interior formatting by Alt 19 Creative

*For my parents, Sandy and Bill O'Handley.
I wish you could be here for this, and so much more.*

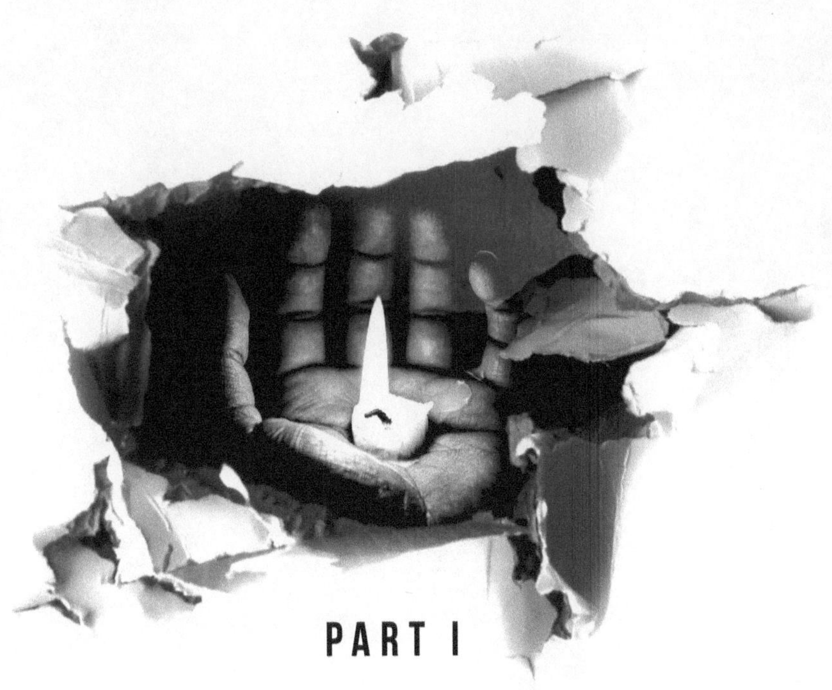

PART I

CHAPTER 1

KEVIN BARTON STEPPED into the kitchen, the morning chill fresh on his cheeks. The calendar might say spring, but the thermometer still dipped close to freezing every night, even though they were already halfway through April.

Monica sat at the table, leafing through a circular, a cup of coffee to one side of her, breakfast dishes stacked in a neat pile. Kevin felt a mild stab of resentment. *She* got to have a leisurely Saturday morning while he got saddled with the job of ferrying kids around.

"What's taking them so long?" he huffed. "It's almost a quarter after. If Dina misses that bus, the Duchess will have my head *and* hers."

"You've got time. They'll be down." She flipped a page. "Why didn't you just tell her no?" And then she added, almost but not quite under her breath, "Goldie."

He bristled at the old nickname. It had been hung on him by a sharp-tongued geology major Kevin had roomed with in college. Kevin had taken it as a compliment until he learned in his own Intro to Geology class that gold was the most malleable metal. Like many—maybe most—nicknames, it could be used with affection but wasn't always very nice.

Kevin marched past his wife, through the dining room and into the living room. He opened the door at the foot of the stairs. Loud music poured out of Kelly's room and tumbled down—a cacophony of guitars, synthesizers, and drums. The falsetto voices accompanying the music might have been the actual singers, might have been his daughter and her friend.

"Girls!" No response. "Girls!"

The music lowered—a little.

"What?" Kelly called.

"We've got to go! The car's running!"

"Be right there."

Kevin returned to the kitchen. Monica had returned her attention to the paper, leaving him to puzzle out just why he was playing chauffeur for the Duchess's daughter instead of tuning up his lawn tractor. It was no mystery, really. Lisa McCray was an imperious woman—which was why Monica had dubbed her the Duchess in the first place—but it wasn't just her presumption of entitlement that had led him to say, "Sure, Lisa, that's no problem," when she had called an hour and a half ago. He told himself she was in a bind, she needed help, it was the right thing to do. And Dina was at his house already anyway, after yet another sleepover. It rankled him, though; there was always somewhere else Lisa had to go, always some other place she just had to be, and while Kevin really didn't mind driving Dina up to the school to catch the bus for her track meet, Lisa did this stuff all the time. And he let her get away with it. All. The. Time. Twenty years later, he was still "Goldie" Barton.

"Relax," Monica said, as he completed his second circuit around the sunny kitchen. "You'll have time to get the lawn done when you come back."

"It's not the lawn I'm worried about. If she misses that bus, I'm not driving her up to Herkimer."

Monica's arched brow refuted his statement.

In the basement, the furnace roared to life. The refrigerator hummed. A voice murmured from the radio, something about the expanding Islamic State. The clock on the wall ticked, the second hand jerking from number to number. Finally, feet thundered down the stairs, and the girls plowed into the room—Kelly short and dark-haired like her mother, and Dina McCray, tall and fair. Dina had a massive backpack slung over one shoulder, a small overnight bag on the other. She wore a warm-up jacket, a pair of track shorts that were almost nonexistent, and electric pink running shoes. She threw an arm around Kelly's shoulder and stooped so they could go cheek-to-cheek.

"I'm so sorry I have to leave my darling Kelly and adored second family," she declared.

"Okay, break it up, we've got to go," Kevin said, though he smiled in spite of himself and the pressure of time.

"Thanks so much, Momma B." Dina bent and planted a loud kiss on Monica's cheek. While Monica was distracted, Dina snuck the last piece of bacon off her plate.

"Anytime, Dina. Good luck at your race. And don't think I didn't see that."

Dina made her best starving waif face, all eyes and sucked-in cheeks as she held the bacon in the air between them. Monica responded with the cold-eyed squint of a gunslinger. They stared each other down while the clock ticked away the seconds, five . . . ten . . .

Dina broke first. She snorted, and the waif was replaced by a giggling sixteen-year-old. "One day, I'll get you," she said, holding out the bacon to Monica.

"Not today, grasshopper." She waved off the slice. "Take it. Better get out of here before you're late."

A burst of static squawked from the radio. The kitchen light went out. Appliances fell silent, leaving them with only the gurgle of refrigerant settling in the refrigerator.

"Power's out," Kelly said, as if they couldn't see that for themselves.

"I wonder why," Monica said.

"Who knows?" Kevin eyed the clock. Ten fifteen, no time to spare. "Let's go, let's go, let's go."

He ushered them out the door to the car. The girls crammed themselves into the back seat, Dina's bags between them. Her school backpack looked about as big as the one Neil Armstrong carried on the moon. Kevin stepped on the brake and put the car in reverse—or tried to. The lever wouldn't budge. He tried again. Nothing.

"What the hell?"

"Quarter for the jar," Kelly said.

"Hell is not a swear."

"It would be if I said it."

The key was in the ON position. Confused, Kevin turned it off then back to the start position. Nothing happened. The engine didn't crank. Worse, the car was totally silent: no buzzers, no bells, no idiot lights flashing.

"Gee, Dad, are you sure there's gas in it?"

"Yes, Kelly, there's gas in it. Give a kid a learner's permit and she thinks she knows everything. We'll have to try Rex."

Rex was Monica's jeep. The girls hoisted Dina's bag out of the car and got into Rex's back seat. Kevin pulled the keys from their hiding place above the visor.

"Sorry, Dina," he said.

"It's okay, Mr. B. What time is it?"

He glanced at his watch. "Ten fifteen. We should be okay."

Something tickled at the back of his mind, something not quite right—besides his car not working for no good reason, that is. He shrugged it off and turned the key.

Nothing happened.

Kevin blew a long sigh to the car's ceiling. "You have got to be f—effing kidding."

"Ooh, Dad, that would have been worth a buck at least."

He forced a smile and tried again. Again, nothing.

"How can two cars stop working at exactly the same time?" He met Dina's eyes in the rearview mirror. "Do you know anyone in town who's on the team? Maybe we can catch them before they leave."

Dina screwed up her face in thought. "Connor Owens?"

"Bleah," Kelly said. "He's a jerk."

"He's nicer at track than in the school. Maybe?" Dina said. "I don't have his number."

Kevin didn't like the idea of putting Dina in a car with someone else—she was his responsibility, after all—but he was out of options. Even if he managed to get the Duchess on the phone, there was no way she'd be able to get Dina to her bus on time.

"Let's go check the phone book."

As he stepped out of the car, Kevin glanced across the road. A hundred yards or so out in the pasture, his neighbor Jake Hillman was elbows-deep in the engine compartment of his tractor. The morning was strangely quiet.

They found Monica in the house loading the dishwasher.

"Why haven't you left yet? You're going to be late."

Kevin had no time for explanations. "Do you know the Owens' phone number?"

"It's in the book. What's going on?"

Kevin pulled their battered address book off the shelf and thumbed through it.

"Cars aren't working. Neither of them."

"What? Why not?"

"I don't know."

"Well, use Bertha," Monica said, referring to the old, wall-mounted landline.

"I know."

"Why does that one work when the power's out?" Dina asked.

"Bertha's old school," Kevin said. "I don't really get all that electrical engineering stuff, but phones—old phones like this one—don't use much electricity, or they run on their own power or something."

Bertha was from the days when telephones had bells but no whistles, or built-in displays, call waiting, or voice mail. She had a long cord that was always getting twisted up, but whenever the power went out, she was there, a trusty old warhorse from a bygone era. Kevin had lobbied hard to get rid of Bertha when they remodeled the kitchen because she didn't fit with the stainless steel and chrome, but Monica had overruled him.

Though the Bartons and Owenses weren't exactly friends, they were acquainted enough to have exchanged numbers. Kevin found the number. He lifted Bertha's handset from the cradle, pinned it to his ear with his shoulder, and reached to start punching buttons.

There was no dial tone.

He jiggled the cradle three, four times, but there was nothing: no dial tone, no static, no crackle or hum. Bertha was as dead as the car—both of them. A cold lump the size of a peach pit formed in Kevin's throat.

"It doesn't work," he said.

Dina pulled her cell out of her jacket pocket.

"What's the number? Oh, that's weird. I thought I charged it last night."
Kelly's phone didn't work either.

"Do you know what time it is?" Dina asked. "That clock doesn't work."

"It plugs into the wall," Kevin said. "It's . . ."

He stared at his watch, his mouth going dry.

"Kevin?" Monica said. "Kevin? What's the matter?"

Kevin lifted his wrist to his ear. Nothing. He took the watch off, shook it, tapped the crystal. The hands were frozen in place, matching the position of the clock on the wall: Ten fifteen.

"Kevin?" Monica's sharp voice jolted him back to reality. "What's wrong?"

He licked his lips and forced a smile. "Sorry, Dina, it looks like you two are going to get a little extra time together today."

The girls looked at each other.

"I'm heartbroken," Kelly deadpanned.

"Totally," replied Dina.

They stared at each other a moment, then fell, giggling, into each other's arms. That made Kevin feel a little better but not much. Monica grasped his arm. He looked down into her beautiful hazel eyes. They were too wide. "What's going on?"

He put his hand against the refrigerator. The metal was cool to the touch, same as always, but it was still as stone. No hum of electricity, no thunk of ice cubes being dumped into the tray in the freezer. All the noises in the house they were used to hearing had stopped.

"I don't know," he said. "Nothing works."

CHAPTER 2

KEVIN INSPECTED THE mess of hoses, wires, and belts that made up his car's engine. Given his knowledge of the workings of engines, this was as useful as fishing in a swimming pool, but he felt compelled to try. He poked at the battery cables. They were tight. There was no corrosion on the terminals, no frayed bits of wire poking out of mouse-chewed insulation. He remembered the crazy Car Talk guys on public radio talking about solving a problem with a car's starter by giving it a couple of whacks with a rubber mallet. There were only two problems with that advice: first, Kevin didn't have a rubber mallet; second, he had no idea what the starter even looked like. And that led to a third problem: he couldn't even look it up on the internet.

He stepped back and rubbed his hand along the back of his neck while breakfast settled unpleasantly in his stomach. Across the way, Jake had evidently given up on his own tractor. It stood alone in the field. All Kevin heard were the sounds of nature: birds tuning up for spring, the gentle swish of branches in a light breeze, the sound of water trickling in the drainage ditches along the road. The only human sounds he heard were the muted voices of Kelly and Dina leaking from Kelly's second-floor window and the crunch of feet on the dirt-strewn road leading up the hill toward his house.

A young man came slouching up the hill. He wore a flat-brimmed baseball cap pulled slightly off-center. Baggy black jeans hung low on his slim waist and pooled into the tops of his unlaced sneakers. The morning sun glinted off a metal ring attached to one eyebrow. He raised a hand in greeting. Kevin returned a nod.

The kid stopped in the street at the end of the driveway. He took off his hat, revealing reddish blond hair shaved close to the skull. Kevin thought he was nineteen, maybe twenty.

"Excuse me, sir. Could I use your phone? Mine's dead, and my car is stuck."

"Oh," said Kevin, caught off guard by the display of manners. "Everything's out. Phone, power, everything."

"Oh, that sucks."

"Yes, it does."

The kid glanced up, smiled, and tipped a two-fingered salute at Kelly's window. The girls, who had apparently been following his progress, disappeared behind the curtains like Whac-A-Mole targets.

"You having car trouble too?" the kid asked.

"Yeah. Neither of them work. I don't know why."

"Yeah, mine too. Only I was driving." He gestured down the hill. "I'm lucky I didn't run off the road."

A bright orange muscle car sat on the county road, about twenty feet short of where Harpur's Hill Road turned off. While it had been pulled as far to the side as possible, anyone leaving town would have to swerve into the oncoming lane to avoid it.

"That's your car there?"

"Yeah."

Kevin frowned. "I think you're going to want move that. What happened?"

"Like I said, it just stopped. I was at my aunt's house last night. Do you know Gail Hester, over on West Street?" Kevin nodded. Gail Hester was a physician's assistant at the hospital; he knew her mainly from the cafeteria. The kid said, "I stayed there last night and was on my way up to Canajoharie. Anyway, I'm coming out of town and the car just up and dies–radio, dash, engine, everything. Steering, brakes—boom, they're gone. And there I am, rolling right towards the ditch."

Kelly's voice came from behind Kevin. "That must have been scary," she said.

Kevin whirled around. The girls stood halfway down the driveway. They hesitated like a pair of squirrels tempted by an offered peanut, wanting to come forward, but nervous and shy at the same time. Kelly's cheeks were flushed as if she'd just run up and down the hill a couple of times.

"It was. I thought I was going to end up with the cows. But I was able to unlock the steering wheel and keep from crashing."

"You're pretty lucky," Kevin said.

"I know, right? All I can figure is the onboard computer blew. It's the only thing that makes sense. Shi-oot." He hauled in the swear before it got all the way out. "I'm supposed to be at work by noon."

Mr. Muscle Car introduced himself as Curtis Pinkney. Kevin left him outside with the girls while he checked Bertha. The phone was still dead.

Power failures were nothing new in Harpursville. Normally, they were an annoyance, an inconvenience of a few hours at most that did little more than make him miss a TV show or go through a mild case of email withdrawal. The worst one he remembered had happened when he was eight or nine, when an ice storm knocked out his part of Long Island for three days in sub-freezing temperature. For Kevin and his brother and sister, it was a grand adventure. They camped out on the living room floor, toasted marshmallows over the burners of a propane camp stove, and listened to music and storm stories on a battery-operated radio.

This was different. It felt all wrong. Power failures didn't knock out cars. Or the land line. Without Bertha, they couldn't even report the problem to the power company. He wasn't even sure if they still had a portable radio in the house. They were in the dark, literally and figuratively.

He poked his head back out the kitchen door. Kelly and Dina kept Curtis company. Despite his professed need to get to Canajoharie by noon, he looked to be in no hurry to leave.

"Kelly, where's your laptop? I need to check something."

"On my desk. It doesn't work, I already checked."

He hurried upstairs. The laptop sat in the center of the desk, mountains of papers, books, and unwashed dishes on either side. He pressed the power button without much hope and got what he expected: nothing.

"Shit."

Monica appeared in the doorway.

"What are you doing?"

"Checking something."

She stepped into the room. Her shirt was smudged with dust.

"I dug Little Joe out of the cellar."

Calling Little Joe a boombox was an insult to the Samsonite-sized blasters of his teenage years; it only took one arm to lift when it was fully loaded with batteries.

"I thought we threw that away years ago."

"You didn't really want to do that."

He smiled. The radio had provided the soundtrack to Kevin's high school and college days. Though the tape deck had long since broken and the antenna had been replaced several times with bent coat hangers, the radio worked well enough that he had been able to use it while doing outside work. But with reception in their area being spotty on a good day, listening to the radio while painting or raking leaves was an exercise in frustration, so Monica had bought him an MP3 player, and the boombox disappeared.

"And?"

"Nothing. I put in new batteries too." She ran her fingers back and forth along her necklace. "I don't like this."

He wanted to tell her it was just a series of bizarre coincidences, but there were two—no, three—cars that didn't work, plus Jake's tractor. Add in his watch, the phone that never failed, Kelly's laptop, and the cell phones—too many things had failed for mere coincidence. He looked out the window, saw the tractor sitting there, half a load of manure cooking in the warming morning. Twisting to the right, he gazed down at the hamlet below. Harpursville wasn't the busiest town in the world, but Saturday mornings saw a fair amount of traffic passing through. Not today. From his vantage point, he had a pretty good view straight down Main Street. Someone rode a bicycle in a lazy circle, but no cars moved. One car sat backed halfway out of a driveway, its rear end jutting into the road. Not the sort of place you'd leave your car if you had a choice. Small clusters of people milled around in groups of two or three.

"I don't like it either," he said. "But whatever it is, I'm sure they've got people working on it. I'm sure it will be over soon."

Monica looked about as convinced of that as he felt saying it.

———

Back outside, he told Curtis, "Everything's out. Computers, clocks, cars, radios."

"Wow."

"Have you seen any cars pass by?"

"I didn't really notice," he said with a sidelong glance at Kelly.

Distracted, no doubt, by the flirtatious company of a pair of sixteen-year-olds. Or one sixteen-year-old, anyway. Dina was part of the conversation, but all the sparks were between Curtis and Kelly.

Kevin chewed on the inside of his cheek. "What are you going to do now?"

"I guess I'll go back to Aunt Gail's house and see what's going on there. See if her phone is working and hope I still have a job. Listen, I hate to ask this," Curtis said, tugging on his ear. "Do you think you could help me push my car off to the side so it doesn't get pancaked? Just in case?"

Kelly volunteered them instantly. "Of course, we'll help."

They set off down the hill. To their left, a dozen or so of Jake's cows watched them pass. When the foursome reached the county road, Kevin looked both ways, but nothing was coming from either direction.

Kelly steered while Curtis, Kevin, and Dina pushed. They got the car to the foot of the hill and as far to the side as the ditch at the road's edge allowed. It wasn't perfect, but it was a little more out of the way.

"It should be safe there." Kevin wiped sweat off his brow, veins throbbing in his temples from the effort. "The road dead ends at the top of the hill, so we don't get much traffic."

Curtis stuck out his hand. "Thanks, Mr. Barton."

"Not a problem, Curtis. Take care. Say hi to your aunt for me."

"Sure thing."

"Dad, Dina and I are going for a walk," Kelly announced.

Dina looked as surprised as Kevin felt. He knew exactly what his daughter was thinking. An idea came to him.

"As a matter of fact, you are," he said. "We're going to the Kwik-Stop. I'm going to need your help with something."

She made a face but didn't protest, and the four of them set off. The hamlet officially began about 100 yards away from Harpur's Hill Road.

Jake's pasture continued on the left. It bottomed out into some swampy ground. Beyond that sat the town office building, a parking lot, and the Feed-N-Seed, a local hardware store. On the right was a huge swath of field that some conservation group bought a few years back to prevent the rumored development of a water park.

Kelly and Curtis soon pulled a few steps ahead. Curtis, to his credit, frequently turned to include Kevin and Dina in the conversation. Kelly, meanwhile, alternated between a rushing flow of words and awkward silences. As they walked, they moved closer together as if they were being pulled together by an invisible string, though they did not quite touch.

Dina leaned in close to Kevin. "I think he likes her," she whispered.

"I think it's mutual."

"What do you think of that?"

"I think I'll have to kill him."

Dina's mouth fell open, then she laughed when she realized he was kidding. He was. Mostly.

Kelly spun around. "What's so funny?"

"Your pants are falling down," he said.

Her hands flew to her waistline. When she found her pants were in fact not falling down, she tossed her head in a very Monica sort of way and stomped several steps ahead. A grinning Curtis, whose pants were falling down, hurried to keep up.

Despite the pseudo-gangsta look, the facial piercing, and the tattoo—there was definite ink on Pinkney's right shoulder— Kevin found himself liking Curtis. He was polite, seemed intelligent, and he looked Kevin in the eye when he talked to him. Most of Kelly's male friends from school were monosyllabic at best, sullen and mute at worst. Curtis was willing and able to carry on a conversation with an adult. Still, Kevin was cautious. He remembered the ulterior motives that governed so many of his own actions at that age. Of course, it was likely a lot of worry for nothing: in a day, maybe two, the blackout would be over and Curtis would be back in Canajoharie. Or so he hoped.

They reached the imaginatively-named Four Corners. Here, the county road crossed Main Street, a two-lane state road that ran down to Algonquin—a medium-sized college town about twenty miles away.

The Kwik-Stop was to the left; Curtis's aunt lived on the west side of the hamlet.

"This is where I get off," Curtis said.

"Why don't you come with us?" Kelly asked.

Curtis looked like he would happily keep them company, but he shook his head. "I need to try and get in touch with my boss. It's been great to meet all of you. Thanks again for helping with the car."

"Dad, maybe me and Dina should walk around and find out what's going on."

Kevin managed not to smirk.

"What do you think we're doing? But not right now. I'm going to need your help with something."

Kelly stuck out her lower lip, but Curtis said, "Hey, it looks like I'll be here for a bit. I'll see you around."

The two of them edged away from Kevin and Dina. Curtis pulled a phone out of his jacket pocket, then he and Kelly laughed when they realized they couldn't exchange numbers or emails or whatever kids did. Curtis started searching his jacket pockets for a pen and paper. Dina got Kevin's attention. "Mr. B., what do you think happened?"

He looked up and down the wide main road of the town. A pickup truck sat square in the middle of the northbound lane. No other cars moved. And it was still too quiet for Kevin's liking. Overhead, a few wisps of clouds drifted by, but not a single contrail sliced the blue sky.

A chill crawled up his back. What if the planes just stopped working in midair?

He forced a smile. "I don't know. But we're going to fix it."

"How?"

"We're going to buy ice."

Her blue eyes clouded in confusion. "How is that going to fix anything?"

"Remember when the hurricane blew through a couple of years back?"

"Ye-e-e-s."

"Our power was out all day. Rumor had it that it could be off for days, maybe weeks. We went to bed, got up the next day, and it was still out."

"We only lost our power for a few hours."

"Yes, well, you live in a privileged community. Anyway, we heard they had power in Algonquin, so we piled into the car and drove down there for breakfast. While we were there, we bought some cheap foam coolers and a bunch of ice so we could keep the refrigerator and freezer cold. And when we got home . . ."

"The power was on?"

"The power was on."

Dina cocked her head, tapped her chin with her fingertips.

"So, we're going to the Kwik-Stop to buy a bunch of ice because you figure if we do, we'll get back to the house and everything will be working."

"Bingo."

"And if it is, what will you do with all that ice?"

He rubbed his hands together.

"Make daiquiris."

———

People were out in force along Main Street. They sat on porches, gathered in small clusters on lawns, or stood on the sidewalk, all talking about one thing: the blackout. The story was the same everywhere: everything was out. No one knew why, but everyone had an opinion.

"North Korea, for sure," said some.

"Sunspots," said others.

"Electromagnetic pulse," said one, with a wise nod of the head. "We've been nuked."

To hear some tell it, the Russians, Chinese, or ISIS would be rolling in to enslave the good people of the US of A any minute. Kevin hustled the girls along. Going to the Kwik-Stop was likely a fool's errand, but he had to try; every minute they delayed gave whoever was working the store that much more time to shut down and go home.

The Kwik-Stop was a freestanding convenience store that stood on the state road just beyond the hamlet's southern boundary. The store was dark. The neon beer signs unlit. A red-shirted employee sat on an overturned milk crate next to the ice chest out front, smoking a cigarette. Kevin seemed forever destined to interrupt Kwik-Stop employees on their cigarette breaks. He always offered apologetic nods to the clerks, who would give him a *yeah, whatever* look before taking one more pull off a half-finished smoke, tossing it to the ground, and grinding it under toe or heel. Kevin suspected more than one clerk imagined his face under their foot.

The kid didn't bother to look up.

"Store's closed." His voice was as flat as the parking lot. The name tag pinned to his shirt said "Troy." He was one of the less friendly employees and a local who lived a few houses up the street.

"Can I convince you to sell me a couple bags of ice? You don't need power to open up the cooler, just the key."

Troy looked at him out of one eye. He took a puff of his cigarette, jiggled it between his fingers, and exhaled a stream of smoke into the morning air.

"Register won't work."

"I just want three or four bags of ice. It's what, two bucks a bag? I'll give you exact change, you won't even have to open the register, just the cooler. Write down the sale on a piece of paper or something and lock the cash in the office. Your boss will probably make you employee of the month for showing initiative."

Troy looked at the nub of cigarette between his fingers, threw it down, and watched smoke curl up from the pavement. Another sigh, another stream of smoke. "All right, I suppose so." He rose, dusted his hands on his khaki work pants. "I'll get the key."

"Thank you."

Troy disappeared into the darkened store.

"Let this be a lesson to you, ladies," Kevin said in a low voice. "Keep those grades up or you might end up here."

"Shoot me first," Kelly said.

Troy returned with the key and unlocked the cooler. Goose bumps rose on Kevin's arm as he reached in. Cold vapor floated up around his face. He grabbed a bag, passed it to Kelly, handed another to Dina, and set two more down at his feet. As Troy locked the cooler, Kevin rifled through his wallet, pulling a five and three singles, figuring eight dollars should cover the cost of the ice. Had Troy been pleasant, he might have given him ten and told him to keep the change for his troubles.

Troy eyed the money, licked his lips with a quick flick of his tongue. "Twenty," he said.

"Sorry, what?" Kevin stared at Troy, who shifted back and forth for a second, then planted his feet and thrust out his chin.

"Twenty."

"Twenty bucks? Five dollars a bag?"

"No, it's two bucks a bag, but twelve for a pack of smokes." He brandished an unopened pack of Camels.

"I don't smoke."

"But I do." He grinned and slid the pack into the breast pocket of his shirt. "Something big is going down. Nothing's working. Lots of people are gonna want ice. Twenty bucks or put it back."

Fading pimples spotted Troy's cheeks. The hairs on his chin were sparse and fine. He was at least half Kevin's age. Kevin tried to make him squirm with an icy glare, but the kid would not budge. If he felt any guilt over this price gouging, he kept it to himself. Twenty bucks for four bags of ice—was it worth the price? If the power was off for any length of time, yes. They had a week's worth of meats and fresh vegetables in the refrigerator, more in the freezer. Managed properly, this ice could get them through several days at least.

Feeling like the world's biggest fool, he jammed the cash back into his wallet and pulled out a twenty.

"I'll be sure to tell your manager about this."

"Hey, it was your idea. It'll be written down as four bags of ice and a pack of cigarettes. Who's gonna know?"

Kevin seethed as they headed for home. The clumps of people outside had reconfigured into new groups, passing time until New York State Electric and Gas could restring the broken wires or repair the blown transformer or reset the relays, whatever it was they needed to do. A few people noted the bags of ice dangling from their hands and hustled off for the Kwik-Stop. It looked like Troy was going to get himself a lot of packs of cigarettes. Kevin fumed, embarrassed at not standing up to Troy's extortion in front of the girls, but he would definitely take it up with the manager when the power came back.

———

Kevin was inside, washing up from dinner as best he could without hot water. Monica stood on the porch, watching the sun set over the hills on the far side of the hamlet. Nuclear sunsets were supposed to be—what, exactly? Spectacular. Extra colorful. Something different. This one looked about the same as any other. She pulled her sweater tight against the chilly air.

Dina stepped out the front door and joined her.

"What a pretty sky."

"Beautiful," agreed Monica. They watched the colors bleed into each other. "Where's Kelly?"

Putting on a stuffy upper crust accent, Dina said, "She's *indisposed* at the moment."

The sun was below the hilltops, the fire all but gone from the sky. Just above the horizon, a strip of sky had turned a deep green.

"Kelly dyed an egg that color one year," Monica said. "She put it in the blue, then the yellow, then back in the blue. She must have worked on that thing for hours. It was the prettiest Easter egg I've ever seen."

Color faded away from the lawn. Smoke twisted up and out of chimneys from the hamlet below. It smelled like autumn, though the spring peepers calling from the swamp at the foot of Jake's pasture told a different story.

"It's creepy, the way everything just stopped," Dina said.

Monica said nothing. Dina rested her hands on the porch rail. One slim finger went up and down, tapping lightly on the wood.

"Did you ever read *The Road*?" Dina asked. "I had to read it for Mrs. Lomongino's class."

Monica pulled her sweater tighter. "I started it, but I couldn't finish. It was just too dark."

The finger tapped on the rail, faster.

Monica's fingers found the satiny sleeve of Dina's warm-up jacket. She pulled the girl close, put her arm around her. Dina leaned into her, resting her cheek against the top of Monica's head. Together, they watched darkness settle over Harpursville. So strange not to see every window lit from within, to not have cars cutting through the dark. A shiver passed through Dina. Monica rubbed her arm.

"Are you cold?"

"A little. This jacket's more for show than warmth, and I guess I left my coat in my locker."

"I'll have to get you one of my sweaters."

Dina pulled away a little, looked down at her with an amused expression.

"Uh, really?"

"What?"

"Here."

Unwinding herself from Monica's grasp, Dina took hold of Monica's hand and straightened her arm. Then she held her own arm against it. At full extension, Monica's fingertips barely reached Dina's wrist.

Monica laughed. "I guess that wouldn't work too well, would it?"

"I'd look like Frankenstein." Dina held her other arm out and moaned from deep within her throat. "Arrrgh."

"The dread pirate Frankenstein." They shared a long laugh. "I'll find something. We can't have you freezing."

"You're the best, Momma B."

A warm feeling spread through Monica's chest. Again, she put her arm around Dina. For the moment, her worries were swept aside. The totality of the power failure—the fact that just about everything was out—had unnerved her. It had set a little mouse loose in her stomach. All day that little mouse had been taking anxious little bites out of her insides with its sharp little teeth. Standing here now, it was easy to believe it was nothing to really worry about, just an ordinary blackout, something that would be fixed within a matter of hours. She gave Dina another squeeze.

"What do you say we go in and get a fire going?"

"Sounds like a great idea to me."

Arm in arm, they went back into the house.

CHAPTER 3

IT FELT LATE, but anything after dark always felt late if the power was out. Kevin said goodnight to the girls—who were bundled up in front of the fireplace, preparing to tell ghost stories—and went upstairs.

Monica had a candelabra with three tapers burning on the night table. She sat up against the headboard, covers up to her chin, her book propped on her knees and angled to catch the light.

"I left a candle in the bathroom," she said. "It's not worth much, but it should keep anyone from killing themselves if they have to get up in the middle of the night."

"I don't think anyone's going to want to get out of bed tonight." Goose bumps broke out on his arms when he pulled off his shirt. "Any colder and it might snow."

"You think the pipes will freeze?"

Kevin paused, his pajama shirt half-buttoned. He usually slept naked, but it was kind of cold for that. Plus, he was uncomfortable doing so when they had guests in the house, especially when the guest was a sixteen-year-old girl. Not that he wanted to be caught by Kelly making a naked dash to the bathroom either.

"I don't think so. I don't remember any freeze warnings for tonight. And it's raining out."

"The weather can change fast."

He stepped into his pajama pants. "Do you want me to crack the taps?"

She snapped her book shut, pushed her reading glasses up to the top of her head. "No, no, I guess it's all right. Just come to bed."

He wanted nothing more than to get under covers—it was cold—but he paused, trying to decipher Monica's tone, body language, and words. Did she really want him to come to bed, or did she want him to open the taps and give her peace of mind? He opted for the former. It was too cold to wander the house.

It was almost too cold in bed, too, at least at first. Kevin scrunched himself into a ball and shimmied over until he was pressed against Monica. She blew out two of the candles and backed into him. He wrapped his arm around her, relishing the heat her body threw, even through layers of nightgown and pajamas.

Monica's hand came around. She stroked his hip, up and down. The reaction was instant.

"Oh my," she whispered, as he hardened against her. "What's this?" Her hand slid down his front. Kevin hissed as her fingers slipped in through the opening of his pants and found him.

"Monica," he said, and his breath caught as she gave him a particularly delicious squeeze.

She rolled over to face him. Kissed him, soft on the lips, and again, long, slow and deep. He ran his hand up her side, found her breast.

Their lips parted.

"Are you sure this is such a good idea?" he said. "The girls might hear."

Even with her face in the shadows, he could see the mischievous glint in her eyes, the eyes that had first captured his attention so many years ago.

"They're downstairs, right?" She pushed him onto his back and leaned over him, her long dark hair falling around them, tickling his face. "Besides, trying to be quiet makes it more . . . exciting, don't you think?"

He did.

He awoke much later with competing urges: to take water in one end and get rid of it from the other. The room was pitch dark. He fumbled in the dark for his pajamas, which had been thrown aside, but couldn't find them. Instead, he pulled the first thing he could find from his night table—a pair of gym shorts and a T-shirt that was too tight across his middle—and felt his way out of the room, walking gingerly so as not to crash into anything. His skin erupted into goose pimples, but at least he couldn't see his breath. At least, he didn't think so.

Dim yellow light danced in the hallway from the candle in the bathroom. Kevin paused, almost shivering, and listened. Deep, regular breathing came from Kelly's room, which was next to the bathroom. With the house as quiet as it was, peeing was likely to sound like someone turning on a fire hose, so he decided to go downstairs rather than risk waking the girls up. He took the candle from the bathroom and made his way down. As he rounded the corner, he saw a flickering light coming from the kitchen and made a mental note to chew Kelly out for leaving it burning. He'd blow it out on his way upstairs, after getting his drink. He paused on his way past and peeked in. Dina sat at the table, a glass of milk and a small stack of cookies in front of her. She held a hand up in front of her mouth but couldn't quite conceal a guilty smile or her milk mustache.

"Oh," he said, his voice sounding rusty. "I wasn't expecting you. Is everything okay?"

She ducked her head and wiped her mouth. Telltale bits and pieces of cookies were everywhere. Black scum floated on the surface of the milk and smudged the napkin when she put it back down.

"You caught me," she said around a mouthful of cookie. "I'm such a pig. It was hot upstairs. And Kelly was snoring. And I was hungry. I didn't wake you, did I?"

"No, no. I just had to . . . you know." He pointed toward the bathroom, his face going warm despite the chill. He reached up and tried to tame his wild case of bed head, then stopped when he felt the way the motion pulled his T-shirt tight up, exposing his belly. The stale odor of sleep and recent sex surrounded him like a noxious cloud, and each movement made it seem ridiculously obvious that he wore no underwear beneath his gym shorts. "Uh, yeah," he mumbled and shuffled off to the bathroom. Though Dina had seen him shirtless and in a bathing suit at the lake plenty of times, he was mortified at how he must look.

Once in the bathroom, he was further embarrassed by how long he stood at the toilet before relief came, and again by the loud splashing of urine that echoed in the little room. The only solace he took was that he didn't rip off a huge, wet fart.

Kevin took extra time to wash his hands, hoping to hear the telltale sounds of Dina leaving the kitchen. When he finally emerged, she was still there, holding a pair of cookies in her palm like an offering.

"Want some?"

"Ted says no," he said, referring to his protruding gut. He and Monica had decided to name it. "I do need a glass of water though."

He filled a glass and drank, standing by the sink. Dina busied herself dunking a cookie in the remnants of her milk. Despite the cold, she wore a tank top held up with a thin pair of straps and a pair of flannel pajama bottoms, pink with little stars and moons on them. Her sandy hair was tied back in a sloppy ponytail; several strands had come loose and hung alongside her face. She rested her chin on her left hand. With her right she dunked a cookie nearly to her fingertips. Her hand went up and down, up and down. He watched the cookie as if it were a hypnotist's watch, up and down, up and down, not quite focusing. With a jolt, he realized he had a nearly unobstructed view down her shirt. He stared—mesmerized by her creamy skin—the tapering shape of her breasts, the darker edge of nipple nearly visible. If he shifted just a little to the left, he might—

Jesus, what are you doing?

He took a huge swallow of water, nearly choked on it. Dina, thank goodness, concentrated on her cookie and didn't seem to notice anything wrong. Kevin grabbed the nearest chair and sat across from her. He studied the jumping shadows the candles threw on the wall behind her, telling himself he had not let his eyes linger on her chest, trying to expunge the image from his mind even as another part of him exulted. The room was so quiet he thought Dina must be able to hear the blood that pounded through him, or worse, the despicable thoughts that tried to be heard in his mind.

"You guys must totally hate me," Dina said, apparently oblivious. "I come over and eat you out of house and home."

He grabbed the conversational lifeline.

"You're welcome to anything here. In fact, I've got a big pile of bills on my desk—you can have them. No? Okay, no hard feelings. And Kelly does snore." He dropped his voice in a stage whisper. "Don't tell Mrs. Barton I said this, but she gets it from her mother."

She drew an x across her chest, rippling the fabric of her top.

"Your secret is safe with me."

Up came the cookie at last. Perfect white drops fell one by one into the glass. Dina put the wet edge of cookie in her mouth and sucked out the milk. The loud slurping noises made him think of porno films.

"Mmph, this is so good. I must look like a total maniac right now." She grimaced and crossed her eyes, turning her pretty face into a grotesque mask. Her lips, gums, and the spaces between her teeth were blackened with cookie bits. Kevin nearly choked on his water again, this time from laughing. With one act, she had reminded him that she was still a kid.

"Thanks for the nightmares." He coughed. "On that note, I'd better go back to bed. Not only am I tired, I'm freezing."

"Do you think the power will be back on tomorrow?"

Logic told him no. There were too many weird things about this blackout for it to be fixed fast. One naggy little voice spoke up from a corner of his mind and wondered if it could be fixed at all. He squashed it. Dina looked small and vulnerable. Her eyes, large and round, glistened in the dim light. Honesty was always the best policy—except when it wasn't.

"I think it will be back on soon," he said. "Maybe not tomorrow, but soon."

"My parents must be worried. I hope they're all okay."

Parents. The word made the hairs stand up on the back of his neck. He hadn't thought of his all day. Was the power out in Florida too? Shit.

"I'm sure they're fine." He put his glass in the sink. "Now if you'll excuse me, I should be going. Goodnight. And I'm sorry you missed your track meet today." It was a stupid thing to say, but he was out of conversation.

"It's okay. I'd rather spend time here. You know, Mom didn't want me running track at all? 'Dina,'" she said, in a bang-on impersonation of the Duchess, complete with one hand flipping around at shoulder height. "'Dina, darling, you just don't have time for it. Dina, dear, running will make your thighs too big.' Too big for what?

"Now she's convinced I'll be getting full athletic scholarships and going to the Olympics or something. It's not as much fun as it used to be."

Though Kevin had no great love for Lisa and Phil McCray, being a parent was like being a cop. He felt obligated to close ranks with them.

"You know she's only looking out for you."

"I know. And I love her to death. It's just that they take all the fun out of everything. They're so serious all the time." She stared down into her nearly empty glass. "I just wish they would lighten up, you know? They just make everything so hard sometimes."

"It's a parent thing. It's what we do."

"Not you and Momma B."

"Kelly's clearly not sharing all the dirty little details of our house with you."

"She shares *everything*."

"And you still like to be here, huh?"

She laughed a little.

"Having kids," he said, "is the most amazing and terrifying thing. And there's a ton of books about how to take care of them and how to be a good parent, and *everyone's* got an opinion on how you should do it, but we're all flying blind. You just do the best you can and hope it's good enough.

"If nothing else, Dina, know that your parents love you."

Her chair scraped on the linoleum. She came to him, kissed him on his stubbled cheek.

"Thanks, Mr. B. You guys are just so great. Goodnight."

She took her candle and disappeared upstairs, leaving Kevin feeling much warmer than the cold kitchen.

———

CHAPTER 4

THE SEX HAD been good. Better yet, it had helped quiet the mouse, and she had slept well. On Sunday morning the power was still out, however, and the mouse returned. As the day wore on, the little mouse grew. By early afternoon it was the size of a rat. It gnawed away at her, sharp, more persistent. The girls, intrigued by the strange novelty of the blackout, had walked into town. Monica was sure part of the intrigue, at least on Kelly's part, was on the possibility of running into Curtis Pinkney again. Kevin split his time between the living room window and the kitchen. He would spend ten minutes or so staring out the window, watching for them—no doubt fretting over Kelly's interest in a boy—then would wander into the kitchen, where she'd hear him jiggle the cradle on Bertha, hoping to get through to his parents.

"Relax," she told him, as he stood once more at the window. "They'll be fine."

He stood there for another ten seconds before sighing and turning away. "Yeah, I know. I just can't help it."

At another time, his worry would have been cute. What he needed to worry about, however, was the power and what would happen if it didn't come back on. The rat took a big bite. It made her afraid, and fear was not something Monica handled well.

Needing something to take her mind—and his—off the situation, she dragged him through the house in search of more candles, more matches, anything that might give them light and heat. The house did not hold heat very well. The little wood stove in the parlor took care of that room but little else. The living room fireplace looked great, but unless you had a bonfire going in there, it spit most of the heat out the chimney.

In a dusty box in the basement, she hit paydirt: a set of hurricane lamps that some distant relative had given them as a wedding gift.

"I can't believe I kept these." She lifted one of the lamps from its nest of mildewy tissue paper, turned it this way and that, inspecting it for cracks. It was a heavy thing, with a gaudy fluted chimney. "I hate this kind of kitschy stuff."

"Do we have lamp oil?"

She pushed aside the paper and found a big bottle of it at the bottom of the box.

"Yes."

Back upstairs, they spread their treasures out on the table: the pair of lamps and the oil, a truckload of candles, and more candlesticks. It was amazing how much crap they had accumulated over the years.

The girls came back a short time later, looking worn out but excited. They had indeed found Curtis Pinkney and spent most of their time hanging out with him. Kevin looked mildly annoyed at the mere mention of the boy.

"Did you actually look around and see what's going on down there? Did you talk to anyone but him?" he asked.

"There's not much to see," Kelly said. "Just a bunch of people sitting around. The Kwik-Stop is closed."

"It's weird," Dina said. "Everyone's hanging out in the middle of the road. It's like a big street fair." She looked from Monica to the refrigerator with the sort of expression one sees on a dog hoping for a handout. "Could I . . .?"

Anxiety took a sharp bite. Scouring the basement for candles and such had driven it off for a while, but now it was back.

"Help yourself," she said. "Just be quick. Don't let the cold air out."

"Oh, we did see Mr. Pierson," Kelly said. "He rode his bike to Emerson yesterday. Everything's shut down. He said he talked to one of the cops up there. They can't get in touch with anybody. Daddy, what's going on? More people are talking about terrorists and nuclear war and stuff. Do you think we were attacked?"

Kevin didn't answer. Brow furrowed, he stared at the refrigerator, where Dina was bent over at the waist, rummaging around inside.

"Oh," he said. "What? Sorry, it's strange seeing the refrigerator door open and no light on. Do I think we were attacked? No."

Dina emerged with cold cuts, mayonnaise, and a jar of pickles.

Monica touched her fingertips to the mayonnaise jar. It was still cool but wouldn't stay that way for much longer. She watched Dina pile ham high on her bread. Did she really need that much?

As if Monica had spoken aloud, Dina peeled a slice of ham off her sandwich and put it back with the rest. A slight blush crept up her cheeks.

"Sorry," she said. "I guess I got a little carried away."

"That looks good," Kelly said. "Okay, you can make one for me, thanks."

Dina stuck her tongue out at Kelly but grabbed two more slices of bread.

"People are talking because they don't know what to think," Kevin said. "I'm sure if we were attacked, we'd know it. Besides, I don't think ISIS could pull something like that off."

"That was before they were being hounded day and night. They're probably the only ones crazy enough to use a nuke, but I don't think they have the capability. Maybe they could blow up a power station or a dam, something like that, or screw around with cell towers, sure. But everything at once? I don't buy it."

It didn't make her feel any better. Monica wanted a reason. *Needed* a reason. If there was a reason, there was a solution. Downed power, overloaded circuits, blown fuses—those things were understandable. And they could be repaired. This?

"We would have known." Kevin's words were firm. He met their eyes, one by one. "Maybe it *is* solar storms or sunspots or something. I've heard they can mess things up pretty bad. I'm sure things will get fixed up soon. Hey, don't put that away yet. I think I'll have some too. Hon? You want some?"

She looked at the dwindling pile of ham, the pickle quarters that had been reduced by three, the bread that had gone from three-quarters of a loaf to less than half in a matter of minutes.

"I'm not hungry."

The rat took up too much room.

——

On Monday morning, Kevin's internal alarm clock woke him because his bedside one could not. He peered through the curtains into a gloomy morning. Nothing moved except a pair of crows, two black shapes against the heavy sky.

"I don't think any of us are going anywhere today," he muttered. Kevin never minded a three-day weekend, but he preferred when they were planned. He dressed and went downstairs into the dark, cold kitchen, set the kettle on the stove for some instant coffee and tried to figure out what he was going to do with himself. Everyone else's internal clocks seemed to be running as well, as the kitchen was soon full.

"I'm glad there's no school today," Dina said. "I'd be the only person wearing the same clothes as Friday."

Kevin laughed, but he had the luxury of clean clothes. His body was another matter, however. He felt a little slimy, like the yellow-spotted salamanders that turned up in the basement each spring. It had only been two days, but he wanted a shower badly.

Light rain pecked at the windows. Kevin floated through the dark, chilly house, looking for a project to take his mind off things; a project that didn't need electricity. Monica sequestered herself for most of the day in the bedroom. The girls had done their homework over the weekend and spent the day largely playing board games. If they were frightened at all by the situation, they kept their fears well hidden.

After dinner, he went in the bathroom to make room for the next day's breakfast. When he flushed the toilet, his inner homeowner's alarm blared. The toilet whooshed, water swirled around the bowl, but something was off. When he went to wash his hands, he knew why. Water flowed from the faucet, but without its usual gusto.

"Oh shit."

He rushed from the room, found Monica on the couch, reading by lamplight with a blanket pulled up to her chin.

"We need to fill everything we can with water," he said. "Every cooler, every jug, every pot we can spare."

"Why? What are you—" The light went on in her eyes. She leaped from the couch and ran to the kitchen. While she clanked around, pulling pots and pans out, Kevin ran upstairs. He gave the bathtub a quick wipe out with a clean towel, closed the drain, and opened the taps wide.

Kelly and Dina emerged from their bedroom.

"What's going on, Daddy?"

"Water," he said. "We're running out."

"How can we run out of water?"

"Because there's no electricity." She blinked at him, confused. "The water we drink comes from the ground," he said.

"No, it doesn't. It comes from up on Caleb's Hill."

"Right," he said. "And do you know how it gets up there? It's pumped out of the ground and pumped up the hill. Then it comes down to us by gravity."

Dina reached for Kelly's hand and took it. They stood together, staring at the slowly filling tub, and Kevin started to really worry for the first time. For the first time, it really occurred to him how dire their situation was becoming.

———

It was absence that woke him. The absence of Monica's breathing, her warmth. Kevin laid in the dark for several moments, listening to the absence of sound in the house and the loud night noises from outside: the trilling and peeping of frogs, the huff of Jake's cows, three quick, sharp barks of a dog from somewhere in town. When he did not hear Monica in the bathroom, he rose and felt his way through the dark and down the stairs. It was getting easier, though he still had the need to keep one hand up in front of him, lest he run into a wall or door.

He found her downstairs, framed in the window that looked out over town. Her nightgown shimmered.

"Hon? Are you okay?"

She didn't answer. He approached, placed a careful hand on her cool, bare shoulder. Dim light deepened the shadows on her face and flashed off the silver chain around her neck that she fiddled with.

"It's going to be okay," he said. "You'll see. Whatever this is, people are working on it. It may take a little while, but they'll get it—"

"Stop. Listen."

He waited, but she didn't say anything. She didn't seem to even be breathing. Beneath his hand, the muscles of her shoulder were like rock.

"What—"

"*Listen.*"

The house was absolutely silent. No ticking, no humming, no furnace rumbling in the basement. All he wanted was to go back upstairs and back to sleep.

"I don't—"

"Shh!"

Kevin tucked his chin to his chest and listened. All he could hear were the frogs, and he was about to say so when he heard another sound. Voices. Two or three of them, he couldn't tell for sure, they were muffled by distance and glass. Then he heard the clatter of a bottle skipping along the pavement and loud laughter. He raised his head.

Outside, a three-quarter moon hung high in the sky. It turned the road into a silver river, striped here and there by the black-fingered shadows of trees. The hamlet was dark, as it had been since Saturday.

Shadowy figures appeared in the moonlit center of the road. Three of them. They bumped and rebounded off each other like numbered balls in a lotto machine.

Glass shattered in the street, and laughter echoed up to them. The figures continued on, louder, not caring that it was the middle of the night.

Harpursville had some rough edges, but aside from Halloween, a one-night orgy of pumpkin smashing and shaving cream pranks, nothing much happened here. People had to go elsewhere to do their carousing, only now there was no easy way to get there.

The kids—and Kevin had little doubt that's what they were, they just had that vibe—had reached Curtis Pinkney's car. One broke away from the others and leaned down over it, peering in through the driver's side window. He tugged on the door handle. Tried it several times to no avail, then circled the car and tried the other side. He said something to the others over the roof of the car.

Monica's fingers tightened on his arm.

"I'm not liking where this is going," she said. "What do we do?"

"I don't really think there's anything we *can* do."

Down below, one of the figures tugged again on the door handle. Then he kicked it with the flat of his foot, two, three times. The hollow crump of the foot on metal was loud in the quiet night.

Monica's fingers dug deeper. "Kevin, you've got to do something, or they're going to ruin that boy's car."

"What am I supposed to do? Go out there and get my ass kicked? It's three on one, and I'm pretty sure they're drunk."

A metallic whump from outside drew his attention back to the window. One kid was doing a river dance on the car's roof. He capered like a monkey at feeding time. Glass smashed as one of the boys hurled a bottle at the car's side. Hooting laughter floated up to him.

"Oh Jesus," Kevin said. "Look at that."

A door slammed. Kevin looked over his shoulder. Monica was gone. "Monica? Monica?"

A flash of movement in the corner of his eye made him whirl back to the window. What he saw took his breath away, then sent him running for the front door and out into the night.

Monica was ghostly in the moonlight, her pale nightgown flapping. She was already halfway across the big lawn, already halfway down the hill to where those boys—not boys . . . maybe men . . . young men, who were likely drunk—jumped around and tried to break into Curtis's car.

"Monica! Monica!"

Kevin flew down the porch steps after her. The grass was cold and wet. It scratched at his unprotected ankles. The frogs, undeterred by the monkey boys jumping on the car, continued their chorus.

"Hey!" Monica's voice rang out, powerful and commanding. Everything—frogs, boys, even Kevin—stopped. "Get away from that car! What do you think you're doing? Get off that car."

To Kevin's surprise, the boys clambered down. They stood together, shuffling and muttering. Kevin's own paralysis was broken, and he jogged the rest of the way down to the group, his chest and legs burning. Huffing and puffing, he put his hands on his knees, his paunch rolling and folding against itself, and struggled to get his breath back.

Monica, all of five-foot-three, marched back and forth in front of the boys like a marine drill instructor. The upstate accent she had tried so hard to lose—that little twang that always struck Kevin as a cross between New England and Canada—was back, as always happened when she was angry.

"You ought to be ashamed of yourselves." She leaned in to get a closer look at them. "Connor, does your mother know you're out here drinking and smashing up cars?"

Though they towered over her and could have easily overpowered her, they stood quietly, humbled. She wore a nightgown that, while not exactly naughty, was thin at best, and Kevin had little doubt she was giving them quite a show, especially given the chilly air. They made no smart remarks. Not one of them raised his eyes off the ground.

"Get out of here, all of you. Get right home, and don't do this again. And give me that." She snapped her fingers at Connor. For a moment, he did nothing, then slowly handed over the remnants of a six-pack.

"Go home," she said, softer now. "Go home'n sleep. Come back to-morrow'n clean up this mess. This car belongs to Mrs. Hester's nephew. You can stop by Mrs. Hester's tomorrow and apologize and offer t'pay the damage."

Amazingly, the three nodded and mumbled words of apology. And if they weren't too drunk to remember, Kevin thought they just might do what she said. If they didn't, it was entirely possible she'd go to their houses and make them do it.

They shuffled off. They still bumped into each other but not with the boisterous élan they had shown earlier. Kevin half-expected them to shout curses and rude comments once they were out of chasing range; instead they melted into the shadows without a word, leaving Kevin and Monica standing in the dark, accompanied by the stars, the moon, and the frogs, who had resumed their mating chorus.

Kevin's arms and legs started to tremble from the combination of cold and adrenaline rebound. He turned on Monica.

"Are you crazy?" He kept his voice low. "Do you have any idea what could have happened to you? Three drunk teenagers, one . . . you."

"I stopped it." She thrust the six-pack at his chest. "*Some*one had to do something."

Without another word, she turned and set off up the hill to the house.

CHAPTER 5

MONICA'S WORDS FROM the night before dug at Kevin like a rock in his shoe. He shifted and squirmed to shake it loose; it periodically jabbed him when least expected. It was stabbing at the tender part of him when he entered the muddy driveway of his nearest neighbors, Jake and Alma Hillman.

Before moving upstate, Kevin thought men like Jake existed only as clichés in TV shows and movies. A farmer, Jake wore flannel shirts, overalls, and heavy work boots. He always had a baseball cap—John Deere, Mack trucks, Stihl—perched on top of his large round head, a bandanna of one color or another hanging out of his back pocket, and it seemed like he could fix anything. "On a farm, you gotta make do with what you got," he once told Kevin.

The Hillmans were affable people who were quick with a smile and a wave. Despite the fact their houses were only a few hundred feet apart, their paths rarely crossed socially. The Hillmans' kids were grown and gone, while Kevin and Monica were still at the stage where their lives revolved around their daughter. The Bartons both worked in town, as the locals called Algonquin. They spent most of their scant social time either there or ferrying Kelly to and from school functions and friends' houses. The Hillmans, meanwhile, were busy running their small beef farm, which looked to be a never-ending job. Jake was most frequently seen riding slowly up or down the street on the seat of his ancient tractor, heading to one of the fields he leased for hay or feed corn, or hauling around plastic-wrapped rolls of hay that looked like giant marshmallows.

Jake sat in a folding lawn chair in the shadow of his house, a glass of water in hand.

"Hey, Jake," Kevin called. "Got a minute?"

"Sure. Come on up."

Kevin picked his way around the potholed surface of the driveway—what Jake called the dooryard. He felt odd about dropping in; while he grew up when life was still largely unstructured and remembered aunts, uncles, and friends coming by unexpectedly, nothing happened spontaneously anymore. His life was now choreographed down to the minute; it typically took dozens of phone calls, emails, text messages, or Tweets to make anything happen. Or it did before the power went out.

Jake waved a big hand at an empty chair, and Kevin sat. Everything about the man was big: big head and hands, big belly, big feet, everything was big except his voice, which was surprisingly gentle.

"How are you guys doin'?" he asked the farmer.

"Oh, we're doing okay. How 'bout you?"

Kevin shrugged. "Not bad, I guess." He leaned forward and rested his elbows on his knees. "What do you make of all this?"

The metal legs of Jake's chair ground into gravel as he shifted his position. "I have no idea," he said. "Word around is ISIS."

Kevin wondered where Jake was getting his information. He wasn't sure Jake had managed to leave the farm at all in the last three days, and he hadn't noticed anyone coming up the hill to visit either.

"I've heard that too. Do you buy it?"

"Nah. A lot of things have gone wrong with th'war, but one thing I think we got right is keepin' 'em from doin' anything outside the Mid-East right now."

"Then what do you think it is?"

Jake lifted his cap and scratched at the top of his head. His mostly gray hair was shaved down to the nub. "I don't know. Sunspots. Magnetic storms. I read about them once. I know they can screw things up pretty good if a big enough one hits. Gamma rays, radiation. Tell you what, I think I better watch for three-headed calves."

Kevin laughed, though the situation was far from funny. Sunspots didn't seem quite right either.

"They always have a good idea when those things are coming," Kevin said. "Solar storms, I mean. Doesn't it take a few days for them to reach us? I don't remember hearing anything about them."

Jake shrugged. "I pay more attention to the weather on earth than the weather on the sun. What I do know is I gotta get corn in the ground soon. There'll be hay and wood to cut, and all this stuff"—he flapped his hand at the collection of tractors and combines lined up under the big pole barn nearby—"is useless right now. I'll tell you what, though." He leaned forward again. "It's a good thing this happened now and not in the middle of winter. As long as the grass keeps growin', I can get by on grazin' alone. We'll be all right, for now. How are you folks set?"

Kevin considered their situation. All their perishables had been stuffed into coolers and packed with the remnants of the ice. The previously frozen meats and vegetables were getting squishy on the edges but would keep a few days longer. As far as he knew, there was still a decent supply of cereals, rice, oatmeal, and canned goods. How long would it last? Monica was already scouring her recipe books, looking for ways to make something from nothing.

Jake said, "We got hens layin' more eggs'n we can eat. I can send some over every couple-three days. And a few of the ladies had calves over th'winter." He rubbed his big hand across his chin. The calloused pads of his fingers across his chin stubble sounded like a zipper. "Some of 'em I think I can wean. These ain't milkers, and they ain't gonna like it. But if I do this right, I can keep milking for a while. Ever have fresh milk?"

"No."

A sunny grin broke over his round face. "Oh, it's a treat, that's for sure. Well, it usually is, anyway. Can't say for sure how it'll taste coming from beefers, but it'll be better than nothin'. Tough part is keeping everything clean. Gotta be real careful about that. Got an old stanchion out there." He was almost talking to himself now, his eyes tracking back and forth as if he were in his barn taking inventory. "It'll be slow going at first—*if* I can even get 'em going at all. You're likely to hear a heck of a lot of bawlin' from over here for a few days. If I can start g'ttin' a few gallons a day, I'll send some over. And I've got a chest freezer outside stuffed full of meat from last year. That stuff's gonna spoil pretty fast. I'll bring some over."

"Jeez, Jake, you don't need to do that."

Jake's smile disappeared.

"You sure 'bout that?"

Milk normally lasted a while in their house, but that was without Dina living there full time. Their current gallon was just about empty. The one week's worth of groceries they picked up on Thursday night would soon come to an end, and the extras tucked away in the freezer were going soft in the coolers. Jake was offering him a lifeline; it would be stupid to turn it down.

"Well, thanks. I appreciate it."

"Tell you what, maybe you folks can help us out," Jake said. "Everything's going to take me and the wife a lot longer than normal, and Alma don't get around so good these days. Water's down to a trickle, and we got to have that. I still need to get a round bale a day out there and need some help. Gonna have to figure out how to do that without a vehicle."

"Yeah, yeah, absolutely. We can do that. Hey," Kevin added, "have you seen Luis and Val?"

Luis and Valerie Silva lived on the last house on Harpur's Hill Road, almost a quarter mile up from Kevin, where asphalt turned to dirt. They were college professors who seemed to spend more time guest lecturing at schools across the country than teaching courses at Oneonta, and Kevin couldn't recall seeing either of them for a while.

"Val dropped by 'bout a week ago, said they were heading out to Maine t'visit the new grandkid of theirs. Guess they'll be visiting a bit longer." Jake pulled his bandanna from his pocket and wiped his nose. "You folks may want to think about getting something in the ground yourself too. And cutting wood. How much propane you got left?"

Kevin wanted to say it had only been about two weeks since their last delivery, but the older he got, the more he found he was wrong about things like time. He'd have to check the bill. They usually went three, maybe four months between deliveries.

"You really think it's going to last that long?"

"If it was just the 'lectric, I wouldn't worry, but it's everything. Something monkeyed with the system. If it was a simple solution, we wouldn't be having this conversation, is what I think." He stuffed his bandanna back into his pocket. "Something else to think about: do you have a gun?"

There were multiple layers behind that question, and Kevin didn't like any of them. Yes, Jake could be talking about getting a gun and taking potshots at rabbits and deer, but as last night's episode had shown, things could easily get out of control with no authority on hand. And Harpursville was a rural town in a rural county in a rural part of the state—how many of his neighbors had guns? How often did Kevin hear gunshots echoing across the valley each November while he warmed up his car in the morning?

"You really think it's going to come to that, Jake?"

The farmer took a long swallow of water and looked steadily at Kevin with his pale-blue eyes—eyes that were faded by many years of sitting up on the tractor seat in the bright sunshine, circling the fields, plowing, cutting, and baling.

"I think it already has."

—

Jake had given him an idea, a way, perhaps, to dislodge those sharp words of Monica's. He was going to *do* something. He inventoried the garage. All the tools—shovels, pitchforks, and rakes—hung in a neat row on the wall. Several pairs of clean work gloves were folded neatly in a plastic bin. Aside from a few flower beds and pots of petunias hung on the porch each spring, the Bartons had never been gardeners. Though Monica had grown up on a farm, she wanted nothing to do with that life, and Kevin never had the time or interest. Now he had the time— and the need. It was a good time to start.

He towed Kelly's old red wagon down the hill, certain he was on a fool's errand. Curtis Pinkney's car sat dented and scuffed but still intact. The boys had not come back to clean up the mess, but they hadn't come back to finish breaking in either. At least not yet.

The Feed-N-Seed occupied an old railroad depot built in the days when Harpursville was important enough to warrant a railroad. It sat at the edge of the hamlet, a low red building with a shaded porch and a corrugated metal roof just across the parking lot from town hall. Kevin had been expecting the place to shut down for years; it appeared to be on its last legs when they moved in. Range wire, horse feed, and electric fence accessories were specialty items for a rapidly dwindling clientele. Yet it had scraped by, and with the Kwik-Stop now closed, it had somehow outlasted every other business in the hamlet. The proprietor, eighty-two-year-old Herman Newberry, sat in a rocker on the porch, the door wide open behind him.

"Hey, Herman, I'm glad you're open."

"Eh. What else am I going to do?" The old man's voice was strong for his age. "I figure this is my going-out-of-business sale."

Herman's face was as leathery and wrinkled as a deflated football. The left side drooped from a stroke he'd had some years before, but he regarded Kevin with bright interest.

"Funny, I seen you passing by more these couple-three days than all the years you been up there."

Kevin scratched at his itchy chin. He hadn't shaved since Friday morning. "Yeah, well, you know how it is, Herman."

"Yeah, I know how it is. Young folks like you always running around, no time to hang around a little place like this and pass the time. What you looking for? I got no propane. Folks bought up all my bottles."

"I'm looking for seeds. Vegetables."

Herman turned slightly so his good eye looked at Kevin dead on. "Huh. Most folks haven't thought of that yet. Come on, let's see what we got." He pushed himself up from his chair and led Kevin into the dark store.

Half an hour or so later, Kevin had loaded up the wagon with a few bags of mulch and fertilizer, a pile of plastic starter trays, and a bag full of seed packets. While Herman didn't price gouge, he did charge sales tax, working everything out in a notebook in an exact, if somewhat shaky hand. It just about cleaned out Kevin's remaining cash.

"That's going to be well worth it." Herman watched Kevin struggle to keep his pile from falling off the wagon. "Here, tell you what, let me throw in a couple of these to help you get out of here." He tottered back into the store and returned a moment later with a pair of bungee cords dangling from his hand like dead snakes. "On the house."

"Thanks, Herman." Kevin strapped his load down. "What's next for you?"

"I suppose I'll stay open till I've got nothing left. I figure in another couple days everyone'll catch on like you. Then I'll have a big run on what's left. After that?" He shrugged.

Kevin saw how little there was to the man. His shirt hung off his shoulders. The legs of his pants looked empty. He thought of his parents. A hard lump formed in his throat. *They're fine*, he told himself. They were a good fifteen years younger than Herman and in much better health. *They're fine.* He cleared the lump, focused on the old man.

"Are you doing okay, Herman? Are you getting enough to eat?"

"Eh. I don't eat so much these days, but I've got a secret." His good eye gleamed, bright and alert like a crow's. "When my wife was ill, we got a few cases of that Ensure stuff. She passed without making a dent in it. Tastes like crap but keeps me going well enough."

Kevin gave an experimental tug on the wagon's handle. Pulling it up the hill was going to be a bitch. He looked up at the old man, who was easing himself back into his rocker.

"What do you think happened, Herman?"

The old man pursed his liver-colored lips and looked off in the distance for a moment, then eyed Kevin.

"Does it really matter?"

———

Harpur's Hill was neither the biggest or steepest hill in the county, and Kevin's house wasn't that far up, a mere two hundred feet or so past where Harpur's Hill Road split off from the county road. It was a tough climb for an out-of-shape forty-two-year-old dragging an overloaded wagon, however, and it was made worse by the skinny years in the town budget that left the road pocked from the ravages of winter. By the time he got home, Kevin's shirt was soaked through with sweat, and his shoulders and legs ached. He sat on the porch and let his heart slow down before going inside. Kelly and Dina were playing yet another Scrabble game in the living room. It was chilly in the house. Kelly wore a thick sweater; Dina had a blanket draped over her shoulders. Kevin was amused to see that both girls had their phones close to hand.

"Hey, girls, I need your help with something. You'll warm up. I promise. Meet me outside."

He felt bad about pressing Dina into service, but Monica was exuding a *leave me alone* vibe. Besides, he figured Dina's participation would make for a more cooperative, cheerful Kelly.

Out in the garage, he pulled his tools down and carried them outside to where the girls waited.

"Oh, come on, Dad," Kelly said when she saw the tools. "Do we have to?"

"Yes, we have to. Come on."

She kept up a steady stream of complaints as they waded through the ankle-deep grass: it was scratchy; it was going to rain; there were too many bugs. Kevin gritted his teeth and surveyed the yard, looking for the best place for his garden. He settled on a swath behind the garage that looked to be both bright and flat enough.

He laid the tools down in the grass.

"Do me a favor, girls. See if you can find something to mark the corners. Rocks, big sticks, logs—anything that will stand out, okay?"

Dina set off at once. Kelly stood with her chin thrust out and her feet spread, an almost perfect copy of her mother's defiant look.

"Why do we have to do this?"

Kevin took a deep breath and fought off the urge to yell at her. He didn't want to embarrass her in front of Dina. He put his hands gently on her shoulders. "This is important, honey. We've only got so much food. You're hungry. I'm hungry. Mom's hungry. Dina's hungry."

"Like that's going to make a difference. What are we supposed to eat *now*?"

His fingers tightened on her shoulders. He forced them open. "We're okay for now. This is for the future. I don't want to scare you, but we don't know how long this is going to last. And as soon as this garden's planted, everything will probably go back to normal."

She smiled. A little, anyway. "Like the hurricane."

"Like the hurricane. Just think, fresh vegetables, all summer long."

"I hate eating healthy." Full smile now. "I'm sorry for being cranky."

"I'm used to it." He hugged her and kissed the top of her head.

"Ugh, Dad, you're smelly."

"You're no bed of roses yourself, kid."

He rubbed her back, kissed her again, then turned her loose to find sticks. Too late. Dina was there with four skinny tree branches in her arms. She smiled at them, but Kevin thought her eyes looked watery.

"Hey, those look perfect, Dina," he said. "Let's stake out the corners."

———

Kevin drove the sharp tip of the shovel into the ground, ripping through the tightly woven roots. He cut a square of turf, then wedged the shovel beneath and levered up. Kelly and Dina dug their fingers into the edge and tugged, peeling the sod off the soil beneath as if it were the skin of an orange. As they lifted, Kevin slid the shovel beneath, slicing the fibrous roots that clung to the soil below, taking great care to avoid the girls' fingers.

He tried making a few jokes at first, but they fell flat. After a few shrieks from Kelly over scuttling spiders, centipedes, and mutilated worms, they worked in relative silence. The only sounds were their grunts, occasional instructions passed between them, and the grass; it gave up its hold on the earth reluctantly, with the sound of ripping fabric. Though the day was cool, all three dripped sweat onto the earth. The ripe smell of their bodies mingled with the damp soil and bruised grass.

"Are we done yet?" Kelly asked. "My back hurts, and I don't feel so good."

Kevin straightened and stretched his shoulders and back. His muscles groaned, his joints popped and crackled. They had made better progress than he expected, but they weren't finished. A square of grass bit into the brown rectangle of cleared ground, making the plot look a little like the state of Nebraska.

"Just a little left." He wiped his forehead with his arm, leaving a dark-brown smudge on his sleeve. "It shouldn't take that much time."

Runners of sweat carved clean trails down their grimy faces. Dina looked tired but okay. Kelly was another story.

"I don't feel good," she repeated. "I'm all shaky. My legs are wobbly, and I'm getting a headache."

She held her hands flat out in front of her. They trembled. Of course, this was the girl who had once heated a thermometer on a radiator trying to fake a fever. She ended up with a burned tongue. Kevin studied her face and frowned. She could fake the shakes but she couldn't fake pale. Beneath the dirt, her skin had a waxy quality he didn't like.

Hunger. None of them had eaten since lunch, and she had worked hard. Kevin cursed himself for pushing them, but he felt compelled to get the garden prepped. He looked at the sky. Heavy clouds were piling up, and the temperature had dropped.

"I'm okay," Dina said. "I can keep going."

He stripped off his gloves. His palms burned and his knuckles were sore. More alarming was the small circle of rubbed-off skin on the webbing between his thumb and forefinger. *That's going to hurt like a bastard later.*

"You know what? Let's take a break and see if Mom's got dinner going. Nice job, girls."

They trudged toward the kitchen door. Dina put an arm around Kelly's shoulders and hugged her. She whispered something that made Kelly laugh and swat playfully at her arm, but there was definitely a wobble to her walk.

Out of habit, he glanced at his watch, but it still didn't work. He pulled it off and jammed it in his pocket, then looked up and tried to reckon the time from the sky: two, maybe three hours of daylight left, he couldn't say for sure. After dinner, they would come back out and finish the job. Weather permitting, they would plant tomorrow or the next day. Eventually, there would be tomatoes and cucumbers and zucchini and green beans and more. What they would eat next week or the week after, he didn't know. That was a worry for another day.

———

Monica cooked pork chops, rice, and a half-serving of barely frozen vegetables. She also forced a cup of hot chicken broth into each of them. Kevin's cramped hands made it tough to cut his meat. Kelly improved with the food, but she still looked ragged.

"It's coming along great out there," he said as he cleared his plate. "Thanks for the help, girls. Just a little more, and we'll be ready to plant."

After dinner, he went into the bathroom and poured peroxide over his blister. It *did* hurt like a bastard.

Monica waylaid him when he came out. She pulled him into the kitchen.

"She can't go back out there again. Not today."

"We need to get it done, Monica."

She lowered her voice, but her urgency came through, loud and clear. "Look at you—you can barely stand up straight. And your hands." She grabbed them, flipped them over. His palms were the color of boiled lobster. "They're practically bleeding. What does it matter if you get that patch of land cleared today or tomorrow? Don't kill yourself."

"We don't know what's coming tomorrow or the day after or the day after that. What if it rains all week? You grew up on a farm. You know there's a short window of opportunity to plant up here."

"She's exhausted, Kevin. *You're* exhausted. Come here."

She led him to the living room. Kelly was splayed on the couch, her mouth open, one arm thrown back over her head, the other dangling to the floor. Kevin recognized the pose from his college days, when he'd find his roommates passed out every Saturday morning.

"Dinner helped," Monica said in a low voice, "but she's not in shape for this sort of thing. And you—you need to be careful. You can't go dropping dead of a heart attack."

"I'm not in that bad shape." She raised an eyebrow. "Look, maybe it's all for nothing. Maybe I get the lawn dug up and the power comes back. Maybe FEMA shows up tomorrow with tents and kitchens and truckloads of food and supplies."

"I hope so."

"Me too. More than anything. But—"

"But."

Her lower lip trembled, just a bit. He pulled her into a tight hug and thought about that last patch of grass that needed to be torn up.

"She can stay in," he said. "I'll finish up. It shouldn't take that long."

He felt her shoulders rise and fall as she sighed. "I'll come out and help you."

He was grateful for the offer but he knew how little she liked digging in the dirt. It was part of a life she had grown up with and didn't really want to go back to.

"It's okay, really," he said. "I'll be okay. There's not much left."

———

The problem with hard physical labor wasn't the work itself—it was stopping, then trying to start again. Stopping gave exhaustion time to settle in and take hold. It gave time for Kevin's muscles to cool down and tighten up. When he returned to the future garden, his legs were as limber as telephone poles and just about as heavy. The shovel felt like it had put on sixty pounds since he put it down. With a great effort, he jammed it into the turf. It barely broke the surface and sent a shockwave up his arms and burned his palms.

Maybe Monica was right, maybe he should leave it for tomorrow.

Footsteps swished in the grass behind him. Kevin turned and found Dina making her way toward him.

"You want some help?"

"Oh. No, I'll be okay. Why don't you go back in and—"

"Momma B. said she didn't need any help, and Kelly's still sleeping." She twisted her fingers together and bounced on the balls of her feet. Kevin didn't want to take advantage of her, but it was clear he'd never get this done by himself. She wanted—maybe *needed*—to help.

"You want to chop or pull?"

"Can I chop? My back hurts from all that bending."

"Well, my arms hurt from all that chopping, so I guess that's a good deal for both of us."

He pulled off the gloves and handed them to her. She slipped her fingers in and wiggled them like some birthday party magician.

"Ew. They're all wet."

"Sorry. I'm a sweaty guy," he mumbled.

She plunged the shovel into the ground, stepped on the edge, and drove it deeper. Then she pulled it out, moved it a few inches down, and repeated the process.

"You're a natural," Kevin said.

"I learned from the best."

He didn't know how she still had any energy left, but she attacked the ground and her cheerfulness rubbed off on him. While two worked slower than three—especially when the two were already tired and sore—the remaining chunk of lawn soon disappeared, and they stood at the edge of a thirty-by-fifteen-foot rectangle of bare ground.

Dina held out her fist. It took a second for Kevin to recognize the request for a fist bump, which he gave at the cost of some pain to his knuckles.

"It's a lot easier with a rototiller," Dina said. "My mom uses one."

She appeared to be staring right through the ground. When she looked up, Kevin saw tears pooling in her eyes. He rubbed at his sandpapery chin, not sure what was called for.

"Hey, I'm really glad we got this done today, Dina. Thanks."

She nodded and blinked, dragged the back of her hand across her nose. "I'm glad I could help. I feel so . . . useless."

"Stop it. You're not useless."

"I feel like it. You guys are so good to me, and I'm just eating your food and getting in the way . . ."

Crap, he thought. *Don't cry.*

"We're happy to have you. Kelly would be insufferable if you weren't here." The joke was feeble, but she managed a wavering smile. "You're always welcome here, Dina. You know that."

"I know. But . . . I miss my family." She sniffed and bent her head.

His fatherly instincts told him to reach out and offer her consolation, but his sense of propriety made him hold back. Somewhere along the line it had become taboo to so much as touch someone else's kid, especially teenage girls, so he stood by and ran his hand along the top of his dirty head while trying to think of things he needed to do. They'd have to rake out the rocks and break up the soil, mix in the additives . . . but that would have to wait, it was getting dark, and the breeze was picking up. A cold drop of rain hit his arm.

Beside him, Dina continued to sniffle. *Ahh, fuck it.* He laid a tentative hand on her back. His abraded palm itched and burned.

"It's okay," he said. "It's going to be okay."

For a moment, he thought she was going to really break down. She took several deep, shuddery breaths and wiped her eyes with the backs of her hands.

"Thanks," she said. "I'm sorry for being such a dork."

"You're not a dork. We're all worried about people." His thoughts turned to his own parents. Were they okay? He'd check Bertha again when they went in. Just in case. "I'm sure they're fine."

She wrapped her arms around herself and nodded.

"Are you cold?" he asked. "We should go inside. Rain's coming."

And it was getting cold. He had thought at first it was just because they had stopped working, but the temperature had dropped; the sky to the west was turning the gray of battleships. The air tasted like winter.

"Okay. Thanks, Mr. Barton. Maybe . . ."

When she didn't say anything else, he said, "Maybe what?"

"Nothing. I don't know."

She didn't make a move toward the house, just stood there chewing her lip and twisting the ring around her little finger.

"Maybe what?" he prompted.

"Well, I was thinking, maybe I should just try to walk home."

"Walk? That's kind of far."

"It's only seven miles. If I leave my stuff here, I could run it. We run that far in track practice all the time."

Seven miles. It was an easy enough trip. Ten minutes in the car, straight up the state road to the end, a couple of side streets, nothing complicated about it. If she ran all the way, it would take her less than an hour. Walking, it would take two hours tops. She would probably be fine.

But.

But they'd never know if she made it or not. What if they let her go, and a week later the power came back and the McCrays called? He heard the Duchess in his head, "Thank you for taking care of Dina this week. I hope she behaved herself. We're on our way to pick her up." Or, more likely, "Do you think you could bring her home? I'm so busy right now." Even thinking about it turned his stomach upside down. How could you tell someone, "Sorry, we let her leave. She should've been home a week ago"?

"I really want to get home, Mr. B." She made a brave attempt at a smile. "My family is totally whacko, but I love them. I need to know they're okay. And you guys are going to get sick of me."

"Impossible."

Was it, though? Part of why the girls could spend so much time together was there were always distractions: TV, the internet, videos, school. Without those things, would they get on each other's nerves? They hadn't yet, but it had only been four days. And then there was something else: they weren't at the breaking point as far as food went, not yet, but they were stretching. Without Dina, their supplies would last a little longer.

She stood before him, her eyes big and round and her hands clasped beneath her chin, a posture of hope. He couldn't resist the look, but he couldn't send her out on her own either.

"Tell you what," he said. "We'll walk you home."

"You don't have to do that."

"Yeah, we do. I wouldn't feel right just turning you loose. No telling what kind of trouble you'd cause on the way home."

It wasn't just her safety he was thinking of. He had no idea if her family was even home. What if she went all that way and found an empty house?

"We'll go tomorrow," he said. A cold raindrop landed on his head and soaked through his thinning hair. "Or the day after, depending on the weather."

"Thank you!" Her bouncy energy was back. She threw her arms around him. "Thank you so much, Mr. Barton!"

Dina hugged him, and he stood there with his hands floating in air over her back, not sure what to do. Again, his cheeks flared. The hug felt good but made him uncomfortable.

"It's okay." He patted her back, once, twice, and she took the hint and broke away. "Now, let's go in before we get soaked."

"Do you think—" She paused and gave him a hopeful little-girl face. "Do you think maybe we could have some hot chocolate?"

It sounded good to him. "We can probably arrange that."

She helped carry the tools back to the garage. A strong breeze clattered branches together and rustled the leaves that were just beginning to unfurl. Thick clouds stretched from one end of the sky to the other. It was getting dark. Not twilight dark, storm dark.

Weariness was taking over again. What he wouldn't give for a hot shower.

A fresh gust brought a scattering of rain. Kevin paused outside the garage, staring at the corner of his roof. A fat drop of water hung off the edge of a shingle, then fell into the gutter.

"Mr. Barton? Is everything okay?"

"Yeah. You should go in now. I just thought of something."

"Can I help you with anything?"

"No, thanks, Dina. This won't take long. Save me some hot chocolate."

Beneath the tool bench he found a stack of buckets that once held joint compound. He pulled them apart, peered inside, and shook out spiders, dried bits of spackle, and dead insects. Wanting to work fast before he got thoroughly soaked and before it got too dark to see, Kevin hurried out and went to the nearest corner of the house.

A rising breeze played with his hair. Tight muscles in his back groaned as he bent and tried to pry off the bottom section of downspout. His fingers, weak from the day's exertions, couldn't get a firm grip.

He stepped back and squinted up through the gloom. The downspout looked loose near the top. He ran back to the garage once more and returned with his extension ladder. The rain was steady now, fat droplets that stuck his hair to his head. A few mushy snowflakes mixed with the rain fell like sodden cotton balls. Rain plastered his hair to his head. Water ran into his eyes, trickled down his back, stuck his shirt and pants to his skin.

Kevin hauled on the rope and ran the extension up until it could reach the gutter above Kelly's second-floor window. He wedged the ladder against the house and climbed. At the top, he leaned against the ladder and wrapped his hands around the downspout. Grunting with effort and fighting to keep his footing on the slippery aluminum rungs, he pulled and twisted while the rain drummed on the roof, on his head, all over him. Snow blobs splattered on his neck.

With one final tug, the downspout came away and fell to the side, taking his balance with it. The ladder pulled away from the house, and Kevin had a brief, dizzying sensation of weightlessness. He flailed and threw his weight forward. The ladder thumped against the wall then began to slide to the right. *Oh shit oh shit oh shit!* If it went over, Kevin would land squarely on the car, and his mind stupidly fixed on how much it would cost to replace the windshield.

Kevin's fingers scrabbled along the wet clapboard, desperately seeking purchase, finding none. He was going over, there was nothing he could do but maybe try to leap over the car at the last minute. Then the ladder caught on a corner molding and jerked to a halt. Kevin clung to the ladder, not daring to move, but the icy rain was everywhere. It sheeted down over his face, into his eyes, his nose, his mouth. It weighed down his jeans and shirt, and it was freezing. If he didn't get down soon, he'd be incapable of moving at all. He glanced at the gutter. Despite the downpour, a mere dribble came through the opening. Kevin reached up with a shaking hand and probed the opening. A mass of slimy black leaves that stank like old farts slopped out and fell to the ground. Cold water followed, gushing over his hand and arm. Kevin crawled down the ladder one rung at a time. As desperate as he was to get out of the rain, he resisted the urge to rush.

Once safe on the ground, he placed a bucket in the path of the cascade. Soon the bottom was covered with gritty, dirty water. He'd have to screen out the roof debris, but it was a start.

Slipping and sliding on the saturated lawn, Kevin ran around the house with his other buckets. Fortunately, the other downspouts came apart without any trouble. Teeth chattering, he hauled the ladder back to the garage, barely able to tell where the cold metal ended and his hands began. Monica met him in the kitchen, dark fury in her eyes.

"What the hell is wrong with you? Are you trying to get yourself killed?"

"W-w-we n-n-n-need w-water."

She shoved him through the kitchen into the little bathroom. His sneakers squelched with each step.

"Strip," she said.

"W-what about the g-g-girls?"

"I'm not going to parade you through the house naked. Just get out of those clothes."

Buttons slipped through his numb fingers. Water coated every inch of skin. It squeezed out of his shoes and socks and puddled around him on the floor. His shirt and pants stuck tight, smothering him. All he wanted was to get out of his clothes—but the buttons, the damn buttons. He couldn't work the fucking buttons, and he had to get out of the clothes. He started tearing at his shirt, raking at his pants, desperate to shed them, not able to do a damn thing.

Monica grabbed his wrists, her fingers hot and strong. "It's okay, it's okay," she whispered. "Calm down. It's okay." When he stopped flailing, she peeled off his clothes for him. Each piece hit the floor with a slap that echoed in the small room. When he was naked, she wrapped a towel around him and held him close until the worst of his shivers passed.

"My God, Kevin, couldn't you have waited until it *wasn't* raining to do this?"

"I j-j-just thought of it."

She rubbed his arms, warming him, until they both realized they were standing in a cold puddle of water.

"Stay here."

She left him sitting on the toilet, huddled under the towel. When she returned, she had sweatpants and a sweatshirt, clean underwear and socks. Kevin pulled them on, marveling over how good they felt, how much of a relief it was to be dry. He stepped out of the bathroom, his hair still wet, his body more sore than he could ever remember, and cold—a down deep cold.

"Come on, the girls made a fire."

Shuffling along like Herman Newberry, he followed Monica to the living room. Kelly and Dina sat in front of the fireplace, illuminated by the glow of the fire and half a dozen candles and lanterns set around the room. The Scrabble board was once again laid out between them. Kelly, he was glad to see, looked far better than she had before.

Every inch of his body ached now. He winced as he lowered himself to the floor next to Kelly. Monica draped a blanket over his back. The dry clothes, the fire, the blanket, all wrapped him in comforting heat.

"Oh, that feels good." He inched toward the fireplace. He wondered how Jake Hillman, a man who had at least twenty years and probably a hundred pounds on him, could haul feed, haul water, haul manure, and do all the other stuff he did. Despite his little paunch, Kevin looked to be in much better shape than the big man, but he felt about a hundred years old. Kelly hugged him from behind, then put her head on his shoulder.

"Are you okay, Daddy?"

"Yeah. I'll be okay, thanks. How are you, sweetie?"

"I'm a lot better. I'm sorry I wimped out."

"You didn't wimp out. You did great today."

She kissed him on the cheek. Dina pressed a mug of hot chocolate into his hands. It was the cheap stuff, made with water, not milk, and way too sweet, but it warmed him from the inside while the fire warmed him from the outside.

The heat soaked into his core, made him feel lazy and good. Mesmerized by the dancing flames, he listened to Kelly and Dina laugh and giggle over their Scrabble game. Even Monica, who had been edgy since Saturday, joined in.

Maybe this isn't so bad, he thought. On a typical night, the three of them would scatter to different corners of the house, watching TV, burying themselves in books and computers, texting and emailing, and Facebooking or FaceTiming—or whatever the app du jour was with friends and family the world over. They lived under one roof but in three different worlds. Maybe when all this was over, he would junk the TV and limit the internet. Maybe they could have family nights where they didn't allow anything but talk time. That would be nice.

Kelly nudged him. "Are you sleeping?"

"Uh, no. Just resting my eyes. What did you say?"

"We're almost ready for a new game. Do you want to play?"

"I think I'll pass." He leaned over and frowned at the board. "What kind of words are *piff* and *floot*, anyway?"

"*Our* words," Dina said.

"I think I'd be at too much of a disadvantage," he said. "Maybe next time."

"Maybe you should go upstairs," Monica said.

Bed sounded like heaven, but Kevin liked being here, close to the fire, close to his family. He leaned against Monica and closed his eyes, enjoying the fire, the candles, the laughing girls, the encircling arms of his wife, even the rain drumming on the porch roof. It felt so good he could almost forget that something really big and strange had happened to the world.

It didn't take long for him to fall into a deep, heavy sleep.

—

Monica listened to the crackle and hiss of the dying fire, the gentle drip of rain on the eaves, and her husband's slow, steady breathing. The girls had gone upstairs shortly after dark. Unlike most nights, when they whispered and giggled until late, they had gone right to sleep, worn out by the afternoon's work. She could have killed Kevin for pushing Kelly so hard. She wasn't used to that kind of work. You didn't train for a marathon by running a marathon. It would take time to build up to whatever the situation would require.

The fire threw shifting, orange light on Kevin's face. She let her fingers play lightly with his hair. It would take a bomb to wake him; he was out, hard.

Poets waxed on about the beauty of sleep, how it smoothed the worries and cares off a person's face, restored them to a childlike state, made them look years younger. What a load of crap. Sprawled as he was, with his mouth hanging open and a glimmer of spittle creeping down his cheek, he looked more like a man who had fallen off a ten-story building than a man in peaceful repose.

She wanted to curl up against him, take some comfort from his warmth and solidity, but floor sleeping had lost its appeal long ago. Instead, she watched the fire burn down and thought about vegetable gardens and rain buckets, a cooler full of melting ice and warming meats, about neighbors offering milk and eggs in exchange for work.

Monica took the hurricane lamp into the pantry. As much as she tried to distance herself from her frugal farm upbringing, keeping a fully stocked pantry was one lesson that had stuck with her, incessantly hammered home by her grandmother, who had grown up in the Depression. Grandmother Willsey hammered a lot of things home, most of which, in Monica's view, was bullshit, but she had listened. You didn't not listen to Grandmother Willsey.

She set the lantern carefully on a shelf and appraised their stores, lifting and shaking boxes to test their weight and assess their fullness. Cereal, pasta, oatmeal. She counted cans: tuna, fruit cocktail, kidney beans. She shifted bags of flour and rice and split peas and lentils, slid them back and forth, making mental notes of how much of this and how much of that. Grandmother Willsey's Depression-era recipes flashed through her mind. Mock apple pie. Cakes without butter or milk, flatbreads.

How far could she stretch this? For how long could she feed three, no, four—she couldn't forget Dina—people?

She stood in the pantry for a long time, chewing the edge of her thumbnail, her eyes crawling up and down the shelves. Finally, she took the lantern and stepped back into the kitchen. After a moment's consideration, she lifted the key for the door off its hook and held it in her palm, smiling at the memory of their first days in their new house. It was a house of doors, each with its own key, and none of the keys were marked. She and Kevin had spent half a day matching keys to locks, and the rest of the day chasing each other around the house, locking each other in and out of different rooms. The game had ended with them making love in the parlor. So many things had ended with them making love in those days.

She closed the door, slid the key in the lock, and heard the satisfying *thunk* of the bolt sliding home.

"You're being totally stupid," she told herself, and her voice sounded extra loud in the quiet kitchen. The rodent gnawing at the pit of her stomach told her something different. She put the key in her pocket and went up to bed.

———

The fire had burned down to sullen red embers when Kevin awoke alone on the floor. Rain pattered softly outside. Someone had tucked a pillow beneath his head and laid an extra blanket over him. He grunted and struggled to his feet, his muscles one big knot. It felt like it took hours to climb the stairs. His knees popped like knotty pine in the fireplace.

He made his way upstairs by feel and crawled into bed, relishing the soft mattress, smooth sheets, and Monica's body heat.

"Kev?"

"Sorry to wake you, honey. Go back to sleep." He settled himself into bed, letting the mattress cradle him.

"It's okay," she said. "I'm not sleeping."

"Sorry about before." He was drifting already. God, he was tired. "I wasn't thinking. It just seemed . . . important."

"It *is* important. I'm—I'm sorry too. What I said the other night—I didn't mean it that way. I was just . . ."

He was floating, spinning slowly like a satellite in space. "I know," he murmured. "S'all right."

"I'm worried about our food," she said. "We've got enough dry goods—rice, beans, cereals, things like that—to last a little while. We've got some apples that haven't gone bad yet, and the frozen meat should hold up a few more days."

He drifted further away, little by little.

"It's not going to last forever," she went on. "And what do we do when the gas runs out?"

"They topped us off just before this happened, right? It should last a couple of months. And there's the barbecue."

"We're using the gas to make hot water for cleaning too."

The panicky tone in her voice brought him back down all the way. He propped himself up, wincing at the spearpoints that pierced him all over. "Jake's going to get us eggs. And milk. And some of that stuff in his freezer will get us through a few more days."

"That will help," she said. "But there's something else."

She didn't continue. Kevin touched her rigid arm but didn't say anything. He knew better than to press her.

When she spoke again, her voice was barely above a whisper.

"What are we going to do about Dina?"

"What do you mean?"

"She eats a lot."

Kevin snorted. Dina's appetite had always been a point of amusement to them. He didn't know if it was being on the track team or a high metabolism, but she ate more like a sixteen-year-old boy than a girl.

Monica rolled over and stared at him. "What?"

"Sorry," he said. "It just sounded funny, that's all. She's trying."

Monica rolled onto her back and stared up at the ceiling. "I know she's trying. I feel bad for even bringing it up. I feel bad for *her*. But what are we going to do when we run out of food?"

"I've got some old shoes in the closet."

She sat up fast. "That's not funny."

"No, you're right. I'm sorry." He took her hand. His fingers were stiff and slow moving. His blister burned like hell. "What would you like to do about her?"

"I don't know." She sighed and stroked the back of his hand. "What can we do? Nothing, I guess. I just needed to say it. I'm . . . I'm . . ."

Scared. He wanted to tell her it was okay to admit, but admissions of that sort didn't come easy to her. Monica reacted to fear by going on the attack. It was a defense mechanism developed by having two older brothers who did everything they could to torment their little sister.

"I keep telling myself it's just a blackout, but it's not. If it were just a blackout, we could drive down the Price Chopper. This . . ."

He found her hand. It was cold. He took it, raised it to his mouth, and kissed the back of it.

"If it's any consolation to you," he said, remembering his conversation with Dina, "she wants to go home. She told me after dinner. She wants to walk."

"Can she do that?"

"Not by herself. That wouldn't be right. I'll go with her, make sure she gets home safe."

He burrowed deeper under the covers while she mulled this over. "When?"

He yawned. Sleep was coming for him again, fast. "Once it stops raining. It's just a little walk. I'll be back by dinner."

She slid back down and rolled to face him. He put his arm over her, kissed her once. His body felt like it weighed ten tons and was going to sink right through the bed.

"I wonder if she'll really be better off with the Duchess than with us," she said. "Can you imagine how *she's* dealing with this? And she's got the other two. Plus that pompous ass of a husband."

"Do you *want* her to stay?" His voice was getting further away.

"I don't know. I mean, I'm not . . . I don't . . . I don't want to sound like a monster, you know? I love the girl. But if she weren't here, we could stretch what we have for longer."

"They may not even be there," Kevin yawned. "Wasn't she running kids all over town?"

"Isn't she always? You can't talk to that woman without hearing about how busy she is. But . . . well, I guess we should try. Her place is with her family, isn't it?"

Dina wanted to be with her family. She belonged with her family. He wasn't crazy about a fourteen-mile round trip. As his locked-up muscles indicated, he wasn't exactly in prime physical condition for it either. Still, she wanted to go home, that much was clear, and Monica wanted her to go—*that* was also clear. She could hem and haw, but he knew she would feel better about things if they didn't have to worry about Dina. They all would. Except maybe Kelly.

A short walk, Kevin thought, as he drifted off. A couple-three hours, as folks in Harpursville said. Like a walk in the park, as they said where he grew up. Home before dinner.

CHAPTER 6

IT RAINED THROUGHOUT the next day, which was probably a good thing. Kevin's arms and legs felt like they'd been filled with concrete, his joints with glass. He could barely straighten his fingers. He spent most of the day in front of the fireplace, hoping the heat would melt his aches away.

The mood in the house matched the weather, sullen and gray. No candle or hurricane lamp could clear the gloom. It was made worse by the nagging feeling of missing out: work, school, parents, friends. Kevin kept imagining his coworkers wondering where the hell he was and why he hadn't called. He tried not to imagine his parents floundering in the dark, preferring to see them instead watching the blackout unfold from their fully powered Florida condo. On the rare occasions he rose and creaked his way to the bathroom, he'd stop in the kitchen and try Bertha. Still dead. Monica was trying to read, but Kevin caught her more than once staring over the top of her book, eyes far away. The girls talked about school a lot, and while they seemed happy for the day off, there was unmistakable anxiety in their voices about assignments coming due, tests coming up, and rumors about the fast-approaching prom.

Scrabble gave way to Jenga, which yielded to Monopoly, but that ended in a dispute over whether there were three houses or four on Ventnor Avenue. Kelly flounced off and barricaded herself in her room. Dina retreated to the den. Even Kevin, who was not looking forward to the long walk, had to admit it was probably best to get Dina home.

"Maybe tomorrow," he said to Monica.

"I hope so," she said.

———

The rain stopped that night. The next morning was fine and clear. Raindrops sparkled on the grass, thousands of rainbows prismed from drops suspended on twigs and branches. Pale green leaves unspooled in the sun. Kevin despaired at what the combination of rainy nights and cool, sunny days would do to his lawn. He'd need to hire a landscaper to get it under control once this was done. The economic recovery from the blackout would be fueled by landscapers, he mused.

Dina came downstairs for breakfast with her small backpack of clothes slung over her shoulder and an extra bounce in her step. She opted to leave the bulk of her schoolbooks with the Bartons.

"You really don't need to walk me home. I don't want to be a pain in the butt." She paused for a bite of eggs. "I appreciate the company but I hate, hate, hate to be so much trouble."

Kelly sat, round-shouldered and downcast. Her dark hair hung like a limp curtain, casting her face in shadow. She pushed her eggs around her plate.

"Cheer up, Kelly," Kevin said. "It's not like you're never going to see her again."

Yet even as he said this, he wondered. Seven miles wasn't much by car. It wasn't a big deal to walk either—*if* you could, say, stop for an ice cream or a soda or to use a bathroom. Without those luxuries, it became a very different proposition. It could be the last they saw of each other for a long time.

Monica, after much consideration, had decided to stay behind. "I feel a little funny leaving the house empty," she told him, and while Kevin understood, he thought she could stand to expend some of the nervous energy that had been charging her up the last few days. "I'll find something to do," she said. "Maybe I'll even rake some rocks out of that garden. Kelly can help."

Kelly's back straightened like she'd been Tasered. "What? No way, I'm going."

They stared each other down. The only sound was the kitchen door swinging shut behind Dina, who slipped away from the fight. Kevin tried his best to fade into the background before they asked him what he thought.

"Mom," Kelly said. "This is my best friend. I'm not going to let her walk home alone."

"Your father will be with her."

"Well, then," Kelly said in triumph, "he'll need someone to keep him company on his way back here."

Monica's mouth opened. Kevin braced himself, but no sound came out. She closed it again, then scooped plates off the table and put them in the sink. Kelly looked as surprised at her victory as Kevin felt. Knowing better than to push her luck, she ran off to tell Dina the good news and to get ready.

They filled water bottles and packed something of a lunch: a couple of apples, a baggie with some homemade trail mix. Monica threw in a half-empty jar of peanut butter and some spoons for good measure.

"It's not much," she said, "but it's better than nothing."

"It's good energy food," Dina said. Her eyes shone with a mixture of excitement and tears. "Thank you so much, Momma B." She bear-hugged Monica. "Goodbye."

"We'll see you again." Kevin thought he heard a catch in his wife's voice. "Be well. Say hi to your parents." She hugged Kelly too. "Be careful out there."

"Why careful?" Kelly said. "It's not like we're going to get hit by cars or anything."

"Just be careful." She looked at Kevin. "Can I talk to you for a minute?"

"Sure. Girls, why don't you wait outside?"

"Oh, here comes the big, romantic goodbye." Kelly dragged Dina outside.

Once the girls were out of earshot, Monica turned to Kevin. "You need to be careful. We don't know what's going on out there."

Kevin frowned. "What are you worried about? It's not like this is *The Walking Dead* or something."

"It's not zombies I'm worried about." She chewed on her thumbnail for a moment, then pulled open a drawer and removed an item folded in a dish towel. She flipped open the cloth, revealing a large knife in a leather scabbard. "Take this."

"What the hell is that?"

"It's my old hunting knife. Take it."

"You want me to skin a bear while I'm out there?" He put his hands up to his shoulders, refusing to touch the knife. "Sorry, no. That's an accident waiting to happen."

"No, it isn't. That stuff the other night with the car was just a couple of kids acting stupid. The power's been out near a week. We're not the only ones running low on food, Kevin. Desperate people do desperate things." She held the knife out again. "Take it."

Resistance was futile. He took the knife, slid it out of its sheath. The six-inch silver blade gleamed. It looked sharp enough to perform microsurgery, sturdy enough to hack off a leg. He clipped the sheath to his belt, easing the knife into the worn leather. The hilt dug into the soft flesh of his side. He put his jacket on, tugging it down so that it covered up the knife.

"You should have that showing," Monica said.

"I don't want to worry the girls."

Her fingers worked at her necklace. "I hope you don't have to use it."

"I'm not going to have to use it. This is going to be easy. We'll be back at"—he looked at the wall clock and grinned—"ten fifteen."

She allowed herself a small smile and hugged him, hard. "Please be careful," she said into his chest. "Come back safe. Keep my baby safe."

"We'll be safe. I've got a knife."

———

They stood in the center of the road, looking down at the hamlet. Kevin considered cutting through the big field across the road from the town hall but changed his mind when he saw how wet the grass was. No one needed a seven-mile hike in wet shoes and socks.

"Let's stick with the road," Kevin said.

Down into the hamlet they went. Dina bounced around them, prattling on about how grateful she was to the Bartons for putting up with her and how excited she was to be seeing her family again. Kelly perked up once they were on the move, and Kevin thought there might be some relief for her. She wasn't used to sharing a room, and she could do without the unspoken pressure to keep her guest constantly entertained.

Herman Newberry sat on his chair in front of the Feed-N-Seed, shaded by the porch.

"Still open for business?" Kevin called out.

"Why not? Still nothin' better t'do."

By the time they reached the Four Corners, their mood sagged like the porches of old houses.

"It's spooky," Dina said.

Harpursville was always quiet during work hours, but there was a hush Kevin hadn't noticed on his two trips in since the blackout. And there were little things wrong with the scene, things that made the skin on his neck and back prickle. A bag of garbage ripped open, the contents smeared over the sidewalk in yellow, red, and brown streaks like a giant's finger-painting. The stench of rot rising from it followed them far down the street. The stop sign at the Four Corners bent out over the road at a steep angle. Beneath the word "Stop" someone had scrawled "the experiment" in blue paint. *That's one rotten experiment,* Kevin thought. The directional sign pointing to Algonquin had been assaulted with a bat or some other heavy object—the surface was pitted, scored, and bent beyond readability. A bed sheet dangled from an attic window like an escape ladder. A shrub had been uprooted from in front of a house. It lay on the lawn like a tumbleweed. A sense of disorder prevailed.

"Where are the police?" Kelly asked quietly.

"Probably trying to fix their cars," Kevin said.

Cops were scarce in Harpursville on a good day, and these were not good days. The town relied on the county for most of its policing needs. State troopers occasionally set up speed traps south of town but were rarely seen otherwise. Kevin imagined they had their hands full in Oneonta right now. If they were even functioning at all.

It was the quiet that was the creepiest. Over the weekend, there had been people on porches and lawns, talking, filling each other's heads with wild speculation about who was responsible and how long it would last. While there had been doom, gloom, and grousing about the in-convenience, there had also been a sort of block party atmosphere to things. Children had played in the street and rode bicycles up and down the road, free of the fear they would end up like the flattened skunks and opossums and turtles. Now, there was a watchful, almost menacing feeling. Kevin wanted to get clear of the town as fast as possible. He quickened the pace.

A hundred yards up from the Four Corners, a little bridge carried the state road over Mill Creek. A white bucket stood at the end of the guard rail where a dusty trail descended to the creek bed. Kevin paused and looked into the bucket. Half a dozen crayfish, each no bigger than his thumb, staked out territory on the bottom.

"Hey!" A scowling boy of ten or so scrambled up the bank, a dripping aquarium net in his hand. "Get away! Those are mine—I caught them!"

"I was just looking."

"Go find your own food," the kid said. He waited until Kevin, Kelly, and Dina put more distance between them and emptied his net into the pail.

They hurried on.

———

Once clear of the hamlet, the road pulled away from the creek and rose slightly, presenting them a nice view of the rolling valley. They were now in what Kevin called the Big Empty: the sparsely populated, very poor belt that ringed Harpursville for several miles in all directions. An area some folks in the hamlet quietly referred to as Hardlucksville when no one from that area was around. More than a few folks in Algonquin applied the name to the entire town. Once, Harpursville had been a thriving town at the heart of New York's hops industry; a blight or fungus of some sort had killed that in the 1800s. Dairy had risen to replace it, only to be smacked down by the Great Depression. In the post-War period, Dairy had surged again, only to be felled by a three-headed monster of falling prices, rising costs, and an inability to convince the kids to stay home and farm.

Kevin and Monica had bought the best house in the worst neighborhood. They couldn't afford Algonquin or some of the towns closer to it, like Oaks Mills, but Harpursville offered them everything they wanted: it was affordable, it was close enough that the drive to the hospital wouldn't be too bad, it was pretty, and it was part of the Algonquin school system, which had a very good reputation. Their real estate agent also told them Harpursville would be the Next Big Thing, that agritourism was coming and the town would be full of apple orchards, craft breweries, or wineries. Home values would sky-rocket. But, time after time, the entrepreneurs behind these schemes chose to base their operations closer to Algonquin instead, which had more tourist traffic, better infrastructure, and a friendlier climate for business. The Great Recession had effectively killed all development for a few years, and the Big Empty was still the Big Empty: a mix of state forests on the rugged hills, abandoned farms in the valley, and a few houses here and there set well back from the road at the end of long, dusty driveways flanked by signs warning of dogs, guns, or both. It sure was pretty though.

The floodplain was open and inviting, the only structure was an abandoned farm, the faded For Sale sign a reminder that the recovery had not really reached this part of the state yet. On the left, trees climbed a steep hillside. Early wildflowers sprinkled the ground, adding a welcome touch of color to the greens and browns that dominated the landscape. A deer crashed through the underbrush and dashed across the road in front of them, its white tail flashing in the morning light. A pair of hawks traced lazy circles high above. Kevin wondered what the animals thought of the sudden silence. Did they relax at all with the volume of the human world turned down so suddenly?

"How are your feet, girls?"

"Great," Dina walked backward in front of them, her arms held out, parallel to the ground, her face turned up to the sun.

"Mine hurt a little, but they're okay, I guess," Kelly said. "Just a little sore."

"Blister sore or achy sore?"

"Achy. I'd love to have one of those cart-thingies, like Cleopatra. With strong men carrying me everywhere."

"Strong men like Curtis?" teased Dina.

"Shut UP!"

Kelly lunged at Dina, who laughed and twisted away. They chased each other around the road, giggling and laughing, before settling down again.

The day warmed. Kevin took his jacket off and tied it around his waist, arranging it to keep the knife out of sight. He still caught himself looking over his shoulder for cars, half-expecting to be surprised by one racing around a curve, but cars, at least for now, were a thing of the past.

A whirring sound came from around the curve ahead of them, coming fast. Kevin pulled the girls to the edge of the road, against the guardrail.

A bicycle sped past at a dangerous speed. Two more whizzed by, one passing close enough to ruffle his hair.

Brakes squealed. The cyclists turned around and pedaled back up until they were even with Kevin and the girls. They were teens, three boys. The biggest wore a blue T-shirt and khaki shorts and looked vaguely familiar to Kevin, with curly red hair and a freckled, round face.

"Hey, Kelly," he said.

"Hi, Dougie," Kelly said, and Kevin put the name with the face: Dougie Austin. He was the same grade as the girls, but big enough to be a senior. The Austins lived up a side road in the middle of the Big Empty, about halfway to Dina's. Kevin remembered now that Dougie's father worked in the hospital. He was an orderly, or a porter or something, someone Kevin knew *of* rather than knew. The other two boys pulled up behind Dougie. One was a younger, skinnier version of Dougie, with similar hair and features. The third was stocky and dark.

"What's going on?" Dougie said. "Whatcha doing?" His cheeks were blotchy from exertion. Sweat darkened his T-shirt beneath his arms and in a V down his chest, making it cling to the top of his large belly.

Kelly shrugged. "Just taking a walk."

"I guess you're all out of power too," Dougie said. "We rode all the way up t'Springfield yesterday. Everything's out."

Kevin had doubts that this boy was capable of a fifteen-mile bike ride. Then again, *he* didn't look to be up for a seven-mile walk.

Dougie continued, "People broke into the Grade A. Totally cleaned it out. My dad says we're being invaded, and everyone should get guns. Hey, do you guys have any guns?"

"No," Kelly said. "I hate guns."

A warning bell rang in Kevin's head. He took a half step forward, putting himself in between Kelly and Dougie.

"We should be getting on," he said. "We've got a lot of ground to cover. Come on girls."

"Yeah, that's cool. See you around."

They resumed walking. Kevin glanced back over his shoulder. The boys had pulled their bikes together. They hunched over the handlebars, heads close together. Sweat prickled the back of Kevin's neck. His hand crept down, touched the solid shape of the knife through his jacket.

The road continued to rise. The land fell away into the valley on the right. Black smudges and scrapes marred the dull metal surface of the guardrail, the scars of careless drivers traveling too fast down the hill. Kevin took another look back. The boys were distant but still visible, still in discussion over something. Dougie's meaty fist punched the air two or three times as he made some emphatic point, then he punched his brother on the shoulder. Kevin pushed the pace, ignoring the burning in his thighs, his heavy breathing, and thudding heart. He wanted to put some distance between them and the boys, though he couldn't quite say why.

They had nearly reached the top of the incline when he again heard ticking bicycle chains. The dark-haired boy shot past, then cut across their path, front tire to the guardrail. Dougie pulled up alongside them. He glanced behind at his brother, glared at him. The younger boy pulled up behind them. Kevin saw that they were hemmed in against the guardrail.

"What's going on, fellas?"

Dougie's blue eyes darted back and forth. The corner of his mouth twitched. "This is a toll road," he said.

"Excuse me?" Kevin said.

"It's a toll road. Like the Thruway. If you want to use it, you gotta pay."

Three seconds passed. Kevin laughed, said, "Toll road. That's a good one." Looking back on it later, Kevin thought it might have worked but for that three second pause.

"No joke," Dougie said. He held out his hand. "Whatcha got in the bags? Let's see."

Kevin thought how Monica, little Monica, had cowed three drunk teenagers. Dougie Austin was big, but he was just a kid—a kid who still called himself "Dougie" at his age. Kevin puffed himself up like the tom turkeys that strutted in Jake's fields each winter and summoned The Voice of Authority.

"There's nothing—nothing in here for you."

His breath nearly failed halfway through. Instead of The Voice of Authority, he had sounded merely indignant. Not even that. Prissy. Weak.

Dougie let the bike fall. It rattled off the pavement.

"Come on, Dougie," Kelly said. "Don't be—"

"Shut up," he said. "Give me the bags and we'll let you go."

There was no fear in Dougie's eyes. What Kevin saw instead was excitement and the conviction common to teenagers, especially boys: that they could not be hurt, that they were immortal. And Dougie had the air of someone who was used to using his size to his advantage.

Kevin's fingers twitched at his side like an Old West gunfighter's. The knife was right there, ready to put a stop to this nonsense.

Rapid-fire thoughts flashed. Quick strike with the knife. Slice through the boy's shirt, deep enough to leave a mark, not deep enough to kill. He saw the boy go slack-jawed in shock, watched the three of them run off, their bicycles forgotten. Then, a line from an old movie floated through his head: "If you shoot him, you'll just make him mad." Finally, Monica's voice sounded. "Keep my baby safe."

"Dougie," he said, through a mouth as dry as dirt. "I know your dad. He works at the hospital too. He's not going to like hearing about this."

Dougie snorted. "Who do you think sent me out to find food?"

"He—he wouldn't want you to get it this way."

"Like you'd know what he wants." Before him, Dougie stood, one hand outstretched, the fingers flexing in a gimme gesture. The boy's free hand drifted behind his back where a kid who watched too much TV might think to stash a gun.

Face burning, Kevin let the backpack slide off his shoulder and held it out.

"Ha!" Dougie snatched the pack. He pulled items out one by one and turned them back and forth in his thick fingers, an archaeologist inspecting artifacts from a lost civilization: water bottles, bags of nuts, peanut butter. Kevin stared at the double yellow line between the boy's feet, hating himself for capitulating, hoping things would go no further.

"Cool."

Dougie put the bag down and turned his attention to Dina. "Here, give me that."

"These are my clothes!"

Dougie reached out and grabbed at the strap. Dina slapped his hand.

"Leave me alone, these are my clothes!"

The dark-haired boy stepped forward and grabbed her arms from behind. Dina shrieked and struggled. Dougie yanked at the backpack.

"Stop it! Let me go! These are my clothes!"

"Stop it! Leave her alone! Dad!"

Kevin's paralysis broke.

"Let go of her!"

He reached for Dougie's beefy arm, tried to wedge himself between him and Dina.

Dougie flung his arm back. Bright yellow stars burst in Kevin's eyes as the boy's elbow connected with his temple and he staggered. A hand shoved him in the chest. Already off balance, Kevin fell back. The back of his thighs struck the guardrail, and he flipped over. Pain exploded in his ribs as he slammed into the ground, driving the air out of his body. The bright blue sky grayed out on the edges. Dina and Kelly's shouts became distant.

Sharp claws sank into his chest. Kevin gasped and struggled to get enough air, struggled to keep the pulsing blackness at bay. Kelly's face appeared in the circle of blue.

"Daddy, are you okay?"

He nodded and managed to gulp in some air. He rolled onto his hands and knees, paused for a moment, then, using the rail for support, he rose on Bambi legs.

On the road, Dougie pawed through Dina's bag. She stood nearby, silent tears streaking her red face, clasping her left elbow with her right hand and beating her fist against her thigh. Angry red marks stood out on her upper arms.

Dougie frowned as he rooted through Dina's things.

"There's nothing here but—whoa, look at this!"

Out of the bag came a pink bra. Dougie held it up before him on tented fingers. He turned it back and forth, poked at one of the cups while the other boys snickered. He held it out at arm's length and cocked his head, like a museum patron studying a masterpiece.

"Looks a little big for you, if you ask me."

"Keep it then," Dina said, her voice bitter. "You need it more than me."

Dougie's crew stifled snorts and smirked at each other. Dougie's face, already flushed from the scuffle, turned a deeper shade of red, and Kevin feared things were about to get worse. Instead, the boy shoved the bra into the bag and threw it at Dina. Her pajama bottoms fluttered to the ground. Dougie grabbed Kevin's backpack and slung it over his shoulder. He picked up his bike and threw his leg over it.

"Come back anytime," he said. "And bring more food. Let's go."

They pedaled up the road, laughter ringing out behind them. Kevin sagged against the rail, powerless. Dina squatted on the ground, getting everything resettled in her bag. She kept her head down. Kelly, caught between helping her father and helping her friend, stood between. Kevin couldn't look directly at either of them.

"Is everyone okay?" he finally managed.

"Yes, Daddy. Are you?"

He nodded. Probed the back of his head for blood and found none. He was lucky. The ground was hard enough to knock the wind out of him but not hard enough to give him a concussion, and he hadn't tumbled all the way down the hill. He dusted off his backside. Breathing was getting easier now.

"Dina." He stopped, not knowing what to say. He settled for the easiest thing. "Are you okay? Did they hurt you?"

Dina shook her head. Again, she stood, clasping her elbow. Her hair had come loose. It hung down so he couldn't see her face, which was something of a relief.

"What should we do?" Kelly asked. She was watching the road where the boys had gone, her eyes large and round. "I don't want to stay here. What if they come back?"

"There's nothing to come back for," he said. "They know we don't have anything else."

Except that wasn't true. They could come back for more *fun*. As for what to do? There wasn't much choice. He took a deep breath.

"I'm sorry, Dina."

She didn't say anything. She walked past, head down, back toward home.

It was a long, somber walk. Every rustle, every crackling twig made Kevin jump and spin around, but they didn't see anyone else on the road. With each step, the knife bumped against Kevin's hip, a silent condemnation of his inaction, his failure to protect them. He wanted to go back and slice Dougie Austin from throat to groin, to cut off the fingers of the boy who left purple marks on Dina's arms. He wanted to fling the knife into the deep woods on the side of the road so it would stop shaming him.

When they got to the house, Dina bolted straight to the den and shut the door. Kelly, probably deciding her friend needed time alone, disappeared upstairs. Monica grabbed Kevin. "What happened? My God, Kevin, what happened to your face?"

He sank into a kitchen chair, heart- and footsore. Monica soaked a dish towel in cold water and pressed it against the lump Dougie's elbow left next to Kevin's eye. He sat for a long time before he could bring himself to tell her, and the telling was almost worse than living through it the first time. He'd been humiliated by a teenaged boy. He'd given up their food and water without so much as a fight.

"I did nothing. They could have killed us, could have taken the girls and . . . could have . . . I did nothing." He punched his thigh. "I did nothing, Monica. Nothing. I just handed everything over." He buried his face in his hands in case the tears that burned his eyes spilled over.

She came around the table and enfolded him in her arms, resting her head against his back. "You lived," she said. "You lived. The girls lived. Where would we be if you'd gotten yourself killed? Listen to me." She moved to his side, gently pulled his hands away from his face. He turned away. "Look at me, Kevin."

He didn't want her to see him like this, but he couldn't fight her. He met her eyes, the eyes that had first captured his attention when they met almost twenty years ago.

"You did what you thought was right. It's shitty we lost that food, but that's better than the alternative." She squeezed his hands. "You lived. The girls lived. That's more important than a jar of peanut butter."

It was not the reaction he expected from her, but it was the one he needed. She was right. He knew the biggest injuries were to his self-respect and Dina's dignity. It could have been so much worse. Would they be so lucky next time? Kevin decided he would not put them at risk again. There would be no *next time*.

———

Dina curled up on the couch in the den, a blanket pulled up to her shoulders, a pillow clutched to her chest. The blanket did little to keep the chill out. The pillow was soft but no comfort.

Dim light seeped in around the drawn window shades. She saw her reflection in the TV screen, a gray outline devoid of color and detail. It was fitting for how she felt right now: gray and colorless. Mrs. Schroeder would like that metaphor; she'd have to remember it for Creative Writing class when school went back in session—*if* it ever went back in session.

Two light taps sounded on the door.

"Dina?" Kelly's voice was soft, tentative. "Can I come in?"

What a stupid question, Dina thought. Of course she could come in—it was her house after all.

She pushed herself upright. The blanket fell away. She left it lying on the couch beside her and dragged the heels of her hands across her cheeks, drying her tears.

"Yeah."

Kelly stepped in, sliding her foot along the floor, wary of obstacles in the dark. She carried a foil-covered plate.

"I saved you dinner," she said. "Hungry?"

Dina felt empty, hollow, but not in a hungry way. The thought of eating made her nauseous. She shook her head.

"That's a first," Kelly said. Dina didn't laugh. "Are you okay?"

"I just wanted to go home." The words scraped against her raw throat. "I didn't mean for your dad to get hurt."

Kelly put the plate on the coffee table and sat beside her.

"He's okay. He didn't get hurt. You saw him."

She hadn't, though, not really. On the way back, she'd kept her eyes fixed on the pavement, had watched cracks and tar blobs and the flattened,

mummified remains of old roadkill pass beneath her feet. She had counted steps to keep the images of Dougie at bay, to drive away her sense
of powerlessness, and to block out the meaning of their failure. When
she lost count at 673, she withdrew into a recent memory. She sat on
the couch in the family room, between Mom and Dad, while her sister
Sara put on a play that involved unicorns and princesses and made no
sense, but it was wonderful all the same. Even Zach, her brother—who
usually avoided anything that had a hint of girlie to it—got involved,
shining a flashlight on Sara like a spotlight.

It made her feel a little lighter, a little better, until they passed back
into Harpursville; then it blew away like fog before the wind and brought
her back to reality. She was stuck. She loved the Bartons dearly, but she
wanted to be home.

As for Mr. Barton not being hurt, Dina knew physical pain wasn't the
worst thing in the world. Her parents never raised a hand to her, but their
constant battles left a different kind of wound. The bruises and scratches
on her arms from Dougie's pukey little friend were nothing compared to
watching Dougie put his hands on her things. The thought of putting
on the clothes he had handled—especially her underwear—made her
shudder. It would be like having his hands right there. She shivered and
wrapped her arms around her knees.

Kelly draped the blanket over her shoulders and hugged her. "It's
getting cold," she said. "Mom and Dad went upstairs already. We should
build up the fire and tell ghost stories."

"We already know each other's ghost stories."

"Oh no," Kelly said. "I've been saving one for just the right occasion,
and this is it: no lights, no power, nowhere to run, mwa-hah-ha. But
first . . ." She peeled the foil back from the plate. A white blob of mashed
potatoes sat on the plate. The faint smell of roast beef reached Dina's
nose. "If you don't eat this, I'm going to eat it myself."

Dina's stomach growled in answer.

"Oh no you don't."

She grabbed the plate, plunged her fork into the soft potatoes, and
popped it into her mouth. "Mmm." She rolled the smooth lump around
on her tongue. "Your mom makes the best mashed potatoes."

Her mother's voice sounded in her head: "Eat slow and you'll eat less." Mom seemed to have a never-ending fear that her eldest child was going to end up as some enormous tubbo. Dina tried to follow her advice now, not because she worried about getting fat, but to make the meal last.

A few minutes later, they settled themselves in the warm circle of the living room fireplace. As Kelly started her ghost story, Dina resolved to do everything she could to be a help. *This is the best possible place you could be*, she thought. *Make the best of it.*

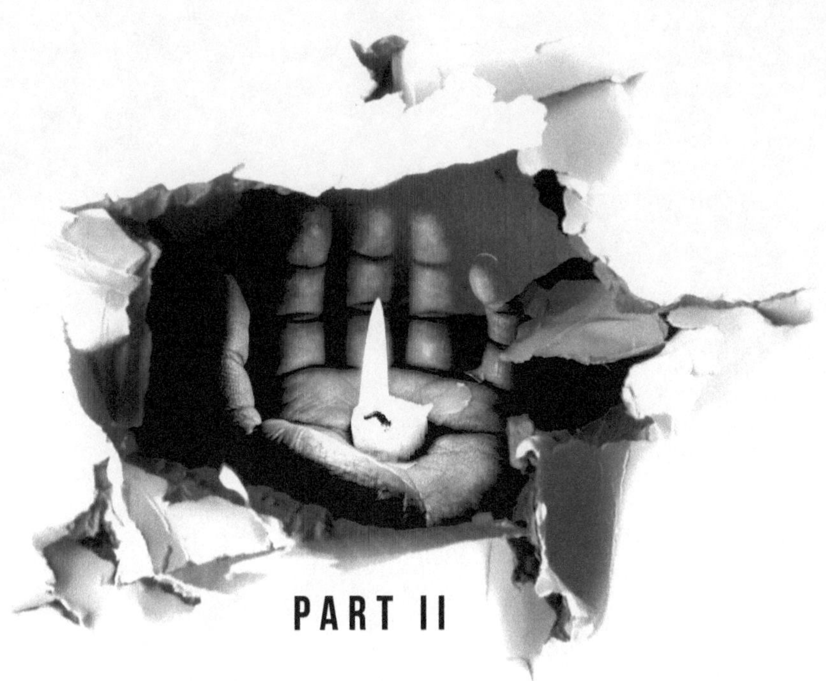

PART II

CHAPTER 7

KEVIN WOKE TO find Monica sitting on the edge of the bed, looking down at him with a tender expression on her face.

"How are you?"

"Sore all over."

He had barely recovered from the digging and the climbing. Added to those aches were sore legs, a swollen cheek, and delicate ribs.

Monica peeled back the covers and lifted his shirt. Her finger traced a circle the size of a plate on his back, just below his right shoulder blade.

"You've got a bruise. How's it feel?"

He flexed his arm and winced, took a careful deep breath, testing his ribs. "It's okay. I don't think I broke anything."

"Jake dropped off some eggs this morning. Come on down."

The physical pains were not the worst though. All night long he had replayed the incident over and over in his head, trying to find the moment it had gone wrong, looking for what he could have done differently. Aside from successfully summoning The Voice of Authority instead of that indignant squeak, the thing he kept coming back to was the pause. It was nothing, really, only three seconds, yet he was certain that in those three seconds he had somehow ceded control to Dougie, had waved the white flag. Had he laughed immediately, had he followed it up with a "Come on, girls" and pushed his way through the loose bicycle cordon and walked up the road like he owned it, maybe this morning it would be Dougie Austin mulling over how he could have made things come out in *his* favor.

These thoughts plagued him all night, and they plagued him as he put on his clothes. He tried to drive them away with a fantasy in which *he* shoved Dougie over the guardrail but found little satisfaction in the idea of beating up a teenage boy. Even a deserving thug like Dougie Austin.

Kevin took the stairs one at a time, partly to appease his sore legs, partly to delay the inevitable. His stomach growled in anticipation of fresh eggs. His throat clenched at the thought of facing Dina.

When he got downstairs, Kelly smothered him in kisses. He hugged her, then had to pry himself from her clutches so he could take care of business.

"Hi, Mr. B." Dina's voice was bright, but her smile looked as real as the ones on Kelly's old Barbie dolls.

"Good morning, Dina. Can I—uh, can I talk to you a minute?"

Monica hustled Kelly into the kitchen, but Kevin needed more space. He went out to the porch, and Dina followed. The first dandelions of the season poked their heads above the ragged grass. Kevin clenched the porch rail and looked down at the little cluster of houses that was Harpursville. He cleared his throat and turned. Meeting Dina's eyes was difficult, but it was better than looking at the purple finger marks on her arms. They were his failure made visible.

"I'm so sorry about yesterday," he said.

"It's okay, Mr. Barton."

"No, it isn't. I didn't think—I didn't think this would happen. Not yet, anyway. It's been less than a week . . ." He rubbed his palm against his stubbled face and forced himself to meet her eyes. "I should have done more."

"I'm the one who's sorry. I shouldn't have asked you—"

"Stop, please. It's not your fault, okay? Okay?" She nodded, but he could tell she would never not blame herself, just as he would never not blame himself. "Dina, I'm sorry you got hurt. I'm sorry I couldn't get you home. But believe me, we're happy you're with us. We're going to get through this, all four of us, together. And I will never let anything like that happen again."

"Thanks, Mr. B."

He couldn't tell if she believed him. He wasn't sure he believed it himself. At the very least, he would do his best not to put her—*any* of them—in that position again.

When they entered the house, Kelly came running over, her eyes huge and round. "Dad! Dad! You have to see this!" She grabbed him by the arm and dragged him into the dining room where Monica was busy with something at the table.

Kevin stopped at the head of the table and scratched at the whiskers under his chin.

"Mom," Kelly said, "when did you get a gun?"

"It's not a gun, it's a rifle," Monica said. "And don't you have a job to do?"

Kelly stuck her tongue out at her mother but pushed back through the swinging door into the kitchen.

"Wow," Kevin said. "I didn't know you still had that thing."

A rifle lay on a piece of canvas spread over half the dining room table. Monica began taking it apart, placing each piece on the canvas in an orderly fashion. She worked slowly at first but picked up speed as she went along.

"You've got your boombox, I've got my rifle."

Kelly poked her head out of the kitchen. "Why did you even have a gun?"

"Everyone had one," Monica said.

"Your mom was quite the shot back in the day," Kevin said. "You want to tell her, or should I?"

A blush spread across Monica's cheeks. She picked up the detached barrel and sighted down it. Kelly came back into the room carrying a plate of scrambled eggs.

"Tell me what?"

"Your mother won a couple of shooting contests at the county fair. And she had—"

"Has," Monica corrected.

"—*has* the county big buck record for a woman. You were how old?"

"Sixteen."

"Sixteen. Same as you." He poked Kelly's nose like he did when she was a baby. Her mouth hung open, a comical mix of shock and horror on her face.

"Oh my God, Mom. You killed Bambi!"

Monica snorted. "That thing was bigger'n me."

"You shot a few back then, didn't you?" Kevin asked.

"I got one every year," she said, with obvious satisfaction. "I outhunted my brothers combined."

"How come you stopped?" Kelly asked.

Though he was ravenous, Kevin paused and watched his wife arrange the parts of the rifle on the canvas. For a moment, he didn't think she would answer.

"My boobs started growing in fourth grade," she finally said, in what seemed like the biggest *non sequitur* in recorded history. "By the time I was twelve—when I started hunting—they were almost as big as they are now. I was miserable. Boys stared and snapped my bra. Girls hated me because I had them and they didn't. People called me 'Moo-nica.' Every time I opened my mouth in class, there was one boy who would say, 'How udder-ly fascinating.' Part of why I loved hunting was because it just got me away from all that."

She poured some oil on a rag and began rubbing it over the barrel.

"By the time I was sixteen, it wasn't so bad anymore. The weird jealousy stuff was mostly over, and the boys had other boobs to look at. And then I shot the buck.

"It was beautiful. Twelve points. Like this." She held our hands about two feet apart. "My father took a picture, and he sent it to the paper.

"Someone stuck it up on the student achievement board at school. The first thing I heard was, 'That's a great rack—and the deer's not bad either.' Then it was, 'The paper lied—I only see two points.' The girls started calling me Sheena."

"Who?" Kelly asked.

"Kind of like a lady Tarzan," Kevin said.

"I took so much shit I just quit. It was just not worth it. That was enough for me."

Kelly wrapped her arms around Monica's neck and kissed her on the cheek.

"I'm sorry, Mom, that's awful."

"You are such a warrior princess, Momma B.," Dina said, drawing a laugh from Monica. "I think it's awesome."

Kelly kissed her again, then said, "You always told me not to care what everybody thinks."

"How do you think I learned?" Monica sighed. "I am sorry I let the other kids get under my skin about it. I loved hunting." She held up the bolt, turned it back and forth, inspecting it for damage. "But we're almost out of meat and we can't rely on Jake for everything. I also think it will be good to have for protection."

Kevin stopped mid-chew as a chill crawled down his back. "Do you think your bullets will be any good?" he asked. "They must be pretty old."

"My father shot World War II surplus for thirty years. These were stored properly. They should be fine."

"Are you going to make us learn to shoot?" Kelly asked.

"I don't know," Monica said. "It takes a lot of ammunition to get good, and I don't want to waste it. Do you want to learn?"

"Ick," Kelly said.

Kevin polished off his eggs. His body still ached, but he felt better. "Hey, girls," he said. "After we clean up breakfast, what do you say we go downtown and see what's going on?"

Kelly and Dina exchanged an uneasy glance that matched how he felt deep inside. Yesterday's events had shaken him badly. He hadn't expected things to go sideways quite so fast, but he told himself it was just that way out in the Big Empty. Harpursville the hamlet wasn't as well off as Algonquin or Oaks Mills, but it was generally better off than the Big Empty, where maybe people didn't have the resources to shop for a week's worth of groceries at a time.

"Come on," he said, forcing extra cheer into his voice. "I want to pay another visit to Herman before he's closed for good. I'll need your help getting things back up here."

Silent communication passed between them, and they both nodded at the same time. Kevin finished quickly and cleared his plate. Monica decided to stay at the house.

"Be careful," she said.

This time he didn't brush her off.

The morning was warming nicely, improving everyone's moods. The girls made dandelion crowns for each other and giggled over something Kevin didn't really understand, and he marveled over their ability to put yesterday's trauma behind them so quickly. At their age, he brooded over slights real and imagined for days. Age and maturity hadn't improved him much, it seemed; Dougie Austin's leering face flashed in his mind every time he caught a glimpse of Dina's bruised arms.

Town hall was deserted and dark. Across the parking lot, Herman sat on his rocker on the Feed-N-Seed's porch. A shotgun lay across the old man's lap. Kevin wondered if everyone in town had the same idea.

"Packing heat, huh, Herman?"

"Protecting my investment. You here to buy or talk?"

"A little of both?"

"Well, I don't have a whole lot left to buy, and I don't have much t'say. What do you need?"

"Chicken wire?"

Herman grunted. "Yeah, I got some. But if you're looking t'protect that new garden of yours, you're better off with deer fence. Eight foot." He patted the gun. "Or one of these. Go on in, see what we got. Don't forget posts. I got some of those too."

Even though the shelves were mostly empty, it took Kevin some time to find what he needed in the dark store. Plus, he didn't know exactly what deer fence looked like. After seeing the price on the posts, Kevin stuck his head back outside.

"Herman, you take credit cards?" he asked, only half joking.

"You want an ass full of buckshot?"

Kevin retreated inside. He picked up a 100-foot roll of fencing and a couple of packages of zip ties. He'd have to improvise on the posts.

Thandie charged him fifty dollars, a deep discount on the sticker price. He skipped the tax this time too.

Kevin counted his remaining cash. It wasn't nearly enough. "Shoot," he said, "I couldn't read the price inside. I can't cover this."

Herman surprised him and said, "Tell you what, just take it. If this ever ends, I'll find you. I know where you live."

"Are you sure?"

"Cash is kind of useless now, ain't it? Nothing t'buy, nowhere t'buy it. Maybe for burning come winter, that's about it."

"Herman, is everything okay?"

The old man looked up at him. Blue veins pulsed beneath paper-thin skin. "You hear about the Kwik-Stop?"

"No. What about it?"

"Some fools broke in there last night and cleaned it out. Wrecked the place too. Smashed up everything they couldn't take. I tell you what, anyone tries that on *me* . . ."

He touched the shotgun with a crooked, wobbly finger, and Kevin had no doubt the old man would shoot someone, though the recoil would probably tip him right over backwards if he fired it.

The old man killed their good mood. Kelly dropped her dandelion crown; Dina quickly followed suit. Kevin, curious about the Kwik-Stop, asked Thandie to keep an eye on their purchases while they checked it out. He was also curious about what folks were saying.

"I'm not going anywhere," Herman said.

No one was out on the street. They heard shovels digging from some backyards, the rasp of a saw, but not much conversation, no laughter. The feeling of being watched was even greater than the day before, and Kevin almost turned for home. Kelly hung on one arm, Dina latched on to the other. They reached the Kwik-Stop and stopped at the edge of the parking lot.

"Shit," Kevin whispered.

"Quarter for the jar," Kelly said automatically.

Every piece of glass in the place—four big windows, the doors, even the light-up sign out front—had been smashed. Broken glass turned the ground into a shining disco ball. In contrast, the Kwik-Stop's interior was a black hole that seemed to suck the light out of the air.

"This is horrible." There were tears in Kelly's voice. "Who would do this?" She tugged on his arm. "Let's go home, Daddy. I don't like this."

"Soon," he said. "I just want to look around."

Glass crunched underfoot as he approached the building. As he drew closer, the smell hit him: spoiled milk, cold cuts gone to the dark side, rotting eggs, rancid butter. Food smells mixed with the rank chemical smell of spilled antifreeze, motor oil, cleaning fluids. Though his breakfast threatened a reverse voyage, Kevin peered in the gaping window.

It looked like the aftermath of a terrorist attack. All the glass-fronted cases were smashed. The coffee machine was overturned. Display racks leaned against each other, toppled like dominoes. Liquids of all colors made patterns on the floor that might have been pretty on a canvas but were unsettling here.

"Someone was really mad," Dina said in a low voice.

Indeed, people were angry, and rightly so. It had been a week—a week? Kevin couldn't be entirely sure, time had gotten slippery, but a week seemed about right, and they still had no idea what had happened. No presidential address on the TV or radio, because there was no TV or radio. Not one county cop, not one state trooper had made their way to the hamlet to explain the situation. All they knew for sure was what filtered back from those who had ventured out from the hamlet, and those who had wandered in: from Algonquin in one direction to Oneonta in the other, nothing worked. Nothing worked, no one knew why, and no one had come to explain. Anything beyond that was rumor. People could put up with a lot, but people hated to be kept in the dark. They were right to be angry.

As Kevin surveyed the wreckage, his mind turned back to the last few days. Dougie Austin's highway robbery. The little boy fishing in the creek. That feeling of being watched as they walked through the hamlet. The skin on the back of his neck tingled, and he wanted nothing more than to get the girls home and off the streets. The people weren't mad. They were scared. And so was he.

"Let's get out of here," he said.

They hurried back up the road to the Four Corners, had just turned on the county road, when Kelly stopped.

"Daddy, what's that?"

"What's what?"

"Do you hear it?" Her voice rose in pitch. "Do you?"

He was about to say no, but then he *did* hear it. A low sound, not so much heard as felt in the center of his chest and the soles of his feet. After a few seconds, he actually heard it with his ears, and the nervous energy that had propelled him away from the Kwik-Stop made him bounce up and down instead. Could it be?

Others heard too. Heads appeared in windows. People stepped out onto their front porches, responding to a sound that, until last week, was so common it was hardly noticed: engines.

"Let's go see!" Kelly screamed. She grabbed Dina's hand, and they flew back to the corner, pogoing in place and hugging each other.

People rushed to the sound like bees to flowers. Kevin sprinted to the intersection and pushed his way through to the girls. He stretched his neck as far as he could, and then he saw the wink of sunlight reflecting off a windshield, and his own voice joined those of the growing throng at the corner, voices raised in whoops of joy and relief.

Trucks roared toward them from the north, headlights blazing and bright even on the sunny day. Olive drab trucks, wide bodied with high, knobby tires. As the first one raced through the intersection, everyone could see the plain white star on the door, and the voices of Harpursville rose in a single cheer: the Army had arrived.

Their passing rattled windows up and down the street, made a few people cover their ears, but it was a beautiful sound nonetheless. It was the sound of salvation. Deliverance. Civilization.

People lined the curb, waving and cheering at the trucks, hugging and kissing each other. A woman next to Kevin burst into tears, and she wasn't the only one. Though he didn't really know her, he put his arm around her shoulder, gave her a quick hug, then let her go. Virtually the entire population of the hamlet watched the convoy roll through, a seemingly endless procession of trucks, and the promise of order restored.

Choking diesel fumes wafted over the crowd, but it couldn't stop the cheering; nothing could, until someone realized the trucks weren't stopping. They passed through the crossroads and continued south, jogging left and right to avoid the stalled pickup truck. They drove through the hamlet, past the husk of the Kwik-Stop and, as quickly as they came, they were dwindling in the distance, heading toward Oneonta.

"Why didn't they stop?" Kelly's desperate tone nearly broke Kevin's heart. "Where are they going?"

"I don't know, honey. I don't know."

The question was being asked by dozens around the crossroads: Why didn't they stop? Where were they going? The crowd broke up into dispirited clumps that spilled into the intersection. The tears of happiness and relief turned to tears of bitterness and frustration; joyous voices turned angry. The unease Kevin had felt at the Kwik-Stop was back.

"Come on," he said. "Let's go home."

"There's more!"

Heads whipped around to follow a pointing finger, and sure enough, there were more. A fresh dust cloud shimmered above the road; the subsonic rumble returned. Almost automatically, people pulled back to the edge of the road. Hope rose again.

"Mr. Barton," Dina said, "what's that man doing?"

A wide-bodied man stood in the center of the intersection. He had a round face with a scuff of brown beard. Kevin recognized him as a technician for Schuyler Energy Services who used to service their furnace.

"Get out of the road, Eli," someone shouted. "You tryin' to get yourself killed?"

The man looked around him and started moving, taking long strides on short legs, but not out of the road. Instead, he moved forward until he was just past the crosswalk on the north side of the intersection. He folded his arms across his chest and planted his feet on either side of the double yellow line.

"Get out of the road!"

A horn whomped, two, three times, and the engines roared louder. The man didn't move.

The lead truck bore down on him.

"Oh my God, oh my God," Kelly murmured. Kevin grabbed her and pulled her close, pushing her head down so she wouldn't see, but he couldn't take his eyes off the scene. He cringed, bracing for the expected impact.

Rubber squealed on asphalt, but the thud of bumper on body never came. The vehicle stopped, mere feet from the man in the street. Trucks piled up behind it, nose to tail, but by skill or miracle, there were no collisions. A collective sigh went up from the crowd.

A metallic voice crackled through a loudspeaker. "THIS IS MAJOR PETTIT OF THE 39ᵀᴴ INFANTRY DIVISION. YOU ARE INTERFERING WITH ARMY OPERATIONS. STEP ASIDE."

The man stayed put.

"I REPEAT, YOU ARE INTERFERING WITH GOVERNMENT BUSINESS. STEP ASIDE OR FACE ARREST."

The man held his hands out in a conciliatory way but didn't leave the street.

"We don't want trouble," he called. "We just want some answers, that's all. And if you're going to arrest me—" He chuckled. "Well, I could use a good meal."

Someone stepped off the curb and took up positions in the road behind him. Then another and another.

Doors swung open on the trucks. Soldiers in full combat gear poured out and took up positions around the caravan. Machine guns bristled from roof turrets. A lone soldier hopped out of the lead vehicle and approached the growing number of people in the road.

"I'm Major Pettit." He did not offer his hand. His voice was firm and carried well, even without the loudspeaker. "This has been a difficult time for you all, but we have orders, and those orders are to keep moving."

Dozens of voices broke out at once, shouting questions. "What's going on? Were we attacked? Was it a bomb? Can you help us? How come you can drive?"

The crowd pressed forward, desperate for answers. Kevin saw the eyes on the nearest soldier widen, saw his finger creep toward the trigger. Despite the trappings of the professional soldier, his clenched jaw and wide eyes told Kevin an important fact: these were not battle-hardened men who could keep cool in a crisis. It would only take a second, a half second, a millisecond, for this group to become a mob, would only take one bad decision or one slip of a finger before bullets started flying. As much as Kevin wanted answers, as much as he wanted to be present for an important event, they had to get out of there.

"Girls!" He tugged on Kelly's arm. "We need to go."

He squeezed through the crowd, towing Kelly along. She let him lead her away from the buzzing crowd, then stopped short.

"Daddy, where's Dina?"

"What?"

They had emerged into an open spot on the street, but Dina wasn't with them. Kevin scanned the crowd, his fear growing in proportion to the volume of angry voices from the Corners. Then he saw her in the mass; a tall girl oblivious to the dangerous combination of desperate people and green troops.

"Dina!" He shouted. "Dina!"

She didn't move.

Kevin gave Kelly a gentle push away from the mob.

"Wait right there," he said. "If you hear shots, run."

Against all common sense, he forced himself forward, back to the scene of impending disaster.

"Dina!"

The crowd had coalesced into a tightly packed horseshoe in front of the convoy. Kevin wedged his way in like a root working through hardpan. Dina was at the very front of the crowd, ten feet from the wide-eyed soldier. Finally, he got close enough to reach out and grab her shoulder.

"We need to get away from here." Her brows drew together as if she didn't understand the urgency. "Now!"

Finally, with a last look over her shoulder, she started to follow him as he again worked his way out of the throng.

With each second, Kevin grew more certain that he was about to hear the firecracker staccato of shots and either take a bullet in the back or get trampled by the fleeing mob.

They finally broke free and reached Kelly. Kevin put his hands on his knees, trying to catch his breath and quiet his racing heart. Once under control, he said, "This is a disaster waiting to happen."

"You think they would massacre us?" Kelly asked. "No way!"

"Kent State," Dina said, surprising Kevin. "We learned about it in US history. Remember?"

Kelly nodded but looked doubtful.

"Things are tense," Kevin explained. "Those soldiers are barely older than you. All it takes is one wrong move at the wrong time."

In confirmation, the buzz of the crowd went up a notch, as if someone had whacked a hive of hornets with a stick. Kevin looked back, saw hands rising as people shouted and gestured.

"I think we should be—"

A short squall of feedback cut him off. Major Pettit's metallic voice sounded through the truck's loudspeaker.

"PLEASE REMAIN CALM. REMAIN CALM. WE HAVE ORDERS TO PROCEED TO BINGHAMTON TO RESPOND TO A GRAVE HUMANITARIAN CRISIS."

"What do you think we have here?" someone shouted. The major plowed on.

"I CAN, HOWEVER, REPORT THE FOLLOWING TO YOU:

"FIRST, WE HAVE NOT BEEN ATTACKED. REPEAT, WE HAVE NOT BEEN ATTACKED. THE PRESIDENT IS IN WASHINGTON. THE GOVERNMENT IS DEALING WITH THIS CRISIS."

"THIS IS THE RESULT OF UNEXPECTED, MASSIVE SOLAR STORMS. I—" There was a brief pause, and when the major resumed, his voice had lost some of its authoritative sound. "I'm no scientist, I really don't quite get all of it. I'm told we were hit by a blast of radiation from the sun that disrupted virtually all electronic systems in the Northeast. Power supplies, satellites, computers—you name it, it's out." Anticipating the obvious question, he continued, "These vehicles here were in shielded bunkers, so they were unaffected by the burst. People are working around the clock to restore the situation. But I have to tell you, we're operating about as well as a one-legged man in an ass-kicking contest."

Maybe it was Major Pettit's attempt at folksy charm, or maybe it was just that people were finally getting some kind of answers after stumbling around in the dark for a week. Whatever it was, the temperature of the crowd dropped noticeably. It wouldn't last, Kevin knew. The army was bound for Binghamton. What was the plight of a hamlet of 100 or so compared to the suffering of a city of 50,000? The fact that they weren't heading to someplace bigger like Syracuse or Rochester, or somewhere more important, like Albany or New York, gave him hope. Maybe this wasn't that big after all.

"We have some food, water, and medical supplies," Pettit said. A sigh passed through the crowd. "I wish," he said, "I wish I could leave it all, set up a medical tent, and get you all squared away. I can't do that. However, we can and will leave some supplies for you, along with the promise that HELP WILL BE COMING."

The crowd cheered. Major Pettit had won them over, but Kevin wondered if they would get stuck at every little burgh between Harpursville and Binghamton. It was a long trip.

A moment later the crowd on Kevin's side of the intersection parted. Four weaponless soldiers gently created a corridor and three vehicles turned onto East Street. Corinne Rowley, a member of the town board, was squeezed into the front seat next to the major. They rumbled down the street and turned in at town hall. They were getting supplies.

CHAPTER 8

THE GIRLS RAN off to join the throng following the trucks. Kevin tried to keep up but was quickly winded. He stopped to rest and nearly got knocked down from behind.

"Sorry 'bout that," said a familiar voice. "You okay?"

"My fault." Kevin looked up into the round face of the furnace man, the man who had stood in the road and stopped the Army. "Oh. Hey."

Kevin felt just the way he had when he met Derek Jeter, his all-time favorite baseball player, at Yankee Stadium as a kid. Instead of telling his idol how much he admired him and politely asking for an autograph, Kevin had stood there with his mouth agape, a game program and pen clutched in his sweaty hands, rendered powerless by the greatest shortstop ever.

The man before him did not emanate star power. He was shorter than Kevin by a good three inches, barrel-shaped, with an utterly un-remarkable face, yet Kevin was just as tongue-tied as he had been by Jeter. This man was a hero. This man had put his life on the line—the double yellow line, to be exact—and stopped the Army, and now they were getting supplies.

"Uh, that was great back there," Kevin said, the tips of his ears getting hot. "Just . . . great."

The man shrugged as if standing up to a battalion of rifle-toting soldiers was no more difficult than filling an oil tank. "Someone had to do *some*thing." He patted his large belly and winked. "I'm wasting away to nothing. Say, you still in the old Tanner place? Still got that old V5?"

"Uh, yeah, we're still there," Kevin said, surprised he remembered where they lived. It had been at least five years since Monica had switched them to a different company. "The furnace is great. It's extra quiet."

"I bet." The man stuck out his hand. "Eli Sobchuk, in case you don't remember."

Now it wasn't just the tips of Kevin's ears that burned. Thrilled by his brush with greatness and embarrassed by being starstruck, Kevin took the offered hand. Though Eli was shorter, his hand seemed to swallow Kevin's, and his grip was strong. They started walking together toward town hall, following the crowd that had streamed ahead.

"That V5's a real good furnace," Eli said. "Hope you get to use it next winter."

"Sheesh, I hope so. We'd probably have to burn half the house down to stay warm."

"That'd be a real shame. My dad did some work for the Tanners. Yeah, that house is a beauty."

They had reached town hall. The army trucks were parked inches apart directly in front of the chunky municipal building. It was a single-story building with a meeting room that could hold about fifty people, an office for the clerk, one for the supervisor, and a couple of spares used on a rotating basis by the other town officials. Half a dozen soldiers stood in guarding positions around the trucks. Though their weapons were pointed at the ground, they were armed, and Kevin didn't like that.

"Hey, talk to you later," Eli said, and gave Kevin a companionable slap on the shoulder. He angled off across the lot.

Kevin searched the crowd for the girls. A booming laugh nearby made him snap his head around, had his half-empty stomach dropping to his knees. That laugh had plagued him for days: Dougie Austin. Kevin twisted and turned, a pulse beating in his throat, but he could not find the boy. The laugh sounded again, and when Kevin found the source, it wasn't Dougie Austin at all, but the middle-aged man who used to tap maple trees and sell his syrup at the Algonquin Farmers Market. Kevin let out a shaky breath and started looking for the girls again. He spotted them alongside the tall form of Curtis Pinkney. Dina waved at him, said something to Kelly that, from the look of things, barely registered and came over to Kevin, smiling like it was Christmas and her birthday rolled into one. Kevin kept his eyes on his daughter and Curtis. They stood close—too close. Kelly twirled a lock of her hair around one finger. Curtis looked at least as interested in her as she was in him, and Kevin felt an ache in his chest. Kelly had never had a boyfriend before, had never really liked anyone before—or she had never admitted to it anyway. He didn't know how he was supposed to feel.

"She's okay, Mr. B.," Dina said. "You can trust her."

"I trust her. It's *him* I'm worried about."

Her laugh was nice to hear after yesterday's disaster. She pointed at one of the soldiers. "Let's get closer. *He's* kind of cute."

"Great, now I'm going to have to chase both of you around."

"I just want to look, that's all."

Dina pushed straight ahead to the edge of the crowd. After a moment of hesitation, Kevin followed. At least from there he could keep an eye on both girls.

The townspeople stood in an arc around the trucks, some ten feet of space between them and the vehicles, as if an invisible wall had been erected. Kevin listened in on the conversation going on between one of the soldiers and some people in the crowd.

"We're like mushrooms," one of the soldiers was saying. "They keep us in the dark and feed us shit."

"Why are you going to Binghamton?" Kevin recognized the voice of Max Carver, a known pot-stirrer. The few times Kevin had gone to town board meetings, Max was the one who challenged every little thing. Whenever Arnie Bitzer, the town supervisor, asked for public comment, all eyes turned to Max, and Max always had something to say. He never ran for town board himself, though, even when he had a chance to run unopposed.

"That's where they want us to go, sir, I don't know why."

"Typical," Max said. "Send help to the city. What about us? We need help here too."

For once, Max got a favorable response from the hometown crowd. The soldier shifted from foot to foot and glanced to the man to his right for help, but none came. He said, "We're here now, sir. Major's gonna hook you up with some stuff."

"And then you'll be gone, and that's it for us."

A mutter of dissatisfaction spread through the crowd. Kevin felt bad for the soldier; it wasn't his fault. They couldn't stop and deliver supplies at every town.

The doors of the town hall opened. Major Pettit came out, flanked by a clipboard-carrying officer and Corinne Rowley. Corinne was the only member of the council who lived within the boundaries of the hamlet; the other four were spread out over the twenty-five square miles of the township. An irascible sixty-something woman who voted with Arnie Bitzer on everything, Corinne looked to Kevin like she wished she was anywhere else. Also emerging from the building was Eli Sobchuk. He huddled up with the major and his assistant in the shade of the entryway. Corinne stood at the edge of the trio, looking pale and insubstantial, and when she reached up to adjust her glasses, her hand trembled.

After several minutes of conference, Sobchuk split away from the huddle. He put his fingers to his mouth and let out a shrill whistle, then waved at someone. The major gave instructions to his assistant; he grabbed two soldiers and opened the tailgate of the truck. The soldiers hopped into the back of the truck. Sobchuk was joined by three young men, one of whom was Troy, the Kwik-Stop extortionist. The soldiers handed down big brown boxes. The men carried them off into town hall.

An angry roar went up from the crowd. People pushed forward, carrying Kevin and Dina toward the trucks. The guards looked suddenly frightened and started shouting for the crowd to keep back. Weapons rose, not to firing positions, but to an alert posture.

Kevin grabbed for Dina's arm and planted his feet against the tide. Bodies buffeted them back and forth, the voices of Harpursville cried out in outrage and confusion, while the soldiers shouted for order and calm.

The crowd teetered on the edge of becoming a mob, an ungovernable force ready to take what it wanted, what it *needed*, no matter the cost. Kevin could feel it in the air, could hear it in the voices around him as the fears and frustrations of Harpursville, like lightning, sought a target, any target, for its pent-up fears and frustrations.

A siren pierced the morning, and the major's voice, commanding and strong, cut through the roar. Just as a lightning rod can draw a bolt and send it safely to ground, the major caught the crowd's attention. He stood on the hood of the truck and spoke through the loudspeaker, calm but firm, and diffused the riotous energy. "WE'RE ALREADY BEHIND SCHEDULE," he said. "WE'RE UNLOADING A LIMITED SUPPLY OF MRES. MRS. ROWLEY WILL SAFEGUARD THESE SUPPLIES UNTIL AN ACCURATE ASSESSMENT CAN BE MADE OF HOW MANY PEOPLE ARE HERE, AND SHE WILL SUPERVISE THEIR DISTRIBUTION. YOU WILL ALL BE GETTING FOOD."

This news was greeted with moans and angry shouts. Pettit stood on the truck's running board. He held his hands up for quiet and got it.

"EACH CARTON CONTAINS 12 MRES. EACH MRE IS A COMPLETE MEAL." He paused and again switched off his authority voice. "Not the tastiest things but nutritious and loaded with calories. This should be enough to get you by until more supplies can be delivered."

"When's that?" Max Carver called.

"I can't say for sure. States that haven't been affected are mobilizing relief units to the area, but it's going to be a slow process. *Our* mission is to stabilize a very specific community, and we have to get a move on. Rest assured all available manpower is working on restoring systems to good working order. Now, Mrs. Rowley here will fill you in a little." He turned and gestured to Corinne, who stood by the doors watching the procession of boxes pass by.

"She doesn't look very happy," Dina observed.

Indeed, she didn't. She tottered toward the front of the truck, her face the color of old bread dough.

Pettit handed her the microphone and pointed at the push-to-talk button on its side. Corinne frowned at it, shook her head, and thrust it back in Pettit's hands. She retreated to a bench next to the building's entrance and sat, where she stared down at her lap.

"Okay," Pettit said. "What we decided is we're going to unload these MREs into town hall and then we need to be on our way. In one hour, Mrs. Rowley and her helpers will distribute MREs to you. You all need to go to your homes and get your family members down here so Mrs. Rowley can get an accurate count and hand them out."

He paused and looked around the crowd.

"I just want to wish you good health and good luck. Help is on the way."

With food so close at hand, people seemed reluctant to break up to spread the word. Kevin wanted to get Monica but worried about leaving Kelly and Dina behind. Things were calm for the moment, but it was a shaky calm, like a truce between Middle Eastern countries. He wanted to be able to get them away if things went pear-shaped. He also worried that he would somehow miss the one-hour deadline and get no food, which was stupid; he could see his house from where he stood. He could be there and back in ten minutes. Dina seemed to read his mind.

"Do you want me to go and get Momma B.?"

"Do you mind? My legs . . ."

"Sure. I could use the run."

"Oh," Kevin said, calling her back. "Make sure to tell the Hillmans, too, okay?"

"You bet." She clasped her hands in front of her chest. "It's really going to be all right now, isn't it?"

Kevin looked at the trucks, at the boxes being relayed into the office building, at the soldiers with their regulation haircuts and neat and clean uniforms.

"You know, I think it is."

———

What to Kevin seemed an overly long time later, nearly 100 people had gathered in front of town hall. Kevin was dismayed at how few people he really knew. These were people he nodded to at the Kwik-Stop, or saw pushing lawn mowers around, or walking in and out of the post office. He could put names with faces, mostly, but he could count the number of people he'd had actual conversations with on one hand. Even after seventeen years, he was a stranger in this town.

Snippets of conversation came to Kevin, much of it not good. Several people had ridden bicycles together to Algonquin, only to find that both the Price Chopper and Walgreens had been cleaned out. "Liquor store too." The person chuckled grimly. "Food, drugs, and booze, the necessities of life." Kevin, who didn't usually butt into other people's conversations, had to ask. "What about the hospital? What's going on there?" The man shrugged. "Didn't get that far. We heard they barricaded the doors, but who knows? We didn't stick around. Place didn't feel safe, you know?" Kevin knew. And he decided he didn't really want to think about it.

The Army was gone. Lined up just outside the door to town hall were several large folding tables. Sobchuk sat with Corinne Rowley, talking. Mostly Eli talking, Kevin noted. Corinne nodded a lot but didn't look like she had much of anything to say. "How are they going to do this?" Monica asked. "Corinne Rowley's in charge? How's she going to hand out food to all these people?"

"It's going to be all right," Kevin said to Monica, whose lips were thin and white. "The major said people were working on it. I'm sure they'll get it fixed soon."

"I love you for believing that," she said. "I wish I could."

"Hey, everyone, can you hear me?" Sobchuk's voice rose above the babble. Kevin watched as he stood, pressed his palms against the tabletop, then clambered up on it. He raised his arms like a referee signaling a touchdown until conversation stopped and everyone was watching him.

"The Army dropped off stuff to help us get through this. We're going to distribute this as best we can, but we need to do it fairly. I know you're all hungry. We're all getting a little thin here." He patted his own belly and grinned. "This is way better than Weight Watchers, right?" Laughter rippled through the crowd, and Kevin's admiration for the man grew. He stood in front of the crowd as self-assured as a lifetime member of Toastmasters International.

"We need to figure how many folks we got here," Eli said. "We'll count you up then pass out the MREs."

"Just give us the goddamned food," Max Carver yelled.

Eli grinned. "We've gone seven days without fresh food, what's another half hour? Here's the thing," Eli said, now looking directly at Max. "If *you* start pushing, everyone's going to start pushing. You want to see this turn into Christmas at Wal-Mart?"

Max scuffed at the ground with the toe of his boot but backed off.

"Okay, what we're gonna do is line up, right acrost the edge of the lot by Thandie's." He pointed with both hands together, swept them apart to show how to line up. "Folks're coming round to get names and numbers per family so we can do this orderly. And then we'll get you your food."

"Who put you in charge?" Max asked. "Where's Arnie?"

Eli tilted his head back to the sky, then leveled his gaze at Max.

"You know Arnie lives halfway t'Algonquin, Max. Why didn't you run out there and get him?" Max just rubbed the back of his neck. Sobchuk said, "I figure, if he hasn't made his way up here by now, he either doesn't want to or wasn't home when this thing hit."

"What about Corinne? She's the ranking board member here. You're not even on the board."

Kevin had an urge to jump up on the table, throw his arm around Eli's shoulders, and say, "If it wasn't for this man, we wouldn't even have these supplies. *He's* the one that stepped in the road and stopped those trucks. *He* put his life on the line, so shut up and line up!"

He didn't do it but he didn't need to. Corinne Rowley rose from her seat behind the table. "I'm the ranking board member," she said, "and I'm authorizing Eli to take charge. Of the rations." Her voice was thin and reedy but carried well enough.

"Thank you, Aunt Corinne," Eli said. He turned his attention back to Max. "Is that good enough for you? Yeah? Okay. So, everyone line up in front of Herman's. Nice and easy, no pushing, no shoving. The faster we do this, the faster you'll get your food, and we'll get you home before dark."

———

Some men are born to greatness; others have it thrust upon them.

The phrase circled around in Eli Sobchuk's head as he walked down the quiet street toward his home, three MREs tucked under his arm. His knees and back ached from all the standing around today; the season's first sunburn left his face tight and raw, and all the talking and shouting he'd done left his throat feeling like he'd swallowed a ten-inch flat file. He was exhausted but elated. He'd done a Great Thing today.

No one had ever thought he was destined for greatness. For all of his thirty-three years, he'd been ordinary, had never stood out. In school, teachers had never sent home notes that read, *Eli could do so much better if he applied himself*—they seemed as satisfied as he was with high Cs and low Bs. In the small pond of Algonquin High School, he was neither big-P popular nor pariah. In sports he was never the star, never the captain, was never called on to take the last shot or pinch hit in the bottom of the ninth or given the ball on fourth and goal with time running out. He had never been asked to be on a board or to run an event. He wasn't a blind follower nor was he a leader. He just *was*, and that had always been good enough for him.

Until today.

Today, he'd stood out from the crowd. He'd done a Great Thing. And that made him wonder: Was I born to this? Am I fulfilling my destiny? Or was it thrust upon me?

An avid reader of history, he knew the world was full of men like George Patton who—convinced they were earmarked for greatness—sought to put themselves in places where they could fulfill their perceived destiny. Eli hadn't been thinking about destiny when he stepped into the road. As he'd told Barton, "Someone had to do something," and that was the crux of it. He *knew* they wouldn't run him over because you couldn't run one man down. The Chinese didn't flatten that guy in Tiananmen Square, after all—but Eli was lead-pipe certain they would've mowed down a hundred men without batting an eye. That old murdering bastard Josef Stalin was dead on the money when he had said, "A single death is a tragedy, a million deaths is a statistic." Eli was pretty sure if even a dozen more had lined up behind him in that road, they'd all be one big red smear on Main Street right now.

He let himself into the kitchen of his small, two-floor house and set his MREs on the table. Three packages, each roughly the size and shape of a baking dish. Beef stew, spaghetti and meat sauce, or Salisbury steak? His stomach growled as he debated which one to break into.

After brief consideration, he decided to ignore the MREs for tonight. Instead, he opened his refrigerator and inspected his supply of TV dinners. Water dribbled out the door in little rivulets and fell onto the damp towels he had laid out. The ice bags Troy had *liberated* from the Kwik-Stop were mostly water now. The single-serving pizza and lasagna boxes were getting a little soggy, but they were still cold enough. The MREs could wait until he absolutely needed them.

He peeled back the plastic cover on the lasagna. It looked like a pile of puke after a pizza and beer binge and wouldn't taste nearly as good as what his ex used to make, but it would fill him up well enough. As he slid the semi-frozen food into the oven and turned on the gas, he wondered what Micki would say if she had seen him handle things today. Probably find something to bitch about.

While waiting for the lasagna, he took a box of cereal from the pantry and wandered into the living room. He sank into the couch, ignoring the bent spring that poked him in the ass. Sitting was a relief to his aching back and knees.

Eli crunched on his dry cereal. How long before the Army came back, and what would happen in the meantime? Things had been changing in town over the last few days. The first few days had been a little like the Fireman's Parade: festive and chatty, and even though a lot of the laughter had been nervous laughter, there had been plenty. Now, though, folks were getting secretive. Suspicious. Instead of loose gatherings at the ends of driveways and in the road, tight knots watched from porches and out windows. It had gone quiet, like in the last minutes before a whopper thunderstorm, and it was only a matter of time before something really bad happened, before someone got killed over a scrap of bread or a bag of rice.

"Someone has to do something," he said out loud.

As he sat in his darkening living room waiting for his lasagna, plans took shape in his mind, plans that could save the town. He didn't think it would take much convincing for his aunt to go along—she was in over her head, that was clear. She once told him she was only on the board for the $15,000 a year. And to keep the folks from "Away" from moving in and taking over.

Despite what Major Pettit had said about help coming, Eli thought this thing would last for months. If they did things the wrong way, the food would be gone in a week. People would get restless. If someone didn't take control now, the Army would come back to a burned-out husk of a town, populated by a handful of stick figures who looked like Auschwitz survivors.

He was lucky. He was a man who lived alone, who lived simply, and had some measure of self-control. How many people around him were gorging themselves on their MREs tonight? How many people were letting their remaining food spoil while shoveling down Uncle Sam's prepackaged food—food which had a shelf life of forever times two? How long before they were banging on the doors of town hall, demanding more? Who would stop it from becoming a mob scene next time?

He thought of Franklin Delano Roosevelt and the Great Depression. His father said the New Deal was the forerunner of today's runaway government, that it was the root of the long-term ruination of this country. Maybe, but it had also been a short-term wonder that put people back to work. It gave them some money and, maybe more important, restored their self-respect. Harpursville needed its own New Deal.

He brushed cereal flakes off his chest and into his hand, threw them into his mouth. Can't afford to waste crumbs. Yes, Harpursville needed its own New Deal. He picked his way around the coffee table back into the kitchen, where the oven was warming things nicely. In the morning, he'd talk to Corinne and get to work on this. She'd go along.

A gentle, lasagna-scented breeze wafted out of the oven. He put on an oven mitt and reached in for the bubbling, sizzling food. Born to greatness? Thrust upon him? Nah. He was going to reach out and grab it.

———

The girls picked through the 12 MREs piled on the kitchen table. It reminded Kevin of Halloweens past, when he and his friends would sort through their trick-or-treat spoils and work out trades. My Snickers for your Baby Ruth. Two packs of Twizzlers for a Milky Way. Milk Duds for Candy Corn and Jujyfruits.

"Beef stew." Kelly pushed it aside and grabbed another. "Beef ravioli. Ugh."

"Two more raviolis," Dina said. She reached for another, then stopped, her eyes getting big. "Oh, they have desserts too! Blueberry pie! They all have desserts. Pound cake. Cinnamon buns—there goes my butt."

"Great," said Monica, but she was frowning. "Do they have toilet paper?"

"It says it does," Kelly said, pointing to a line on the package. "How big is a single serving of toilet paper, do you think?"

Kevin's optimism was waning. Twelve MREs, three per person per household—it wasn't much. These weren't family-size frozen dinners. Three days per person.

"Steak and potatoes!" Kelly hugged the brown bag to her chest. "Can I have this one? Please, please, please."

"We shouldn't rip into these just yet," Kevin said.

"What? Come on, Dad, why not?"

"We have stuff we should use before it goes bad."

"Oh, Dad—"

"He's right," Monica said. "Use it or lose it. Let's put these away so we have somewhere to eat." She unlocked the pantry door. "Come on. Put them in."

Use it or lose it. There was so much to think about. Out by the garage, one garbage can was full, the other nearly so. What would they do with it? Monica mentioned toilet paper. He hadn't thought of that. How much was left? He wondered if they'd be wiping their butts with the seven years of tax forms and bank records filed in the basement. Laundry. Water. And, of course, food. How long could twelve MREs last? Jake had been sending over a few eggs, but would chickens lay them forever? He knew nothing about chickens except that he'd kill for some of the Colonel's extra crispy thighs right now.

"The Army said they'd be back." Kelly made a pouty face, but she put the MRE down.

"Yes, they did," Kevin said, "but it's going to take time."

"How much time?"

Kevin shook his head. "I don't know, sweetie. I think we just need to be prepared to be in this for the long haul, that's all."

Having killed the mood in the house, they scavenged the cooler for the last usable meat.

CHAPTER 9

ELI SOBCHUK WOKE to the sound of feet on his porch. He struggled against the sagging couch to a sitting position and blinked in the dim light of the living room. Last night's lasagna-encrusted plate sat on the coffee table, alongside three empty cans of beer. When the front door began to creak open, he grabbed the plate, ready to throw it, Frisbee-style, at the intruder. Like most Harpurites, he didn't lock his doors; he'd never had a reason to. The world had changed, however; it might be time to start.

A shadowed face poked through the door.

"Eli? You up?"

Eli let out his breath as he recognized the voice of his cousin, Roger Fields.

He put the plate down and rubbed goop from the corners of his eyes. Three beers weren't normally enough to leave him with a hangover, but times weren't normal. He had the fuzzy, disoriented feeling he associated with staying up too late and getting up too early.

"Yeah, I'm up." His shirt had ridden up over his belly in the night. He tugged it back into place. "What time is it?"

"How the hell should I know?" Roger came all the way into the room. He was eleven years younger than Eli, but they had gotten close the last few years. "It's still kind of dark. Anyway, you gotta come."

"All right, all right. Give me a second, would you?"

"Yeah, but hurry. Before anyone else sees."

Eli stretched and walked through the kitchen, eyeing the coffee maker on his cluttered counter. Most days coffee was his only breakfast. Instant was all he had now, but at least he had a lot of it, courtesy of Troy. The Kwik-Stop's storeroom was bigger than it looked.

Chilly air slapped him fully awake as he crossed the yard to the back fence. There he unzipped and peed the previous night's beers away. Water. Public health. Trash. Burials, because someone was going to die, if they hadn't already. He tried to think of the people he hadn't seen at town hall yesterday: Addisons. Crisps. Teddy Melville. Silvas. Who else? He'd have to make a list, send someone to check on them all. For all he knew, those folks could all be rotting in their homes right now, and more would surely follow. Without decisive action, they'd either kill each other or die of cholera.

Eli found Roger skulking on the front porch, gnawing on a granola bar. He was six feet tall when he stood up straight, which he rarely did.

"What's so important?" Eli asked. "And what are you doing up so early?"

"Just walking around, seeing what's what. You know." With a sly grin, Roger reached into his jacket and pulled two light brown eggs from his pocket.

"I don't even want to know where you got those." Eli could think of at least three backyard coops within a hundred yards of the Corners. "Just don't get caught. Things could get real ugly real fast around here."

Safety. Law enforcement. Jesus, there was a lot to do.

Roger led him down the street. The sun was just breaking above Harpur's Hill. Long shadows stretched across the hamlet. The angle of light and crisp air made Eli think of September; the red and yellow tulips lining the long walkway to Corinne's big house told a different story.

"Up there," Roger said, pointing. "By the door."

Corinne's house was set well back on one of the largest properties in the hamlet. A pair of giant cedars flanked the front steps, casting deep shadows on the porch, but even from here, Eli could make out a darker shape on the walkway beneath the trees. He squinted, took a step forward, stopped.

"Is that . . .?"

"Yep."

"Shit."

Eli trotted up the walk into the shadows.

His aunt lay on her left side, her body curved like a question mark. Her mouth was half open, her cheeks slack. Eli knelt beside her.

"Aunt Corinne? Are you okay? Corinne?"

He grabbed her arm, meaning to shake her, but one touch confirmed what he already knew. Her arm was too dense, like with a sack of wet sand. Her face was a study in gray: gray hair, gray skin, gray film over her empty, staring eyes. He stepped back, wiping his hands on his pants.

"What do you think?" Roger asked. He stood about ten feet away.

"She's dead."

"I know that. I mean, what do you think happened? You think she just"—he lowered his voice—"dropped dead?"

Eli studied his aunt's body. Corinne wore the same clothes as yesterday. There wasn't any blood that he could see, either on or around her.

"Yeah, that's exactly what I think. Heart attack maybe. She wasn't looking too good yesterday."

A guilty thought circled in his mind. After everyone went home yesterday, Corinne locked up town hall and sat on the bench in front of the building, her three MREs beside her. He'd asked if she was okay, if she needed help getting home. She said no, she was okay, she just wanted to sit a little while, so he left and went about his own business. Maybe if he'd stayed with her . . .

Wait a minute.

"Where are her MREs?"

"What?"

"Her MREs. She had them when I left her. It doesn't look like she ever got in the door. They should be here."

Roger scratched his pointed nose and looked off down the empty street.

"Roger. Did you take them?"

"Uh . . ." Eli grabbed his cousin by the jacket and shook him.

"Hey, get off!"

"Jesus Christ, Roger, get them and bring them back here. If someone finds out you have them, they'll think you killed her for them."

Roger's face went nearly as pale as his dead aunt's. "I didn't kill her, Eli! No way!"

"Keep your voice down. I know you didn't, but don't you see how it will look?" It was apparent his cousin didn't get it. He gave him a shove down the walkway. "Go get them and bring them back here."

"It's not like she needs them anymore," Roger sulked.

Eli closed his eyes and took a deep breath. "Just get them. Before someone sees you. Hurry up."

Roger looked like he was going to say something else but stopped himself. He squirmed into the dense shrubbery to the side of the porch and returned a moment later with Corinne's MREs. And her bundle of keys.

"I still don't see why I can't keep them," he said. "Finders keepers, you know?"

"What are you, eight?" Eli grabbed the keys and shoved them in his pocket. "Put the meals up on the steps. Make it look like she dropped them. You've got to be smarter than this, Roger. There's no law, there's no one in charge. If folks thought you'd killed her, they'd probably drag you off and string you up."

The street was still silent, unmoving, but it wouldn't be for long—without electricity, people were going to bed and getting up early. And older folks—which Harpursville had plenty of—were always up early and poking their noses out the curtains. Eli sat on the top step of the porch and regarded his dead aunt. In times of crisis, people needed something to hang onto, they needed to be led. Aunt Corinne wasn't all that effective, but she was the closest thing they had to an authority figure. Now they had nothing, no one.

But they could have someone.

"Roger, go get your brother and a couple other people. Divide up the town. Knock on every door. Tell everyone there's an emergency meeting at town hall, everyone's got to come."

Roger ran off. Eli sat on the porch with his aunt's body and pondered the words that would help him seize greatness.

———

The Bartons and Dina stood together near the edge of the crowd in front of town hall. Unlike the carnival atmosphere that had prevailed when the MREs were finally passed out the day before, faces were grim, and more than a few people wiped tears from their cheeks. Tables were once again set up in front of the building, but this time Corinne Rowley's body lay on them, a sheet pulled to her chin.

"I'm not really surprised she kicked off," Monica said in a low voice. "She looked terrible yesterday."

"She sure did," Kevin said.

Monica chewed on her thumbnail for a moment. "Why are we here? We've got things to do."

Kevin knew she was anxious to try out her rifle. And Kevin was supposed to help Jake with some kind of project today that the big farmer said would help them both.

Eli emerged from town hall with a stepladder. He set it up behind the table and climbed up, waving his arms to quiet the crowd.

"Friends." His voice showed the strain of yesterday's shouting, and he spoke more quietly. "This morning we were shocked to find our beloved Corinne Rowley had passed away unexpectedly."

Someone sobbed nearby.

"It's hard to believe she's gone," Eli said. "She was a great lady who loved this town and its people."

Monica nudged Kevin. He looked down to see her mimicking Corinne's trademark scowl and suppressed a grin. Corinne had loved the people of Harpursville all right, particularly those who could trace their lineage back to the days of Captain Phineas J. Harpur and the original settlers, but she was no friend of *flatlanders* and people from *Away*. On more than one occasion, she had opined that voting privileges should only be extended to those who had three generations of continual residence in town.

Eli continued, "As her closest living relative, I'm going to take my aunt's body over to the cemetery and bury her when we're done here. But I wanted to give you all the chance to say your goodbyes. I know she meant a lot to many of you."

"I can't believe we came down here for this," Monica muttered. Kevin, who had met Corinne Rowley face-to-face on several occasions and found her to be thoroughly irascible, was inclined to agree. But Harpursville was a small town, and many of its people had blood connections; they both understood it was good to be seen at such an event.

People filed past the makeshift bier. Some paused to pray. A few dropped tulips or daffodils on her body. The Bartons paused briefly. There was no coffin, no satin pillow, no soft music humming through hidden speakers, just Corinne Rowley lying on a table. Sixty-four years old, someone had said. Same age as his mother. His breath caught. Corinne's face blurred, and he hurried away, biting his lip. Monica caught up to him, searched his face, and understood. She hugged him tightly while he composed himself.

The parking lot was eerily quiet. When the last person had paid their respects, Eli climbed the stepladder again.

"Thank you all," he said. "I know my aunt appreciates it, and so do we."

As he was stepping down, someone called from the back of the crowd, "What now?"

"What now? Well, like I said, we're going to take Aunt Corinne up to the cemetery and bury her. Then we'll go home and raise a glass to her memory."

"No, no," the person called. Kevin looked back but couldn't see who was asking, nor could he recognize the voice. "I mean, who's in charge?"

"I don't know."

"Who's got the keys to town hall?" That was Max Carver, no doubt about it.

"Oh, I've got those." Eli reached into his pocket and held the keys up. They flashed in the morning sun. "I don't know what to do with them."

Once more, the voice from the back called out. "You should take over."

"Oh jeez," Sobchuk said, "I don't—"

He was interrupted by a handful of voices shouting in agreement. "Take over!"

Two voices became three, then five. More voices joined in, chanting "Take over, take over," then shifting to a new cry: "Eli, Eli, Eli."

Sobchuk ducked his head and waved dismissively, but the chant built up. Kevin felt himself nodding to the beat of it. Eli Sobchuk? Why not? He stopped the Army. He brought them food. He was a hero. Why not Eli?

Eli held up his hands for quiet. It took a long time.

"I don't know," he said. "I don't know about politics. I don't know about running a town or anything like that, but I'll take over"—he raised his voice over the outburst of cheers—"but only if no one else wants to."

Not even Max Carver protested.

"Well, all right, I guess," Sobchuk said, and the cheers were deafening.

"Just like that?" Monica said to Kevin. "Just like that?"

Kevin looked down at her. She stood with her arms folded tight across her chest, glaring straight ahead. "What's the problem?" he asked. "You should have seen him yesterday. He was . . . amazing."

She shook her head, her mouth set in a firm line, her eyes flinty. "I don't like him. I know his type."

"What does that mean?"

She didn't answer. Kevin meant to press her, but Eli started speaking again.

"I know one thing my aunt would want to see. And that is for us to continue working together. We're in for hard times, people." He paused and looked around, meeting eyes, seeming to acknowledge each and every person gathered there. "Benjamin Franklin once said, 'We must all hang together, or assuredly we shall all hang separately.' Of course, he was talking about a very different time, but the idea is the same: we have to face this as a group. As a community. Not as individuals. If we all work together, we'll make it through until this mess is fixed, whether that's next week, next month, or next year. But if we don't stick together . . ."

Kevin was transfixed. The man was brilliant. The only sound in the parking lot was Sobchuk's voice.

"I know we'll come through it," Eli said, his voice strong and assured. "And when the Army *does* come back and when the power *is* turned on again, we'll still be here, stronger than we are today."

The crowd exploded, swept up in Sobchuk mania.

When they'd calmed down, he said, "As it turns out, I do have some ideas. I was going to run them by my aunt today, but . . . well, I guess I should run them by you first."

———

Eli stood on the ladder, head down, stroking his beard, gathering himself. Careful, he thought. Harpurites are an independent bunch: farm stock, country people, salt-of-the-earth types who believed in personal responsibility and small government. They believed in helping their neighbor but had too much pride to ask for themselves. He was banking on their generosity of spirit. Everything depended on voluntary participation.

He raised his head and surveyed the faces spread out before him.

"We're living in a tricky time right now. No money, no stores, no jobs, and no telling when we'll get our power back, or when anyone will be back with more food or more water.

"Right now, there are two important things for us to do. First, stay calm. We need to have confidence that everything is being done to fix this mess. But we can't sit around scratching our asses. We can hope and believe that it'll be fixed soon, but we have to act like it isn't. We have to prepare for the long haul."

The faces before him turned from excited to grim, but Eli thought it was the right play.

"This town was founded by ten families who came out of Massachusetts. They fought off wolves and bears and mountain lions, wrangled with Indians, dealt with disease and cold. They made it, and we'll make it, too, but it's gonna be hard.

"I'm not gonna lie to you. Right now, we're not a whole lot better off than those first ten families were. In fact, we're probably worse off. Technology made us soft; now we're going to have to live a whole lot harder than most of us have lived before."

What Eli saw on their faces was the same thing he saw on his customers' faces when he showed up in the middle of a frozen February night, his toolbox in one hand, a jerry can of #2 in the other, ready to get their furnaces running again: hope. It was the big-eyed look of men and women bundled in sweaters and flannels and winter coats who had spent several hours dealing with sinking temperatures in drafty old houses on a subzero night. "Can you fix it?" they'd ask. And he always could. An hour or so later, he'd walk out of the house on a wave of gratitude, a hero, until the house warmed up and they forgot all about him again.

They wouldn't forget him this time. He could fix this.

"Here's what I want to do," he said, and he laid out his plans.

—

Kevin couldn't stop marveling.

Sobchuk the furnace man showed more intelligence, initiative, and foresight than Kevin would have believed possible. It was a plan to put people to work, to give them jobs that wouldn't pay off in cash, but in survival. It was brilliant.

The only part of his proposal that caused grumbling was his plan to sweep the hamlet's vacant houses to appropriate food, clothing, blankets, tools—anything useful.

"I don't like it either," Eli said. "It goes against everything we believe in. But there are folks who left town for the weekend, and we all know they're not coming back just now. Those things aren't doing anybody any good sitting in empty houses. Let's put those things to use for all of us."

He promised another distribution of MREs in a few days, then set out sheets of paper for job signups. "We'll post them down here tomorrow. First workday is the day after," he said. "We'll make it through this. Now if you'll excuse me, I've got to go bury my aunt."

Kevin watched as Eli and several others hoisted the table bearing Corinne Rowley's body up on their shoulders and set off toward the cemetery.

"Wow," he said. "That was . . . that was just incredible."

Kelly said, "Dad, I'm going to volunteer for the garden."

"What? You can't do that."

"Why not? He said he wants at least one person from every family helping out."

"We need you at home," Kevin said. "Our garden has to come first. And the Hillmans need our help too."

"I hate working with the animals."

"And you hate gardening too."

"I like gardening now."

"It's okay, Mr. Barton," Dina said. "I like the animals. I can do that stuff myself."

"See?" Kelly crowed. "Besides, you heard Mr. Sobchuk. They'll give me lunch every day."

"I just don't think it's a good idea."

Kelly's face darkened with righteous anger. She opened her mouth to reply, but Monica stopped her with a single raised finger. She took Kevin by the arm and steered him to the side.

"I know what you're going to say," Kevin said. "The answer is no."

"Okay," she said. "Why?"

"It just doesn't . . . it's not . . . it doesn't feel right," he said. "We need her around the house. There's just too much to do."

"Like what?"

"The garden."

"How much time does that really take, Kevin? You already did the heavy work on that."

"Jake and the animals."

"Kelly is afraid of the cows. It's not safe to work with animals if you're scared of them. Dina says she can handle it. And she's not coming out hunting with me. There's not much to do inside the house now either."

Kevin linked his fingers together at the back of his head and walked a tight little circle, looking for the right words. *It just doesn't feel right* wouldn't cut it.

"I thought—I thought I saw Dougie Austin here yesterday." Just the mention of his name made Kevin's gut feel loose and crampy. "What if he's here?"

"Then we'll deal with him. Together."

She was so sure, so firm, and Kevin knew it was true. It made him feel better but also worse, like a little boy hiding behind his mother's skirts.

He glanced over at the girls. Curtis Pinkney had joined them. The impact of his presence on Kelly was immediate. She looked brighter, happier. It hurt him a little, right behind his sternum. As for Curtis, he looked more puppy than predator. Monica followed his gaze.

"Is that what this is about? Are you worried about him?"

"No." Monica regarded him from beneath raised eyebrows. "Okay, maybe it's a little bit about that, but it's . . . it's everything."

Monica squeezed his arm, soft, reassuring. "She'll be okay. She's probably safer walking into town now than she was standing at the bus stop. We just need to establish some ground rules, that's all. She's growing up, Kevin. She needs to start experiencing life."

"You think this is a good time for her to be experiencing that part of life?"

"Well, why not? She's scared, Kevin. Maybe some romance will take her mind off all this. And we'll save some food in the deal." She chewed her lip. "If Dina would volunteer, we could save two meals a day."

It was decided, and he knew it; but he still didn't like it. Though Kevin agreed with Sobchuk that they needed everyone working together, and though he promised a peaceful, safe environment in Harpursville, complete with some kind of patrol to ensure law and order, Kevin didn't like the idea of Kelly being on her own. Three images kept returning to his head: Dougie Austin leering at Dina's underwear; the looted, stinking husk of the Kwik-Stop; and three boys jumping up and down on Curtis Pinkney's car.

The whole world was teetering. It could go completely to shit at any time, and Kevin didn't want Kelly too far away. He wanted to put his foot down, wanted to stand firm, but his resolve blew away under Monica's steady gaze. She wasn't wrong. Neither was he, but his counterarguments abandoned him.

"All right," he said. "We'll try it."

She rubbed his arm. "She'll be okay, you'll see. Though I don't know how that little turd is going to deliver on his promise of lunch."

CHAPTER 10

KEVIN STOOD IN front of Luis and Val Silva's house, a stack of collapsed moving boxes salvaged from his basement under his arm. Except for the overgrown lawn, the two-story home was as elegant as ever, the last outpost of civilization before Harpur's Hill Road turned to dirt and disappeared in the dense woods of the state forest above. He knocked out of habit, though he knew no one was here.

Something brushed his leg. Kevin jumped and dropped his boxes, then laughed. Franklin, the Silvas' white and gray tabby, looked up at him hopefully.

"Hey, Franklin."

The cat didn't respond. Neither did Val or Luis. Kevin knocked twice more, then tried the door. It was locked. The Bartons were one of a rotating cast of friends the Silvas asked to take care of Franklin when they went away. Kevin hoped whoever was on the case this time had left the key in its proper place. He stood on his toes and ran his fingers along the upper edge of the lintel until he found it.

Kevin stuck his head in and immediately recoiled, choking on the stench of spoiled food. Franklin dashed in past his ankle. Now that he was on the comfortable turf of his living room, the cat turned in circles and meowed at Kevin, the tip of his tail flicking in time to his hunger dance.

Eyes watering in self-defense, Kevin clamped his hand over his mouth and nose. Once he was certain he could keep his lunch down, he called again for Luis and Val. Nothing but the sound of empty.

Kevin retreated to the porch and took deep, cleansing breaths. He pulled his shirt up to cover his mouth and nose and re-entered the house. Franklin slalomed through the legs of a chair and meowed again, a raspy, unpleasant sound. His needle-sharp teeth showed white against his pale pink tongue.

"Hang on there, big guy," Kevin muttered. "I'll get you in a minute."

Though his business was in the kitchen, Kevin took a quick turn through the first floor, then went upstairs, compelled to check the rest of the house. He took each step slowly, leaning forward, clutching the banister, listening hard, but all he heard was the flat thud of his feet on the uncarpeted treads. He didn't like the sound of it. He felt dirty, like a sneak, a burglar, even though what he was doing was necessary.

Images from TV crime thrillers sprang into his head: Val and Luis dead in their bed, the sheets stiff with blood. Murder-suicide. He froze. Maybe just double murder. Someone could be poised behind that door, crouched in that closet. He wished he had Monica's knife. He called out, "It's Kevin Barton. Just checking up on you."

The only response was an echo and a plaintive meow from Franklin.

After a moment, he forced himself forward. Franklin zipped past his feet to the top of the stairs and raked his side against a corner. The odor wasn't so bad here; he took a relieved gulp of air.

Now feeling more like a peeping Tom than a burglar, Kevin checked each room. No bodies, no blood, no crazed killer leaping out from behind a bed. Satisfied that no one was here, Kevin descended to the first floor and went to the kitchen, doing his best not to breathe in the rot.

Clouds of tiny fruit flies swirled around a mass of blackened, shriveled bananas and shrunken brown apples in a ceramic bowl on the kitchen table. Shiny green flies performed aerobatics around his head. Franklin's mewling reached a fevered pitch. Kevin turned in a circle in the center of the room, trying to figure out where the cat food would be, trying to keep his nose and throat shut tight against the nail polish smell of dead bananas.

He pulled open a tall cabinet to the right of the oven. The collar of his shirt slipped off his nose and face. He stood and stared, open-mouthed, unmindful of the flies, the dancing cat, or the stench of spoiled food.

The cabinet was a miniature supermarket, stocked floor to ceiling. Cereals, crackers, rice, sugar, and canned goods stood in neat rows. Familiar faces stared at him from brightly colored labels: the Quaker Oats man with his Mona Lisa smile; Keebler elves; Paul Newman's twinkling eyes on jars of pasta sauce and salsa; even good old Cap'n Crunch was there, sailing through a sea of sugary cereal. All the symbols of prosperity and wealth were there, artifacts of a civilization that might be lost forever. Despite the nausea-inducing smells in the kitchen, Kevin's stomach growled. He wanted to dump it all onto the floor and make angels in the boxes and cans and jars and bags. The water that came to his eyes now was not from the stink.

"Look at all this stuff," he said, no longer bothered by the empty house sound. "Wow."

Cornmeal and flour. Rice. Beans, dried and canned, in every conceivable color: black and red, pink and white, green. Stuffing mix. Canned peas, canned carrots, canned peas and carrots, beets, corn—whole and creamed—and coffee, blessed coffee, the big can at home was almost empty. Tuna and sardines. Canned olives. Unopened jars of mayonnaise and applesauce. He pulled things out with shaking hands and put them on the table, waving away the flies, feeling like a man who won a shopping spree at a supermarket without a time or cart limit. Franklin jumped on the table and headbutted a box of macaroni to the floor.

"Sorry, forgot you were there for a second, big fella."

He pulled a can of cat food from a stack and set it on the counter. Franklin thumped to the floor and took up a post by an empty bowl. Kevin opened the can and dumped its contents into the bowl. The cat promptly parked himself three feet away and stared off to the side through half-closed eyes.

"Better enjoy it while you can, cat. I think this is going to be your last feeding for a long time."

As if he understood, Franklin sauntered to the bowl and began to eat.

Kevin got to work. He unfolded his boxes and started loading them up. After a moment's consideration, he placed the stack of cat food cans in the box as well. Would they ever get so desperate they would eat cat food? Or the cat, for that matter? He hoped it wouldn't come to that. When the pantry was empty, he went through the cabinets. In one he found an open bag of bite-sized Milky Way bars. Cap'n Crunch, Milky Ways—who knew the Silvas had such a sweet tooth? In another, he came across a wad of several hundred dollars in a coffee can. He left the cash and took the candy.

He knew he shouldn't do it, but the bag was already open.

The chocolate was pure heaven. He closed his eyes and leaned against the counter, savoring the way the sweet, delicious chocolate melted on his tongue. He had a second, then a third, then something tapped at the window, and he jumped, shoving the bag behind his back. Instead of someone catching him indulging his guilty pleasure, he found nothing more than a branch waving in a sudden breeze. Still, the message was clear: time to leave.

He hauled the boxes outside and stacked them with care on the wagon, strapped them down with Thandie's bungee cords. It would take several trips to get this down the hill. Then, feeling worse about this than about taking the food, he scooped up the cat and set him outside.

"Sorry, buddy," he said. "I'd take you home, but I can't feed you. And you've got the equipment to survive out here."

Franklin sat on the porch and began licking his paw. Kevin pulled the wagon out to the street. The boxes teetered, but the bungee cords kept them in place. It was all he could do to keep the wagon from dragging him down the hill.

Kelly and Dina sat on the front porch of his house. They looked up at the rattle and squeak of the wagon wheels and bounded across the yard to meet him.

"What's that, Daddy? Oh. My. God!" Kelly bent down and started rifling through the boxes, squealing in delight. "Oreos! I'm dying for Oreos!"

"Hold on, girls, hold on. These aren't for us."

Kelly's smile slid like snow off a roof.

"What do you mean? The Silvas aren't using it."

"Right. But this is going for everyone. You heard Mr. Sobchuk."

Dina held a can of black olives against her cheek. She caressed the can, then put it back in the box. Kelly clutched the package of cookies. Her bottom lip stuck out.

"When are we going to get to use this? It's not fair!"

Kevin put his hands on her shoulders and looked into her eyes, so much like Monica's. Could he feel more bones in her shoulders? Was there a shadow on her cheeks that hadn't been there before? Was her shirt a little looser than last week? No, that was stupid, it was too soon for that. Yes, they had cut back quite a bit, yes, the junk food was long gone, but it was surely his imagination. Still, a voice spoke in his head. *Why should I starve my child? I got to it first, it should be mine.* But even as he thought this, he knew Sobchuk was right; everything hinged on cooperation, on community. He saw Sobchuk again, standing in the road in front of the convoy. Without the oilman's actions, Harpursville might have already turned into an outlaw town, dissolved into a band of Dougie Austins and Troy Fieldses. Sobchuk was right; they had to stick together, and this was part of sticking together.

"Fair doesn't really play into this," he said. "Is it fair that someone else doesn't have an empty house next door? Or a neighbor with cows and chickens?"

He hugged her. The packet of cookies crinkled between them. Kelly's body was stiff and unyielding.

"I'm sorry, sweetie. We have to take care of ourselves, but we have to look out for others, too, the way Jake and Alma are looking out for us. Besides, we *will* get to use this."

Kelly pulled back, the cookies still clutched in her hands. She glanced at Dina, who nodded at her, almost imperceptibly. Kelly's mouth twisted down. She flung the cookies at the wagon. They bounced off the box and fell to the ground.

"Fine, take them. Who cares if we starve as long as *they* have food."

"It's not like that—"

She was already running to the house, her dark hair streaming out behind her. Windows rattled when she slammed the door behind her.

Kevin bent to retrieve the cookies. The package was intact, but broken fragments made a kaleidoscope sound when he shook it. He put them back in the box and straightened to find Dina watching him.

"What? Do you think I'm wrong?"

She bit her lip. "I don't think so . . ."

He waited for her to complete the thought. When she didn't, he said, "But?"

She shrugged and looked off to the side.

"Look, Dina, you don't have to be diplomatic. If you think I'm being stupid, just say so."

"No, I don't think you're being stupid at all. I mean, it's the right thing to do, I guess. It's just . . . it's just all so scary. What if—"

He waited, but she just stood there, twisting her fingers together.

"What if what?" He took a breath and tried again, softer this time. "What if what?"

"What if we *all* run out? I mean, everybody? Of everything?"

She looked small and young and afraid. The last of his anger dribbled away.

"That's why we're doing this."

The door slammed again. Monica strode down the driveway with the purpose she had shown last week when the boys were trashing Curtis Pinkney's car.

"What's going on?" she demanded.

"I'm taking these down to town hall. It's from Luis and Val's place."

She poked through the boxes, just as the girls had done moments ago.

"We could use all of this. Pancake mix? We're almost out. If we have it, it could cut our flour use. We only have half a bag. Canned tomatoes? Pasta? Noodles? We could use all of this."

She straightened, hands on hips, and Kevin could see her lips moving as she did some silent calculations. She reached down and unhooked a bungee and started wrestling with a box. "Here, give me a hand with this."

"What are you doing?"

"We can't give all this away, Kevin. This can last us weeks if we're careful. Maybe long enough to hold us over until you start getting something from your garden."

"We can't take from this, Monica. It's for everyone."

She snorted. "Do you really think it's going to be used for everyone? Do you really think that?"

"Yes."

Her hazel eyes softened. The deep lines around her mouth smoothed. She reached out and stroked his rough cheek with her soft hand. "You are such a sweet man. You believe the best of everyone." She took her hand away. "This will be just like your taxes. They always say it's going to help you and me, and it goes into some fat cat's pockets."

Kevin summoned a mental image: Sobchuk standing in front of the Bradleys or Hummers or whatever the Army drove. He imagined himself in Sobchuk's place, saw Monica behind the wheel of the lead vehicle. She would stop. He could make her stop. Sobchuk had been the immovable object—he could be that too.

"If we pool this stuff with everyone, we'll all benefit. It will help everyone. Didn't you hear anything he said this morning?"

"I heard him. He was big on ideas but short on specifics. What do you think is going to happen once he's got all that stuff piled up down there? Who do you think it's going to help? What are we supposed to do, go down there once a week with a shopping list? Kevin," she said, her voice softer now. "Our priority has to be here, this house, this family, first and foremost."

In his head, the grille of the truck smashed into his midsection, flinging him far down the road, leaving behind an empty pair of shoes. Again, he heard the humiliating laughter of Dougie Austin and his friends as they rode away with their loot. He believed in Sobchuk, believed in his vision for getting them through the crisis, but Monica didn't. He'd tried to explain to Monica why Sobchuk's plan would work, why they needed to cooperate, but he couldn't articulate it. In truth, Sobchuk hadn't *really* explained how he'd do it. Kevin was trying to be the immovable object, but Monica was the irresistible force. He lowered his head, raised the white flag. Monica was graceful in victory.

"We're not keeping it all," she said. "We'll split it. Here, help me."

She sifted through the boxes. Anything that was already open, she took. Two bags of flour? She took one. Four cans of creamed corn? She took two. She passed them to Dina, and when Dina's arms were full, she scampered to the house, looking more than happy to escape.

"Is that all there is?" she asked. Kevin shook his head.

Through the afternoon, they repeated the scene until the Silvas' house was empty.

In the end, he was left with a little more than half of what he'd started with, and even less pride. As Monica hoisted the last box in her arms, and he prepared to make his way to town hall, he took the package of Oreos and placed them on top of her pile. "Give these to Kelly. Call it a peace offering."

———

Eli was at town hall when Kevin towed his diminished but still sizable load to the door.

"Well, well, what's this?" Sobchuk walked around the wagon, eyeing the boxes. "How many houses is this?"

"Just one," Kevin said, not quite maintaining eye contact. "The Silvas'."

Eli turned to a handful of men who stood nearby. "Now see fellas? This is what I've been talking about: neighbors helping neighbors. Good man."

He clapped Kevin on the shoulder. Though it had been at least a week since the man had last worked on an oil burner, Kevin thought he could still detect the sharp traces of fuel oil on him.

"Nice job, nice job. All from one house? That is how you do it." Sobchuk chucked a thumb over his shoulder at the group behind him. "These knuckleheads hit five or six houses and didn't get near as much."

Now Kevin recognized the men from around. There was Henry Chambers, who looked like a meaner version of the first President Bush and could be anywhere between 50 and 80, depending on how you looked at him; Troy, the infamous Kwik-Stop price gouger; and a sharp-faced young man who looked like a slightly older version of Troy and slouched like he didn't want to be seen.

Kevin felt both proud and embarrassed at being singled out.

Troy dropped a great dollop of brown spit on the ground.

"I guess they do their shopping on Friday night," Kevin mumbled.

Sobchuk laughed. "Yeah, and no skimming off the top either."

Kevin felt his face flush, but no one seemed to notice. They were all looking at the sloucher.

"I didn't skim," the man said. "Someone else got to those houses first, that's all."

"Yeah, yeah, whatever you say, Roger. All right, let's get this stuff inside."

Kevin wanted to help, but they had some kind of system already in place; he was afraid of getting in the way. Everything came out of the boxes, and Henry wrote it down in a spiral notepad. When the wagon was empty, Sobchuk thanked him for his help. Kevin was about to leave but decided to ask him the question that was on his mind, the one that Monica would probably want to know. "What next?"

Sobchuk scratched at his wiry beard. "Way I figure, we'll sort through all this stuff and get an idea of what we got. It'll be thin for a bit, but we'll get things going. First town meal should be tomorrow, about midday. What do you think of that, Chief?"

"Sounds great. Who's cooking?"

"Brenda, Henry's wife. You know, she does all the firehouse breakfasts." He frowned. "You ever been to the firehouse breakfasts? I don't remember seeing you there."

"No." Kevin rubbed the back of his neck. "We always meant to, we just never made it."

It was always on the list of things to do. The firehouse breakfasts were on the first Saturday of every month, a fundraiser for the department, or sometimes for a family that had fallen on hard times. But something always seemed to come up: they overslept; Kelly had a soccer game; they went to visit Kevin's parents. Eight years, and they still hadn't made one.

"Well, come on down. Hey, maybe your wife or little girl would like to come and help out. I'm sure Brenda could use the help. Wait a minute." He narrowed his eyes. "Didn't I see your name on the list? For the garden, right?"

"Yes. No, I mean, that was my daughter."

"Oh, right, right. Well, I guess we'll be feeding her then. Are you doing any hunting or anything? I don't recall seeing any other Bartons on any other lists."

"Actually, if anyone in my family is going to go hunting, it would be my wife." Troy snorted and spat again. Feeling his face get hotter, Kevin added, "Jake Hillman needs a lot of help at his place, so I'll be helping him out a lot."

"Neighbors helping neighbors. See, fellas? That's what's going to get us through this. Say, thanks for the help. We'll be seeing you around."

Kevin felt ridiculous pulling the wagon behind him, and when a burst of laughter rolled across the lot behind him, he was convinced it was directed at him.

CHAPTER 11

KEVIN SAT IN his kitchen early the next morning, picking at a crust of homemade bread, Kelly's goodbye kiss still warm on his cheek. She would be doing the same work in the hamlet that she had done under protest just a week ago—a week? Was it that long? He wasn't at all certain how long it had been. Though he knew it was right, it was hard to watch her walk out the door.

"What are you doing today?" Monica had her rifle zipped up in its carry case, ready to head into the woods at the top of the hill in pursuit of something. Kevin liked the idea of Monica wandering around the woods about as much as he liked Kelly running off to town, but she had a rifle, a knife, and an attitude.

"I'm helping Jake bring us running water down from the creek. I swear, the guy's an agricultural MacGyver."

"When you live on a farm, you learn to be creative."

Dina shouldered the door open. She brought in a plastic jug of milk, a half-full carton of eggs, and the smell of barn. Bits of hay clung to her hair. She kicked off her sneakers and left them with the pile of other shoes to one side of the door.

"Omelets for lunch and milk for—whatever," she chirped. "It takes me forever to milk though."

"Is that why the cows were making so much noise?" he teased.

She stuck her tongue out at him and set the eggs and milk on the table.

"They are loud, though, aren't they? Mr. Hillman was really fast. He did one cow in like five minutes. I think it took me twenty. It was fun but it feels really weird." She shook her hands as if she were drying nail polish and cast a longing look at the bread.

"Did the Hillmans give you anything to eat?" Monica asked.

"Eggs."

The smallest of sighs escaped from Monica, like the hiss of steam from a radiator, and she nodded at the loaf, giving her permission. Dina smiled, grabbed the knife, and sawed through the bread, cutting a wafer-thin slice. Monica looked her up and down, frowning.

"Those clothes are filthy, Dina."

Her jeans were more black than blue at this point and stiff with dirt.

"I know, but—"

"Go put something else on. I'll wash them later."

"Oh no, Momma B., I can't ask you to do that."

"Nonsense. Go change. Leave anything you need washed in the laundry basket in the bathroom." Dina hesitated, looked like she was going to apologize or protest, then thought better of it. She ran out of the room and up the stairs. Monica stared at the ceiling, tracking her movements by the creaking floorboards overhead. "I don't know where she gets the energy."

She sighed, louder this time, and cracked an egg in a pan for Dina.

"I know you want to get out there," Kevin said. "Why don't you let me to do that?"

"It's okay. Honestly, it's too late already anyway. I need to be out there before dawn. I just want to get in the mindset again, maybe find a good spot. Funny, isn't it? All those woods up there, and when was the last time either of us took a walk?"

The egg sizzled. Monica left the stove and opened the window. A cool breeze helped clear the fertile aroma of barn from the room.

"Before you go to Jake's, can you get some water for me?"

They still had a few jugs and a wading pool full of tap water outside, but that was for drinking, not washing. There had been little rain so the rain buckets were empty. Washing water meant a trip to the pond behind the Silvas' house.

"Yeah, I'll do that." He flexed his shoulders. Since the blackout, *sore* had become his default state. "I can't wait until we've got this thing set up at Jake's. Life will be a lot easier."

"Life isn't getting any easier any time soon."

She put the egg on a plate and set it on the table. They sat in the quiet kitchen for what seemed like a long time.

"What's taking her so long?" Monica grumbled. "Her egg is going to be cold."

Dina appeared as if summoned by her words. She wore her track uniform: tiny shorts that barely reached her thighs and a tank top molded to her chest. She paused in the door, one arm crossed in front of her, her knees pressed together, her cheeks reddening.

"It's all I have," she said to the floor.

Though she had run in front of hundreds in this skimpy uniform plenty of times, it was a completely different context. Kevin interested himself in the view out the window.

Monica said, "Are you running track or playing beach volleyball?"

"It was bigger when I got it. I think it shrank."

"Couldn't have shrunk that much. Do the boys wear the same thing or do theirs actually cover something?"

"Theirs are bigger. Looser."

Monica snorted. "Figures. Well, at least it's warm out."

"I can start working on my tan." Cheerful again, Dina took the seat next to Kevin, modesty forgotten with food on the table. "Thank you so much, Momma B." In between mouthfuls, she said, "I'm going to weed after breakfast. Is there anything else you want me to do?"

"Maybe you can help Mr. Barton bring water down from Silvas' pond."

"It's okay," Kevin said. "I can manage by myself."

"I don't mind." Dina sopped yolk up off the plate with her bread. When she was finished, the plate looked cleaner than it had coming out of the cupboard. Kevin studied the wall clock, frozen at ten fifteen, but could still see far more leg than he wanted to.

"We'll go in a couple of minutes," he said, hoping she'd discover something else to do.

"I'll be outside." She flashed out the door.

Once she was out of earshot, Monica said, "I can't believe they make girls run in those things."

Kevin said, "I can't believe she brought that enormous backpack and only had one set of clothes in it."

Monica laughed. A genuine laugh that warmed Kevin up. He thought it might have been the first real laugh he'd heard from her since day one. She said, "When you have time, I think you'd better see if you can find something for her to wear."

"Me? She can't fit in my clothes."

"At least she'll have room in yours. Anything of mine or Kelly's would be just as bad as those painted-on shorts." She took the rifle to the pantry and locked it in with the food. "There are some boxes of stuff you outgrew a couple of years ago down in the cellar. See what you can find."

"If this keeps up, I'll need them myself."

———

Eli Sobchuk emerged from the dark interior of town hall into a bright, sunny morning. Sixty people, nearly two-thirds of the hamlet's pre-blackout population, milled around, ready to work. Not bad. He had hoped to get one person per household to volunteer; instead, entire families had turned out. Whether it was a sense of duty, the promise of a free meal, or simple boredom, he didn't know and he didn't care. They were here, they were ready, and so was he.

He had stayed at town hall until well after dark the night before with his handpicked crew: Henry Chambers, Roger and Troy Fields, and Vance Johansson. They had pored over sign-up lists, divvied up tasks, and planned the day. Roger was head of security, mainly tasked with organizing patrols and keeping the town safe. Troy had sanitation, a task he'd bitched about to no end. Vance would run hunting and lumbering; "woodscraft", he insisted on calling it. Eli didn't give a damn what he called it as long as he brought in food and wood. Henry was his right hand, his chief deputy. His uncle never said much, but when he did, it made sense.

Brenda Chambers ran the midday meal, Cassie Magglio the garden. What they really needed was a doctor, but doctors just didn't live in

Harpursville. It was just a little too far from Algonquin, had a little too much dirt beneath its fingernails. Instead, they lived right in Algonquin itself or turned seasonal camps on Algonquin Lake into luxurious homes or bought up failed dairies in hamlets like Oaks Mills. While it was true half of Harpursville worked at the hospital, most were orderlies, porters, and maintenance types. But even if they'd had a doctor or a couple of nurses, they didn't have much in the way of supplies.

He smiled and walked toward the gathered throng.

"Folks," he called out, raising his hands for attention. It thrilled him how quickly they quieted for him. "Folks, I want to thank you for volunteering. I'm proud to be part of a town that cares so much."

He worked the line while each of the team leaders called people to their crew. "Thanks so much," he said, shaking hands with people. "We can't do this without you." Everyone greeted him with smiles, everyone leaned over and lingered, hoping to shake his hand, to thank him for taking charge and giving them hope. He made contact with just about everyone, until the lot was empty, save for Troy and his group: four sullen-looking teens and a couple of middle-aged men.

"Come on," Troy was saying. "We've got to do this."

One of the kids looked like he'd swallowed a piece of dog shit. Eli approached.

"Hey," he said, nodding at the unhappy one. "Connor, right? Connor Owens? What's the trouble?

"I didn't sign up for this," Connor said. "I don't want to be hauling garbage around."

Eli nodded. This was where things would get tricky, balancing what people wanted against what the town needed.

"I understand completely, but here's the thing," he said. "Sanitation is going to be more important than just about anything we do. It ain't pretty, but we're going to have to haul garbage, and we're going to have to put dead people in the ground. If we don't, we'll end up with rats and disease. We're also going to have to find a clean, reliable source of water, and we're going to need to keep garbage and dead people away from it. If you boys figure out a way to do that, you'll be bigger heroes than George Patton."

Connor said, "Who?"

"Never mind. Now, we tried to give everyone their first choice, but that wasn't always possible. It won't do to have forty people running around shooting up the woods, will it?"

Connor glanced at his friends, shook his head. "No."

"Right, 'cause the last thing we need is someone getting shot. Now you fellas need to be patient and do your best, and I promise, we'll rotate your jobs and get you onto something you like better in a little while. That okay?"

Though the boy still didn't look thrilled, he nodded. "Yes, sir."

Sir—that was unexpected and gave Eli an unexpected boost. He clapped his cousin on the shoulder. "You got this?"

"Yeah."

"All right then." He thought for a second. "You know what? Why don't you take Henry along? He's got some thoughts on this water thing."

"Cool."

With that straightened out, he wandered to the shady side of town hall. A few folks had lugged the big metal grills from down the fire department along with bags of charcoal. The charcoal would only last so long, so Henry was going to jerry-rig a fire pit out of cinderblocks. Linda Gibson doused the coals with a godly amount of lighter fluid. Nearby, Brenda Chambers and two other grandmotherly women worked at a table, chopping onions, potatoes, and carrots into small pieces. No one wore hairnets or gloves. There was no county health department to worry about; no USDA to put its stamp of approval on whatever it was they were cooking, and no one would complain. Except maybe Max Carver.

Linda leaned over to stick a flaming piece of paper into the coals, rewarding Eli with an eyeful of cleavage. It triggered memories of a particularly satisfying summer when they were in high school, when her chest had been familiar ground—what had that been, fifteen, sixteen years ago? His old man was right, time did go faster the older you got. She caught him looking, and straightened, adjusting the front of her blouse. Despite popping out three kids by the time she was 24, she looked pretty good. Fifteen years ago, he decided, when they were seventeen.

"Can I help you with something?" she said.

"Oh, you could help me out with something, all right." He winked. "Just like old times."

She blew a loose strand of hair back from her face and looked him up and down.

"You're either pretty desperate or pretty sure of yourself, talking that way to a woman with fire in her hand."

He opened his mouth to say something like, "I've got something hot for your hand," but held back. He didn't want to give one of the grandmas nearby a heart attack. Instead, he offered Linda a lusty grin, then stopped to chat with Aunt Brenda and the other ladies as they chopped and diced their way through the vegetables. Next, he drifted his way across the road to check on the progress of the garden, his mind returning to Linda Gibson as he walked. It occurred to him that the word she used, *desperate*, wasn't far from the truth. Since his first time, he didn't think he'd ever gone more than a month without getting any. Until now. The last time he'd gotten laid had been St. Patrick's Day, when he'd had quite a fun time with a girl from one of the colleges in Oneonta. It was now closing on two months. Desperate indeed. Focus, Eli, he thought.

A hand-painted sign at the edge of the field brought him to a stop. He stood there for a moment, musing over the two-by-three-foot piece of plywood. It had been painted with a sunflower and a pumpkin. The words *Sobchuk's Acres* stood out in bright green against a plain backdrop.

"Like it?"

He turned and was face-to-face with Cassie Magglio, a retired specialist from the Cooperative Extension. With her long gray braids hanging down either side of her broad face, her floppy hat and oversized sunglasses, she looked like a relic from Woodstock, and she might have been for all he knew. She knew her way around a garden though.

"You should have named it something else." He surveyed the field and was surprised at how much of the grass had already been pulled up. "How'd you get so much done so fast?"

She laughed in a witchy cackle that matched her looks. "Girl power," she said. "Actually, I rounded up a few folks yesterday afternoon, and we started sod busting. I've been after Arnie for years to turn this into a community garden."

Cassie left him to go help someone with something. Eli wandered out into what yesterday had been the outfield of Harpursville's baseball field.

Other than a few boys who were too young to be left alone or do other jobs, the entire crew was girls. They worked with rakes and pitchforks, turning over the soil, pulling up rocks, yanking out turf. Grass and rocks were thrown into wheelbarrows and piled up on the side.

Where were the young, single women? Eli wondered. They were either old and ugly like Cassie, too young, or too married.

"We have a demographics problem," he muttered. Like many rural towns in the state, Harpursville had too many people above fifty. They'd been talking for years about how to keep young people from leaving or how to get young families in, but it seemed everyone wanted to live somewhere else.

He came upon a girl in a yellow tank top and tan shorts. A red bandanna kept her hair out of her face. She chopped at dirt clods in the newly exposed soil with a long-handled rake, singing as she worked. She picked up a rock, turned and tossed it, nearly hitting him.

"Oh my gosh, I'm so sorry! Are you okay?"

"My fault," he said, holding up his hands. "I wasn't paying attention."

"No, it's my fault. I was in my own little world."

She was short, dark-haired and dark-eyed, and though she looked familiar, he couldn't quite match a name to her face.

"I just want to say thanks for helping out down here. You're doing a real service for the town." He stuck out his hand. "Eli Sobchuk."

She pulled off her glove and shook his hand with damp fingers. "I'm Kelly Barton."

"No kidding? Last time I was up at your place you must have been . . . so high." He held his hand about waist level. "Look at you, all grown up."

A water bottle hung from the belt loop at her right side. The weight of it pulled her shorts down a bit, showing a little bit of pale belly. She saw him looking, reddened, tugged at the hem of her shirt.

"I, uh, I should get back to work."

Girls were funny, he thought. They wore skimpy little outfits for you to look at, but when you did, they got mad. Or pretended to.

"Don't let me hold you up. Hey, thanks again, and say hi to your folks."

"I will."

"Oh, you dropped your glove. Behind you."

"Thanks."

She bent to pick it up. Not terrible, he thought, but a little wide in the wrong places. Her face was almost pretty. A shame she hadn't inherited her mother's tits—that woman had a first-class rack.

He walked away, nodding and chatting with others along the way, but his mind went back to Monica Barton. He'd wanted her the moment he'd seen her, and she'd wanted him, he was sure of it. She'd given him the signal, like shooting a big red flare up into the night, but when he made his move, she backpedaled. Too bad. Still, she'd given him quite a show.

He reset his sights on Linda. Women like it when you were persistent.

CHAPTER 12

TIME HAD GOTTEN slippery since the blackout. Monica wasn't counting days, exactly, because it was hard to keep track of days without meetings and weekends and due dates; instead, she calculated based on MREs. She had delayed breaking into their original supply as long as she could. When she did use them, she spaced them out, with at least one day in between to keep from using them too fast, and Sobchuk had doled out another set to each household. Based on that, she figured it was about three weeks since the creepy little troll had taken over, and somehow, Harpursville still stood.

From what she gleaned from Kelly and on her own infrequent trips down the hill, three or four people had died, older folks who ran out of medication, and a handful had taken to the road, chasing rumors of electricity in Pennsylvania. They'd also gained about an equal number of people who'd come in from the Big Empty. Sobchuk had somehow also delivered on lunch for the crews every day. Sometimes those meals were little more than vegetable stew, according to Kelly, but they were more and more supplemented by meat from the hunting parties that had had far more luck than Monica. So far, she'd managed just one turkey and a snapping turtle she'd beheaded when she found it laying eggs on the roadside. It didn't go far. She had to get something bigger. Had to.

She stood in the center of the kitchen, chewing on her thumbnail and watching the light drain slowly from the room. The fancy track lighting they installed when they renovated the kitchen was no help. Not anymore.

"A little help?"

Kevin's muffled voice came through the door. She pulled the door open, and he came in, carrying a large pot of steaming water held in his mitted hands. Though they still had propane for the stove, Monica had invoked strict conservation measures: the stove was for cooking only. Wash water was heated outside on the firepit. As it was, every time she lit the stove, she expected the flame to shrivel and die.

Kelly's laughter floated in from the front room. Curtis had invited himself to dinner. He'd come with three sunnies and a bass he'd caught that day. Smart boy, that Curtis. And stupid woman, that Monica: The Silvas had a cute little pond up behind their house, one they had dug for their kids to swim in and skate on when they were little that was now mostly used as a backdrop for sipping cocktails when they were actually home. That pond was full of fish. Monica knew there were no fishing poles in her own house; she hated fishing, and Kevin was no outdoorsman. She would bet her right arm that the Silvas had poles and tackle, and if *they* didn't, Jake would. She would check tomorrow, after coming back from the woods.

Kevin set the pot on the stove, his face lobster red. He frowned in the direction of the front room.

"Isn't it Kelly's night to help with cleanup?"

"Let them have some time alone. They're not going to get in any trouble out there." She fit the stopper in the sink. "Can you fill that? About halfway? Thanks."

"Is Dina with them?"

"For heaven's sake, they don't need a chaperone."

She wished he worried as much about their food as he did about Curtis. He had this crazy notion that everything was okay, that it would all be all right. The meat in Jake's freezer had long since spoiled, they were living on eggs and a trickle of milk and the things cobbled together from their rapidly dwindling pantry. Hunger was an unwelcome guest that never really went away, even after a relatively full meal like tonight's. It was like that annoying kid in school who followed you everywhere, talking nonstop, hurrying to keep pace when you sped up to leave her behind. Let Kelly have some fun, let her have something to take her mind off it all. Kelly's excitement over Curtis did *Monica* some good too. She liked Curtis, and she liked the way her daughter seemed to be blossoming.

"Okay," Kevin said, "but is she out there?"

"I don't know where she is, Kevin," she said. "Just fill the sink. Please."

Muscles jumped out on his arms as he hoisted the pot and carefully poured water into the sink. Steam floated and swirled around him. He squinted and blew it away with noisy puffs.

"Good?"

"Yes. Thanks."

Footsteps echoed and Kelly and Curtis came in. The rangy young man rested one hand on Kelly's shoulder. He was becoming bolder in his displays of affection. Monica hadn't seen them kissing, and Kelly hadn't confided in her, but the way she looked after they said their goodbyes told her everything she needed to know about that. She tried not to wonder how far they'd gone or if they were being careful. She'd had the talk with Kelly a few years back, but back then it had seemed more like a thought exercise. Maybe it was time for a refresher.

"I have to get going," Curtis said. "Thanks so much for having me."

"So soon?" Monica said. "I wish I had something for dessert, but . . ."

"It's okay. I just hope I didn't impose."

"You brought dinner—that's never imposing. Are you sure you can't stay longer?"

"I'm on patrol tonight. I have to get ready. But thank you again."

Monica was sold on him. He treated Kelly well, showed proper respect for her and Kevin, and he was cute. Especially now that his crew cut was growing out. It also helped that Curtis had ditched the baggie jeans in favor of something better fitting. He'd also ditched the hoops in his ears and eyebrow after seeing someone lose half an ear when they got it caught on a branch in the woods.

"Be careful out there," she said.

"We watch out for each other."

Kelly said, "I'm going to walk Curtis down to the corner."

Kevin's lower lip pushed out. Monica shooed them out before he could manufacture a reason to keep her home.

"Just to the corner," he called after them, putting as much iron in his voice as he could manage. "And don't be long."

She watched him watch them.

Despite himself, she could tell Kevin was warming to him too. He no longer adopted that stiffened, puffed-up posture men got when they felt threatened. He chewed on a stray hair from the mustache he had given up trying to shave. While she didn't mind the facial hair, she could do without him using it as dental floss.

"She'll be fine."

"I know. I just . . . I don't know."

"We've got bigger worries than Curtis."

Starvation, for example. The garden was coming along; was doing quite well, in fact, but they were still weeks away from harvesting anything but field greens. Now she regretted letting Kevin take anything down to town hall at all, even though those supplies were helping to feed Kelly once a day. She wished Dina would go, too, and had dropped some not-so-subtle hints to that effect, but the girl showed no inclination to do so.

"We're doing okay, hon," Kevin said. "Really."

"How can you say that?"

"Because it's true. We're going to be okay."

He opened his arms. She wanted to go to him, wanted to rest her cheek on his chest and feel his heartbeat, as strong and sure as his conviction. She wanted to believe, like he did, that the Army would come back, that help was on the way, that it would all be over soon. She wanted to believe but she couldn't. She wanted him to hold her but she couldn't. She turned back to the sink.

"I'd better get this done before the water gets cold."

"You want help?"

He came up behind her, put his arms around her and pressed tightly against her. In recent years, his rounding belly would fit nicely into the curve of her back. But Ted was shrinking rapidly. Something else was growing, though.

"You don't really want to do dishes, do you?" he said.

He kissed her neck, slid a hand up and cupped her breast. It sent a thrill through her, and she leaned back, felt him growing harder still against her. It was something she'd been feeling a lot more lately. At night, he'd slide into bed and snuggle against her. She'd feel his heart thumping against her back and soon enough she'd feel him poking her. He rubbed his thumb along her nipple.

"Oh," she breathed. "How can you think of that now?"

He mumbled against her neck, sending tingles all through her. She wanted to strip off her clothes and have him right there, right now. But that little mouse of anxiety started nibbling again at the edge of her rib cage. Its sharp little teeth gnawed away, and she lost the mood. She peeled his hands away and slipped out of his grip.

"I'm sorry," she said. "I just—I can't. Not right now."

"It's okay." If he was disappointed, he disguised it well. As always. "Maybe later?"

She forced a smile. "Maybe. Go play in the garden before it gets dark."

His arms remained around her, at a safe level. "I love you."

"I know. Me too."

She went to the sink as he left, squeezed a precious drop of their diminishing dishwashing soap into the water, and frothed it up. She took a deep breath, inhaling the lemon-scented water, relishing the momentary quiet.

Solitude had been harder to come by since the blackout. Someone was always close at hand—Kelly, Kevin, or Dina—or she found herself helping out Jake and Alma. Hunting was the only time she got to be alone with her thoughts, but the increasing pressure she felt to provide did not do anything for her peace of mind.

Her full belly was hollowed out by the gnawing reminder of her latest failure, of several early morning hours concealed in a thicket overlooking the intersection of several well-worn deer trails. Nothing had moved except for chipmunks and squirrels and songbirds. Squirrels were an option. There were dry woods on the south-facing side of the hill that were loaded with oaks—and squirrels. While Monica was confident she could hit a squirrel, both weapons she carried into the woods—her Winchester and Jake's shotgun—were far too much gun for tree rats. She feared she would be spending rounds to do nothing more than spatter squirrel guts around the woods. Maybe it was a scent problem; she was smelling pretty ripe these days. She'd have to find a way to mask that.

She was mostly through the washing when the door opened behind her, and Monica knew it was Dina.

Monica took a deep breath and turned. Dina smiled shyly. A small wicker basket hung over one arm. She wore her ridiculous track shorts, must have changed into them just after dinner, but at least this time she also wore one of Kevin's old T-shirts. Black mud streaked her legs from her bare feet to the midpoint of her calves.

"Look what I got, Momma B."

She tipped the basket and dumped a squirming tangle of thumb-thick centipedes on the table. Monica shrieked. The handful of cutlery she'd been holding hit the floor and exploded in all directions.

"Get them out of here!"

She shrank against the counter, feeling the hideous crawl of bugs over her skin, skittering up her back, on her neck.

She blinked. She wasn't looking at impossibly large centipedes, she was looking at . . . roots. Mud-streaked roots with wiry hairs sprouting from them. Monica pressed her wet hand to her chest, trying to quiet her pounding heart and tried to laugh, because if she didn't laugh, she might start yelling.

"I'm sorry, Mrs. B.," Dina said, looking confused and a little hurt. "I didn't mean to upset you."

"It's not your fault, Dina. My brothers—my brothers used to put bugs in my things, all the time." Grasshoppers, spiders, crickets—all had made appearances in her bed, her dresser, her lunchbox. And especially worms. "I'm okay with bugs when they're outside. Inside—"

"I didn't know. I'm so, so sorry. Let me get those."

They collected the silverware and put it back in the hot water. Monica approached the table and eyed the things on the table. They were yellowish white and segmented like centipedes, but stiff, not squirmy. What she had thought were legs were little white root hairs.

Dina spread them across the table. Drops of water glistened on them.

"I washed them before I came in. I didn't want to get the house dirty."

They both glanced at her streaked legs and feet. Little chunks of gray mud lay on the floor around her, left a trail to the door. Dina laughed in a sheepish way. "I'll sweep up when I'm done."

"What are these, anyway?" Monica asked, poking at one with the tip of her finger.

"Cattail roots. They are so cool, Momma B. You can eat them, you can make flour from them, you can boil them like potatoes. They're really good for you too. They would have been better if I got them earlier in the spring, but . . ." She shrugged. "I just didn't think of it then. They're growing all around the Silvas' pond."

It had been this way for a week now. Dina kept presenting her with dandelion greens, unknown fruits and nuts, seeds, and flowers gathered from all around the house and the woods up the hill. She lined them up on the table the way Franklin used to line up headless mice at Val's door. And though Monica already knew the answer, she asked anyway.

"How do you know all this, Dina?"

"Nature camp."

Monica's knowledge of woodland foraging pretty much began and ended with "don't eat it if you don't know what it is." She approached Dina's findings with caution, but the girl hadn't steered them wrong so far. But she was exhausting, and she was always around.

"I don't really know what to do with them."

"I could cook them."

She almost squashed the idea immediately. As weary as she was of coming up with tasty ways to make something out of nothing, she was loath to give up the kitchen, even for one meal. It was her territory, her domain, and it felt like she had precious little of that left.

But Dina looked so hopeful, it almost broke her heart. Monica had to remind herself that the girl was suffering, too, forced to live here while her family was who knew where, doing who knew what. If they were even alive at all.

"Sure, Dina. Why not?"

Dina almost exploded. "Thank you! They'll be really good!"

"I'm sure." Monica mustered a smile, though in truth she had serious doubts about the tastiness of cattail roots. For the second time she said, "Well, I'd better get back to this before my water goes cold."

She returned to the sink, plunged her hands back into the warm water and began rewashing her silverware, but she could feel Dina's continued presence behind her. *Please, just go already.* The thought was there before she could stop it. It made her feel small and mean. She just wanted some space.

The furtive squeak of a foot on linoleum came to her over the sound of sloshing water. Monica tried to ignore it and looked out the window, but she also saw Dina's ghostly reflection in the glass. She scrubbed viciously at gunk on a knife. Shining fish scales winked at her from the bottom of the sink. She squeezed her eyes tightly for a second, opened them, and turned once again. Dina was still there, her fisted hands pressed together just below her chin.

"Is everything okay, Dina?"

"I just wanted to say thank you, Mrs. Barton. I know it hasn't been easy having me here. I'm just . . . I'm just really, really grateful."

Guilt rose in a slow wave, hot and thick like bile. Monica swallowed it down, licked her lips, and smiled. It was the kind of smile you put on when the photographer says, "Just one more," and you've already posed for a dozen just-one-mores—not fake, not exactly, but not quite genuine either.

What's wrong with me? All the girl needed was some reassurance, but Monica found it hard to give. Looking at Dina now, she was reminded of one of Kelly's favorite childhood books, *If You Give a Mouse a Cookie.* Kelly made her read it over and over to the point where she almost had it memorized. Give a mouse a cookie, and he'll want some milk. In a glass. With a straw. On and on it went, the mouse always asking for something more while the poor boy in the story turned his house upside down to accommodate him. Dina was the mouse—the mouse who consumed one-quarter of everything they had. She would eat one-quarter of the cattail roots she was so excited about. She would drink one-quarter of the milk and eat one-quarter of the eggs Jake would send tomorrow. She ate one-quarter of the sunnies Curtis brought, drank one-quarter of their water.

A war raged inside her. On one side was Momma B., loving and caring, who had welcomed Dina with open arms from the day she met Kelly's instant best friend when she was just eight. Momma B. had stroked Dina's forehead and sung her back to sleep when she woke from a nightmare on her first sleepover. Momma B. wanted to sweep her up now and tell her it was all going to be all right.

On the other side was a cold quartermaster counting every scrap of food, every glass of water or milk, every pinch of flour and salt. *That* one looked at Dina as a mouth—a gaping, chewing, needy mouth to feed, a body to clothe and keep safe, a guest who had long overstayed her welcome.

She's sacrificing, too, Momma B. said, but the quartermaster would not be silenced.

Sure she is, it said, *but so is everyone. How much better off would you be without her? How much healthier would Kelly be without her?*

One touch, said Momma B. *We'll both feel better.*

She couldn't do it.

"We're happy you're here. You don't have to thank us."

Dina wanted a hug. Momma B. wanted to give it to her, but the quartermaster would not yield. That one-quarter of everything stood between them like a Jersey barrier on the highway. She reached out and gave Dina's arm a light squeeze, then went back to the dishes, her guts sending up a fresh wave of fishy-tasting guilt. After a moment, the door opened and closed gently, as Dina took care not to let it slam. The gunshot crack of the screen door was one of those silly little things that set her teeth on edge, a sensitivity inherited, no doubt, from her own mother. Kelly did it constantly. Sometimes she'd even stick her head back in and say, "Sorry, Mom," then run back out and let it slam again. Dina never slammed the door. She loved Dina for being so considerate. She hated her for being so considerate. She attacked the dishes with her sponge.

Monica let the bitter taste of guilt fill her. She deserved it. It wasn't Dina's fault.

With the dishes finally finished, Monica pulled the plug to drain the sink. As the water swirled down the drain, she looked out the window. Long shadows slanted across the garden, cutting black stripes across the rows of the plants that Kevin was sure would sustain them.

Kevin stood at the edge of the garden. He looked good, tan and fit. His hair was too long, but not yet out of control. A squarish patch of gray flashed in his beard, just below his mouth. He hadn't worn a beard since college. She hadn't liked it on him then—it made his face look too long—but now it suited him. Age on a man's face, she thought, gives him character. It speaks of experience and confidence.

He put his hands on his hips and twisted left and right, stretching his back. His T-shirt was tight across his chest but loose in the belly.

Ted was a mere bump instead of a belly. Lean, ropy muscles showed in his arms. The blackout had melted away much of the excess weight he'd built up over the last few years. He looked healthy. Happy too. This life agreed with him. She envied his ability to enjoy it.

Dina came over and stood beside him. She was nearly as tall as he. In one hand she held a pile of loose greens. They flopped up and down as she talked. Her hair was pulled back in a tight ponytail that highlighted the bones of her cheeks and made her neck look long and graceful. The sleeves of her borrowed T-shirt were rolled up to expose her tanned shoulders. Even streaked with mud, her legs gleamed in the evening sun, seemed to stretch for miles.

Monica glanced down at her own stubby legs, at the hips that just seemed to get wider and wider. She felt an ache in her chest, a pang for her lost youth, and something else she couldn't pin down.

Outside, Kevin said something that made Dina laugh. The girl lit up as if she had a hundred-watt bulb inside of her. A finger of bile, hot and sour, touched the back of Monica's throat as she watched the two of them laugh and joke as if there was nothing at all wrong with the world.

CHAPTER 13

ELI SAT ON the top step of Linda Gibson's porch. Out on the dark road in front of the house, three dim figures passed, members of the night patrol. They moved in well-disciplined silence, no chatter or goofing around. Initially, they'd mostly approached it as an opportunity to goof around playing at soldiers, but after Max Carver had been relieved of his rifle, ammunition, and the deer he'd shot by a trio of better-armed strangers in the woods on the northwest side of town, Eli had lit them up. "We're building something here, something great," he'd told the crew. "We can't let anyone waltz in here and take it away from us. Our lives depend on it." He was pleased with how they'd embraced the importance of the job, and how quickly they'd adapted their tactics. They scoured the roads and fields and woods around town, watching and listening. When they found groups of strangers, they kept eyes on them, and made contact when necessary. Some groups were only interested in getting someplace else; these they escorted through town. Some tried to set up camp in an abandoned farm or house. They were politely asked to leave, and if they refused, were given strong encouragement to do so. On Eli's orders, all groups encountered were questioned, in search of a few qualified people—doctors and nurses, mostly—who could be invited to join the community. So far, they had turned up no one, and so far, none of the encounters had resulted in any loss of life or serious injury.

A candle flickered in an upstairs window across the way. Otherwise, the homes on this street were dark. With no late shows to watch, no Netflix, no Internet porn, folks went to bed early.

He popped open a fresh beer. Lukewarm foam poofed. Eli slurped it away before it could drip down over his fingers. Warm beer wasn't great, but the only thing worse than warm beer was no beer.

"Kind of reminds me of high school," he said. "Remember?"

Beside him, Linda made a noise through her nose that he took as a yes.

"Good times," he said. "Good times."

Good times indeed. A time when they had no real responsibilities, when they spent long nights in the woods in front of a bonfire, radio playing, people smoking, drinking, making out. Endless summer nights; a time he thought would never end.

Linda set her beer down between her feet. "I find myself wondering the same thing now that I did then," she said.

"Yeah? What's that?"

"Where'd you get the beer?"

"What'd they used to say on *The Sopranos*? It fell off a truck."

"Right," she said. "I expect it helps having a cousin with keys to the Kwik-Stop."

"Don't ask, don't tell. Remember that one?"

He shifted to ease the bite of the porch floor against his ass. It also put his hand close enough that he was almost—but not quite—touching Linda's fingers. All part of the game. She picked up her beer and took another sip. This time, she rested her elbows on her thighs and dangled the can between her knees. Her back curled. An invitation to a hand?

Part of the fun of pursuit was the anticipation of the payoff. Eli had been working Linda for days now, but his lack of progress was frustrating. This was far different from the Oneonta bar scene. Despite being an ordinary-looking guy with an ordinary job, Eli was very successful when it came to bedding women. He chalked it up to three things: he was generous with his smile, generous with drinks, and he wasn't afraid to get shot down. His "I don't give a fuck" attitude seemed to play especially well with the college girls in Oneonta, who were either adventurous, careless—or drunk.

Linda was none of these things, however. She listened to him when he needed to unload and was not above slipping a little extra on his lunch plate, yet he had not been able to get past the purely social boundary, what the kids called "The Friend Zone." Not even a goodnight kiss.

He leaned over and brushed the hair back from her face, let his finger linger on her soft, cool cheek. Time to push his chips to the center of the table.

He moved in.

She pulled back.

"What are you doing, Eli?"

"What?"

"I mean, really, Eli, what are you doing? What do you want out of me?"

He took a large swallow of beer.

"I just thought, you and me, you know, we have history." He took a large swallow of beer. "What do they say? We made beautiful music together."

"That was years ago," she said, and she sounded tired. "And there's a reason we didn't stay together."

"I just thought maybe we could have a good time, you know? Like old times."

"Where are you going to be when the kids wake up in the morning?" She gave him a moment to answer. He didn't. "Those kids will be up with the sun, looking for breakfast. Who's going to feed them? You? Who's going to give them a bath? You? Who's going to get them dressed?"

"First, who do you think's feeding your kids? Me. And what's wrong with a little fun? Everything's working fine. We're on top of things. Hell, things are probably running better in this town right now than when Arnie was banging that damn gavel once a month and saying, 'It's not in the budget, it's not in the budget, it's not in the budget.' That's why we're the poor stepchild in this county.

"Besides, if things are going to shit, wouldn't you rather go out with a smile on your face?"

"We're not sixteen anymore, Eli. This isn't experimenting or sowing wild oats or whatever you want to call it, not for me. You haven't changed a bit. Our world has fallen apart, and you're just looking to get laid."

She stood, wiped her hands on her pants, and looked down at him. "I'm not looking for any commitment, Eli. I'm not looking to get married. I just don't need any distractions right now. And I don't think you do either. Good night. Thanks for the beer."

The door closed quietly behind her.

Ah shit. Give me diamonds, give me money, give me kids, there was always an agenda. This was why he preferred the college girls: they weren't looking for husbands, they weren't gold-digging, they were just looking for fun. And they had firm tits and tight asses. No sags, no bags.

He drained his beer, then picked up Linda's half-full one for the walk home. His cock stood at half-mast, reluctant to give up the dream of action, but dream was all that was left for tonight. Eli walked down the street, the beer hanging from his fingers.

Linda was a lost cause. Who did that leave? Who else was single, the right age, and good looking enough? The sad fact of life was that Harpursville was aging, which wasn't necessarily a problem; Eli had no problem bedding a cougar. But the women around here were too married. Eli set the beer on his kitchen counter and went up to bed. Maybe things would look better in the morning.

—

They didn't. A mountain of dishes rose from the kitchen sink, plates and bowls stacked in an untidy pile, held together by luck. Mouse turds lay scattered across the countertop. A wet, sour odor hung over everything. Cobwebs gathered dust in the corners.

Cleaning was never his specialty. Before the blackout, Eli's housekeeping regimen consisted of running the dishwasher when it was full, wiping down the table and counters a couple times a week, and swabbing out the toilet when the rim was more black than white. Since his unanimous election, he hadn't had time for any of that; he was out early and home late, when it was too dark to really see what he was doing. As he looked around the mess of his house, he felt something he hadn't felt since stepping into the road nearly a month ago: down.

What he needed was someone to take care of his house, someone to get it back under control so he didn't feel like he was living in a pigsty. He just didn't know who; that was the problem.

He found a foil-wrapped packet on the counter. In it was an extra hunk of trout from yesterday's lunch, courtesy of Aunt Brenda. A good woman, Aunt Brenda. She spent hours every day at the town hall creating tasty, filling meals out of whatever they had on hand, yet she still kept her house spotless, even though she couldn't run a vacuum or dishwasher.

The trout passed the smell test. He flipped the chunk of fish onto a reasonably clean plate and set the foil aside for future use. Who knew when the next shipment of tinfoil was coming?

When he finished his meal, he placed his plate on the stack carefully so it didn't cause an avalanche. This was no way to live. He needed clean plates, clean clothes, a clean place to live, but he had no time. He needed someone to take care of it for him.

Outside, the air was heavy and warm. By Eli's estimate, it was the first week of June, a time when they traditionally got their first blast of hot and humid, and he made a mental note to remind Troy to make sure the field crews had plenty of water. They didn't need anyone dropping dead of heat stroke. They couldn't afford to lose any able bodies.

"Hi, Eli."

"Good morning, Mr. Sobchuk."

"How are you today, Eli?"

The people—his people—greeted him as he walked down the street. They offered him warm smiles, looks of hope and optimism, and, once in a while, a bit of homemade bread or some other fresh-baked goodie. He protested, but they insisted; so he always took it. It would be rude not to. He called them by name and asked after their kids or their parents, but always most of his mind was on the problems of the day. Wood and game, fish and water, sanitation and safety. Who needed a fresh propane cylinder, and how many were left? Is anyone sick? Were there any accidents? Is it time to hand out more MREs? Did anyone die overnight? It seemed he was better at solving the town's problems than his own.

The sun hung just above the crest of Harpur's Hill when he reached town hall. Eli shielded his eyes with his hand and gazed at Jake Hillman's farm complex: red barn with its gray metal roof, the sun gleaming off the silo roof, the couple's modest white farmhouse. Closer by rose Kevin Barton's Victorian, the normally well-manicured green slope of lawn dotted with pink and white and purple weeds. Eli frowned. Barton's kid worked in the garden. Every morning, she dragged a red wagon down the hill with a gallon or two of milk from Jake. Other than that, he never saw any of them in town. They were in their own little world up there. Barton seemed like an okay guy, and he had come through with a big load from that other house up the hill there.

Eli gathered his crew in the small meeting room outside of the supervisor's office. He ran his meetings quickly without much chitchat or debate. After getting the reports from his team and giving out the day's orders, he said, "Hey, has anyone checked in on Jake Hillman lately?"

No one had.

Eli drummed his fingers on the table, thinking.

"What about Barton?"

"Who?" Vance said.

"You know, Barton. Kevin Barton. Moved into Tanner's place seven, eight years ago. That's his kid bringing the milk down. Works in the garden."

"Oh." Wavy lines formed in the middle of Vance's head as he thought. "I don't know."

"Maybe you know his wife." Eli held his cupped hands out about a foot away from his chest. "Monica Willsey, she was. Her family's from over Bowman's Corners."

"Her I remember," Vance said. "Nope, haven't seen her around."

Eli scratched at his chin, momentarily distracted by the thought of Monica Barton's body. He refocused.

"All right. Get on out there and get to work. Uncle Henry, you're with me. Let's you and me pay a visit up the hill and check in on those folks."

CHAPTER 14

THE DAYS HAD settled into a routine. It wasn't exactly a comfortable routine, but it was a routine, and that helped everyone. Dina was out before sunrise, milking a handful of cows, feeding chickens, and helping with chores around the barn. Bartons, Hillmans, and one McCray met each day for breakfast and to plot out the rest of the day. Kelly went into town to work in the community garden, dragging a wagon loaded with milk for the town. Though he was busy most of the day, Kevin watched anxiously for her return all afternoon.

Once her work in the barn was finished, Dina spent most of her time searching for wild edibles in the woods and fields on the hill. While a lot of her findings looked questionable to Kevin, she hadn't poisoned them yet. Whether it was the plants or just their meager diet, everyone suffered through bouts of horrible, gut-cramping diarrhea followed by days when it was all anyone could do to squeeze out a few rabbit pellets. At least, Kevin mused, they hadn't gotten to the point of eating their own crap like rabbits. Kevin noticed that Dina never roamed too far. Though she didn't say anything, he was pretty sure it was because of what had happened with Dougie Austin.

Monica spent most of her time in the woods, searching for a consistent source of meat, and mostly coming up empty. As much as Kevin assured her they were doing well, her frustration grew. She was increasingly irritable and becoming more and more withdrawn.

Aside from working in his own garden, Kevin spent most of his time working with Jake. The excitement Kevin felt when first learning to cut trees was over. Now, it was just another job, though one of crucial importance. Jake was obsessed with wood and having enough for the winter. As a veteran of fifteen upstate winters, Kevin was fully on board.

They were taking a midday break. Kevin left the big man in his dooryard and walked across the road to get a snack, check the garden, and have just a few minutes to himself.

As he approached, he caught a flash of color through the weeds that were shooting up along the road edge. Dina was in the garden, and he felt his spirits lift a little.

He enjoyed her company. She was lively and quick-witted and gave off a positive energy he sorely needed, especially with Monica's frequent dark moods.

But she was wearing her track outfit.

The shorts were a second skin. The top showed off her tan shoulders, most of her middle, and hugged her breasts. When she wore it, Kevin had to work to staple his eyes to her face or the ground or some point on the horizon just over her head, lest they roam where they shouldn't. It was embarrassing. This was his daughter's best friend, she was family, but he couldn't seem to help himself. He didn't want to be uncomfortable around her, didn't want her to feel uncomfortable around him.

He stayed in the road, then walked quietly up the driveway. Dina didn't see or hear him. Kevin made it safely to the side porch where he found a bright orange sports jug sitting. It was empty. He'd have to bring it over to Jake's to refill it. Carrying five gallons of water from Jake's might have given him a heart attack two months ago. Not anymore. This blackout had been good for some things.

Movement from down the street caught his eye. Eli Sobchuk was coming up the hill, accompanied by the reedy Henry Chambers. Kevin put the jug down and made his way back down the driveway to greet them.

Eli's face was red and slick with sweat. Henry looked cool and dry despite his long-sleeved cowboy shirt and jeans.

"Whew." Eli wiped his brow with the back of his hand. "Kevin Barton. Haven't seen you around the last little while. Your girl is a nice kid. She's doing great work down there."

"Thank you." Sixteen years as a parent, Kevin still felt the rush of pride at having his daughter praised. And then, because he felt like he needed to explain his absence, he added, "We've been pretty busy keeping up with things here."

"Sure, sure, I know how it is. I'm glad we ran into you. I wanted to run something by you."

"Sure thing," Kevin said, puffing up even more. *He wants to run something by* me! "What can I do for you?"

"Well, Thandie says you got a good start on your garden. How's that coming along?" Eli looked beyond Kevin. "Looks pretty good from here."

Kevin followed his gaze. About half the garden was visible from where they stood at the end of the driveway, and it did indeed look good, lush, and green. Tiny yellow tomato flowers winked at them from the foliage.

"I got a little lucky, to be honest," he said. "This stuff's all new to me, so we're kind of stumbling a bit. Jake and Alma have been a big help."

"Neighbors helping neighbors," Eli said. "See, Uncle Henry? He gets it." The older man looked unimpressed, his expression as blank as a chunk of marble before the sculptor goes to work. Eli directed his attention back to Kevin. "That's what's going to get us through this, don't you think?"

"Absolutely."

"So, neighbors helping neighbors," Eli said. "Summer's just getting started, but you know they're short up here. That killing frost comes mid-October if we're lucky, sooner if we're not, and then it's a long ass winter. We don't know when—or if—the Army's coming back. Maybe they will, maybe they won't. The thing is, we can't count on anyone but us, right?"

"Right."

"So, I've been thinking. See, we got a lot of folks like you who went and popped some plants in the ground, and we've got the patch where your girl's working, but I'm worried about a feast-or-famine sort of thing happening, you know what I mean? We need to lay in a store. It sounds funny right now, when we've got so little, but in a couple-three weeks we're going to be up to our eyeballs in zucchini. But when September, October, November comes 'round . . ."

Kevin understood exactly what Eli was driving at, and he was once again thankful that this man was here. Most people were thinking in terms of today, tomorrow, maybe next week. Eli was planning for the long haul.

"So, I'm thinking of a community root cellar, sort of like a food bank," Eli said. "That way, if you find yourself with more tomatoes than you can eat, you bring them down. We've got a few folks who are real whizzes with canning. We build a supply, it's there for the lean times. If everyone pitches in a little bit, everyone benefits."

Eli had been wearing an easy sort of smile through most of the conversation. Now, his expression turned grim.

"If winter comes 'round and things aren't back to normal—and I don't think they will be—we're going to need people as healthy as possible, or else."

The three men were silent while the idea sank in. There was so much to do. Wood, food, water, clothing—he wondered how the settlers and the pioneers had managed; it just seemed like an impossible thing.

"So," said Eli, back to his more jovial demeanor. "What do you think? You in?"

Sharing food with everyone, helping everyone out, neighbors helping neighbors—the idea was great in principle. It was the right thing to do, he knew, but Monica's reaction when he had brought the supplies from the Silvas' house still stung. That was bad, and they had only been a week into this then. She would flay him if he gave anything away. But Eli was right; you could only eat so many zucchinis in a day, and you could only keep them fresh for so long.

"I like the idea, but . . ." He rubbed the back of his neck, not quite wanting to admit that he'd have to talk it over with his wife. "I think so. I mean, I'm happy to give if we've got extra, but—"

Eli gave him a hearty clap on the shoulder. "Good man. Like I said, we've got to stick together. You're doing pretty well here. You've got plenty of resources, a nice big garden. What's wrong with . . . what's wrong with . . . with . . . my, my, my."

Eli's eyebrows disappeared beneath the shaggy hair falling across his forehead. He was looking at something over Kevin's shoulder. Kevin turned. It was Dina, who had come into view in the garden.

Her back was to them. She was bent over, pulling weeds.

Eli whistled low, the sound of a falling bomb. "My, my, my. That's not—who is that?"

"My daughter's friend." Kevin shifted to block Eli's view. "She was visiting us when the power went out."

Sobchuk craned his neck in an attempt to get another look at Dina, but Kevin stayed in his way. He gave up and grinned at Kevin.

"Now, see, that's exactly what I'm talking about. You got some good resources here. Good garden, good neighbor." He licked his lips. "Extra help. You're a lucky man. A man in your position could share a little, don't you think?"

Kevin suddenly wanted the two men gone.

"Listen, I've got things to do."

"I bet." Sobchuk's little white teeth gleamed. "Oh, hey, listen, I forgot. Two nights from now, we're going to have a little party at town hall. Sort of a morale booster, you know? Got a few folks who play acoustical instruments putting on some music, just a chance to maybe forget some troubles, you know? Uncle Henry here calls a pretty mean square dance. Bring the family." He shot another glance past Kevin. "Bring everyone. Alrighty, we got to get moving."

"Right," said Kevin. "See you around."

"Oh, and don't forget about that food bank idea, okay? Talk it over with the wife."

"Yeah. We'll do that."

The two men ambled up toward Jake's house. Despite his claim of having things to do, Eli sauntered along, obviously trying to watch Dina through the shrubbery, who was picking through the foliage of a tomato plant in search of bugs.

Kevin was still hungry, but as he watched Sobchuk watch Dina, the empty space in his gut was replaced by a hard knot. He wondered if he could find a way to lose Dina's track outfit.

—

Monica wanted nothing to do with the little troll or his food bank plan. How could you give anything away when there was so little to give? How would he share it fairly? It burned her to admit that the idea was good and it burned her to admit that Sobchuk had, somehow, delivered on his promises, including distributing supplies, feeding the workers, and keeping people safe.

She hadn't wanted to come to his party, but Kevin convinced her. It burned her to admit that maybe the little troll was right about it being a morale booster too. Getting out of the house for something other than hunting or helping with house and farm chores was good for her. If she discounted the pinched, dirty faces and the not-quite-clean and increasingly baggy clothes of her neighbors, it could almost pass for a normal Friday night at the Grange.

She was chatting with Gail Hester. Gail was a fireplug of a woman with bleach-blonde hair and the squarest jaw Monica had ever seen on a woman. As a Certified Nursing Assistant, she was the closest thing Harpursville had to a doctor—and she was exhausted.

"I don't know if I can do it, Monica," she said. "I've got nothing to work with. I'm stitching people up with sewing thread. Nothing's sterile. It's only a matter of time before someone gets an infection, and I'm going to have to do an amputation." She took a gulp of her drink, fruit punch laced with a liberal shot of vodka. "This is the closest thing I have to anesthetic. And some old cough medicine. And I've given up on Ryan."

Ryan Merkley had been sent out three days ago on his bicycle on a desperation run to the hospital in Algonquin to beg for medicine or, if that failed, to raid any empty homes he found along the way. He still hadn't come back.

"Anyway, I guess on the bright side, I've never seen my nephew so taken with a girl before. Kelly's such a sweetheart."

Monica decided to do a bit of fishing. "Has Curtis had a lot of girlfriends?"

"Oh, not really. I can tell you this though, Sybil Harrison was throwing herself at him for a while, and he completely ignored her. He's only got eyes for Kelly."

Sybil had once been part of Kelly's crowd, though she had never been Monica's favorite. They'd had a falling out over something a couple-three years back. Kelly never really explained it.

Talking about Kelly and Curtis was much better than discussing amputations and cough syrup. That, the little bit of booze in her own cup, and the music from Max Carver's *ersatz* band made her feel even better. It had been a while since she'd heard music. Monica sipped her drink, talked to Gail, and allowed herself to relax, just a bit. And then she caught sight of her husband and Dina.

It should have made her glad, the fact that Kevin and Dina had grown close. After all, it kept Dina out of her hair a bit, gave her some room. But as she watched them, her mood curled at the edges like a singed piece of paper, and the sound of the music and Gail's voice became indistinguishable from everything else.

They stood a little apart from the crowd, deep in conversation.

Most people stood at angles to each other when they talked, an open way that encouraged others to join the conversation. Kevin and Dina faced each other directly, closing everyone else out. Kevin's hands sketched shapes in the air, and she could tell from his gestures that he was telling the story of his Uncle Bobby juggling wine bottles in the liquor store. Dina spread her delicate fingers over her mouth as she laughed. She wore one of Kevin's favorite old T-shirts, a paint-spattered thing he had stubbornly refused to throw away even though it was thin enough to see through in the shoulders and far too tight across the now-vanished Ted. He loved that shirt, always swore he'd lose enough weight to wear it again. Now that that day had finally come, he'd given it to Dina. It was another one of those little mouse bites deep inside.

She forced her attention back to Gail but kept glancing at Kevin and Dina every few seconds until she couldn't take it anymore.

"I'm sorry, Gail. I just remembered something. Excuse me a second."

"Oh, sure. I'll talk to you later."

She threaded her way through the crowd, aiming for her husband. She didn't get too far before she found herself face-to-face with Eli Sobchuk. She stopped short, her throat squeezing tight.

"Evening, Missus Barton. How are you?"

She crossed her arms over her chest, an involuntary reaction that made her angry with herself. Being leered at was nothing new; she had long ago grown comfortable with her body and had found effective ways to deal with men who felt her up with their eyes. Sobchuk was different though. He made her skin crawl in a different way.

"I'm fine."

"We haven't seen you in town too much these days." He drew closer, not quite invading her personal space, but she took a half step back anyway. "I'd almost think you didn't like us down here."

"We're busy."

"So your husband says. I expect having an extra mouth to feed keeps you hopping."

"Dina's a big help."

"So I've heard." He tipped his head in their direction. "Your husband seems quite . . . fond of her."

Monica found her gaze being dragged back once more to Kevin and Dina.

They were both looking down at something on the ground. Dina crossed her left foot over her right knee and tried to look at something on the sole of her sneaker. She bounced up and down on the right foot, waving her free arm like a squirrel on a skinny branch waving its tail. She lost her balance and started to tip. Kevin's hand shot out and caught her, his fingers curling around her upper arm. He said something, probably a smart-ass remark like, "Think you can manage to stand?" and they both laughed. Was there color in her cheeks that wasn't there before? Did Kevin's fingers linger on her arm longer than necessary? Monica's throat pinched tighter.

"Looks like *someone's* getting too comfortable," Sobchuk said.

She whirled on him. "What the hell is that supposed to mean?"

"Huh? Oh, I was talking about the Pinkney kid and your girl. They make a cute couple." He tipped an imaginary hat. "Enjoy the rest of your night, Missus Barton."

Maybe it was the way Dina stood. Too close for normal conversation. Maybe it was the way she reminded Monica of certain girls in high school who hung all over the boys, doing their best to get noticed—the girls who laughed the loudest and twirled their hair the most and wore the tightest jeans and sweaters. Maybe it was the way her legs snaked out of her shorts (not *her* shorts though; these were a pair of Kevin's old shorts, held up with one of Kevin's old belts). Or maybe it was the way hunger and hard work had sanded away the veneer of girlhood, the last baby fat, leaving a grown woman in her place.

Eli strolled away, stopping every few feet to greet people and press the flesh like a veteran politician. The band started on an old Bill Monroe tune. Chuck and Elva Corbett started doing a lively little step dance. It was sweet, but Monica's good feelings had drained away, leaving her empty. When she looked back to where Kevin and Dina stood, she saw they had been joined by Kelly and Curtis, and Curtis was indeed looking quite comfortable; he had one lanky arm draped over Kelly's shoulder, their fingers entwined. Even Kelly's obvious happiness could not fill her up again.

Dina had made room for the pair by shifting closer to Kevin. Not touching but close. Too close.

The skin on the back of her neck prickled. She turned and found Sobchuk watching her from thirty-odd feet away. He winked in a way that made her want to go home and take a shower. She put her back to him and walked away, but his words thudded in her head like her footfalls on the pavement. *Someone's getting too comfortable.* They accompanied her as she walked over to the party of four. They echoed in her ear as she slid into the space between her husband and her daughter's best friend. She looped her arm around his waist, he looked down at her and smiled, put his arm around her. Dina smiled at her, too, a smile full of affection, devoid of threat, rivalry, or competition. But all Monica could see was her husband's hand on Dina's arm, and Dina's flushed cheeks that may have been from the effort of hopping on one foot or from the reddish glow of the setting sun or from something else entirely.

Someone's getting too comfortable, Monica thought. But who?

CHAPTER 15

KEVIN SET A piece of window screen over an empty bucket. He poured roof water from another bucket through the screen, straining out crumbly bits of shingle, a yellowing leaf, and several unfortunate bugs. Roof water was for flushing toilets, but Kevin figured the less junk going down the better. Between the coarse leaves now passing as toilet paper and the low volume of water pushing it through the pipes, he was afraid of stopping up the pipe. The last thing he wanted to have to do was dig an outhouse.

Kevin straightened and stretched his back, more out of habit than need. His back, arms, legs—they no longer hurt from hard work the way they once did. From the corner of his eye, he saw Roger Fields shuffling up the hill. Roger stepped into the dense tangle that had once been Kevin's lawn and flipped open a butterfly knife. He whipped the blade back and forth, cutting a swath through the knee-high weeds and grasses. Bright white Queen Anne's Lace fell as he carved himself a path. Kevin's neck prickled. Roger Fields was not one of his favorite people. He carried himself more like a sullen middle schooler than a man in his early twenties.

Kevin intercepted him well short of the house. As far as he was concerned, the farther away from the house, the better.

"How are you, Roger?"

"Eli wants you at the hall."

"Eli?"

"Sobchuk, man."

"What does he want?"

"How the hell do I know? He just told me to come get you."

Courtesy dictated that Kevin invite him in and offer him some water, but the thought of Roger Fields in his house was even more distasteful than the reality of him on his lawn. Roger decapitated a few more weeds, then began cleaning a dirty fingernail with the blade tip.

"Tell him I'll be right there," Kevin said. "I just have to finish something up here."

Roger made a *tsk* sound and shuffled away, muttering as he went. Kevin waited until he was well down the road before going inside.

Monica was in the kitchen, hands on hips, frowning over a large pile of greens on the cutting board.

"She's going to drive me crazy," she said.

"Who?"

"Dina. Look at all this stuff. Plantains. Dandelions. More cattails. We're turning into rabbits. What the hell am I supposed to do with it all? I don't know how to cook this stuff."

Kevin circled behind and put his arms around her. Her back and shoulders were rigid against him. He rested his chin on her shoulder.

"She's just trying to help."

He kissed the side of her neck, flicked at it with the tip of his tongue, enjoying the salty taste of her. She squirmed but not quite in a *go away, you're bothering me* sort of way, so he slid his hand up and cupped her breast. She left it there for a moment, leaned into him a little, then grabbed his hand and moved it down, clamping it to her waist.

"You have been awfully active lately," she said. "What's gotten into you?"

"I don't know. Maybe pioneer living agrees with me. Anyway, you should be glad she's so willing to help and isn't a stereotypical sulky teen."

She sighed and looked at the pile of odds and ends on the table. "I know. She just takes so much energy, that's all. I'd like us to be able to have a full, decent meal again. I'd *like*—"

When she didn't continue, he said, "You'd like what?"

She rotated in his arms so they were face-to-face and lowered her voice. "I'd like to have our house back to ourselves. I just want things to get back to normal."

He kissed her forehead, wrapped his arms around her. Her body was stiff, and so was he.

"We all want that."

"Even you?"

"Well." He leaned into her, just a little, enjoying the sensation, and the way his heart rate kicked up a notch. "Who says *everything* has to go back to the way it was?"

She pulled away from him. "Not now. There's just too much to do."

"I can't, anyway," he said. "Eli wants to see me about something in town."

She wrinkled her nose. "*There's* someone who doesn't want things to go back to normal. What does he want with you?"

"I don't know. Roger Fields just came by and said Eli wanted to see me about something."

"Fat boy can't make it up the hill without his truck, huh?"

She picked up her knife and began chopping at the pile on the cutting board.

"What's your problem with the man? Every time his name comes up, every time you see him, you get all . . ."

She stopped chopping. The kitchen was silent. "I get all what? Bitchy? Is that the word you want?"

He grabbed a plate and hid behind it. "Don't stab me, don't stab me!"

She glared at him for a second, then the hard lines around her mouth and eyes softened. She brandished the knife like a fencer, though she kept it well away from him. To Kevin's delight, she actually smiled, and it hurt him to realize just how little he'd seen that lately.

"Bitchy is not the word I want," he said. "And I'm not just saying that because you have a knife."

She pooched her lower lip out in an exaggerated pout. "Good thing." Again, the knife thocked against the cutting board, echoing.

Bitchy wasn't the word he was looking for. She responded to Sobchuk almost the way she did to spiders, ants, and other multi-legged creatures that got in the house. Disgusted. Revulsed. Repelled. He chose his words carefully.

"I just don't understand why you hate him so much."

"And I don't understand why you worship him so much."

"I don't worship him."

"Uh huh."

"I don't! I admire him, sure. Even you have to admit he's done a great job."

She pushed the pile of chopped roots to the side and went to work on the next mystery item, a leafy green that smelled like parsley. "He's done a great job of setting society back fifty years."

"Huh?"

"How many women are out cutting trees? Or hunting or fishing? Or on his little advisory council, or whatever he calls it?" She snorted. "Right, none. The way I hear it, they're all in the garden or cooking. 'Women's work.'"

Kevin thought it best not to point out that she was doing almost all the cooking in their house. It might earn him a hole in his chest.

"And where is all that food we brought him?" she went on. "How much have we seen? We haven't gotten nearly as much as we put in."

"But we *have* gotten some."

"A box of powdered milk? Big deal. Milk is something we have plenty of."

It was more than that, and she knew it. She also knew, because she was normally a sensible person, that it would be impossible to share everything equally. Eli Sobchuk had an impossible job, and he was doing it really well.

"Go," she said, waving the knife over her shoulder. "Just be careful. Don't give anything away or commit to anything without talking to me. Family first."

"Don't worry," he said, and there was just enough irritation in his voice to make her stop chopping. "Don't worry," he said, softer now. "I'll be back in a little bit."

"Before you go, can you do me a favor? Go get the girls. They're fishing."

"Sure."

Once he was away from her, he gave voice to his frustration, said out loud all the responses to her arguments; the responses that were never quite there when he needed them. Or, rather, that he never quite dared to say. Letting them out helped a little but also made him wish he could stand up to her better. Monica wasn't a shrew. She wasn't a bitch. She *was* a bit hardheaded, but her mind could be changed. The issue was his own desire to avoid confrontation.

As he walked up the path to the pond, he heard the sound of splashing and laughter. Not the sound of girls fishing, that was for sure. He stomped up the path to the pond, making as much noise as he could so they would know he was coming. Kelly had let it slip that they had been skinny-dipping on more than one occasion. "You don't take a bath with your clothes on," she had rationalized, though Kevin supposed it would do the clothes as much good as it did the girls at this point.

"Girls!" he hollered. "Are you decent?"

"Never," Kelly yelled back. "But we have clothes on."

The pond was kidney-shaped, about thirty feet long. A short wooden dock stuck out into the middle. Two towels lay on the dock, along with two fishing poles and a little cooler for the catch, which was empty. Out in the middle, Kelly was treading water. Dina's feet stuck up nearby, kicking frantically.

"How's the water?" he asked.

"Great," Kelly said.

"Aren't you supposed to be fishing?"

She shrugged. "We tried, but nothing was biting."

Dina's feet disappeared. A cloud of bubbles roiled the surface followed by Dina. "There's a cold spot right there," she said. "Oh, hi, Mr. B. Are you coming in?"

It looked inviting, that was for sure, and he could certainly use a wash, but he didn't have time. "I can't. Sorry to break up the party, girls, but Mom needs you back at the house. I think she might need help with dinner."

"Dinner?" said Dina. "Last one out is a rotten egg!"

She was a strong swimmer and beat Kelly by a wide margin. She hauled herself out on the dock like a seal.

The track outfit was now a bathing suit, which seemed appropriate. She bent to retrieve her towel and wrapped it around her middle. "The water was really nice." She twisted her hair in a makeshift braid and squeezed the water out of it, trying to write her name on the dock. Her neck was long and graceful. "You should have come with us."

"Are you trying to say I need a bath?" Kevin lifted one arm and sniffed at his armpit. "Phew. Yeah, I guess I do."

"Dad, you're so gross." Kelly had reached the dock. She climbed the ladder, picked up her towel, and the three of them left the pond together. Gross was exactly how he felt.

———

Eli was waiting for him in the public meeting room. He sat in the supervisor's seat, his workboot-clad feet up on the desk. The space looked like a Salvation Army thrift store. Boxes, jars, and bags of goods taken from the empty houses of Harpursville sat in organized piles in the center of it all. An assortment of sheets, pillows, blankets, and quilts were stacked halfway to the ceiling on one wall. Clothing in all sizes, shapes, and colors was piled on tables along another. Pairs of shoes and boots were lined up like animals marching onto Noah's Ark. Tools and hardware surrounded the desk.

"Not bad, huh?" Eli said. "Kinda like Wal-Mart, only nicer."

Eli came out from behind the desk and extended a hand. His grip was strong, and that wasn't the only thing that was powerful about him. Sobchuk was barrel-shaped, big across the chest and belly, but it wasn't about size. Kevin had three, maybe four inches on Eli, but he felt small in comparison. The man had presence. It was certainly something he'd never had when he came over to check the furnace.

"You work up the hospital, right?" Eli asked.

"Yes. Or I did, anyway. If this ever ends, maybe I will again." He hadn't given it much thought, not in a while. In the first week or so he had thought a lot about what wasn't getting done: the grant reports and applications, donor management, annual appeals. Now there were more important things to worry about.

"Not a doctor, though."

"No, I worked for the foundation. I wrote grants, organized dinners and events, donor appeals, that sort of thing."

It was important work. He was proud of what he did, but it sounded lame as he described it. Blue-collar guys like Sobchuk had a way of making him feel inferior. They were friendly enough but displayed a thinly veiled disdain for the paper pushers and bureaucrats like Kevin. *I'm a college-educated man with a high-paying job, a beautiful, intelligent wife, a terrific daughter, and a great house. Why should I feel inferior to these men?* Yet he did.

"Can't say there's a whole lot of call for 'development' these days, but you've been getting your hands dirty lately."

"It's hard to avoid," Kevin said, and he was proud of the scabs, scars, and calluses he was gaining.

Eli offered Kevin a chair then straddled one himself, resting his arms on the backrest.

"You're an idea man," Eli said. "I've got an idea I want to run by you."

Kevin leaned forward, hoping he could prove himself valuable to this man.

Eli thrust his chin out, scratched beneath it with stubby fingers. "So, here's the thing. You're a good guy. I know you believe in the same things as me, as far as what's going to save this town. Neighbors helping neighbors, right?"

"Sure."

"You and Jake Hillman are working together to keep his farm going. You went up and brought back a shit-ton of stuff from Silva's. And you didn't skim. Not too much, anyway," he added, with a wink.

Kevin rubbed at his suddenly hot face and looked away. "Oh, uh . . ."

Eli waved it off. "Don't sweat it. You still brought more out of one house than my cousins got from four. Between you, me, and the lamppost, I'm probably lucky I got anything out of them at all. I tell you what, between what they skimmed off those houses and what they busted out of the Kwik-Stop, they've probably got the best-stocked basement in Harpursville."

"They did that?"

"Yeah, and it didn't take a *CSI* guy from the TV to figure it out." Eli popped up his thick thumb. "One: the lock wasn't broken. Two: the window glass? Was all outside the building, not in. It was an inside job, as they say, and Troy's the only one in town with a key to the place.

"Anyway, that's neither here nor there. I leaned on him, and he's kicking stuff back to the town, so it all comes out in the wash, right? But I want to talk about you. You're a good team guy. Your kid's helping out here, you're helping Jake, you get it: neighbors helping neighbors.

"But here's the thing." Sobchuk leaned forward. "*I* could use some help. Me, personally. I'm so busy with things here I can barely take care of myself."

"Well, you know, I'm sure with all the work going on, you'll be taken care of—"

"It's not that kind of thing that's worrying me," Eli said. "We've got lots of wood, the smokehouse is going good, and we've got a twenty-foot-high pile of road salt, so we'll have meat and fish well into winter if game gets thin. If this farm works out as well as Cassie Magglio says it will, we should be able to do some canning and stockpiling stuff in root cellars, and Jake says he'll slaughter a couple-three cows when things get real tight. To be honest, he's going to have to—no way he can manage the whole herd through the winter. 'He who defends everything defends nothing.' Come winter, Herman's going to show us how to cut ice from th'ponds. Tough old bastard will probably outlive us all. Anyways, I think we'll do okay, as a town. I'm talking about *me*. Yeah, people give me a bit of food here and there, which is awfully nice, but my house is a mess, I can't keep up with it. My clothes are ready to walk off on their own. I need some help. I've just got no time for my own self."

Kevin frowned, not understanding what any of this had to do with him.

Eli scratched at his chin again. "What I need is someone to help me out around the house. Domestic help, I guess they'd say. Now, the way I figure it, you've already got your wife and your girl, and you're working with Jake and *his* missus, so between you all, there's more than enough to run two houses. But you've got an extra *body* up there. I'm thinking maybe we can arrange something."

"I'm sorry." Kevin felt more than a little dense. "I'm not quite following you."

"An exchange. See, you got that girl. I got a need. Maybe she can come down a couple-three days a week and take care of my housekeeping. You know, cooking, cleaning. And whatnot."

It almost slipped past him. As it was, it took a few seconds before the emphasis on certain words—girl, body, need, whatnot—sank in. And then he remembered the hungry look on Sobchuk's face when he'd seen Dina in the garden. His stomach clenched. *Is he asking what I think he's asking? I must be reading something into this that isn't there.*

Sobchuk continued on as if he was trying to sell a reluctant homeowner a Schuyler Energy Platinum Plus Maintenance Program. A program he had talked Kevin into, come to think of it.

"See, that girl up there, she's taking up space and eating your food. Look at you." He pointed at Kevin's midsection. "You're getting skinny. She's taking food out of your mouth. She's taking food out of your wife's mouth and your kid's mouth. You're sacrificing your own health, and the health of your kin, for her, and you don't have to. She can work for me. I can take care of her. She'll get her meal." There was a little gleam in Eli's eye. "And, you know, when winter comes, and we're passing out wood rations and blankets and cooking up one of Jake's cows, you might find a little extra coming your way: a little more wood, a couple-three more blankets, maybe a bigger helping from the lunch pot. You see what I'm saying? Neighbors helping neighbors."

Kevin's fingers and toes were going cold.

"Let me make sure I understand," he said. "You want me to trade a girl for some blankets and wood."

"I'm just looking out for everybody's interest here. It's a win-win situation."

"Who wins?"

"You win—you get rid of a mouth. I win. I get . . . help."

"And Dina?"

"She'll get food, just like everyone working for th'town. She'll have something to do with her day. Heck, if she wants, she can stay with me. I've got room." He grinned, showing small, even teeth. "Who knows, maybe she'll learn some valuable skills."

Had Sobchuk been more delicate, Kevin might have believed this to be an honest idea worth thinking about. *Our leader needs my help.* How could he resist? The man stopped the Army, for God's sake, brought them all emergency rations, and had kept the town functioning. But Kevin was not some crude-talking buddy from Schuyler, and he didn't believe people could be swapped like baseball cards.

"You want me to trade her so you can have sex with her."

Sobchuk held up his hands. "Hey, now, who said anything about that? Of course, I do have a way with the ladies, and if she were amenable . . ."

"She's sixteen, Eli."

Sobchuk laughed. "As my dad used to say, 'If there's grass on the field, they're old enough to play ball.'"

Kevin's jaw fell open.

"I'm kidding, I'm kidding," Sobchuk said. "It's just locker-room talk. Man, you should see the look on your face. Hoo, boy."

He rose and paced the room, his heavy boots thudding loud despite the carpeting.

"Look, it's simple, I've got more than I can handle here with everything going on. She can help out at my house, and she can maybe pop down and help Gail Hester too. Gail's trying, but she's no doctor. We've got no medicine, and I'm not sending anyone else out to try to find some. We can't spare the bodies. I don't know exactly what happened to Ryan Merkley, but you don't need to be a rocket scientist to figure it out." The big man grimaced. "Hell, someone could get an ingrown toenail, next thing you know, we're chopping off their leg.

"Look, I'm offering her a job. A place to live. Food. It takes her off your hands, and I gotta tell you, your wife doesn't look too happy to have her around. You really can't say no to that."

Sobchuk beckoned to Kevin. Robot-like, he rose, followed the big man toward the door.

"Tell you what, take a couple-three days to think it over. If the power comes back on, or Major Pettit or some other army guy comes through and tells us this is ending, forget it. No harm, no foul, right? If that happens, then maybe next week or next month I'm back to fixing furnaces, you're back to pushing your papers around the hospital, and she's back wherever she comes from.

"But you and I both know that's not going to happen. So, three days. That should be long enough for her to pack and for you to say a proper goodbye."

Feeling like he was in a bizarre dream sequence in a movie, Kevin allowed Sobchuk to propel him through the door and into the parking lot. The light hurt his eyes. Eli stood beside him.

"You know, Barton, we had a couple of folks pass through the other day who were coming from up in Herkimer. Patrol caught 'em breaking into Randall Weams's house. You hear 'bout that?"

Kevin shook his head.

"One guy told Roger that Herkimer was all but burned to the ground. Looting, shooting, raping—pure chaos, to hear it told. And it's that way all over. Take a look around—what do you see?"

Kevin saw Brenda Chambers, Linda Gibson, and two other women cleaning up the lunch area. Across the road, a handful of women, girls, and children moved along the rows of crops. It sickened him to realize that Kelly was there most every day, closer to this scumbag than she was to the safety of home and family. Over by the highway department garage, a group of men split wood and stacked it on a pile that dwarfed what Kevin and Jake had accumulated so far. Smoke billowed out of the smokehouse Thandie built, spiraling up and forming a gray smudge against the bright blue sky. The thock of axes on trees echoed down from the hill on the south side of the village.

"I don't know," he said, looking into Sobchuk's round, grinning face. "What do I see?"

"You see satisfied people. They're satisfied because they have work, food, and wood. They're satisfied because they're safe and because they're not just sitting around waiting for the world to end. And why do they have that? Because of me. I'm the one who gave them all this, Barton. I'm the one keeping things together right now. And every person in this town knows it.

"You've got yourself a nice little thing going up there, Barton: a couple kids working their asses off for you, a wife cooking and cleaning for you. Jake and his wife at your beck and call. It's like your own little kingdom up there." Sobchuk slapped him on the back, all smiles and good cheer. "Well, we're the empire. Thanks for stopping by, see you in a few days."

———

The sun beat on Kevin's back as he walked home. It cooked him from above while hot asphalt cooked him from below. Inside, he was colder than February.

Offended—that was the right word for it—he was offended by Sobchuk's proposal, though he couldn't decide what offended him more: that Sobchuk thought Dina was a piece of property he could trade for or that he believed Kevin was the sort of man who would agree. It made him shudder.

The most horrifying thing was he had almost gone along with it. So much of what Sobchuk said had made sense. If the man had presented his idea plainly and without the innuendo, the locker-room talk, Kevin—old, malleable "Goldie" Barton—might have been swayed. He might have taken the idea back home and floated it at the dinner table. And then?

And then, Monica would have gone for it. It was terrible to admit, but it was true, for as much as she loathed Sobchuk and loved Dina, anything that stretched their food these days was all right by her. She doled out portions like Scrooge paying Cratchit and watched every mouthful Dina took. How often had she moaned about how much more they would have, *if only*? And when was the last time she had touched the girl, given her a hug or even a smile? Dina kept trying, and Monica, hung up as she was on Dina's food consumption, kept pulling away. Presented with Sobchuk's offer, she might well pack Dina's bag and hold the door open for her. And Dina would have agreed because she felt the weight of Monica's gaze upon her.

The sweat went cold on his forehead and his stomach collapsed on itself. Kevin staggered to the edge of the road and spewed the remnants of his meager lunch into the weedy drainage ditch. Two, three heaves, until there was nothing left inside but thick, sour spit. Tears leaked out of the corners of his eyes. He wiped them away with a shaking hand and bent over, waiting for more, but he was finished. A dull cramp settled in below his ribs.

Beyond the ditch, a dozen or so of Jake's cows grazed, their heads lowered to the rough meadow grasses. Tails and ears twitched away the flies that sought a blood meal.

"That's me," he said.

A black-and-white cow lifted her head and regarded him through long-lashed eyes. Its jaw worked side to side, mashing up the grasses it had pulled up from the ground.

Cows never changed expression. They regarded everything—people, cars, bicycles, dogs—with the same mild curiosity. Kevin normally admired their stoicism. Now it just pissed him off.

Standing on the edge of the ditch, his frozen core started to thaw.

"Do you know what's coming for you?" he said to the cow, in a voice rough from vomiting. "When Jake takes you back behind the barn, are you going to go with that same stupid look on your face?"

She lifted her head a little more, like an old woman peering through the bottom half of her bifocals.

Stupid. So stupid. They just wandered around the field all day, every day, eating, pissing, and shitting. It didn't even matter to them if the grass they ate was just pissed on by another cow—they went right on eating. They paid no attention to anything but the grass and the twin strands of barbed wire that separated them from the road.

The thaw was now a full boil. Everything he should have said to Sobchuk ran through his mind like a highlight reel. He grabbed Sobchuk by the ears and drove his round, grinning face down to his knee, splintering Sobchuk's nose, felt the warm spurt of blood on his leg. He punched Sobchuk around the room, smashing the carefully ordered boxes and bags and jars, while spitting curses and telling the man he could take a flying fuck at a rolling doughnut. He would never agree to such an arrangement. Sobchuk's ruined face became Dougie Austin's. He grabbed Austin by his shirt and snarled into his face, "Keep your hands off my stuff, punk!" Saw a chastened Dougie and his friends ride away in panic. He saw himself take the lead and drive Connor Owens away from Curtis Pinkney's car while Monica watched from the porch. He cowed Troy Fields at the Kwik-Stop when Troy shook him down for cigarettes. All the times in his life when he'd let people walk over him flooded back and were changed with a word, a withering look, a well-placed fist.

Reality came back. Monica drove those boys away. Dougie Austin walked off with their food. Eli Sobchuk expected Kevin to deliver Dina to him in three days.

"Fuck!"

More cows picked their heads up. Bits of grass hung from their mouths, but their expressions still didn't change.

Kevin leaped across the ditch, throwing his arms high. "Heeyah!"

Clods of black earth flew as they turned and thundered away, a mini stampede across the pasture. It wasn't nice, but Kevin didn't care—he was just happy to have something take him seriously for once.

He re-crossed the ditch and continued walking, head down. Dusty pavement passed between his feet. At Curtis Pinkney's car, he stopped. Yellow pollen dulled its once shiny surface. Multiple Kevins stared back from the spiderwebbed glass of the driver's side door. No one had messed with the car since Monica scared the hell out of those boys. People took *her* seriously. No one messed with her.

Monica. What was he going to tell Monica?

"The truth," he said to his reflections. "You have to tell her the truth."

Knowing what Sobchuk was really after, Monica would have told him to fuck off. She would have left him with no doubt whatsoever what he could do with his trade. And then? Then she would pour the milk all over the ground, smash the extra eggs, salt the earth in the community farm. Her unexplained dislike for Sobchuk would become biblical. Unless he could find a way to defuse her, she would make all of Harpursville pay for the sin of its leader.

He couldn't chance that. There were men, women, and children in the hamlet relying on that small amount of milk, and Dina was relying on *them*. On *him*. He wouldn't let her down. Not again.

Still not certain what he was going to say, he entered the house. Monica was at the stove, tending to something bubbling in a saucepan. It had a wet, spicy aroma that made his stomach roar, despite the lingering cramp from his roadside hurl.

"Smells good," he said. "What's cooking?"

"Stew. Vegetarian. Because I can't shoot for shit and the fish weren't biting." She chewed on the ragged end of her thumbnail. "God, I would love some decent onions."

"Yeah, well."

"Yeah, well."

She gazed down at the pan, momentarily far away. Her hair was up in a sloppy bun, the back of her neck nicely tanned. Kevin wanted nothing more right now than to feel her arms around him and take comfort from her.

"What did the troll want?" she asked suddenly.

"Oh. Nothing. Just wanted to talk about the root cellar."

"Hmm." She was lost to him again. He stepped closer.

"Hon? What's wrong?"

"It's just not enough." She swept loose strands of hair back from her face. "We're running on empty, Kevin."

"Things are ripening. It's going to be all right, you'll see."

She reached for the lid to cover the stew. It slipped from her fingers and crashed to the floor. She cursed, snatched it up, and slammed it on the pan. Seconds later, she removed the lid and stirred the stew. He watched her eyes move back and forth and knew she was calculating portions, splitting it into fourths and, perhaps unconsciously, thirds.

Tell, or not tell? What would she do? He looked for a third option, one that ended well for all parties.

"Where are the girls?" he asked.

"Huh? Oh, upstairs, changing." She looked at him, really looked at him, for the first time since he returned. It took a great effort to meet her eyes; it felt like she could see right through him. "Are you all right? You look a little pale."

"I'm just a little tired, that's all. The walk up and down the hill wore me out."

"You need more to eat. We all need more to eat. We're going to be eating grass soon."

"Listen," he said. "Jake's got to cut hay soon. He's going to need a lot of help with that. Between that and all the other stuff we need to do, I think we should keep Kelly here for a while. We're going to need all hands on deck."

"Yeah, fine." She poked at the stew and sighed. "This is ready. Would you call the girls?"

"Yeah."

He went to the foot of the stairs and called the girls down. Their cheerful response made him smile despite the situation. Kelly would stay home to help cut hay, which would solve one worry. For now, anyway. As for the rest? Sobchuk had given him three days. Surely, he could come up with a solution in three days.

CHAPTER 16

DINA SAT ON the porch, her back against the house. The evening had turned cool and pleasant. Something tickled her bare foot. A daddy long legs spider crawled over her ankle and onto her shin. She watched it climb, marveling over how its spindly legs could hold its body up. When it reached her knee, she scooped it up in her hands and put it back down on the floor. It ran off toward the edge of the porch.

The screen door opened and closed. Heavy footsteps sent vibrations through the floorboards. Mr. Barton.

"Oh, I didn't realize you were out here." He plucked at his beard. "Uh, mind if I join you?"

"It's your house. Oh." She covered her mouth with her hand, too late to stop the words. "I'm sorry. I didn't mean that the way it sounded."

"You're fine, Dina. It's your house, too, you know. Though Mrs. Barton and I do get to play benevolent despots to your and Kelly's groveling peasants. So, do you mind if I join you?"

"Absolutely, your lordship."

"You can say no. I won't be offended."

Kelly had tried to get her to play a board game. Dina begged off, told her she wanted to be alone, but if she really wanted that, she would have slipped off to sit by the Silvas' pond or gone up into the hayloft in the Hillmans' barn or wandered off in the woods up the hill, not come out on the porch, where she knew Mr. B. came every night to sit.

She wanted company, needed company. But Kelly was in that boring stage where all she wanted to talk about was Curtis (and Dina couldn't begrudge her that, but sometimes, she just didn't need to *hear* about him), and Momma B. was prickly like a porcupine. Being alone was not what she wanted, not now.

"It's okay," she said again.

He pulled one of the chairs around and sat, half facing her.

Dina stretched out her legs. They were browned by the sun and embarrassingly hairy. Her feet were pallid in comparison, set off from her legs by a noticeable shoe line around her ankles. Shoes. Her track shoes, never meant for everyday use, were wearing out. The sole of the left was starting to peel. The tip of the right was fraying. Soon, she'd be able to play peek-a-boo with her big toe. The shoes she had worn to school the day before the blackout looked great, but you couldn't wear them when shoveling cow flops or digging in a muddy garden. What would she do when her sneakers wore out?

She fingered the hem of her shorts. Not her shorts, Mr. Barton's. Mr. Barton's shorts, Mr. Barton's shirts. She was grateful; the Bartons took care of her, they fed her, they made her feel welcome—mostly—but she wanted to go home. God, she missed her family. She missed her house, she missed her own bed, she missed her things.

Ever since the disastrous attempt at going home, Dina had been living with a weight in her chest. It wasn't so bad when she was busy. In fact, it lightened when she was milking cows, playing Scrabble or Monopoly with Kelly, or baking bread with Mrs. Hillman. It never really went away, though, and sometimes it grew. It grew on rainy days. It grew when Mrs. Barton chewed on her thumbnail and stared out the window, or when she found her in the pantry, her grim eyes scanning the shelves. It sometimes grew when Mr. B. teased Kelly and vice versa. It grew when she needed something that no one, not Kelly, not Momma or Mr. B., not Jake or Alma, could give her. It grew and it hurt.

"Well, look at that."

Mr. Barton's voice was little more than a breath. Dina looked up. He sat on the edge of his chair, his neck stretched to see beyond the porch. She shifted to see what he was looking at.

"Slow, slow," he whispered, holding his hand up. She edged forward and peered through the railing.

Ten feet or so away, the tall grasses and weeds swayed and bent, though there was no breeze to move them. A flattened trail meandered and curved back toward the house.

"What is it?"

A fat brown woodchuck sat up. It stared at them with beady black eyes. With a sharp whistle, it rushed for shelter beneath the porch.

Mr. Barton leaned over the railing. Dina joined him. He pointed to a hollow beneath the lattice.

"That's where it went."

"How could that fat thing squeeze through there?"

"They're boneless."

"What?"

He kept a straight face for about three seconds, then they both laughed. Mr. Barton redirected his attention to where the woodchuck had gone. It stayed out of sight.

"I wonder," he said.

"Wonder what?"

"I wonder what woodchuck tastes like."

Neither of them laughed. It was no joke.

"My mom—" A lump formed in her throat almost immediately. "My mom would probably say it tastes like chicken."

"Everything different tastes like chicken. I wonder if Jake has any traps. He's got everything else under the sun over there." Mentioning Jake seemed to remind him of something. "Listen, Dina, I hate to do this to you, but I think we're going to have to ask you and Kelly to steer clear of town for a little while. Jake's going to need help cutting hay, and we're going to be really, really busy, so—"

"Okay."

"Okay?" he said. "That's it? You're not going to have a tantrum or anything?"

"I could if you want me to."

"Please, no. I think I'm going to have a whopper on my hands when I tell Kelly. Thank you for being reasonable."

They returned to their places, him in the chair, her on the floor.

"It's okay." She picked up a brown piece of dead grass and used it to trace shapes on the floorboards. "I don't like going down there, anyway."

"Where, town? Really? What about your friends?"

"I don't really have friends here, Mr. B. Besides Kelly."

"Oh?"

"Nope."

Dina was only too happy to stay out of town. While she liked Curtis just fine, she didn't like playing chaperone, and Kelly really didn't need one. There was also the fact that she had been persona non grata with Sybil Harrison and her friends ever since Dad had hooked up with Sybil's mom during intermission at the school play two years ago. Her one attempt at reopening her friendship with Sybil had not ended well. "Come near me again, and I'll cut you," Sybil said. She wasn't sure if she really believed her, but at the little town party, Sybil had given her the evil eye and made a slashing gesture. Best not to mess around.

Sybil's threat wasn't the only thing keeping her out of town though. Simply put, town gave her the creeps. Even though things were better now than before the Army had come, the memory of the burned-out Kwik-Stop, that feeling of being watched by unfriendly eyes, stayed with her. Each time she and Kelly went down there, she felt exposed, vulnerable. She expected Dougie Austin to leap out from behind every bush, even though he lived a couple of miles out of town. It was stupid but true.

A light breeze brought the sweet smell of wood fires from town. It smelled like fall, of dry leaves, brown and red and yellow, and jumping in the big piles Dad had raked. She and Tyler and Sara would grab huge handfuls of leaves and throw them in the air. They would have leaf fights and stuff each other's jackets full until they looked like three scarecrows running around the yard. When they had had enough, they would help Dad rake them up all over again. Once or twice each autumn they would gather the leaves and burn them while drinking hot apple cider. "It's our own little harvest festival," Dad would say, and she'd huddle into him for warmth and watch the flames leap into the air and inhale the spicy smell, maybe her favorite smell in the whole world.

With her eyes closed, the sun felt almost like the leaf fire. *God, I miss them.* Her father could be such an asshole, but she missed him. She missed them all. The weight in her chest throbbed. She pulled her legs up and hugged her knees, resting her cheek on them.

"Dina?" Mr. Barton's voice was cautious. "Are you okay?"

She nodded but was betrayed by a tear that escaped her clenched eye and slid down her cheek. She wiped it away with the back of her hand, then let her hair fall forward so he couldn't see her face.

The chair creaked. His voice came from a little closer.

"Are you sure?"

Not trusting herself to speak, she gave him a one-shouldered shrug.

"Oh boy," he said. "I was afraid this would happen."

"What?" Her voice was thick and cloggy.

"You and Kelly. You're spending so much time together, you're becoming the same person. She's the shrugmaster. If I say, 'Kelly, do you want some ice cream?' Shrug. 'Kelly, do you want a million dollars?' Shrug. 'Kelly, Ryan Gosling is here for you, should I let him in?' Shrug."

She smiled. A little.

"I know this has been really hard for you. Being here, stuck with us ogres, not knowing. I think that's the worst thing." His voice got quiet. "Not knowing."

"You guys are great, Mr. Barton," she said into her knees. "Really, really great. But I miss my parents. And my brother and sister."

That weight in her chest stretched like a waking cat. It spread out, sank its needle-sharp claws in her heart, and tore at it. It kept growing, kept taking on weight, and filled her up—chest and stomach, arms and legs, and then her throat and mouth, ears and brain, eyes and nose. It filled her until she had no room left, then it started to leak from her eyes in hot tears and threatened to send runners of thick, ropy snot out of her nose. *No, no, no, do not cry.* Once she started, she might never stop.

She curled herself around her knees, turned her face away from Mr. Barton, and slammed her eyes shut against the tears.

"I know," he said. "It's okay."

His hand, hesitant and unsure, touched her, gently, between her shoulders.

She wanted contact, *needed* it. She wanted to lean against him, wanted him to loop his arm around her shoulder, maybe rest his cheek against her head the way he did with Kelly. For all her father's faults, he was unsparing in his affection, was quick and generous with hugs and kisses. She yearned for that kind of comfort now, yearned for the sort of hug Mr. Barton and Kelly shared on a regular basis. Momma B. once accepted and returned Dina's hugs and kisses happily; now she was a board, a steel beam, a porcupine. Dina needed more.

"I miss them," she said, in a watery voice. Another tear rolled along the side of her nose. "I'm sorry—"

"No, no, it's okay."

He rubbed her back in a semi-circle, a warm arc that went from shoulder blade to shoulder blade. It made swishy sounds against the fabric of her shirt.

He said, "My parents—" He stopped, cleared his throat. "I have no idea what's happening with them. I hate to think what it might be like for them."

She turned her face a little. He was perched on the edge of his chair, staring through the porch rails, maybe picturing his parents in their house in Florida, just as she pictured her family in the little house in Oaks Mills.

"I hate to say this, because it just sounds so . . ." His hand stopped moving. "I try not to think about my parents. I mean, not at all. It's like . . . it's like if I don't think about them, maybe it didn't happen down there, you know?"

She nodded.

"I want to believe they're okay, no problems. They're both pushing seventy, but they're healthy—were healthy, anyway, but . . . I don't know. It's easier not to think about them."

"They're in Florida, right?" she asked, and he nodded. "Maybe it didn't happen down there. We don't know for sure, right?"

"Right. We don't."

"I can't *not* think about my family. This might sound silly, but—"

"Girls are inherently silly."

"That's why boys love us. That and boobs." She laughed at his suddenly red face. "It's okay, Mr. B., we all know it."

A dozen boys she knew in school would milk her comment for all its worth, so to speak. She wondered if a sixteen-year-old Mr. Barton would laugh off her comment, make a snappy comeback, or stumble and stammer, like he was now. The comforting hand was gone from her back; it was now tugging at the gray patch in his beard.

"Anyway," she said, trying to get back to where they were. "When I think about my family, I like to picture them in their own garden. Mom had it all planned out. She was going to try potatoes this year. She's probably really happy too; she's been threatening to go vegetarian for years."

She saw them in her head. Mom kneeling over a row of carrots, a hot-pink foam cushion keeping her knees clean, that silly straw hat she loved, casting a great round shadow on the ground before her. Tyler hauled a basket overflowing with zucchini while Sara picked cherry tomatoes—and ate every other one. Red juice stained her fingers and chin. And Dad—beard or no beard? No beard, she decided, he would find a way to keep clean-shaven—carrying a bucket of water from the goldfish pond. Colorful clothes hung, drying from a line stretching from the house to the big maple in the back corner. The cast-iron pot they used for hot cider on leaf-raking weekends hung over a fire, savory steam mingling with smoke.

"The power of positive thinking, right?" she said.

"Right."

The sinking sun shone in their faces. The heavy thing had shrunk again, had retracted its claws, for the moment.

"Do you think it will ever go back to the way it was?" she asked. "Do you think I'll ever see them again?"

"Your folks are smart people, Dina. I'm sure they're alive and well, and that all of them are doing fine. So, yes, I think you'll see them again."

He looked her directly in the eye as he said this. He seemed so sure; she could almost believe it. She smiled.

"Thanks, Mr. B., I feel better now."

"So do I. Except for my butt. I'm losing too much padding, and this chair is too hard." His knees cracked as he pushed himself up. "Well. Now I suppose I should walk into the lion's den and tell Kelly."

Dina stood and brushed off the back of her shorts. "She'll be okay," she said. "Just explain it to her the way you did to me."

"Good idea. Maybe you should be around to help pick up the pieces, just in case." She nodded. "Thank you. Oh, and Dina? I'm glad you're with us. I mean, I'm not glad you're with us, but I'm glad you're with us. Well, you know what I mean."

"I do. Thanks, Mr. B. For everything."

She wanted to hug him or give him a kiss on the cheek, but she settled for a fist bump.

CHAPTER 17

KELLY TOOK THE news far better than Kevin expected. She protested, but it wasn't a shouting, crying, foot-stomping scene, especially when Kevin told her Curtis was welcome to come up and visit any time. That mollified her quite a bit, though Kevin also took it as a sign of the way the blackout was maturing her. And Kevin wasn't exactly lying about Curtis being welcome. It allowed him to keep a watchful eye over both of them, and, he had to admit it, he liked Curtis. How long he could use haying as an excuse he didn't know; Jake himself was vague about how long it would take.

"I've only got a couple scythes," he said. "And I've never cut by hand. My biggest worry isn't cutting it, it's what to do with it once it's cut. I can't bale it or roll it. I hope I can remember how to build a proper hayrick or it's all for nothing."

"Why do you even have scythes?"

Jake grinned. "I'm a sucker for old farm equipment."

With both Kelly and Dina taken care of, two weights were off his shoulders. How to keep Kelly out of town once haying was done was a worry for another time. Meanwhile, he rose extra early each morning and lugged the milk down to town hall himself, a task Kelly was more than happy to give up. Each trip was made with dry mouth and hammering heart; he didn't know what he'd say to Sobchuk if he saw him. He knew what he *wanted* to say though. Eli was nowhere to be seen, however, and Kevin dropped off the milk on the shady side of town hall and retreated up the hill as quickly as he could.

The night before deadline day, Kevin slept poorly. Every time he drifted off, Sobchuk flashed before him, winking and grinning in his "just us guys" sort of way. He rolled left, rolled right, fluffed his pillow up, punched his pillow down. After a while he finally dozed, then woke drenched in sweat; though he could remember no nightmare, and the bedroom was cool and comfortable.

He sat up, picked his sodden shirt away from his chest, and flapped it to cool down. Monica sighed.

"Sorry, hon," he said, "I didn't mean to wake you."

"I wasn't sleeping." She was on her side, her back to him. "What's the matter?"

Tell her. The thought exploded in his head, so loud he half-expected her to say, "Tell me what?"

The whole story of Sobchuk's proposal nearly spilled out, but he thought of Monica's reaction earlier that evening when Dina hugged her and called her Momma B. She had gone as rigid as the maples he and Jake were taking down on the hillside. She patted—not stroked, not squeezed, not one smidgen of comfort in that touch—Dina's arm and smiled the tightest of smiles. Kevin couldn't remember the last time she had actually called Dina by name. Lately, she had developed a way of talking sideways to Dina when she talked to her at all.

She's under a lot of strain. One of Jake's hens had stopped laying, so the farmer put it on the chopping block, and they had rotisserie chicken for dinner. They ate well that night, but Monica took it as an indictment of her failings as a hunter. He didn't want to add to her worries.

"Nothing," he said. "I'm just really hot tonight."

Even in their post-have-sex-at-the-drop-of-a-hat years, she would have made a snappy comeback of a sexual nature.

"It's warm."

Dim light from a thinning moon filtered in and around the curtains. He sank back down and stared at the ceiling. Monica's breathing was slow and deep. Her actual sleep breathing had a totally different rhythm. She didn't want to talk, and he was happy to oblige. It was easier that way.

—

Sobchuk's deadline came and went. For the better part of a week, Kevin jumped at every sound. He had trouble eating, though he was ravenous. Wherever he was, he found his attention wandering down the road, toward the hamlet, and nearly sawed through his thumb as a result. Nothing changed down there. Smoke rose from Brenda's noon meals, Thandie's smokehouse, dozens of chimneys, and backyard fires. People moved this way and that, with town hall the center of activity. Kevin kept expecting to see a posse marching up the hill, Sobchuk in the lead, but the closest anyone got (besides Curtis) was Roger Fields's patrols along the county road. When a week passed without a word from Sobchuk or a second summons to town, Kevin breathed easier. Maybe he had misunderstood or Sobchuk found someone in the meantime.

Monica became his biggest worry. She slept worse than he did. During the moments when there wasn't much to do—and Kevin tried to make sure they all had downtime—she couldn't sit still. When she wasn't in the pantry inventorying supplies for the umpteenth time, she was flitting from room to room like a caged bird. Despite all the time she spent outside, she paled. He tried to reassure her about their food situation, but even bringing in the first basket full of peas from the garden did little to improve things.

After a particularly hard day felling trees with Jake, Kevin collapsed into bed and fell almost instantly into a heavy sleep. It was a blessed relief after a week of nighttime anxiety. He woke to Monica shaking him. Hard. He struggled to sit up, feeling like he'd slept for days.

"What? What's the—"

She shushed him with a finger on his lips, then tapped his ear. Moonlight lit up half her face in pale light. Kevin held still, straining to hear over his rapidly beating heart. From somewhere below them, out on the porch, he heard a hollow clunk, a furtive scuffle.

"It's probably just—" *A possum*, he was going to say, but there was another clunk, followed by a distinctly human curse. The hair stood up on the back of his neck. Someone outside. On their porch. Were the doors locked?

The sheets sighed as Monica slid out of bed. He heard the scratch of a zipper being pulled up. The floor creaked and she was beside him, her breath tickling his ear.

"Get the bat and meet me downstairs. Hurry, and be quiet!"

"What—"

"Shh!"

In the dim light, he saw Monica's dark outline had sprouted an antenna—her rifle.

He reached out, tried to catch her arm, but she was already gone, her feet whispering on the runner, then the stairs creaked as she descended. Another clunk sounded from outside. He grabbed the bat from where it leaned up against the night table and followed her downstairs. She met him in the living room, the rifle held at port arms.

Their *house of doors* had two doors that opened on the wraparound porch. The front-front door was on the street side. Scuffling noises came from near the back-front door where Kevin had been stacking their firewood. Monica pointed from Kevin to the back-front door. Next, she pointed to herself, then toward the front door. He leaned down to speak into her ear. "You can't—"

"Someone's stealing our wood." Her voice was low and full of anger. "Count to thirty so I can go out and get behind them. We'll catch the bastards."

Before he could tell her how crazy she was, she was pulling open the front door and slipping through like a ghost. He had no choice but to follow her plan.

Kevin edged his way to the back-front door and peered through the glass. *Thirty, twenty-nine, twenty-eight . . ..* There was just enough of a moon to outline a man-shape bent over the woodpile. Kevin's mouth went dry. *Twenty-seven, twenty-six, twenty-five . . ..* The shape straightened, shuffled to the edge of the porch, passed something down, crept back for more. *Nineteen . . . eighteen . . . seventeen . . .*

"Son of a bitch," Kevin muttered.

In the old world, in the world of constant noise where there was always a car on the road or a plane in the sky, where electricity hummed through wires and appliances drew power twenty-four hours a day, his whisper would have been lost in the background noise. But the world had changed. The world was quiet.

The shape outside straightened, like a deer in a field that's caught a dangerous scent. A voice hissed, "Go, go!"

He didn't think. Kevin yanked the door open. Warm, humid air rolled in, carrying a wave of cricket song. He stepped out. *Please, let this work.* He held up the bat and sighted down its length like it was a rifle.

"Don't fucking move," he growled. Something cold and slimy popped beneath his bare foot.

Hands raised, the man in front of him backed away. "It's not that dark out here," he said. "You can't fool me with that bat or two-by, or whatever it is."

Kevin swallowed dry spit and took a sliding step forward, still holding the bat like a gun. A ratcheting click, a sound familiar from scores of TV cop shows, stopped him short.

"Just go back inside," the man said. "Nobody needs to get hurt."

Kevin went tingly all over. He was aware of everything: the squeaky wheel of a wheelbarrow or cart, the soft caress of night air on his face, a creaking board, chirping crickets—he heard it all, felt it all. The man in front of him was backing away, sliding his feet along the wooden floorboards. Moonlight winked off the barrel of a gun trained on Kevin's head.

"You won't get away with this." Kevin's words, maybe his last, came out thin and reedy.

Monica's voice, on the other hand, was cold and deadly.

"Put that gun down, or I'll put a bullet in your ear, George Morris. I can see you."

The man swore. He said, "I ain't George Morris, but you better be careful, lady. I've got a gun pointed right at your fella here. He's threatening me."

"You're on our porch, stealing our wood. I'd say I have every right to kill you. And you down there." Monica raised her voice to be heard by whoever was pushing the wheelbarrow or cart down the lawn. "Stop, or I'll put George down."

The squeaking stopped. Kevin hoped the other man didn't have a gun too.

"I'm backing up, real slow." The man's voice wavered, but the gun trained on Kevin didn't. "And I'm leaving. Nobody needs to get hurt."

There was no waver in Monica's answer. "George, you know I'm a damn good shot. I'll take the tip of your nose right off, even in the dark."

George Morris—or whoever he was—was pressed up against the railing now. Kevin still couldn't see Monica around the corner of the house. His feet were frozen to the floorboards, his breath locked inside of him. His fingers all but squeezed sawdust out of the bat.

"Let's be reasonable here," Maybe-George said.

"I'm not—"

The handgun boomed and spit fire, the muzzle flash turning night to day for an instant. It left a tapestry of purple and green blotches in Kevin's eyes that blotted out everything. Over the ringing in his ears, he heard the crash of a body falling into shrubbery, Maybe-George yelling, "Go, go, go!" and shrieks from upstairs.

"Monica!"

He sprang at Maybe-George and went sprawling over a stray piece of firewood. Fresh sparks exploded in his vision as his chest and chin slammed into the porch floor. The bat flew out of his hands and skittered away. Kevin scrambled to his feet and stumbled forward.

"Monica!"

The rifle cracked twice, a puny sound compared to the handgun's bellow.

"Damn it!" she shouted.

Far below, at the road, there was a clatter of wood and curses. Kevin blundered to the corner of the house, half-blinded from the muzzle flash and dizzied by his fall. Monica had one leg thrown over the railing and was preparing to chase the men. Gunsmoke hung in the air, making the porch smell like a Fourth of July fireworks show. Kevin grabbed Monica's arm. She slapped at his hands, trying to tear away.

"Let me go, damn it, let me go!"

She was a wild thing, thrashing and cursing and twisting in his arms. Afraid in her rage that she would turn the gun on him or crack him in the face with its butt, he pinned her arms and held fast.

"Monica," he said again. "Monica. Monica." He kept saying her name, trying to get through to her.

"Mom? Dad? Where are you? Where are they?" Kelly's voice was shrieky.

"Did he shoot you?" Kevin asked. "Are you okay? Put down the gun. Put down the gun. Please, put it down."

"Let me go, damn it, let me go."

"Put it down. Just put it down. They're gone. They're gone. Put it down, Monica. Please, put it down."

She finally stopped struggling but quivered in his arms. "Okay. Okay," she said. "Safety's on. Let me go. I'm okay."

He released her but remained poised to grab her in case she should make a dash for the road. "You're okay?" he asked. "Are you sure?"

"Mom? Mom!" Kelly was in a near panic.

"We're out here," Kevin called. "We're okay."

"That son of a bitch!" Monica stomped back and forth across the porch, cursing in ways he hadn't heard since college. "I'm going to go down to that asshole's house tomorrow and cut his fucking balls off! Son of a bitch!" She stopped in front of him, as if she just realized he was there. "Are you okay?"

"I'm okay, I just tripped. Super Klutz."

He tried to laugh, but nothing was funny. His legs wobbled, and he grabbed the railing for support. Monica resumed her pacing.

"I couldn't get out fast enough." There were tears of frustration in her voice. "Goddamn it. That was George Morris for sure. I don't know th'other, but we'll find out."

"Mom? Dad?" Kelly's shaky voice came from behind. "What happened?"

"We're okay," Kevin said in a low voice. "Someone just raided our woodpile."

"What? Who?"

"I don't know."

Kelly appeared on the porch, Dina on her heels.

"Did they shoot you? Where's Mom? Is she all right?" Kelly started to cry.

"We're okay, honey. We're okay."

Monica leaned the rifle against the house with care, making sure it wouldn't fall, then she reached for her daughter. Kelly folded up against her. Monica cradled the girl's head against her chest. Kevin put his arms around both of them. Kelly shuddered in one arm, Monica vibrated with adrenaline in the other. He kissed the tops of their heads in turn and tried to stop his own shaking.

In the dark behind them, Kevin saw the humped shape of the wood-pile. It was still considerable. It didn't look like they'd gotten away with much; more important, no one had gotten hurt.

"It will be all right," Kevin whispered, over and over. "We'll be okay."

They stood that way for a minute or two, then he caught sight of Dina on the outside of it all, her arms twined in front of her, her eyes huge and frightened. He took his hand off Kelly's back and held it out, inviting her into the circle to take comfort from them all and give what she could. She hesitated for a second, then joined them.

—

All four of them spent the rest of the night in the living room. No one could sleep but no one had anything to say. Jake, roused by the exchange of gunfire, stopped to check in, his shotgun cradled in the crook of his arm. "I tell you what, I had flashbacks to 'Nam," he said. He didn't stay long, as he didn't want to leave Alma alone. When it was light enough to see, Kevin assessed the damage. The thieves had not made much of a dent in the woodpile, but every missing stick was time, sweat, and blisters. Every stolen piece meant that much more work to do. More alarming was the shooting. George's shot—if it was George Morris, and Monica was dead certain it was—had torn a chunk out of a column several feet above where she had stood. Realistically, it wasn't that close, and Kevin thought that Maybe-George had been shooting to scare, not kill. But even one bullet flying around their house was one too many for him.

Monica was less concerned with being shot at than the theft.

"We have to do something about it," she said.

The four of them sat slumped around the table as dawn's light crept into the kitchen. They poked at ersatz pancakes and stared at the world through red-rimmed eyes. Monica's hair stuck up in clumps. She had lack-of-sleep bruises beneath her eyes and red spots high on her cheeks. Instead of calming down, each passing hour made her angrier.

Kevin's chest and jaw ached from his fall. Both palms were scraped. They burned, and he wondered how he was going to manage the saw with Jake today.

Monica shoved her plate to the middle of the table and stood. "Someone else can have this. I can't eat." She paced the room like a zoo tiger. "We can't let them get away with it," she said. "We have to do something."

Monica stopped and faced Kevin, her little fists balled up on her hips. The hands that had fired a rifle at a man last night. "What do *you* think we should do about it?"

He felt like a steelworker on an I-beam forty stories above New York City. There was a delicate balance here, and he knew it. Harpursville had been peaceful since the blackout, with everyone working together for a common goal. If it *was* someone from town, it had to be dealt with, quickly and severely. Without action, this could become commonplace.

But what kind of action was justified? Monica would love to kick in Morris's door and start shooting. Or she'd want him kicked out of town or forced to give up his wood and his gun. Hell, she might even demand his hands. Kevin was afraid her reaction would threaten the foundations of peace that Sobchuk had established. There was only one solution he could see.

"Well?" Monica said. "What do you think?"

They all looked at him. He cleared his throat.

"I think we need to talk to Sobchuk."

Monica rolled her eyes. "I think—"

"I know what you think." He tried to cut into some of the tension in the room. "I know you'd like to go down there and, what was it you said last night? 'Cut his fucking balls off', I think it was. That'd be great; you could make a pair of earrings out of them."

"Dad!"

"Sorry, sweetheart." He turned his attention back to his wife. "Honey, we need to be careful. If we just go down there and shoot him, we'd be opening up a big can of worms that I don't think anyone wants opened. Next thing you know, it's total war. Let's go talk to Sobchuk."

"Right," she said. "Let's go talk to Sobchuk. And you know what he's going to say? 'Where's your proof?' And you know what? We're not going to have any proof except for my word. I know George Morris. I was friends with his sister growing up. I was at their house lots of times. I know his voice. I know it was him, but you know what a woman's word is worth for a guy like Sobchuk? Jack shit."

"We've got evidence," Kevin said. "Wheel ruts in the grass, a chunk blown out of our porch. Four witnesses—"

"Four witnesses against George Morris, who, by the way, used to work at Schuyler."

"Why would George steal our wood? What does he have to gain from it?"

"I don't know." She grabbed empty plates off the table and scraped the few crumbs left into the sink, hard enough to practically take the finish off them. "But go. You go, go and talk to your hero and see what he says. See where it gets you." Dishes clattered. She stomped up the stairs and slammed the bedroom door, leaving a heavy silence behind.

"I have to go milk," Dina said in a small voice. She slid out the kitchen door, leaving Kevin and Kelly alone. They sat for several minutes, listening to the sound of Monica moving back and forth in the bedroom.

"I think she's running laps up there," Kevin said.

Kelly smiled, but it was not an especially happy smile. Her face was wan in the pale morning light. "I'd love to do what Mom said," she said. "Daddy, I'm scared."

He put his arm around her. "I know, sweetie. I know. We all are. But you understand why we can't just go after Mr. Morris, right?"

"Yeah, I guess. But what if we find out it was him?"

"Then Mom gets a new pair of earrings."

"That is completely disgusting."

"It is." He kissed her. "Let's go see if we can catch a crook."

By light of day, it was apparent that this had been a well-planned effort. Trails beaten through the grass suggested a wagon or small cart had been used to carry off the wood. A sheet of plywood had been laid across the ditch at the road's edge. In the road, a handful of splits lay scattered about, apparently lost in the flight from Monica's rifle. Kevin and Kelly searched the edge of the field across the county road, but there was no evidence anyone had gone through it during the night. They went up and down the county road in both directions, but the trail was lost. They picked up the splits in the road and carried them up to the house. Kevin went back for the plywood; plywood was always useful. Finally, they moved all the wood to the basement. It was hard, dirty work. When they were finally finished, he went to see Sobchuk.

———

Eli weathered the first storm, though in truth it wasn't much of a storm. Barton came in, looking more tired than angry, asking what could be done about The Crime of the Century. After careful questioning, Eli offered sympathy and an apology.

"We're a little thin on the ground right now," he said. "Patrols were chasing down some stragglers out on the state road and missed the whole thing up your way." He sent for George and his wife, got their stories, and sent them on their way. Then he conferred with Uncle Henry while Barton cooled his heels in Arnie's old office.

"I'm sorry, Mr. Barton, but there's not much we can do. George seems pretty well alibied, as they say. Honestly, it was probably stragglers who saw your wood and got bold. You're kind of out there on the edge of things, and there's been a lot more folks out on the roads lately. From what I'm hearing, the rest of the world is getting pretty scary."

Barton tried to restate his case, but there just wasn't enough evidence. In the end, he went away unsatisfied but understanding. He was a reasonable man, after all. As for the girl, she never came up. Eli's proposal was obviously the last thing on Barton's mind, and Eli wouldn't say anything with Uncle Henry around. That could wait.

On a normal day, once work details were assigned, Eli was in the habit of cruising the town, seeing people and being seen, giving little pep talks, passing on his approval at the work being done, pitching in here and there. Today, however, he changed his plans. Hurricanes usually announced themselves with a little bit of wind and rain before the big blow. He didn't need a weatherman to know the big blow would soon arrive.

"Let's stick close, Henry," he said. "I have a feeling this ain't over just yet."

They stepped outside. To the left, four boys gathered around a chopping block. Connor Owens spit into his hands and rubbed them together. He picked up an axe and brandished it like a circus strongman.

"Watch and learn," he told his smirking friends.

He made a show of lining up the axe with the center of the log, then pulled it way back. Loosing a grunt that echoed off the highway garage, he swung. The axe head made a black streak in the air as it whipped up and around. The blow caught the edge of the log. A splinter flew off in one direction, the mostly intact log went the other, and the axe thunked into the block. Connor's friends started giving the red-faced boy a load of good-natured shit.

"Damn fool is gonna take his foot off," Uncle Henry muttered.

"I think we better teach those boys about log splitting," Eli said. They ambled over to where Connor, red-faced and cursing, struggled to pull the axe out of the chopping block while his friends jeered.

"Man, you really suck at that," said one of the boys, a big red-haired kid whose family finally gave up trying to scrape by on their own a few weeks back and had come to town. Eli couldn't quite remember his name, he just called him Big Red, but he'd been keeping an eye on him all the same. He was a bit of a bully, and Eli didn't want bullies disrupting a system that had been working pretty well so far.

"Morning, fellas. How's it going?"

The boys quieted, squared their shoulders, and stood a little taller. A few months ago, they might have nodded at Eli if they'd passed him in the road. Maybe. Then they'd probably snicker behind his back about his oil-stained coveralls and make snide comments about *real jobs.*

Eli frowned at the small pile of splits and the larger pile of logs waiting.

"I finally get you fellas on woodcraft, and this is what you give me? I thought you boys knew how to split wood."

Despite the rebuke, he kept his tone light. The work needed to be done, but he didn't want to shame them or make them resent him. More flies with honey and all that. The boys shuffled their feet and made subdued jokes about each other's skills as lumberjacks. Eli let it go on for a minute. He glanced up the hill toward Barton's house. As expected, Barton's woman was coming down fast. It was a wonder he couldn't feel the ground shake beneath her stomping feet. She was coming in hot, as they say.

"Here's the thing about splitting wood," Eli said. "It's about precision and placement, not brute force. Let the axe do the work. Here, watch."

He rocked the axe back and forth, loosening it from the grip of the chopping block.

"That's quite a swing you got there, Connor. You almost split the earth. Here, set that back up for me, would you?"

Mrs. Barton had reached the bottom of the hill, a few hundred yards away, no sign of slowing down.

Connor replaced the log and stepped back. Eli rested the sharp edge of the axe against the center of the log.

"There's natural weak points in any piece of wood. That's what you're trying to find."

He set his feet, filled his chest with air, and swung the axe in a smooth, easy motion. The axe head whickered down, then sliced the log in two like soft butter. The two halves of the log jumped apart, stood on end for a second, then wobbled and fell.

He handed the axe to Connor.

"Let the axe do the work. Remember, boys, precision and placement."

He stepped back and watched. Connor's next swing was much better, the one after that even better.

"Nice job, boys. Carry on."

He turned, and Monica Barton was homing in on him like a Predator drone on an Al-Qaeda compound. He enjoyed the view while he could; he'd have to make sure to keep his eyes up.

Now the fun part.

"Keep an eye on these fellas for a few, would you, Uncle Henry? Looks like round two is about to start."

He met her near the building's front doors. She stopped, her chest heaving. Sweat glistened on her forehead, her cheeks, and her upper chest. Damn, he was horny.

"Good morning, Missus Barton, what can I—"

"Cut the shit. Why aren't you doing anything about George Morris?"

"Let's talk inside, where it's cool." She didn't budge. They'd have to do it out here. Fine. "I'm real sorry about last night. But as I told your husband—"

"I know what you told my husband. And I *know* that was George Morris on my porch last night." She set her feet. "What are *you* going to do about it?"

She was outraged—and rightly so. In the old world, stealing a little wood was petty larceny, a couple hundred dollars fine, if that. But the world had changed. Though it didn't sound like the thieves made off with much, it could be a matter of life and death in the new world.

He scratched at the edge of his beard. "Your husband said there were two men. Did you see th'other?"

"No."

"Hear a voice? Anything?"

"No."

"Then I'm afraid my hands are tied here. George says he was home, his wife backs him up. Your husband wasn't positive it was him. You're the only one saying it was him."

She put her fists on her hips. Her shirt stretched tight across her chest. *Eyes up. Eyes up.*

"Maybe I need to have a talk with George myself."

"No, you won't."

"Excuse me?"

"You need to stay away from George Morris, Missus Barton, if you know what's good for you."

She stepped toward him. Aside from an impressive rack, she had an impressive set of balls. Bigger than her husband's, certainly. Eli wasn't sure if it was a turn on or a turn off.

"Are you threatening me?"

"No, ma'am. I'm just saying we can't have frontier justice here. You go see George and what? Cut off his hand? Hoyt Paynter says Roger Fields stole eggs from his chicken coop. Cut off his hand. Herman says Bruce Vietch pissed on the side of his house. What are we going to do, cut off his dick? Pardon my French.

"If Hoyt had proof, if Herman had proof, if you had proof—and I mean definitive proof—I'd do the cutting myself. We can't let something like this go unpunished. But this thing we've got going here, it's fragile. Even though things're good right now, people are on edge. It wouldn't take much to break things. We need to keep the peace. And that means we need the same standards of proof we always had. Innocent until proven guilty is even more important than it used to be, don't you think?"

She blinked, surprised. She was just another one of those people who saw his grimy hands, heard his upstate accent—or learned he never went to college—and assumed he was dumb as a stump. Flatlanders like Barton all seemed to think the locals were sister-banging hillbillies and dumb-ass rednecks. Monica Barton should have known better, she was local. Even the gnarliest-looking folks, the ones with the missing teeth, the wobbly eye, and the genetic limp, had more beneath the surface than looks would suggest. Maybe she'd been *Away* too long or maybe Barton had fucked the country-wise out of her. He'd like to put the country back into her.

Careful. She'd had a hard-on for him since he'd seen her prancing practically naked around her kitchen. He knew she could be a bitch—she'd almost gotten him fired, after all—but he hadn't realized how dangerous she was until he'd heard that shots had been fired. Monica Barton was a wild card, but he had cards of his own to play. From behind him came the thock of an axe on wood and a cheer from the boys. Sounded like they were getting the hang of it.

Precision and placement.

"Look," he said, and almost—almost—put his hand on her arm. It was an unconscious gesture. His hand descended toward her upper arm, but he saw her eyes lock on it. He adjusted course at the last minute, dropped it to his belt instead, like he'd meant to do that all along.

"It was probably just stragglers. There's been more of them about the last couple-three weeks, and they're getting desperate. We've caught some folks trying to raid the Farm. They're keeping the patrols real busy right now. I wish I could say we'll catch 'em, but . . ." He spread his hands out to show there was only so much he could do. She wanted blood. He had none to give. He offered the next best thing. "Would it help if I had some wood delivered to you from town supplies? Replace your losses?"

He could see her thinking it over. He had stopped her cold with his little speech about frontier justice. Now, most of the steam was out of her.

"It's not what I want," she said. "But I suppose so."

"Okay. I'll have a couple of fellas drop off a load this afternoon. And please, keep your distance from George, okay? I'll keep my ear to the ground, and I promise you, if I hear anything or find any evidence at all that he was behind this, I'll take care of it right away. Same for you. If you find anything—*anything*—that connects George or anyone else to this, bring it to me. And I'll make sure we get extra patrols put on your end of town, okay?"

She wasn't happy but she was calm. Calmer, anyway. She hadn't gotten what she wanted, but she had at least gotten something. Now it was his turn.

"Great. Oh, by the way," he said, as if he'd just thought of this. "Did your husband mention my proposal from last week? About . . ." He drew a momentary blank. He could picture her tight little ass but couldn't come up with her name. Donna? Dana? Dina? That was it. "Dina? The one living with you?"

Her eyes narrowed. "What about her?"

"I'm looking for help around the house. He didn't tell you this? Huh. Anyway, I know she's living with you, and I know things are tight for everyone, food-wise. I just thought she could come down and do some cooking and cleaning—"

She snorted. "Women's work."

"Hey, now, it's not like that at all. I just don't have the time to do any of that, and I thought—"

"You thought she could do it because she's a girl. We're not born knowing how to sew or bake or do the wash. It's not genetic. We have to learn these things. You could learn it just as easily. Join the twenty-first century."

She was winding up again. He needed to lower her temperature or redirect her anger away from him.

"What do you think I've been doing since my divorce? All I'm saying is I don't have the time for that stuff, and I'm only going to get busier." He spread his hands wide to encompass everything here: the woodpile, the smokehouse, the food pit, the garden across the way, the whole damn town. "I just need some help. A few hours a day, that's all. It must be awfully hard having an extra mouth to feed."

The twitch at the corner of her mouth told him he'd found the mark. Placement. Precision. She was smart, angry, and she didn't like him. Finesse, not force.

"If she comes down to work for me, you'll get her out of your hair for at least one meal a day, maybe two. That'll stretch what you've got a lot further. She can stay with you if you want, go back to your place at the end of the day, or I've got a spare room, whatever. Huh. I'm surprised your husband didn't mention it. I guess he likes having her around."

"We all like having Dina around." It sounded like an automatic response. "She's a big help."

"I'm sure." She raised her hand to her throat, fiddled with a necklace, eyes far away.

"Anyway, I promise to keep an ear out about George. And you think about the girl. Dina."

"Fine."

She stalked off without a backward glance or a thank you, but Eli didn't mind. He enjoyed the view, thought his point had been well made. Once she was halfway up the hill, he ambled back to the woodpile, ignoring Henry's questioning glance. Connor set up another log and swung. The axe struck, dead center. Two even halves fell to the sides. Eli clapped.

"Nicely done, fellas," he said. "And that is how you split a log."

CHAPTER 18

THEY HAD TO board the windows—today, now, before *they* came back, looking for something more than firewood. Kevin mounted the stepladder.

"Hand me that plank."

Monica passed him a two-by-four. He pressed it against the window frame with one hand, fished a nail out of the pocket of his Home Depot apron, and began hammering, lightly at first, to get the nail started.

Tap, tap, tap.

It went in crooked.

"Shit," he said around a mouthful of nails. He was terrible with hammers. Kevin pushed the nail upright and started again. *Tap, tap, tap.*

"Mr. Barton?"

Tap, tap, tap. The nail was going in straight and true. Now he was in the groove.

"Mr. Barton?"

He looked down at Monica while driving in the nail.

"Why are you calling me that?"

Tap, tap, tap.

The edges of his vision fuzzed and blurred, and the light went out of the day. The hammer, nails, and board were gone. The stepladder disappeared from beneath him, and he fell through the dark—and landed in bed. The dream slipped away; all that remained was a whispered voice calling his name, and the *tap, tap, tap* of a fist knocking on his bedroom door in woodpecker bursts.

"Mr. Barton?"

Dina's voice, quiet and anxious. He thrashed his way out of the covers, listening for intruders. Monica's side of the bed was empty; she was downstairs on the night's first watch. Kelly was next, then him, and, finally, Dina.

"Mr. Barton?"

She was keeping her voice low, but fear made it crack a little.

"One second, Dina."

He fumbled through the dark, checking to make sure nothing was hanging out of his shorts. When he pulled the door open, he shielded his eyes against the flickering candle in her hand.

Her words tumbled out. "I'm so sorry to bother you. I had to pee and something itched and when I scratched it, I felt something on the back of my neck and I think it's a tick and Mrs. Barton said to get you."

It took a few seconds for his sleep-fuddled brain to sort the rush of words. She hopped from foot to foot, her eyes big and teary.

"Oh, yeah," he said, when he pieced it all together. "Yeah, I imagine she would. Here, let's take a look. In the bathroom. The light will be better."

The mirrors and tiled surfaces in the bathroom reflected the candlelight and improved visibility, but not by much. He lit an oil lamp and adjusted the flame. That helped. After a moment's consideration, he closed the door most of the way so the light and their voices wouldn't disturb Kelly in the next room.

"Okay, let's see what we've got. Where is it?"

"On the back of my neck. Right near the hairline." She shuddered. "I hate ticks!"

"It's okay," he said. "Maybe it's not even a tick. It's probably just a . . . I don't know, a scab or a blackhead or something."

"You don't get blackheads on your neck."

"Sure you do. At night, all the blackheads get together on the back of the neck for meetings and parties."

It was stupid stuff, but she managed a shaky laugh. She pushed her hair up to the back of her head.

"Is that okay?"

"Yeah." He lifted the lamp. "I just have to make sure I don't set your hair on fire. That's no way to get a haircut."

He brought the lamp as close as he dared. Fine hairs on her slim neck glowed golden in the lamplight. There were smudges of dirt here and there, and he considered making a joke about now knowing why his mother used to nag him to wash his neck, but he'd been around teenaged girls long enough to know better. And who was he to throw that stone? There was dirt ground beneath his nails and in the creases of his fingers that he thought would never come out.

"Whereabouts is it?"

She bunched her hair up in one hand, probed her hairline with the fingers of the other.

"There. Right under my finger. Oh, it's gross." Her shoulder blades fluttered like wings. One of the thin straps on her tank top shifted. No tan line. Kevin wondered how she accomplished *that*—and where.

"Uh, move your finger."

There it was; a dark brown spot the size and shape of a sesame seed. He put his fingers on her neck, pushed more hair out of the way, and leaned in for a closer look. Her skin was soft beneath the pad of his thumb, her hair silky.

Her shoulders twitched. "That tickles."

"Sorry."

Porcelain and tile and glass magnified the heat thrown by the candle, the lamp, and their two bodies. A bead of sweat trickled down the center of his back. He bit his lip and refocused. The tick was nestled in right at her hairline.

"Hello," he muttered.

"Did you find it?"

"Yep."

"Is it . . .?"

He angled his thumb, caught the back edge of the tick with his nail, and pushed. It lifted like a hinged flap. It was attached but barely.

"It shouldn't be hard to get out. Just keep your hair up for a minute."

He gave her shoulder a brief, reassuring squeeze. Standing there in her tank top and shorts with both hands pushing her hair up off her neck, she looked a little like an unhappy pinup girl. He turned away and opened the medicine cabinet, pushing aside bottles of cough syrup, boxes of adhesive bandages and expired cold medicine, tubes of creams and pastes of all kinds until he found the tweezers, the good ones that used to pry splinters from Kelly's hands and knees when she spent most of her time crawling around the floors.

"Am I going to get a disease or anything?"

"Nah." He set two packets of alcohol swabs on the vanity. "To get a disease from these things, they need to be feeding for hours. This one just got started."

"How do you know?"

"Nature camp."

She stared at him, eyes big and round and solemn, then giggled when she got the joke.

"I grew up on Long Island," he explained. "That's like Ground Zero for ticks. Trust me, I learned a lot about them."

While he spoke, he tore open an alcohol swab and wiped down the tweezers, his nostrils twitching at the sharp smell.

"Okay, here's what's going to happen. I'm disinfecting the tweezers and then I'm going to pull the tick out very carefully. When it's out, I'll swab the bite. The tweezers and the wipe will be cold. You'll feel a pinch and a pull and that's it. It's not going to hurt at all. Promise."

"What if you can't get it?"

"Then I guess I'll have to cut off your head." She laughed again, a little louder this time. "Okay, here we go."

Dina was too tall for him to work comfortably while standing; though the tick wasn't deeply embedded, he needed the right leverage. He frowned and surveyed the space.

"Here, sit on the edge of the tub and lean over. Keep your hair up and out of the way."

While she sat, he slid the lamp as close to the edge of the vanity as he dared. He looked down on her curved back and neck, trying to figure out the best angle in the limited space. Finally, he settled for one foot in the tub, one out, and bent over her. Gently, he placed his left hand on her neck, pressing against her warm skin to stretch it a little tighter so that he could get the tick more easily.

At the cold touch of the tweezers, she inhaled sharply, her back momentarily rising into him. He sucked in his chest and stomach, trying to pull away. Sweat beaded on his forearm. A drop rolled down the side of his face. His heart thundered. Taking a deep breath to steady himself, he inhaled her scent. It was a mix of soap and pond water and sweat that smelled a little like vegetable soup. He clamped the tweezers on the tick's body.

"You're doing great," he muttered. "Just keep your head tipped forward."

He exerted slow, steady pressure on the tick, pulling it back while rocking it gently side to side. His left arm lay along her spine, his fingers spread the hairs away from the tick. At last, the tick came out. A tiny white speck of skin was clutched in its jaws or whatever it had for a mouth, a gruesome souvenir of its visit to Dina-land.

"Got it. Don't move yet, keep your hair up."

He placed his left index finger next to the bite and reached across her to drop the tick, tweezers and all, into the sink. His stomach slid over her back, and he felt the rough fabric of her shirt, the sharp edge of her shoulder blade, and her hot skin through his own T-shirt. He grabbed a fresh alcohol swab and tore it open with his teeth.

"Sorry," he mumbled. God, it was hot in here. "Okay, this is going to be cold."

Goosebumps sprang up on her neck as he scrubbed the bite with the swab. When he was finished, the only sign of the tick was a small red bump. He stepped as far back as the little room would allow, his skin fever hot.

"Done," he said. "You want to see it? Uh, the tick, I mean."

She made a yuck face but nodded.

The tick was crawling aimlessly around the bowl of the sink. Kevin plucked it out with the tweezers and held it out with a slightly wobbly hand.

"That's disgusting."

"You should see them when they're full."

"Gross. No thanks." She poked again at the back of her neck. "I'm sorry I was such a baby."

"Is that your first tick bite? Really? Everyone's a little freaky when they get their first tick bite. I remember mine. It was a field trip we took in third grade." He folded the tick into the alcohol pad and ground it into bits with the tweezers. "We were on the bus, ready to go home. All of a sudden, someone says, 'Hey, what's this?'"

He peeled the pad open. Now in four or five distinct parts, the tick's parasitic, disease-spreading life was at an end. He threw it in the garbage can.

"The teachers get all of us off the bus so we can check for ticks. No one knew what we were looking for. We'd been crawling around, rolling on the grass, all that kid stuff. I saw something on my pants and absolutely freaked out." He was rambling and he couldn't seem to stop. "Ah, ah! Get it off! Get it off! I was convinced I was going to die. The other kids called me 'Tick Boy' the rest of the year. Trust me, you were much better than I was."

Dina smiled, looking much better than she had when she woke him up. "Tick Boy, huh? I'll have to remember that."

He turned away, opened the medicine cabinet to put things away. Glancing up, his breath caught. Dina was reflected in the mirror. Yawning, she locked her hands together over her head and stretched. Her shirt rode up, exposing her pale, taut belly, perfectly smooth save for the dimple of her navel. Her breasts pushed at the thin fabric. Each looked like a perfect fit for his hand. His palms itched.

Mortified at the direction of his thoughts, Kevin swung the door all the way open and busied himself with cleaning up, desperate to be away from her.

"Anyway, now you know what to look for. I don't think we have a lot of them here but anytime we're working outside, we should remember to check for them." He was rambling again. "Check especially behind your knees, under your arms, your"—he cleared his throat—"groin. Places that are kind of out of the way. You and Kelly can check each other's backs."

"How's the patient?"

Monica's voice caught him by surprise. His hand jerked. A jar of cold cream and a flattened tube of some old ointment clattered into the sink.

"Uh, she'll be fine. It, uh, came out easy."

He spent a long minute rearranging things in the cabinet, feeling like he did whenever a cop fell in behind him on the interstate. When he closed the cabinet, Monica was reflected in the mirror. Her eyes flicked between him and Dina, who was again poking and prodding at the back of her neck.

"I'm sorry I freaked out, Mrs. Barton. I'm going downstairs for a drink of water. Does anyone want some?"

Though Kevin felt like he'd just walked one hundred miles through the desert, he said, "No thanks. I'd better rest up. I'm on watch next, right?" Monica nodded.

"Goodnight. Thanks again, Mr. B."

"No problem. Goodnight."

She took the candle and smiled at Monica as she passed. Kevin lowered the flame on the oil lamp, plunging them into darkness.

"Oh," he said. "Maybe that was a stupid move. Marco. Marco."

"Polo."

He took a few tentative steps forward, his hand out in front of him. Two steps, three, and his hand connected with the soft firmness of her breast.

"Oh," he said. "Mr. Right, meet Miss Left."

She put her hand over his and squeezed, once. It felt wonderful. Then she peeled his hand away.

"Is she okay?" she asked in a low voice.

"Sure. Why?"

"I don't know. She looked kind of . . . funny. You didn't leave the stinger in or anything, did you?"

"Ticks don't have stingers. How's everything downstairs?"

"Quiet, thankfully. Go back to bed. Get some sleep." She put her arms around him for a quick hug and kiss. "Oh, my. You're . . . awake."

"Uh, well, you know. You. Me. A dark room."

She was silent for a moment. Then, "I'm still on watch."

She disappeared back down the stairs. Kevin felt his way back to the bedroom. *Ticks. How could I have forgotten about ticks?* They were outside constantly—he should have thought of them.

In the bedroom, he stripped and ran his hands down his chest and belly, slid them along his thighs and calves. A shiver of pleasure followed his hands. *Stop it.* He felt along his back, stopping to probe every bump and blemish, finding nothing but a scattering of pimples, mosquito bites and scratches from working in the woods. He combed his fingers through his hair and fingered the backs of his ears. There was nothing there that shouldn't be there, except his erection, which wouldn't go away. It was like being a teen all over again.

It's this life, he told himself. As he and Monica settled into semi-sedentary near middle age, their sex life had settled, too, had become less frequent, though not less passionate. Sitting at a desk all day, sitting in front of the TV at night, it had dulled him, dulled them both, and the growing flab around his middle made him feel shy and self-conscious at times. Now he was out in the fresh air. The exercise had all but stripped away his fat; Ted was all but gone. He was tired all the time from the physical labor but energized at the same time, including sexually.

He climbed into bed. The cool sheet fluttered down and settled over him. He tried to think his erection away by cataloging everything he would need to do tomorrow: water, wood cutting, fishing, if there was time. He tried to let the crickets and frogs lull him to sleep, but the exhaustion that claimed him earlier was gone. Awake. He was awake and didn't want to be, and every breath, every move sent ripples of sensation through him that only served to keep him up. Resisting only took energy that he would need in the morning, so he summoned an image of a woman that didn't look at all like anyone he knew and did what he had to do to get to sleep.

<h1 align="center">CHAPTER 19</h1>

JAKE AND KEVIN rested on a felled tree in the heat of the afternoon. An eight-foot-long trailer sat nearby. In days gone by, Jake would load it up with household garbage and the assorted by-products of the farm that could not be reused or recycled and haul it to the dump; now it was piled high with stovewood-length logs, the morning's work. At least a week had passed since the raid; Kevin wasn't sure of the exact number. Sobchuk had made good on his word and delivered a generous pile of wood—far more than what had been taken. At night, patrols ranged up both the county road and the town road that ran past Kevin's house and dead-ended at the top of the hill. Though there had been no further incidents, the Bartons kept up their night watch. Haying was taking longer than expected, so Kelly was still sticking close to home, which made Kevin happy. Sobchuk had never mentioned Kelly. He preferred to keep her away from the man all the same. He just didn't know how long he could make that last. Dina, meanwhile, was obsessing over ticks, constantly twisting and turning to see if one of the little beasts was crawling up the back of her leg or imploring the nearest person to check her back. She also kept asking Kevin to check on the bite, which itched. Kevin had become all too familiar with the back of her neck.

Jake took a long drink from his thermos. "We had a real bad winter, oh, must have been back in '58 or '59," he said. "By the time spring came, we were burning hay, cow flops, anything we could get our hands on. That was a bad one."

He pushed his cap back on his head and scratched at his wrinkled forehead. The big man's face was the color of varnished cherrywood.

"All's I can say is I hope this winter is an easy one or we might lose a lot of folks."

Kevin nibbled on a hard-boiled egg, trying to make it last. They were cutting into the woods—forest, really—that ran up over the hill and down into the big river valley on the other side. There were bigger trees in the forest interior, but Jake preferred felling trees out into the field. Less chance of a falling tree getting hung up in another on the way down, and they could work on limbing and bucking without fighting through the underbrush. The drawback was they worked out in the heat of the sun, and summer had shown up early this year.

The warm sun made Kevin sleepy, and he started drifting. He was hungry and sore and tired. Drop-dead tired. Though someone was always awake in the house, his sleep had again become fitful. He woke to creaks and clunks, real and imagined, heard gunshots and voices that weren't there.

Jake slapped his big hand against his thigh, snapping Kevin awake. "This is no good. No good at all."

"What's the matter?"

"All of it. The whole thing." He mopped his forehead with a red bandanna. "Listen. Me and Alma've been talking about something off and on. After your little episode th'other night, we thought the time was right. We think you all should move in with us. Kind of combine households."

Kevin stared at his friend, not knowing what to say. He pictured the Hillmans' house, tried to imagine six people living there. It was not a small house by any means, but it wouldn't be an easy fit.

"I appreciate it, Jake, but are you sure? No offense, but your house is half the size of ours. If anything, it would make more sense for you two to move in with us."

They looked down the hill. Though Jake's simple but functional two-story farmhouse was half a football field or so closer to where they sat, it looked small in comparison to the Bartons' graceful Victorian.

"But that's the problem," Jake said. "What have you got—ten-, eleven-foot ceilings? Big rooms, big windows, lots of drafts. And what have you got for heat?

"Our house is smaller," he continued. "That's an advantage. It was built for wood heat. We pack that stove full and bank her down the end of the night, she keeps the whole house warm. In the morning, she's got a good bed of hot coals and the house warms up fast. And Alma's cooked on it for years. When we first moved here, power went out all the time. She got real good at it.

"I know it ain't easy giving up what you're used to, but it's smart. Think about it and talk it over with Monica."

"I don't want to put you and Alma out," Kevin said. "You'd be adding four new people to your house."

"Bah." Jake flapped his big hand at Kevin. "If there's any strain it'll be on you all, having to adjust to us old fogies."

They both stared down the hill. From this vantage point, Kevin could see Monica, Kelly, and Alma Hillman working in the south field, dragging a tarp piled high with cut hay toward the barn. Kevin straightened a little, an alarm rising since Dina was nowhere to be seen, and then he relaxed, a little. Since she was up so early, her job in the middle of the day was to take a nap. Sobchuk hadn't mentioned his proposal when Kevin had gone down to report the wood theft; Kevin didn't know if he had forgotten, found someone else, or if he had imagined the whole thing.

Jake shifted a little on the tree and spat into tall grass at his feet.

"You know, there's another reason. That business th'other night." He nodded at the collection of buildings in the hamlet beyond their homes. "Folks down there are maybe a little safer cause they're close together. We're up on th'edge of things. Predators always go for the ones on th'edges. And you got a lot of doors and windows to watch out for."

Kevin scraped at the bark on the tree with his heel. He knew exactly what Jake meant. Since the raid on the woodpile, Kevin had been looking at his house in a whole new way. Still, Harpursville overall felt safe. As far as Kevin could tell, Sobchuk had made good on that promise at least.

"Do you think Sobchuk can keep it all together?" he asked the farmer.

Jake shrugged. "Maybe, maybe not. I've got to admit, he's done good so far, but we haven't hit rock bottom yet. Ready?"

Reluctantly, Kevin slid off the log and dusted himself off. Each man grabbed hold of the trailer's tow bar. Together, they began the difficult process of wheeling it down to Jake's dooryard, where they would split the wood—literally and figuratively.

"I never had much use for Sobchuks myself," Jake said, grunting with effort. "I went to school with his old man. Howard. Smart fella, but mean like a fisher cat. He'd say anything to anyone if he thought it could get him something. And you know what they say about apples and trees."

"They may not fall far from the tree, but they can roll away," Kevin said. "He did get those rations." A voice in his head, one that sounded an awful lot like Monica's, said, *and he tried to trade for Dina; why are you still defending him?*

"Yeah, well, he's got more guts than his old man, I s'pose. You'd not get Howard Sobchuk steppin' in front of a speedin' truck, that's for sure. Push someone in front of it, maybe. I don't know, I'm just not sold on him. Neither is Alma. And if there's one thing I know, it's to trust her instincts. Anyways, think about it. We just think it'd be safer."

"I'll sound Monica out on it," he said. "No promises though."

They stopped talking then because the hill got steeper, and it took too much energy to keep the heavy trailer under control. Once they got to Jake's, they took turns splitting the logs and dividing the wood into two piles. Kevin helped Jake stack his share but decided to leave his half on the trailer for now. Just in case. The more he thought about it, the more he liked the idea of moving in together. They were functioning as one household as it stood. It would definitely be safer, more efficient.

———

"We're not moving," Monica said when he brought it up later. "No way."

It was the reaction Kevin expected. This was their house, their first house, and she loved it. She wasn't going to move out, no matter how much sense it made. He marshaled the ideas he had rehearsed ahead of time.

"We can pool our resources."

"We're already doing that," she said. "I don't want to share every aspect of my life with them."

"It will be safer," he told her. "We'll have six people looking out for each other."

"And what are we going to find when we come back here when this thing is over? We've put too much work into this house to abandon it, Kevin."

"We're not abandoning it. We'll be right across the street."

"It's not 'right across the street'. It's a hundred-fifty, two hundred feet up the road! You can hardly see it from there, especially with the way the weeds have grown up. We can't keep an eye on it from over there."

"We'll be keeping an eye on it. Someone will be here every day in the garden."

They were out on the porch after dinner. The sun was still high in the west, shining through the haze of wood smoke that rose from chimneys and backyard fire pits in the hamlet. Once one of his favorite aromas in the world, Kevin could barely smell it now.

"I know they mean well," Monica said. Her shoes clip-clopped on the porch as she paced. "I just don't think it's the right move. We'd come back and find all the boards stripped right off in the middle of the night. Or squatters living in it."

He tried to think of the right way to frame his arguments. It had all made so much sense when he talked to Jake about it earlier. It wouldn't be easy but it was right. At the same time, Monica's counterarguments made sense, too, though he suspected her real issues were twofold: privacy and control. She valued them both too much to give them up easily. She needed to be in charge and she needed space.

"Maybe," she said, after a moment's pause. "Maybe . . ." She stopped, chewed on her chapped bottom lip. Kevin allowed himself a glimmer of hope.

"What?" he prodded.

"Nothing. Never mind."

"Tell me. Come on."

Her lips came together in a fine line. Whatever she was thinking, she had decided not to say it. A syringeful of sodium pentothal wouldn't get her to talk now. He decided to go back to the original point of the discussion.

"We really should do this. We really need to consider it."

"I have. No."

She walked off to the end of the porch and started once again exam-ining the spot where Maybe-George Morris had jumped the rail. Kevin sighed—*quietly*—and sank into a chair. She was stubborn but she was smart, and he was sure she would see the wisdom of the move before long. She just needed some time.

He had no idea how little time it would take.

CHAPTER 20

MONICA COURSED BACK and forth across the tracks left by George Morris and his crony. Days had passed, weeks had passed, it happened yesterday—she really couldn't tell anymore, but the path still had a fresh, beaten-down look to it. She zigzagged across the trail like a hound on a scent, hoping for some scrap of hard evidence to shove under Sobchuk's pug nose.

Laughter and delighted shrieks sounded from behind the house. The girls were supposed to be washing up after dinner; it sounded like they were mostly carrying on. Dina's laugh beat loud against Monica's eardrums.

Evidence; she needed to find evidence—but of what?

A slideshow of sorts played on auto repeat in her head: images of Kevin and Dina, narration provided by Eli Sobchuk. Kevin and Dina, alone in a parking lot full of people. *I guess he likes having her around.* Dina in her tiny little track shorts, one long, tanned leg extended in front of her. *Someone's getting too comfortable.* A laugh. A hand on an arm. *Your husband seems quite fond of her.* Kevin's favorite T-shirt hanging off Dina's tanned shoulder.

She shook it off, returned her attention to the trail. Grasshoppers and crickets fled before her. She kicked at the grass, scanned it for something—a shred of cloth, a footprint, a dropped wallet—but there was nothing to be found, same as yesterday, same as the day before that, and the day before that. It was a fool's errand, yet she had to do it—for justice and to keep the other thoughts at bay.

At the edge of the property she paused, looked up and down the county road, and jumped across the ditch. To the right, the road climbed a shallow grade and disappeared around a curve. Trees leaned out from the hillside for light, turning the road into a tunnel. To her left, the road went on past the dusty hulk of Curtis Pinkney's car and on into the hamlet. Beyond the car, half a dozen or so of Jake's Herefords grazed placidly in the low pasture.

Nothing to see here, just like every other day. Back across the ditch she went and started up her back trail. *A fence*, she thought. *We could use a fence.* Maybe Jake had some spare barbed wire they could string up. Any obstacle was better than what they had. Of course, a fence was useless when the threat was inside.

Why hadn't he told her about Sobchuk's offer? It wasn't like him to keep secrets from her. Or maybe he'd never had one to keep before.

I guess he likes having her around. Kevin and Dina bent over a game of Scrabble after dinner—when had that started? He'd never been one for Scrabble. *Someone's getting too comfortable.* Dina shoulder to shoulder with her husband, marveling over a speckled egg she brought over from Alma's henhouse. Dina, lifting her hair off the back of her neck and asking him to inspect, yet again, her tick bite. *Your husband seems quite fond of her.* The two of them sitting side by side on plastic lawn chairs by the garden, passing a water bottle back and forth.

She pressed her hands against her temples, trying to squeeze it all out of her head.

"Honey? Are you okay?"

Her eyes flew open. Kevin waited for her up near the house, his brows drawn together in worry. The girls' laughter carried over the yard.

"Just a headache, that's all."

"Did you find anything?"

"No."

"I'm sorry."

She stopped a few feet short of where he stood. The grass struggled for a foothold on the thin soil on this part of the lawn. Her heart beat up in her throat, too fast. She had to ask.

"Why didn't you tell me about your meeting with Sobchuk?"

He frowned. "I did."

"Not the one about the wood. The one before that. When he offered Dina a job."

Dry grass rustled as he shifted his feet.

"How did you hear about that?"

"He told me."

The corner of his mouth twitched in a humorless smile. "He called it a job, huh?"

"Is it true?"

"Yes." The word slid like the tip of a knife between her ribs. "It's true, but—"

"I think we should do it." The words tumbled out of her, and as they came, she felt her emotions getting away from her too. "I don't like it. I don't like *him* but I think we've got to do something. It's another meal a day that we don't have to worry about. More, if she stays down there. We should do it. We need to—we're going to run out of food, Kevin."

He raised his face to the sky and stroked his chin, a new gesture he picked up since his beard grew in. She could tell by the way he narrowed his eyes that he didn't like the idea, but she thought he'd go along with her.

"No. No way. We can't." He twisted a few strands of beard between his fingers. "Honey, there's something you don't know."

The knife tip slid deeper. Her fingernails dug into her palms, sharp little pinpricks of pain.

"Sobchuk has . . . other ideas . . . for Dina. He doesn't just want her to work for him. He wants her—" He threw a quick look over his shoulder, but the girls were somewhere behind the house and making far too much noise to hear him anyway. "He wants her for sex."

It took her a second to grasp what he had just said.

"What? Are you sure?"

"Yeah. He made it very clear. I mean—yeah, very clear."

Sobchuk was a dog, she knew that, but she just assumed his tastes ran toward older women. It should have been a relief, yet a vision popped into her head, strobe light quick: Dina and Kevin in the cramped quarters of the upstairs bathroom, both of them flushed. Of course they were red in the face—it was warm in there. But why was the bathroom door closed? And why was he so clumsy when she opened the door? He had looked like a child caught in some forbidden act. Why had he closed the damn door?

He must have seen something on her face. He came closer and peered down at her. "What's the matter, hon? Is everything okay?"

"No. No, everything's not okay."

She pushed past him, five, six paces, then turned. The hill was steep enough here that she was almost eye level with him.

"I'm not . . . I'm not comfortable with the situation, Kevin. I'm not comfortable with *her*."

His expression went blank. "With who? With Dina?"

She nodded.

He put his hands gently on her shoulders. Warm hands, hands that were stronger than they had been, hands that were rough with calluses. Funny, she'd been determined to get away from farm life and farm men, and here she was, living with a man who had turned into one. Farming for their life.

"It's going to be all right." He squeezed her shoulders, turned her around and began working the tight muscles of her neck with his thumbs and fingers. "We'll be okay. The garden's going well. There's milk. There's eggs. Fish. There will be meat, either from one of Jake's cows or you'll get something, I know you will. We're making it, Monica. We're not going to starve. We're doing this. And she's contributing as much as anyone."

"It's not just the food, Kevin."

His hands stopped.

"Then what is it?"

She opened her eyes and turned to face him. The house loomed behind him, the pastel Victorian that turned out to be far more house than they needed, the big house that had become too small. She took a deep, steadying breath, ready to lay it out there for him, ready to tell him the terrible thoughts that had crept into her head. He would be shocked. Hurt, too, but that couldn't be helped. Then he would laugh it off, tell her she was being silly. But when he realized how upset she was, he would agree. He wouldn't like it (and, let's face it, the Momma B. part of her didn't like it either, but this was no time for sentiment) but he would agree. Compromise was his strong suit, after all. He was a wonderful man, but he hadn't changed that much since college. He was still Goldie Barton.

"Maybe," she said, "maybe she could go to Jake and Alma's."

"Dina? Why?"

"It would make things easier."

He dropped his hands from her shoulders, put them on his hips.

"That—that's a half measure, honey. It doesn't solve the problem. Besides, Dina's our responsibility, not theirs. We can't just pass her off to someone—even the Hillmans—for our convenience."

He just didn't get it. She took a few steps up the lawn toward the house so that she was closer to eye level with him and took a deep breath, ready to put it out there.

"Save me, save me!"

Dina came tearing around the house like the Devil himself was chasing her with a pack of matches, but her shriek was one of delight, not terror. Kelly came hot on her heels, a sloshing bucket of water in hand. They raced past. Dina doubled back and ducked behind them, seeking shelter from Tropical Storm Kelly.

"Save me, save me!" she cried again, though she didn't look like she wanted saving.

Kelly advanced, the bucket held in menacing fashion, a wicked gleam in her eye.

"Girls," Monica warned. "This is not a good time."

"I'll go when she goes," Kelly said.

"I'll go when she goes," parroted Dina.

Monica backed away.

Dina took refuge behind Kevin. He stood with arms half raised like a tree.

"Come out, come out," sang Kelly. Her dripping hair left dark streaks on her shirt. She faked a throw. Water splashed at Kevin's feet.

"You wouldn't dare," Dina said.

"Oh, wouldn't I?"

They circled him, Kelly with the bucket poised, Dina matching her movements to keep Kevin between them. She used Kevin the way a squirrel uses a tree to shield itself from a hungry hawk. She feinted left, then right. Her paws scrabbled up to his shoulders, and she popped up and stuck her tongue out at Kelly, who faked another throw.

Dina peeked out from beneath Kevin's right arm. Water flew. It hit Kevin square in the chest with a great slap and sheeted around him, soaking him to the skin and leaving Dina remarkably dry.

"Oh," he gasped. "That's cold!"

The girls took off. "Sorry, Dad!" Kelly called over her shoulder, and they were gone, gales of laughter trailing behind them as they disappeared around the house. The empty bucket lay on the ground at his feet.

Kevin's shirt clung to him. Water ran down his arms and off his fingertips. Silver drops gleamed in his beard. His shorts, heavy with water, hung low on his hips and Monica was again reminded of how much weight he'd lost—how much weight they'd all lost. He peeled the front of his shirt from his chest and wrung it out; a mini waterfall cascaded over his feet. He grinned at Monica, held his arms out, and advanced in a zombie shamble. "Gimme some sugar, baby."

"Don't."

Unlike the girls, he heeded the warning in her voice.

"What's the matter?"

"Nothing. I just don't want to get wet."

For a moment, she thought he was going to grab her anyway. Part of her longed for it, longed to feel his wet chest pressed to hers, longed for a moment of frivolity. He chose caution. As always.

"Okay, spoilsport. I'd better go change into something dry."

He started toward the house, feet squishing over the now-soggy ground but stopped when his foot connected with the bucket Kelly abandoned in her flight to safety. A sly smile spread over his face. He bent, picked up the bucket, and grinned.

"In a minute."

He snuck off in search of water—and revenge.

Monica retreated to the porch and watched The Great Water Fight rage across the lawn. Alliances formed and broke. Kevin and Kelly stalked Dina; Kelly and Dina ganged up on Kevin; Dina and Kevin chased Kelly; everyone chased everybody. When it was over, all three were waterlogged, muddy, and loopy with what might have been their first moments of pure, unadulterated joy since the blackout. The girls went to the pond to wash off the dirt and grime they'd picked up slipping and sliding on the lawn. Kevin went upstairs to dry off and change.

Monica sat in the now quiet evening, thinking, oddly enough, about the checkbook. She dutifully recorded deposits and payments, kept up with ATM withdrawals and debit card purchases, and all the associated irritating fees. Every once in a while, she would find an error. Big mistakes—ten or twenty-five dollars—were usually easy to find and fix. Those typically resulted from forgetting to record a check or, more likely, a direct withdrawal or purchase. What drove her crazy was finding herself three, four, five cents off; that was real trouble. It seemed insignificant but it mounted up over the months, and those kinds of errors meant a painstaking trip back through the register for what was usually a simple error in math.

Kevin was a good man, Dina a good girl, but there was something off in the equation. Three cents here, five cents there, multiplied over days and weeks and months. It circled in her head like a squirrel around a tree, a girl around a man, an annoying little thing that kept getting bigger and had to be corrected before it did real damage.

———

Dry and comfortable again, Kevin found Monica on the porch rocker, feet curled beneath her. She stared into the distance, chewing on her thumbnail, her eyes far away but moving back and forth like she was speed-reading. A small vertical line creased the gap between her eyebrows. When was the last time she had read? In all the years he'd known her, she'd never been far from a book or an e-reader. It was one of those small quality of life things that maybe made a difference in people's moods.

He sank into the chair next to her. The water fight had been fun. Youthful energy had surged through him, boosting his spirits as well as his heart rate. Jogging, biking, the gym—all the exercise programs he had tried and abandoned over the years—felt like a drudgery to be endured. This was the way to exercise, a half hour of joyous abandon. Of course, now he was tired. Very tired.

His breathing quickly slowed to match the rhythmic creak of Monica's rocker. His thoughts drifted into a morphine-drip slowness as sleep came creeping. He was sorry Monica had not joined in on the fun—she needed to let go a little, to loosen up.

"When did he ask you?"

He blinked and looked around, vaguely disoriented. "Huh?"

"When did he ask you? Sobchuk? About Dina?"

He rubbed his eyes and yawned. "Oh. I don't know. It's hard to keep track of time. Before the haying started."

"Was it that day Roger Fields came up here?"

He searched his mind, trying to pin it down. It was hard to keep track of time in the new world, the world without clocks and calendars, computers and phones, and his brain was sluggish. "Yeah. Yeah, that's right."

"And you're sure you didn't misunderstand him?"

"Who, Sobchuk? No, he hinted at first, then became quite clear. And when I told him she was only sixteen, he said, and I quote, 'If there's grass on the field, they're old enough to play ball.'"

"Huh? What does that—oh. Oh."

"He tried to play it off as 'just us guys joking', but, yeah."

The light was dimming. A large spider rappelled down an invisible thread from the edge of the porch roof. It came down in fits and starts, two, three inches at a time. It stopped, hung in midair for a moment, then began climbing back up.

Monica's finger jabbed him in the side. "Kevin!"

He'd been drifting off again. "Sorry, sorry. What did you say?"

"Why didn't you tell me?"

"I don't know. You've always been kind of funny about Sobchuk, and I was afraid you'd go and nuke him or something if I told you what I wanted. It was stupid of me, but everything—what?"

The creaking had stopped. Monica's feet were flat on the floor. She leaned forward, her eyes locked on his, cold as a frozen lake.

"What's the matter?"

"What *you* wanted? Tell me, Kevin, what *is* it you want?"

"What do you mean?"

"You said, 'if I told you what *I* wanted.' So what is it you want? Do you want her? Is that it?"

Kevin shook his head like a boxer trying to clear the cobwebs after a good punch to the jaw.

"What? I said 'he.'"

"No, you said 'I', Kevin. You said, 'what *I* wanted.'"

She rocketed out of the chair and stomped to the other end of the porch. Kevin, feeling like Dorothy waking up in Oz, followed.

"What is this about, honey?"

She stood at the rail, her thumbnail once again in her mouth, one arm curled across her midsection.

"Monica?"

She turned sharply. "I don't like the way she is with you."

"What? Who?"

She put a hand on his arm. Made her eyes go soft and dewy, batted her lashes. "'Oh, Mr. B., that's so interesting.'" She covered her mouth with a dainty hand and giggled. "'Oh, Mr. B., you're so funny.'"

Kevin swallowed, but his spit was gone, vaporized by the heat that had crept up his neck. "So I make her laugh. I'm a funny guy."

"You're not that funny. She's flirting with you, and you love it. You're strutting around here like Jake's rooster. It must be so wonderful for you, having someone hanging on your every word." She twirled her hair around one finger and bounced on the balls of her feet in a cruel parody. "'Look at these eggs, Mr. B, aren't they pretty?' 'Oh, I'll help you weed the garden, Mr. B.' She can't stay here. She can go to Hillmans'."

She stood with her feet spread wide, her arms folded across her chest, her eyes bright and challenging. Kevin still didn't know how he had gone from sitting peacefully on the porch to standing on the edge of some dizzying precipice. All he could grab onto was that she wanted to send Dina away.

"We can't do that. Dina is our responsibility, not theirs."

"And what about your responsibility to me? To Kelly? You're willing to put her before your family?"

"I haven't—"

"You let Kelly go to town!" She all but shouted it. The line between her brows had become a deep, dark crevasse. "*He* wanted a girl to screw, and you let your daughter go to town anyway. You son of a bitch! He could have taken Kelly, and you would have let him."

"How can you say that? I would never—"

"Because that's what you did!" Her voice echoed in the quiet evening. He wondered how far away it could be heard. "She has to go, Kevin. I can't have her in this house."

He took a deep breath. She didn't understand; he couldn't seem to make her understand, but there was only one answer to this.

"No."

Silence fell, the sort of silence that comes right before a heat wave-breaking thunderstorm.

"I see," she said at last. "Then I guess I have no choice."

She pushed past him and strode toward the door.

"Where are you going?"

"I'm taking Kelly and going to Jake's. You can stay here and have your little midlife crisis if you want but don't look for me when it's over. You care about that girl more than you care about your own daughter."

"That's ridiculous."

"Is it? Is it really?"

"Yes. I care for Dina. So do you. Don't pretend you don't—"

"*My* priority is my family—"

"You're not acting like it."

"—but when push comes to shove, she's not family. *I'm* family. *Kelly* is family. Dina is not."

She looked like the woman he loved, but in just five minutes she had turned into a stranger. Except, it wasn't just the last five minutes. It had been since day one of the blackout. He reached for the woman she had been.

"Just a year ago," he said, "just a year ago, you were ready to take her in when Lisa left Phil. Remember that?"

It had been another acrimonious moment in the McCrays' marriage. This time, Phil having been caught with an OR nurse. Lisa had asked if Dina could stay with them for the weekend while she retreated for some soul-searching—and, she hinted, house hunting in Jersey, where her family was. During the weekend, Monica had been extra generous with affection for Dina, and on Saturday night, when the girls were sequestered in the den watching a Disney Princess marathon, she had floated the idea of taking Dina in at least for the remainder of the school year, maybe even the remainder of her high school career, if it came to it.

In the end, it hadn't come to it. Lisa and Phil came to their senses (if that's what you could call it) and got back together, and the Barton household held steady at three.

"Just a year ago," he repeated. "Remember that? What's changed?"

Her look was hot enough to peel paint off the side of the house.

"A year ago, the two of you weren't making eyes at each other."

Kevin let out a noisy breath. "We're not making eyes at each other."

"I know what I'm seeing."

"Give me some credit, for God sakes. She's a kid, Monica. A kid."

"She doesn't look like a child. Don't tell me you haven't noticed. Now I know why you've been walking around with a hard-on all the time."

The shot landed hard, knocked some of his breath out of him. At the same time, the back of his neck burned a bit. More than a bit.

"That's uncalled for," he managed.

"Is it? Is it really?"

"Yes, it is." And then, hoping like hell the girls were still up at the pond and out of earshot, he said, "Fine. You want the truth? Yes, I've noticed, okay? Happy? Just like I've noticed that Kelly has grown up, and *you've* noticed Curtis Pinkney's muscles. That hardly puts me at Sobchuk's level. I'm not flirting with her. I'm not interested in having sex with her."

"Monica, we have to stick together. It's the only way we can get through this. You can't do this."

"You did this, not me. The minute you chose that girl over your own daughter."

"I didn't—"

"And what's going to happen if he decides to come marching up here and take Kelly? What then?"

"First of all, he doesn't want Kelly. Second, he won't come marching up here. He's not that stupid."

"And if he does? What are you going to do, fight him?"

The possibility of a fight with Sobchuk was preposterous. But Kevin knew fighting wasn't just about fists, it was about will. He wasn't going to bend. Not this time.

"If I have to."

"Right," she snorted. "You couldn't even fight off Dougie Austin."

All the bad things he'd felt and thought about himself that day came back. This time, it hardened his resolve.

"We're not kicking her out, Monica."

"I'm taking Kelly to Jake's house. Maybe that's why you were so hot to have us all move over there, so you could sneak back over here. You won't have to sneak around now. Have fun playing house with Lolita."

He caught her arm as she turned away.

"Monica—"

She whirled, her right hand balled into a fist and cocked behind her ear.

"Let me go, Kevin." Her voice was low and dangerous. "Let me go now. You're no fighter, but I am."

He let go.

"Monica. Please."

"At least Phil McCray has the decency to bang grown women. I'm not the Duchess, Kevin. I'm not taking you back."

She yanked the door open and stomped into the house. Kevin stood for a moment, listening to doors slam, debating whether he should go after her or not. He stood there for a minute or two, then sank back into the chair and watched the sky change colors. He knew not to go after her, not yet. She needed to cool down, that's all. She would think about it, realize how wrong she was, and come to her senses. Despite the terrible things she had said—the most hurtful things she'd said in the eighteen years of their marriage—he loved her. He could forgive her, *would* forgive her. They would find a way to get back to where they had been.

High over the hill beyond Jake's cow pasture, the first star glimmered in a periwinkle sky. Kevin closed his eyes and made a wish.

—

There were not many times Kevin wanted a drink. This was one of them. Several times over the next hour or so, he considered going to the liquor cabinet and pulling a bottle. Any bottle would do. Drinking, though, would be a very bad idea.

Kevin Barton, the Peacemaker. "Goldie" Barton, who bent to those around him. He was the one who blinked first, stepped back, was last through a four-way stop sign. His first and last fistfight was in second grade. When the insurance company balked at paying for Kelly's broken arm when she was six, he grabbed the checkbook. Monica grabbed the phone and went to war, raining fire and plague on the unlucky soul who denied the claim—and they paid up. He was Nice Guy Kevin; the one people counted on to help out in a pinch, even when it put him at an inconvenience. Had he been less nice, less accommodating, maybe the Duchess would have gotten her ass over to the house and taken Dina home before the blackout. Maybe he would be sitting here with his wife and daughter instead of reviewing the tire fire his life had become.

He didn't know what Monica told Kelly, how she convinced her to go to Jake's, but they had gone. From his seat on the porch, he had heard only the slam of the kitchen door, the scuff of two pairs of feet on the driveway, the questioning tone of Kelly's voice, and Monica's sharp replies. He could not hear the actual words nor did he particularly want to. He heard them go and the world was quiet when they'd gone. It settled down to full dark. Stars came out, and he sat. Fireflies danced above the lawn, flickering like so many party lights. There was nothing festive about the evening, however.

"Mr. Barton?"

Dina's voice was small, childlike. Frightened. He gripped the arms of the chair to steady himself.

"Come on out, Dina."

The door creaked. Her footsteps came, light and delicate, as if she thought the porch was strewn with broken glass and barbed wire. She sat on the edge of the rocker, shoulders hunched, her hands clasped between her knees, toes pointing inward.

"Well, I guess you know something isn't right," he said.

She nodded.

He cleared his throat and rested his elbows on his knees, put his face in his hands and spoke through his fingers. "Did Mrs. Barton . . . did she say anything to you?"

She shook her head, picked at the frayed edge of his old khaki shorts she wore. "When we got back from the pond, she took Kelly upstairs. A little while later, they left." She finally raised her head, looked directly at him, and even though it was dark, he could see she was reliving all the other times this had happened in her life, all the times her mother or her father had sat her down and told her they needed to take a break from each other, they couldn't be together right now, they loved each other, but . . .

"Did I do something wrong? If I did, I'm so, so, sorry, and I'll do anything to make it up to you guys."

You stood too close. You laughed at my jokes. You needed a father.

He chose his words with care. "Mrs. Barton thinks it will be safer for her and Kelly over at Jake and Alma's house for now."

"Then why is she mad at me?"

"She's not mad at you, Dina. She's mad at me. And she's not so much mad as scared."

"Scared? Momma B.? She's like the bravest person I know."

"Brave people are scared all the time. Only stupid people are never scared, and she's not stupid. You know about 'fight or flight', right? She fights. But when she fights . . ." He tried to think of the right way to put it. "She doesn't always discriminate between friend and foe. She's more like a hurricane than a lightning strike. You're just an innocent bystander."

Up in the sky, the star he had wished on was lost in a field of thousands, maybe millions. They spread like diamonds on black velvet, cold and beautiful. He wondered if any satellites still circled the earth, taking pictures and sending them back to . . . what? Were they getting an interplanetary busy signal? A recorded voice saying, "The number you are trying to reach is not in service?" Or had they stopped functioning at the same time the power went out?

The rocker scraped as Dina stood. "*I* should go live with them," she said. "I'll go and they can come home. You guys should be together. I'll get my things and go tell them."

"No, Dina. No. It's not that easy. She needs time, that's all. We'll just go on and make the best of things, you and I, and wait for her to come to her senses. I'm sure she will. Just wait."

For a moment, he thought she was going to call bullshit and leave anyway. He held his breath, waiting. Finally, perhaps eager to please the closest thing she had left to a parent, she said, "Okay, Mr. Barton."

She sat again, and it should have been nice; a warm, early summer evening lit by stars and fireflies, perfumed with wood smoke, pleasant company. He and Dina had spent a lot of time out here on the porch, talking, and though she hadn't mentioned it, he supposed that was also something Monica had a problem with.

Dina said, "Do you want me to keep the first watch?"

"No. I don't think I'm going to sleep tonight. If I need to, I'll wake you."

He ended up sitting there all night.

———

Monica jammed her clothes into drawers, heedless of organization or folding, thankful only that Jake and Alma had been up and willing to take them in unannounced and without question. She couldn't spend another night over there. Of course, she would need to go back; her packing had been too haphazard, but she would wait until she knew both of *them* were out.

Kelly watched from a chair in the corner of the room, arms folded, legs crossed, right foot bouncing fast. She was pissed, but thankfully, hadn't argued too hard about coming. Compliance was in her nature, inherited from *him* and, like him, she generally knew enough to get out of Monica's way when she was riled.

"Okay," Kelly said finally. "Now we're here. Why?"

Kelly had not protested, but she could only be held off for so long. Monica didn't know what to say. Reason was returning, and she knew she couldn't throw *him* completely under the bus. He was Kelly's father, after all; you don't take a teenage girl away from her father—and her best friend—without a damn good reason. Which she had. She cursed Kevin for putting her in this situation.

It was all the worse because he had always been her anchor. As much as he could infuriate her with his acquiescing ways, he had always been a steadying influence, a safety valve. She was wind and fire, and he was earth, solid and stable.

"Your father and I have had a . . . disagreement . . . and have decided it's best if we not be around each other for a while."

"What kind of disagreement? And what does it have to do with me? Or Dina?"

"It doesn't have anything to do with you."

"We're a family. It has everything to do with me."

"I'm just trying to protect you, and this is the best way to do it."

"Protect me from what? From Curtis? I thought you were on my side about him. I'm not stupid, you know. I'm not going to get pregnant."

"That's not what I'm worried about."

"Then what is it? This is so not fair."

Kelly rose and went to the window, arms folded, her back ruler straight. Monica stood slightly behind her, both their pale reflections in the glass. A sachet on the dresser filled the room with a spicy cinnamon smell that covered up the odor of cow from the nearby barn. Mostly.

"This is better for everyone. We can pool our resources with the Hillmans, help each other out," Monica said, her cheeks burning at using *his* argument, the same argument she had recently rejected.

"Then where's Dad and Dina? They should be helping us. They should be here too."

"Yes. They should be. But your father—"

The word stuck in her throat like a pill. She turned away, put her hand on the bedpost as if the solid wood could give her the strength.

"*What*, already?" Kelly insisted. "What's going on?"

"I didn't want to tell you this, because it's going to sound mean and hurtful, and I don't want that. But you need to know the truth about him. I—" Again, her voice failed her, and for the first time, tears threatened. *I will not cry.*

She gripped the bedpost harder and turned now to face Kelly. "When I was little," she said, "my mother and grandmother used to stay up late and make bread. They'd mix the dough, let it rise, shape it, all that stuff. They did it so it was ready to go in the oven first thing in the morning. And they'd talk."

For a moment, she was there again, a girl of ten or twelve, lurking in the shadows, warm with the yeasty smell of bread dough and girl talk.

"They talked about people, some that I knew, some I didn't, and a lot of what they talked about, I didn't understand. Mostly, I just loved to listen to them. They were different with each other in the kitchen at night than they were in the day. Nicer.

"One night, they were talking about someone, and it took me a minute to realize it was about my father. Grandma Willsey said, 'All men are the same, dear. It's just their nature.' That was when I learned Dad was having an affair.

"Mom accepted it like it was just the way of the world, but I could see how much it hurt her. And I swore if I caught any man cheating on me, that was it. No second chances."

Kelly stared at her, open-mouthed, for several seconds, then barked an unkind laugh.

"Is that what you think? Really? Oh my God, Mom. What is this, some kind of joke? That's not like Dad at all. Even if he wanted to, who's there to cheat with? He never goes to town anymore. It's just us and the Hillmans up here." Surprisingly, she had the awareness of her surroundings to lower her voice, and added, "You think he's having an affair with Alma Hillman? *Really?*"

Monica said nothing. It took a few seconds for Kelly to understand. She gave her head a shake as if a fly were buzzing around her ear.

"No. Way. Just, no way. You're wrong. You are so wrong. That's just disgusting."

"It is. It is disgusting. But that's why we're here, and they're not."

She reached out, but Kelly slapped her hand away, her face twisting in revulsion.

"What's disgusting is that you can think that. Of either of them. There's something wrong with you, Mom. Seriously wrong."

"Keep your voice down. What's wrong is your father. I've seen too much."

"What have you seen? Have you caught them making out? Have you caught him feeling her up? Have you caught them *fucking?*"

"I don't have to see that. I know your father better than you—"

"You don't know him at all. How can you think that of him? How can you think that of *her?* She idolizes you, Mom. Oh my God."

She pushed past Monica and went out the door. She got momentarily lost in the unfamiliar hallway, turning left and right until she recognized the room that had been set aside for her. Monica followed, keeping her voice low. Jake and Alma's bedroom was downstairs, but Monica knew how funny sounds could be in old farmhouses like this one.

"I've seen enough of this in my life, trust me. The signs have been there for weeks. My father pulled this shit all the time, and my mother always took him back. And look at Dr. McCray."

"Dad is nothing at all like Dr. McCray. You're totally wrong."

Monica caught Kelly's hand and stared deep into her daughter's eyes. *So much like him.* It almost hurt to look at her, to see him there in the turned-up end of her nose, the arc of an eyebrow, the point of a chin. It hurt, but it did not diminish the love she had for her daughter or the lengths she would go to protect her.

"I wish I were wrong, Kelly. I wish with all my heart I was wrong."

Kelly looked into Monica's face. Her lip rose in a sneer. "Get out of my room, *Mother.*"

———

She hadn't intended this, but once she'd started, everything had come pouring out. Like a tsunami, her rage had picked her up and pushed her along. It had crested on the porch with *him*, but it had enough energy to carry her through the long moments of waiting for Kelly and shepherding her to the Hillmans'. Now, it was receding, and like every great disaster, it left behind shellshocked survivors to survey the wreckage of the storm through hollow eyes and with empty hearts. Monica had not thought this through. She had gone *nuclear*, as her father used to say, and now she was going to have to figure out how to explain it—and how to live with it.

In every great disaster, be it fire or flood, tornado, or tsunami, there comes a moment when the crisis ends. The waters seep into the ground, flow back into the rivers and creeks. The shrieking winds diminish, then become a gentle breeze that sighs an apology for the missing roof shingles and upturned trees. The fires burn down to glowing embers that can be doused with a little water or a well-protected boot.

Left behind are the survivors. They survey the wreckage of their homes and lives with sunken eyes and hollow hearts. They salvage the keepsakes that they find and talk bravely to the news crews that descend on them of starting over, of rebuilding, because what else can they do? Survival is the human condition.

Monica Barton was the storm. She hadn't intended for things to get out of hand, but they had. The rage had come, and she had let it take her. Like a tsunami, it was unstoppable. It had carried her far.

But now the waters had receded. She was no longer the storm . . . she was the survivor.

Kelly had asked her 'Why?' The bigger question in her mind was, *what now?* She paced the dark and unfamiliar bedroom. She had not been prepared. She had been so angry that she had not packed properly. In fact, she realized now she should not have packed at all, she should have sent Kevin packing. He was the one who should be here now.

And what of Dina?

"She idolizes you, Mom," Kelly had said, and Monica knew it was true. She had always felt a secret flush of pride at being 'Momma B.', at being the safe port in Dina's stormy life.

PART III

CHAPTER 21

KEVIN WOKE, BLEARY-EYED and sluggish, his mouth dry and sticky, as if someone had stuffed a wad of cotton in it. It sure felt like a hangover, though he'd had nothing to drink. He'd sat on the porch long into the night, heedless of the mosquitoes that whined in his ears and pricked his skin with their needle noses. He sat when the clouds rolled across the moon and the air chilled, and he sat when thunder echoed off the hills and lightning turned his surroundings into an eerie negative image of the world he knew. Sometime in the depths of the night, Dina crept again to the door and offered to take the watch. Again he refused and sat some more. Only when the wind whipped the rain beneath the protective cover of the porch did he finally give in. He went upstairs, didn't bother to wake Dina. Fuck the wood, he'd thought. Let them take it. Fuck it all. Everything had fallen apart.

Leaden legs carried him to the window. Droplets sparkled on the porch roof. Far below, wet grass, heavy from the rain, bent. Overhead, the clouds were breaking up into strips of white, with clear blue sky showing between. Another beautiful day in Harpursville. Kevin leaned his head against the cool glass. The bed called him, tempting him to return and curl up under the covers, but the morning had already advanced far beyond his normal wake-up time. Better to focus on the things to be done than the things that had happened. And maybe it would work out. After all, he'd wanted them to move in with Jake and Alma, and now half of them were safely over there. He pulled on cleanish clothes, cataloging the things to do, and trying to figure out how to work with Jake while maneuvering around his angry wife.

She'll come back. He believed this, *had* to believe this. She was a smart woman, a sensible woman—and she loved him.

Dina's voice floated to him from downstairs as he started down. She sang in a pretty but slightly off-key voice, some song he vaguely remembered from the Top 40 radio station. Once, he knew all the bands, all the songs, all the words, but the pursuit of a career and all the worries of day-to-day adult living—jobs and cars and mortgages and health insurance and child-raising—had pulled him from that world. Now that world was gone, maybe forever.

He found her in the kitchen, setting a pair of plates out on the table and still singing.

She startled when he came in. "Oh!" She dropped a fork to the floor. Her face reddened. "You didn't hear that, did you?"

He forced a smile. "Don't stop on my account. You have a nice voice."

"Oh, please." She turned a deeper shade of red. "You're just being nice." And then, "Can I make you some breakfast?"

Though his stomach felt unsettled this morning, Kevin knew he couldn't afford to skip a meal; there was too much work to be done, and he needed the energy. Still, the prospect of Dina making him breakfast twisted his stomach up in a way that went beyond his general ill feeling. Monica's voice in his head; *have fun playing house with Lolita.*

"That would be great, Dina. Thanks. Do you need help with the fire or anything?"

"Nope, it's already going. Just sit."

She grabbed a pan and hustled out the door. Kevin poured himself a small glass of milk. Fresh from the udder, it was rich and creamy, but seemed to congeal in a sour mass in his stomach.

He put his face in his hands. Again, he replayed the argument with Monica in his head, tried to figure out how it had gotten out of control so fast, and wondered if there was any way to fix it. One tiny slip. One stupid little word.

Someone knocked on the door. Kevin jumped, caught unawares. Jake Hillman's big face peered in through the screen.

"Anybody home?"

Kevin considered telling the farmer no, go away, come back some other day, but they had business to attend to. His situation extended beyond the confines of their home. He leaned back, let out a deep breath, and invited Jake in.

Jake squeezed through the door, wearing his standard uniform: big T-shirt, fading overalls, solid work boots, battered baseball cap. As he crossed the threshold, he pulled off the cap. Kevin pointed to the chair opposite him, and the big farmer sat.

"Can I get you something to drink? Milk or water is all I have, I'm afraid."

"Naw, I'm good thanks. I tell you what, I'd kill for a big glass of OJ."

Kevin could almost feel the pulp on his tongue. He tried hard not to think about the things he missed from the old world, especially not the foods. Like orange juice. Potatoes. Salt. Coffee. He focused on the brass buttons on the front of Jake's overalls in an attempt to drive the images and remembered tastes of lost foods out of his mind.

"I know why you're here," Kevin said. "I'm really sorry, Jake. I know it's a big inconvenience—"

"Aw, forget that. I invited you to stay in the first place." He twisted his cap in his hands. "I was just a bit surprised is all. I sort of expected you'd all arrive together."

"Yeah." Kevin scraped his thumbnail over a thin skin of something that had dripped and dried on the table. "Yeah, about that—"

"Look, it's none of my business. You don't have to tell me if you don't want to. I'll listen, but . . ."

But I'd rather not was the unspoken end of the sentence.

"Thanks, Jake, I appreciate it. It's . . . complicated, and to be honest, I'd really rather not get into it."

The look of relief on Jake's face nearly made Kevin laugh.

"I tell you what," Jake said, "it's a lot easier dealing with cows than women. You pretty much always know what a cow's thinking. Anyways, I don't mean to sound . . . I mean, I know things are tough right now, but I'm just a bit worried over how this"—the cap flopped in his hand as he gestured at the kitchen—"is going to affect things round here."

"Well, the good news is we got half of us over to your place." Kevin rubbed his tired eyes. "I wish I could tell you it was all part of my master plan, but it was not. I think things will blow over in a few days. I'm just going to have to steer clear of Monica until it does."

Jake scratched his cheek. "Well, I suppose we'll just have to work around things, that's all."

The door squeaked open. Dina stood on the threshold, eyes flicking from one man to the other, a plate of eggs in one hand.

"Oh, hi, Mr. Hillman. I didn't know you were coming. Do you want some eggs? I can make some more."

"Aw, that's all right, sweetheart. Don't trouble yourself. I've got to be getting back to things." He grunted and pushed himself up from the table. "I'm going to get started cutting upside of Silvas' today."

"Okay. I'll be up as soon as I'm done here. And Jake? Thanks."

Jake waved and stepped out. The kitchen grew quiet.

Dina set a plate in front of Kevin. A pair of eggs stared at him with jiggling, golden eyes. Beside them was a stack of thin, misshapen pancakes, and a strip of dried beef.

"Pancakes? How did you make them?"

"Cattail flour. They didn't come out so great. You should eat while they're still warm. My camp counselor said that cattails are brain food. They're supposed to make you smart."

"I need all the help I can get right about now."

She stood by the side of the table, twisting her fingers around as she waited for him to eat. *Have fun playing house.* He put his fork down.

"Don't you like it?"

"It's fine. Just . . . sit, please. You're making me nervous."

"Sorry." The chair scraped over the linoleum, a loud, spine-wracking sound, and she sat, still watching him, hands working furiously.

He had to eat, not just because he needed it for his health, but because the eggs and pancakes weren't just food, they were an apology of sorts. If he refused the food, if he shoved away from the table and left the house, it would be like blaming her for everything, and it wasn't her fault. There was plenty of blame to go around, but none of it rested on her slim shoulders. Finally, he had to eat so he could get out of the house and put some distance between them. He needed that right now.

He picked up his fork and took a bite of pancake. It was crumbly, a little dry, but tasty.

"Mm. This is very good. Thank you."

She beamed. The taste brought his appetite back in force. He tore off a hunk of the dried beef with his teeth. Smoky. Eggs with thick, golden yolks. So good.

"You should eat." He swabbed the plate with some of the pancake, soaking up the yolk.

"I ate before. I'm okay."

"You're not hungry? Really?"

The joke was flatter than the pancakes. She looked away and fiddled with the hem of her shorts. Kevin focused on his plate and power ate.

"That was really good," he said when he finished, sitting back. "Thank you."

"Not as good as Mrs. Barton's."

"It was fine." He reached out, intending to pat her on the arm, but Monica's face flashed in his mind, making batty eyes at him. He scratched his cheek instead. "I'll take care of cleanup and then I have to catch up with Jake. What are you up to today?"

"Mr. Barton, why did she leave? It's because of me, isn't it?"

He placed the plate in the sink and turned. She looked very small and childlike, which was something of a relief. Monica's ultimate conclusion was far off the mark, yet part of it rang true. Dina had grown up physically. Somewhere along the way he'd *seen* that, and though he didn't want to acknowledge it, he had been looking at her differently. He ran his hand over his face, felt a crumb of pancake in his beard and brushed it out.

"I told you why last night."

She took a deep breath, gathering herself, hands clasped on the table.

"One day, my parents are madly in love. The next they're ready to kill each other. And they never tell us the truth. I've always loved being here. You guys are just so . . . so . . . everything is always so right with you." She looked down at the table for a moment. "Last night was the first time I felt like I was back home.

"I used to think everything was my fault," she continued. "I know better. My parents are just screwed up, and it's not my fault. But this is different. I can tell."

"No. It's not—"

"Mr. Barton, please don't lie to me like *they* do."

He let his eyes drift around the room, skipping over the now useless appliances—refrigerator, dishwasher, toaster, microwave, stove. Finally, he found the wall clock, frozen at ten fifteen. Ten fifteen all day, every day. Maybe ten fifteen forever. Whatever the clock said, whatever time it really was, it was time for the truth. Or most of it, at least.

He took a seat directly across from her.

"This whole thing, the blackout, I mean, has put us under a lot of stress. And if you want to be technical about it, you're part of that stress." He held his thumb and forefinger a quarter inch apart. "But one little part. Very small."

"I'm sorry."

"Don't be. Everyone's lives are out of order, yours more than ours. At least I know my wife and daughter are safe. But you . . ." He tailed off and could see she knew exactly what he meant. "The fact that it's all out of whack plays into it, yeah, but this is about Mr. Sobchuk."

"The big boss man?"

"Yes, him. Well, he's done some good things for this town. He's really helped keep it together. If it wasn't for him, this town might not even—" Kevin stopped short, disgusted that he couldn't seem to stop defending the man. "Anyway, a couple of weeks back he told me he was looking for . . . help. Stuff around his house. Cooking and cleaning. He said he was too busy to keep up with his house."

Kevin plucked at his wiry beard. His cheeks were hot, like he was standing in front of a blazing fire.

"He saw you here one day and said he wanted you. Said it was for housework, but . . . well, it was for more than that. He just—he just wanted you. For something else."

He couldn't quite bring himself to say it, but he didn't have to. The smooth skin of her forehead wrinkled, and she looked very much like her mother at her most disapproving.

"Sex? With me?" She pulled her hands up in front of her chest. "Eww. That's just gross. He's so old. Yuck. Oh God, Mr. Barton, that's just horrible." Then she surprised him. She giggled. "I mean, I guess I should take it as a compliment, but eww!"

It didn't explain why Monica had left and Kevin had no explanation except the "we're all under stress here." He decided to see if she could make that connection. She did make a connection, and it was not one he expected.

"Mr. B., do you think that's why the wood got stolen? To punish you for not . . . I don't know, giving me up?"

"Huh?"

"If he asked you, and you said no, do you think maybe *he* stole the wood? Like a punishment? Or to scare you or something?"

"No," he said. "No, that's ridiculous. I mean, everything he's done since he stepped into the street has been to help this town get by. There's no way."

"Are you sure?"

"Sure, I'm sure."

But was he sure or had he just not dared to consider it? As Monica had pointed out, George Morris was one of Sobchuk's work buddies. Kevin even remembered George dropping by once when Sobchuk was there on a service call. After the job was done, the two of them stood by their trucks in the driveway, yukking it up while George smoked a cigarette. Then there was the way George acted when summoned to town hall to answer to Kevin's charges. He hadn't acted at all like a man unjustly accused of a crime. There had been no anger or indignation; he'd just said, in effect, "Nope, I was sleeping all night."

Would Sobchuk stoop to such a thing? Kevin couldn't square the image of him staring down a speeding military convoy with someone who would arrange a midnight raid on a woodpile. Yet he had tried to get Kevin to swap Dina for a few bundles of wood and some deer steaks. Far more powerful men with far more to lose had done worse.

"I don't know," he said slowly. "Maybe."

Dina pushed away from the table in a rush. She ping-ponged around the kitchen, bouncing off cabinets, counters, and useless appliances, finally coming to rest in front of him, her lip quivering.

"If he sent someone to steal wood, what's to stop him from just coming up here and grabbing me? Why me, anyway?"

"It's okay. It's okay. He won't. He wouldn't dare." *Wouldn't he?*

"*This* is what you and Mrs. Barton fought about, isn't it?" She pressed her hand to her neck. Her pretty blue eyes, wet with potential tears, probed his face.

"Yes." It wasn't a lie. They had fought about this. He just prayed that she wouldn't find the final puzzle piece because he didn't know how he would answer for that.

"Okay, then," she said. "I should just go."

"Go where?"

"Home. I can make it."

"No. Absolutely not. If it wasn't safe four, five days after this all started, what do you think it's like now?"

"I can cut through the woods—"

"Dina. You've heard what Curtis has said. It's not safe out there."

According to Curtis, the patrols were coming across more and more stragglers. Most were heading south, chasing rumors of electricity and FEMA camps in Pennsylvania. Many told tales of being hounded on the roads by gangs, of robbery, murder, rape—even cannibalism. Kevin's experience with Dougie Austin and Maybe-George Morris left him inclined to believe most of it, though he drew the line at cannibalism. For now. As Curtis said, "It's getting rough out there." Cops had always been scarce in the county; as far as anyone knew, now they were nonexistent.

"Fine," she said. "If I went off with this guy, she'd be here, right?"

"You're not going with him."

She stopped, fists on her hips, feet planted wide on the tile floor. "What if I want to go?"

"Don't try to martyr yourself to save my marriage. Mrs. Barton will come back once she has time to cool off and think things through. Besides, I won't let you."

She resumed her circuit of the kitchen, talking as much to herself as to Kevin. "I should go. I should just go, and then you and Mrs. Barton and Kelly can get back together. It's all my fault. I'll get my things and go."

"You're not going with Sobchuk and you're not running away."

At last, The Voice of Authority had come. It stopped her cold.

Kevin took her firmly by the shoulders and looked her in the eye. "I can't do a thing to keep you here if you really want to leave," he said. "And I don't blame you if you don't want to stay. My track record at this whole protection thing is pretty shitty, I know, but I'm done backing down.

"I promised you I would keep you safe. I will not let anything happen to you. But I can't protect you if you leave. Trust me." He released her shoulders. "Please."

Little by little, the defiance went out of her.

"Okay," she said. "I'm just—I'm really, really sorry."

"It's not your fault. Everything's going to be okay. We just have to stick together."

There was still doubt on her face, but she nodded. While Kevin cleaned up his plate, they plotted out their activities for the day. *It's not ideal*, he thought as he left the house a few minutes later to meet up with Jake. *But it will have to be good enough.*

CHAPTER 22

MR. B. HAD decided that, since it was just the two of them, keeping watch didn't make sense anymore.

"It's just too disruptive," he said, so when they settled in for the night, they propped dining room chairs under the doorknobs like in the movies and strung old cans across the windows. He kept a baseball bat next to his bed; she kept a fireplace poker next to hers. Every morning they checked the perimeter of the house for signs of intruders; so far, they had found none.

She had moved out of Kelly's room and into the spare bedroom. It was a little further from the top of the stairs, a little closer to the master bedroom. This made her feel a little safer, and it hadn't felt right being in Kelly's room when she wasn't there. Not that she slept all that much; neither of them had since Momma B. and Kelly moved out. She would turn in shortly after dark, drop-dead exhausted. There she would lay in her borrowed bed in her borrowed room, tossing and turning, listening to the old wooden house settle around her, listening to him pacing downstairs. She could follow his restless feet by the creaking floorboards as he traced a path through the house, front door to the back-front door to the kitchen door, kitchen to parlor to dining room to living room. She sometimes dozed, but her brief moments of sleep were broken by violently colored dreams that woke her with a start, heart pounding, unable to remember anything beyond yellows, reds, and blues. At some point, she would hear him climb the stairs, and she would curl herself into a tight ball, certain that he would stop outside her room, and after a brief pause, he would open the door and step in. He would stand at the foot of her bed and say, "Dina. It's time."

It didn't happen. Each night he climbed the stairs, his feet heavy on the treads, and he would move past her door—without stopping—to his own bedroom. After a few minutes, the tension would seep out of her body, and she would sleep then—sometimes well, sometimes not—and in the morning, they started their routine all over again.

The days were not much better. How many days since Momma B. and Kelly had left? She couldn't say. The days and weeks had turned into a big ball of wibbly-wobbly, timey-wimey stuff, as they said on *Doctor Who*, a show she'd never been super crazy about, but she'd give her left eye to watch now, just for normalcy. More than anything in the world, she wanted to sit on the couch in her family room with a big bowl of popcorn in her lap, watching bad TV and surrounded by her family. Each day melted into the last, but each day was endless, worsened by the fact that the easy conversation and laughter she and Mr. B. had always enjoyed had disappeared. Dina tried to be cheerful for the both of them—it was a skill she had honed in the fractious environment of her own home—but it took a tremendous amount of energy, energy that she just didn't have anymore, especially now that she knew. A day (or two or three) after the big blowout, Kelly had managed to drag herself out of bed before full light and appeared in the barn where Dina was getting ready to milk the big Hereford she called Camilla. After the tears and the hugs and more hugs, Kelly had told her the truth. The full truth.

"I mean, it's totally ridiculous, right?" Kelly said, and Dina, who found that Kelly's words had crushed nearly all the air out of her, could only nod and say, "Right."

What might have hurt more than the idea that Momma B.—dear Momma B., her favorite mother not named Lisa McCray (though she often temporarily supplanted Lisa McCray as her favorite, depending on the home situation)—could think that way was how Kelly had searched her face, the slight pleading note in her "right."

So, she and Mr. Barton moved around each other in the house, doing what had to be done to get through the day: milk those cows, sweep that barn, cook this food, weed that garden, rinse (ha, there had been little of that; she was a dirty, stinky mess with tangled hair and hollow cheeks) and repeat.

Tonight's routine had been the same. She had gone to bed. Mr. Barton paced the floors below. She dozed off and on, woke to the sounds of his feet on the stairs, clutched the sheets to her chest and squinched her eyes tight enough to see golden starbursts on the black. The sound of the blood rushing in her ears blocked out the sound of him in the hallway. *This* time, he would stop. *This* time he would come in and say, "Dina, it's time. You have to leave," and he would kick her out to fend for herself. But the door didn't open, not her door anyway. Instead, she heard the soft click of his own door closing just a few feet down the hall, heard the muffled rustling of sheets and a groan as he settled into bed, and she started breathing again.

She turned onto her back, sniffed, swiped at her leaking eyes with the back of her wrist. Outside, a confused bird—a robin perhaps—sang from a tree in the backyard. Its song rang clear in the night, cheerful in the dark night, but lonely too. From the next room she could now hear Mr. Barton snoring loudly, sleeping for once. She was glad to hear that sound—he desperately needed the sleep.

It had taken Dina most of her life to understand that her parents' problems were not her fault. Her father couldn't keep his dick in his pants, and her mother had tied her identity so completely to being Mrs. Dr. Phil McCray that she would do anything to maintain that life, even as it made her and everyone around her miserable. Dina had tried her hardest to be the glue that held the family together, the shining light that burned away the bad. But she'd finally understood she couldn't change them, and that had been freeing. But this was different. She *was* the cause of it. Even before Kelly told her, she had known she was to blame. She could read the room. After all, it was a necessary skill in her house. She just hadn't known *why*. After Kelly told her, her emotions had pinballed wildly back and forth, from anger and hurt—*how could she think that of me? Of him?*—to guilt and self-loathing: *Maybe I did something wrong. Maybe I do want what she thinks.* The only way they would patch things up would be if she were gone.

The night Momma B. had taken Kelly, Dina had packed every-thing she could carry and stowed the backpack beneath the bed. In the morning, after Mr. B. had *explained* what had happened (leaving out the most important part) she had been ready to go and she would have. She would have slipped away in the night but for two things: she had promised Mr. B. that she wouldn't and—plain and simple—she was scared. Curtis had told them stories of more stragglers than ever on the roads, some well armed and aggressive, and on more than one occasion she had heard volleys of shots in the night that was not someone shooting at a herd of deer that had wandered in. Even if she did evade the bad people out there, she wondered if she'd find anyone at her home when she got there. Mr. Barton assured her that her family was okay, but she wasn't so certain. They might have been home when the blackout hit but maybe not. Despite her mom's passion for gardening, she didn't think her parents were really suited to this lifestyle. They were smart—really smart—but the wrong kind of smart. Part of her decision to stay was because it was easier to hold to the illusion that her family was safe at home. That still left the question of what to do next.

Would I go with Sobchuk if I were starving?

The thought made her stomach do a backflip.

Sobchuk would offer her food and a place to live. In exchange. She remembered a date with Robbie Parsons last year. He took her to the movies at the mall in Oneonta. He bought her a slice of pizza before the film, bought her ticket, bought her popcorn. After the movie, they had to wait for Robbie's father to pick them up.

"Shoot, I got the time wrong," Robbie said. He jingled loose change in his pocket. "I thought the movie ended later. It's going to take my dad about a half hour to get here. What do you want to do?"

Normally, she would suggest walking the mall, but it was after ten and the stores were all closed. A security guard stood nearby, thumbs hooked over his belt. "Mall's closed, kids, gotta wait outside."

Other kids who were similarly dependent on parents for rides gath-ered in little clumps in front of the mall, finishing sodas and popcorn, talking in excited tones about the movie they had just watched. People with their own cars streamed across the mostly empty parking lot.

Robbie put his hand on her shoulder and leaned close. His breath tickled her ear.

"I know where we can go to be alone. Interested?"

"Here? Where?"

"Around back. There's some real private places there." He wiggled his eyebrows at her.

Dina *was* interested. They had made out a couple of times, and she liked it. She liked *him*, he was nice, but sneaking off to a dark area behind the mall?

"I . . . I don't think that would be such a good idea."

The grin slid off his face, but he said, "Oh. Okay."

"Not because of you," she hurried to add. "It's just . . . you know."

"Sure. It's okay."

So he said, but he brought it up a few minutes later. Again, she said no, a little more firmly. After his third request and her third refusal, he got annoyed.

"I paid for everything tonight. I should get something out of it."

"You got the pleasure of my company," she said lightly, dropping a curtsy. He muttered something under his breath about the night being a waste, so she told him to fuck off. Poor Mr. Parsons must have felt like he was driving Mr. and Mrs. Winter home, it was so cold in the car.

"He was so stupid about it," she told Kelly the next day. "I wasn't rejecting *him*, I was rejecting the location, you know? But once he made it seem like I was, like, *obligated* because he bought me a movie ticket, that's it, I'm out of there. I mean, give me a choice, right? Otherwise, it's just rape."

"My body, my rules," Kelly said. Kelly got it. Kelly understood. Her other friends? Not so much. They gabbled on about their own experiences, the hookups at parties and school dances, and April Marsh said she didn't mind giving someone a hand job for a nice night out.

"It's messy but whatever," she shrugged. "It's no big deal."

April went on to tell Dina that her romantic notions of love and sex were out of date. "You're so cute, Dee," she said, "but get with the times, girl. Everybody's doing it."

But Dina wouldn't get with the times on this. Quid pro quo wasn't going to be the basis of her relationship with anyone.

She rolled over again, wrapping herself in sheets even though it was a warm night and listened to the near-empty house and the full world outside.

"Things have changed."

She whispered the words so low she barely heard them herself. She imagined them as a physical thing, letters floating in air, light and curvy like a snake, glowing powder blue. The colors were pretty and friendly and warm, but they spoke of the cold reality of the new world, a world she didn't like.

Mrs. Barton—her beloved Momma B.—had tried to kick her out, and Mr. B. had said no. Another question formed, another she was afraid to ask but had to: What if Momma B. wanted to come back but would only do it if Dina was gone? Mr. Barton pledged to protect her, but would his desire to reunite with his family overcome his promise to her? She didn't think he would kick her out, but the world had changed . . . and so had its people. In all her wildest dreams and nightmares, never had she imagined that Momma B. could accuse her of such a thing.

The idea of Sobchuk pawing at her, putting his mouth all over her, being *in* her made her shudder. Leaving and trying to survive on the road would almost certainly lead to a worse fate. What did that leave?

"Things have changed," she said again. She didn't like the implication, but wasn't trading favors part of life? Her father was fond of saying, "You gotta give something to get something, kid." God, she wished she could talk to him, wished she could ask, "Is *this* what you meant? Is this what you wanted for me?"

A tear trickled down the side of her face. It nestled in the hair just above her ear. She was an orphan. Worse yet, a *girl* orphan, powerless in this new world.

Powerless wasn't the same as helpless, however. She took a deep, determined breath.

"Things have changed, Dina." She said it a little louder than last time, but it made no difference to the crickets and frogs and coyotes—or the man sleeping down the hall. Their noises continued on as before. "You have to take care of yourself. You'll do what needs to be done and you will survive."

She *would* survive, and it would be on her terms. Mr. Barton would be kind because he cared for her. She remembered how he had removed the tick, how careful he had been, how he had calmed her with his story of his own tick experience, how his hands had worked so expertly on the back of her neck. She would make herself indispensable to him, in whatever way it took, because Sobchuk was worse, the road was worse, finding out that her whole family was dead was worse.

She rubbed at her watery eyes with the heel of her hand. "My terms," she whispered to the room. "The world has changed, but that much hasn't."

She closed her eyes. Outside, the robin sang its lonely song in the night. Inside, Mr. Barton snored, slow and steady. She slowed her own breathing to match his, and after a while, she fell asleep.

———

Jake Hillman wondered if he would last the winter. Starvation wasn't his worry. There was enough beef on the hoof to feed them for a long time, even without fridges and freezers, and Alma was a whiz with canning. The basement was stuffed full of mason jars of carrots and beans, tomatoes and beets, plenty left from last year with more to come. They weren't eating as well as they used to, not by a long shot, but they were getting by. Food wasn't the limiting factor most people thought.

No, more likely he'd work or worry himself into the ground before he starved. Farm living was hard on the body, always had been, always would be, and Jake had been at it since he was old enough to walk and his ma had him spreading chicken feed.

Funny thing though. He might actually be safer now that the heavy machinery—with its whirling blades and spinning contraptions and grinding gears and spinning belts that were hungry for fingers and hands and were also quite happy to catch up a loose tail of a shirt and take a whole man—was sitting unused in the pole barn or rusting in the field. His spine even felt a little better not jouncing along in the hard seat of his tractor. But the walking, the hauling, the swinging of axes and mauls, the dragging of saws across countless logs, it was wearing him down, taking a toll on a body that had already been stepped on by cows and kicked by a horse and survived a rolled tractor. Over the years, he'd bashed his thumbs and fingers with countless hammer blows, torn open his flesh on bob wire, and been stepped on by cattle. All of these injuries had built up and left a man who was both remarkably healthy and remarkably battered and was currently very afraid.

Pulling the Bartons into the fold had helped a lot, but this latest development, the unexpected arrival of Monica and Kelly Barton, was like a big old rock in the field, the kind that busts up a plow blade and brings the day's work to a halt. It was disruption they didn't need, made worse by the way everyone was tiptoeing around, taking the long way, peeking around corners to make sure the way was clear. It would be funny if it weren't getting in the way of work.

Little Monica Barton, meanwhile, was fearsome when she was riled up, and the woman was riled up. He could hear her prowling around upstairs, a cat on the lookout for mice.

"I think you need to talk to her," Alma said from beside him.

"Me? Wouldn't this be better as a woman-to-woman kind of thing?"

The candle on her bedside table flickered, casting the room in a pumpkin glow. Alma sat with pillows propped against the headboard behind her, hands folded on top of the sheets.

"I have to be the sympathetic ear," she said.

"So you want me to play bad cop? She's liable to brain me."

"Jake Hillman. Are you afraid of her? She's just a bitty little thing."

"So's a yellow jacket, and I don't want to run afoul of one of them either."

"I don't think she'll get mad at you. Not if you approach her right."

"Well, you know how I like to approach a nest of yellow jackets: at night and from a distance."

It wasn't really that he was afraid the little woman would physically hurt him. Sixty-three years on God's green earth had taught him the last thing you wanted to do was get involved in someone else's mess, especially a marriage mess. As far as he was concerned, what happened between a man and a woman was best kept between that man and that woman. Of course, nine times out of ten, someone else's marriage mess had no bearing on him. It was harder to be neutral when you had a stake in things, and Jake had a big old stake in this—their lives were tied together. Plus, he liked the Bartons, and wanted them to work things out. Of course, given what he'd heard through the air vents and walls, he wasn't sure it *could* be.

"Do you think he did what she thinks?"

The bed creaked as Alma adjusted her position beside him. "He hardly seems the type," she said. "And I've never seen anything inappropriate between him and her, have you?"

"Naw, I think that girl's as innocent as a lamb."

"Well, I don't know about *that*, but I know *her* type," and Jake knew she was referring to Monica now. "She's stubborn, hot-tempered, and proud. That's a dangerous combination."

Jake sighed. Monica's footsteps sounded on the front stairs as she came down. The kitchen door squeaked open, flumped closed, and something clattered in there as she set about doing whatever it was she was doing down there. Making bread. Cleaning. Piling wood by the stove for morning. Doing something, anything maybe, but think about what brought her here.

"The problem with her type," Alma continued, "is they can't admit they're wrong, even when they know it. She probably just needs a little time to think, but summer's almost half over and there's not a lot of time to fix things. She just needs someone to give her a nudge is all."

Jake pulled the top sheet up to his chin and watched the flickering shadows. She was a sensible woman, Alma, and he knew she was right. But he had no idea how to nudge Monica Barton. And maybe Kevin *had* done what she accused him of. If that was the case, would he want that man living under his roof?

"I still think you'd be better at this than me."

Alma smiled at him sweetly, and after forty-one years together, it still made his old heart skip a beat.

"You know I don't like to meddle."

She kissed him on the cheek and blew out the candle.

CHAPTER 23

THEY WERE CUTTING hay. Again. For like the third time this summer. Kelly didn't mind the work—in fact, she liked the rhythm of it, sweeping the scythe back and forth through the knee-high grass, the *whick* of the blade slicing through the stalks, the watermelon-rind smell that rose from the cut hay around her. She even liked the grasshoppers and crickets that buzzed and chirped in the field and the yellow-and-black butterflies that danced around her head and the electric blue swallows that swooped overhead, snapping those same insects out of the air. The scythe became a metronome, and she sang songs in her head in time to it, some songs that she made up, some that she remembered from the ancient days of radios and iPods and YouTube. Haying was calming, and she needed calm. It gave her space to think, and she had precious little space in the Hillmans' house. And what she thought was she needed to see Dad.

She was in Jake's east field, a big L-shaped pasture carved out of the woods between her house and the Silvas' property. She worked the scythe, Alma Hillman followed, raking the cut grass into a windrow. Later, they would come back and spread it out to dry and would repeat the process of spreading and piling until Mr. Hillman decided it was ready. Then they loaded it onto tarps and dragged it across the road and built haystacks.

Mrs. Hillman called out to Kelly, interrupting her latest internal song. "Sweetheart, I need to go back and rest a bit," she said. "My back is kicking up a real fuss today."

"Oh, sure, Mrs. Hill—Alma." The Hillmans insisted she call them Jake and Alma, but Kelly had a hard time fighting against a lifetime of training. "Do you need any help?"

"No, I'll be all right. Why don't you just cut to the end of the row there, then come back for lunch? I'm sorry to leave you with this, I should be good this afternoon."

"It's okay, Alma. I hope you feel better."

Mrs. Hillman walked slowly out of the field, one hand pressed against her lower back, and Kelly felt sympathy for the older woman, mixed with a healthy dose of resentment for her mother, who was probably off moping in the woods. The first cutting had been relatively easy. Everyone had pitched in, and it went fast. This cutting was going to take forever because her mother had gone and blown everything up. Everyone was acting like Mom was made of glass or something, and instead of six people working together, everyone was trying to avoid each other. Dina snuck in and out of the barn each morning like a skittish cat, and Dad, she didn't know what he was up to, she hadn't seen him in what seemed like weeks.

And then there was Curtis. Not long ago, the L word had almost slipped out through his lips, and it had sent shivers of delight and terror through her. But since that evening, she hadn't seen him, and she wondered if he was ghosting her and she didn't have anyone she could talk to about it now. Without Dina around, she had no one to share her hopes and fears with. And that was on Mom.

Fuming over all this, she lost her rhythm, started hacking at the grass, caught the tip of the blade in the ground and twisted her wrist. Oh shit. She picked up the scythe, cleaned the dirt off the tip of the blade, and checked to make sure she hadn't broken anything. That would be big trouble.

And though she knew the work was important, with Mrs. Hillman out of sight, Kelly seized her opportunity. She carried the scythe to the edge of the field, leaned it carefully against a tree, and ran through the field for home. Her real home. She ran through the pasture to the little chunk of woods at the edge, cut through the cool dark beneath the trees, and burst through the tangle of bushes at the property line like the Kool-Aid Man coming through a wall.

Dad was in the garden. He jumped and whirled around, eyes wide, then broke into his big, goofy Dad smile that she loved. And she burst into tears.

"Oh, honey, don't do that." His arms were around her, and he kissed the top of her head. She just let go, bawled into his chest, tears of anger and frustration and overwhelming sadness that had been held in for the weeks they had been apart. "Oh my God, I've missed you," he said, crushing her. She cried like she did when she was a little kid, and he held her and smoothed her hair, and she wrapped her arms around him and squeezed with everything she had until she had cried herself out. Finally, with a great effort, she pulled back and looked him up and down through misty eyes.

Looking at him, she understood now why her grandparents always gushed over how much she'd changed since the last time they saw her, even when it wasn't that long between visits. Since Mom had taken her away, the picture of him in her mind had reverted to what he was before the blackout. It was like looking at one of those before and after pictures on a weight-loss site. He was thinner. Ted, her little brother, was just a memory. Dad's hair was down to his shoulders, touched with silver at the temples. His beard was thick, with one white blotch just off-center of his chin, but it didn't quite cover his hollow cheeks. There were bruisy-looking shadows under his eyes.

"I'm so glad to see you," he said. "How are you? And how's Mom?"

"I'm okay. And she's nuts. I'm coming home, Dad. This isn't right."

His smile dimmed. "You can't, Kelly. Not now."

"What? Why not? I can't live with her, Dad. She's miserable. And who knows what she'll come up with next."

"That's why you need to stay there. She needs you, Kelly. She'll come around but she needs you until she does."

"You know what she said about you, right?" He nodded. "How can you defend her?"

He winced, then looked off toward the Hillmans' house, which could barely be seen through the screen of trees and shrubs. For one second,

Kelly's heart sank. *Oh my God, it's true.* No. She knew it wasn't. It couldn't be.

"Because she's not herself. All of this"—he waved his hand at the garden, the house, the world—"has been really hard for her."

"Bullshit, Dad. It's hard for everyone."

"Quarter for the jar."

She didn't smile. He took her hands in his. The pads of his fingers were scaly and hard, not at all like they used to be. But nothing was.

"Yes, it's hard for everyone," he allowed, "but for whatever reason, it's been extra hard for her. I know this is a lot to ask of you but go back. As hard as it is, be there for her. We'll hold down the fort here until she comes to her senses, and then we'll all be together again. You'll see."

She wanted to tell him he was deluding himself. Mom wasn't one to apologize. But in the end, she was cut from the same cloth as her father.

"Fine," she said. "I'll go back. For now. But if she doesn't wake up soon, *you're* going to wake up one day and find me sleeping in my bed."

"Just be patient. She'll come around." He kissed her again. "Do you want to see Dina? She's inside."

She wanted to see Dina. Desperately. Now that she had the chance, she hesitated. The last few times they'd been together had been uncomfortable. Ridiculous as it was, Mom's accusation had been like a fart in polite company: everyone notices, no one wants to talk about it.

"I'd love to but I'd better get back," she said. "The hay needs cutting, and I'm the only one to do it."

But she didn't go back to work and she didn't go back to the Hillmans' house for lunch, even though she was furiously hungry. Instead, when Kelly pushed through the bushes back into the woods, she went just far enough in to hopefully be out of Dad's sight, then cut left. She crept through the woods for another hundred feet or so, then cut left again and started working her way downhill, trying to be as quiet as the Iroquois who used to stalk the forests. Her own house was still visible through the trees on her left. A flash of color caught her eye. Through the trees, she saw that Dina had joined her father in the garden. Unable help herself, she hid behind a large tree and watched them for several minutes.

They worked at opposite ends, backs to each other, not talking. There were no furtive glances, no *accidental* bumping into each other, no words exchanged. They each acted like they were totally oblivious of the other's presence.

If Mom could see this, she would realize how stupid she was being.

She crept away and resumed her trip to town. When she reached the road, she jumped the ditch and dashed across, feeling like an outlaw. The community garden was largely empty at this hour. Cassie Magglio was there, however. The older woman pushed her oversized sunglasses to the top of her head.

"Where have you been, Kelly dear? We missed you."

Seeing Cassie, seeing the way the garden was progressing, made Kelly realize how much she missed working down here.

"We've been really busy up there," she said, waving up toward the hill. "I don't have much time right now. Have you seen Curtis?"

Cassie smiled. "I should have known that's what brought you down here. I haven't seen him today. Try across the way."

Town hall was also largely deserted. The fire pit was quiet and cleaned up, though she caught a faint whiff of charred meat. It made her mouth water. A group of men were gathered near the woodpile. One of them would surely know where Curtis was.

"Kelly!"

He stood near a big bucket of water, his head and shoulders soaked and dripping. He grinned, the grin she was coming to love—could it be love, really? Seeing him made her feel full inside, full enough to burst.

He ran to her, engulfed her in his long, strong arms. His shirt was wet and stuck to his back. He smelled of hard work, but it was a good smell—*his* smell. Then he kissed her, and it was just as good as the first one. Someone near the woodpile whistled at them.

"Where have you been?" she said, trying not to make it sound accusatory. She didn't want to be one of *those* girlfriends. "You never come see us anymore."

"We've been super busy. I've been doing night patrols, but I've been helping out in the days in the woods too. A couple of guys got hurt, and they needed some extra help." He put his arm over her shoulder. She reached up, twined her fingers into his, almost pulled his hand down onto her breast. "Besides, I'm afraid your dad might shoot me."

She snorted. "Mom's the one with the gun. If you do come up, we're over at the Hillmans' across the street. Mom flipped her lid."

And because he was her boyfriend and because it seemed like further explanation was needed and because she really needed someone to talk to, she gave him the lowdown. She held back the most embarrassing details, though; that was just a little much yet.

They sat together for a while in the shade of the equipment shed. Curtis draped his arm over her shoulder, and she felt safe, comfortable, warm, lazy. But she knew it was only for a little while, at least for today.

"I have to go," she said. "I really need to get back."

"I've got some time off right now, let me walk you back."

"Well, I kind of have to sneak back. My parents are really weird about me being in town right now. If they see me walking up the street . . ." She drew her finger across her throat. "Come with me through the garden to the road at least."

Arm in arm they passed in front of town hall, and Kelly felt for a moment like they were any normal, happy couple out for a weekend stroll. When they got to her crossing point, they said goodbye with a kiss, and then a few more. Ten minutes after that, she was once more cutting hay, warmed by the afternoon sun and that last kiss.

———

Perhaps it was luck that Eli happened to be standing at the window of his town hall office when the Barton girl passed by, but Eli viewed luck as a neutral thing: it wasn't good or bad, it just *was*. Whether it turned out good or bad depended on what you did with it. As far as he knew, none of the Bartons had set foot in the hamlet since Monica Barton had thundered down after The Crime of the Century. Eli hadn't forgotten them, or that sweet young girl living with them. He'd just been busy putting out fires of one sort or another—and thinking about his next play.

She came into view, meandering, her head turning this way and that, and he *almost* tapped on the window to get her attention, *almost* invited her in for a little sit-down; but something stayed his hand. Instead, he stood in the darkened room, fingers spreading the slats on the venetian blinds, light and dark striping his face, and watched.

"What will you show me, hmm?"

Barton's girl drifted through the lot like dandelion fluff. Then she straightened like someone had jolted her with a cattle prod, and her face practically exploded in the biggest smile Eli had seen in weeks.

Of course. The Pinkney kid.

Eli chuckled as he watched them wrap around each other. When they finally separated, they stared into each other's eyes with gloppy expressions.

"That girl's got it bad. And so does he."

They moved across the lot, sat in the shade of the shed for a while, but Eli had seen enough. He left the window, dropped into the big, plush supervisor's chair and put his feet up on the desk. He picked up Arnie Bitzer's gavel and turned it over and over, occasionally tapping his palm with the smooth wood.

Abe Lincoln said, "If I had eight hours to chop down a tree, I'd spend six hours sharpening my axe." Preparation was the key. Though he didn't have to satisfy any political base or boost poll numbers with this demographic or that special interest, he had to play it smart, had to do this right. Harpursville had been free of the chaos that had taken root in the wider world, and it was because Eli had worked hard to make it that way. Getting the girl would require finesse. He wanted the girl but couldn't risk what he had built.

Eli's mind dwelled on the lovebirds. Pinkney was a good kid, a hard worker, honest and smart, who fit in pretty well and had made himself valuable. In the dark room, Eli grinned.

"I think Mr. Pinkney needs to stop in for a little visit," he said to the empty room.

CHAPTER 24

MR. BARTON DECIDED they should spend their afternoon fishing at the Silvas' pond.

"We need something a little different," he said. "Man—and woman—can't live on bread alone."

And so, they sat on the grassy verge of the pond, just a few feet apart, using fishing poles and tackle that had been liberated from the Silvas' basement.

It was the perfect setting. Birdsong rang out from the woods. Frogs called from the reeds and cattails ringing the pond. Bright green dragonflies zigzagged over the water's mirror-like surface. Every so often they heard the plop of a fish leaping after some unfortunate critter. They never saw the fish in the air, just saw the rings spreading away. It was romantic, like that scene in *The Little Mermaid*.

They weren't very good at it. Mr. Barton confessed that he had never learned to fish, and once Momma B. had thought of the pond, he had been largely too busy helping Jake with tree cutting or something. Dina's father had tried to teach her—once. As much of an outdoor girl as she was, she found she didn't want to be directly responsible for taking a life. That was a luxury she could no longer afford.

Neither of them had luck catching the bass and bluegills at first, and Dina had no luck with her own brand of fishing. She kicked off her shoes and stretched her legs out in front of her. Hiked her (borrowed) shorts higher up her thighs. Tied a knot in her (borrowed) shirt, exposing her flat midsection to the warm sun and Mr. Barton's gaze, rolled up the (borrowed) T-shirt sleeves to expose her shoulders. She planted her hands in the rough grass behind her and arched her back.

He cleared his throat. "I'm going to try my luck over there." He took his pole some twenty feet down the shore. Dina refocused her efforts on her own pole while wondering how to do this. Getting the attention of boys at school was easy, and she'd had plenty of men look at her and say things that were borderline inappropriate since she'd turned twelve—you pretty much just had to be breathing. This was completely different, and she was at a loss. She tried to put it out of her mind by narrowing her focus to where her fishing line disappeared beneath the surface, hoping that by not thinking about it, a solution would present itself.

"Oh! Oh! I've got one! I've got one!" Mr. Barton's excited voice startled her out of her thoughts. The tip of his rod was bent toward the pond. The tight fishing line cut a sharp V through the water as the panicked fish darted back and forth. Muscles jumped out on his arm as he yanked the fishing rod back.

"Use the reel," Dina shouted. "The reel!"

He looked at her, mouth agape, eyes blank. She dropped her pole in the grass and ran toward him, forgetting her chief objective. As she ran, she spun her hand in a tight circle. "The reel! The reel!"

"Oh, right!"

He started cranking. Dina pulled up beside him, holding her breath. Without thinking, she placed a hand on his arm. His muscles were as taut as the fishing line. The reel clicked as he worked it, reminding her of a windup robot toy her brother had.

The fish burst out of the water in a shower of sparkling drops. He yanked the rod back. The thrashing fish landed in the grass, flipping and fighting. For several seconds, they stood watching it. They caught a fish, now what? Dina's paralysis broke first. She jumped on it, pinning the slick, wriggling fish to the ground with both hands. It was torpedo-shaped, a foot and a half long, and surprisingly strong.

Mr. Barton fell to his knees beside her and worked the hook out of its gasping mouth. They were shoulder to warm shoulder, their faces inches apart, panting with excitement and effort. His hand partly covered hers as he grasped the fish's head.

Her heart raced, a stopwatch ticking down to a moment fast arriving. The hook came free with a gruesome ripping sound.

"Let's get it in the cooler," he said. "Wait here."

She kept her hands wrapped around the still struggling bass while he ran for the cooler. He came back, red-faced and grinning, the first honest smile she'd seen in weeks. He put the cooler down and flipped the lid open. She dropped the squirming fish into it with a plop, and he slammed it shut. They looked at each other with identical, idiot grins.

He caught her hand and held it high.

"Your new fishing cham-peens," he intoned, like an announcer at a boxing match.

Their hands were together. Their forearms touched. Their faces and chests were inches apart. All she had to do was lean in, just a few inches more.

Everything went fluttery inside. She hesitated, trying to read the look on his face.

Do it now!

He let her hand go and fell back on his backside, still grinning, but far away. The moment was lost.

"I'd better get this thing secured." The lure was a silvery, fish-like thing with multiple dangling hooks. He picked it up with dainty fingers. "That was great, Dina, thanks. I can't believe I forgot the reel. Let's see if we can catch some more."

She scrubbed fish slime off her palms onto the grass, berating herself. The setup had been perfect. She couldn't let that kind of opportunity pass again.

They fished for a while longer, and he was more like himself than he had been in a while, more chatty, making goofy jokes, and smiling a lot more. He caught a second bass, smaller than the first. She caught nothing. At dinner, though she was hungry, she couldn't eat. Every time she tried to swallow, her throat shrunk to a pinhole. She put her hand to her chest and forced the food down, felt the lump of fish work its way down, inch by slow inch, until it joined the rest of dinner in a squirmy mess in her stomach.

"Are you okay?"

Mr. Barton's voice made her jump in her seat. She nodded and looked at her plate, glanced at him through a curtain of hair. He frowned, and she dropped her gaze back to her fish.

"Are you sure?"

She managed a smile, met his eyes for a few seconds. "Just a little tired, that's all. That was a lot of excitement."

"Sure was." He scraped at the bits of fish left on his plate. "I don't know if it's from catching it yourself or if bass is tasty, but this is really good, don't you think?"

She slid her plate to the center of the table. "It's okay. I'm not much of a fish eater, I guess. You should finish it."

His grin faltered. "Are you sure you're all right?"

She nodded.

Furrows appeared across his forehead. "I give you a hard time about eating a lot, but you know I'm only kidding, right? I don't want you to think . . . I mean, you're not . . . ah, Jesus."

"It's okay," she said. "Don't worry."

"You're sure you don't want this?" She shook her head. He pulled her plate to his side of the table and dug in. She listened to the scrape and clink of his fork on the plate, listened to his sounds of satisfaction as he ate. She had let a golden opportunity slip past at the pond. She couldn't do it again.

When he finished, he got some hot water from the pot on the fire outside and poured it into the sink and started washing up.

She watched his shoulders flexing as he scrubbed and rinsed, cold inside.

Forget it, a voice in her said. *Just get up, go outside, and start picking bugs off the plants. Make good use of what's left of the day.*

You gotta give something to get something, kid, said a second voice.

She stood and grabbed the table edge for support. *This is not me. This is not the sort of thing I do.* But if she didn't, would she find herself in a far worse position?

Mr. Barton whistled a nonsense tune as he scrubbed at the dishes. She found herself right behind him, unaware of having taken the few steps needed to get there.

She reached with trembling hand and touched his shoulder.

He dropped the plate. It sent a wave sloshing over the side of the sink to the floor. He spun around. Up close, she saw the lines at the corners of his eyes, the deepening seams around his mouth, the gray that was taking over in his beard and spreading from his temples. *He's old like my father.* Dinner threatened to fly back out the way it had gone in.

"You scared me, Dina." Red spots appeared high on his cheeks above his beard. His Adam's apple bobbed. "Is something wrong?"

Forget everything. Do what you have to do. That was how she would get through this. Her heart rabbited the way it did right before the starting gun at a track meet. Her resolve turned slimy like the fish, threatened to slip through her fingers. She couldn't let that happen. She stepped forward and kissed him.

Maybe he recognized what was coming and dodged. Maybe some deep-down part of her rebelled and made a last-second course correction. Whatever the cause, she missed. Her lips found the crinkly hairs at the side of his mouth. *Oh shit, I botched it!* She slid her mouth to the left, scraping against his beard and mustache, finally found him. His lips were dry and pressed together. She took a deep breath through her nose and inhaled his smell, so different from the boys at school who doused themselves in Axe. Mr. Barton's smell was mellower, tinged with sweet wood smoke.

She pressed herself against him, wrapped her arms around his neck and kept kissing. His lips softened and started to open to her, and she wondered if she should slide her tongue in or not and if it would hurt or not when they did it— and then the tears started. They leaked from the corners of her eyes and rolled down her cheeks hot and fast, but it was too late to stop now.

Hard, strong hands clamped on her shoulders and pushed her firmly away. She opened her eyes. The kitchen shimmered. Shame overwhelmed her then. She tried to run, tried to pull away, but he held her tight and there was nowhere to go, and her legs, her legs turned into rubber bands and wouldn't carry her away and she would have collapsed completely, but he was holding onto her and oh God, she didn't want to do it, and he was going to make her do it now anyway and then he was going to kick her out anyway and it was all for nothing.

"Dina." His voice was thick and heavy. "Dina."

"Oh God. I'm so sorry," she said through her hand.

Again, she tried to twist away, but he held onto her and he guided her across the room, lowered her gently into a chair. She put her face in her hands—blocked out the kitchen, him, and the world—and cried into them. It all came out, everything she had been holding in since the day they failed to get home. She cried for her parents, for her brother and sister—who could be dead for all she knew—and for everyone who had died because of this stupid blackout. She cried for the life that was gone, the life that looked a hell of a lot better than what she now faced. He would kick her out for sure. She had betrayed his trust, broken up his marriage and family, and now what choice did he have but to turn her out? He would probably deliver her to Sobchuk himself. "You can have her," he would say. "She's a little slut." And she would deserve it, wouldn't she? She'd deserve to be stuck slaving for Sobchuk, cleaning his house and working his garden and cooking his meals by day, and getting raped by him all night.

She cried until all her breath was gone; still there was more, but she couldn't cry because there was no air. Little spots appeared in the blackness, spiral galaxies and starburst patterns against her closed eyelids.

"Breathe, Dina." His voice was buzzy and far away.

She opened her eyes. The kitchen floor between her feet was reduced to a bright circle the size of a plate, surrounded by swirling gray and black.

"Breathe," he said, louder this time, right by her ear, and she did. She took in a great, big whooping breath; it made a horrible sound, but her lungs were full. She started crying all the air right back out again, and then his arms encircled her, his hand stroked the back of her head. He told her it was going to be okay; everything was going to be fine, don't worry, it's all okay. But it wasn't okay, it wouldn't be okay, not ever again.

She didn't know how long she cried but she finally finished, sat there, empty like the husks of cicadas they found on the trees in summer.

"Here." His voice was kind. He pressed a glass of water into her hand. She couldn't look at him; she kept her eyes down, looked at the geometric shapes on the kitchen tiles, squares with little fleur-de-lis. She found patterns in them, lines and diagonals and squares, and occupied her mind with them. Anything was better than what she had just done. She took a tiny sip of water.

The kitchen was hot. Her whole body was hot but most of all her face. All she could think was *I blew it*, and she wondered if maybe he would at least let her slip out the door and try her luck on her own out there somewhere. She would live in the woods like an outlaw, stealing ears of corn from gardens and living on wild berries while working her way toward home. Seven miles by road, shorter as the crow flies. There were a lot of woods between here and there. She started plotting a route in her head, imagined traveling by night. How many days would it take? Three? Four? She would take the fireplace poker from upstairs for protection.

The water was tepid and tasted of metal, but it soothed her raw throat. She just wished she had something to blow her nose in—paper towels, napkins, toilet paper, and tissues were far in the past. As if the thought had shown up in a cartoon word balloon over her head, Mr. Barton pushed a cloth into her hand, an old dishrag. She wiped her eyes and nose, then with a great, unladylike snort that would have made her mother faint, she spat a foul-tasting gob into the cloth and washed the taste away with another gulp of water.

She lifted her head a fraction, glanced at him out of the corner of her eye. He leaned against the useless dishwasher. She looked down at his scuffed and fraying sneakers.

"Are you okay?"

She shook her head.

"Well, you have to be." His voice was stern, no-nonsense, a very un-Mr. Barton-like tone. She picked her head up a little more, looked at him a little more directly. "Our survival depends on it, Dina. You've got to pull yourself together. There's a lot of work to do, and I can't do it alone. So you've *got* to be okay, got it?"

She nodded, sniffed, took another drink of water and managed to meet his eyes.

"I'm . . . I'm so sorry, Mr. Barton." Her throat felt like she'd gargled with glass. Fresh tears welled. "I just thought . . . I thought . . ."

There was no way to save face, no lie that could smooth it over. She took a deep breath and finally met his eye.

"I was afraid. I thought you were going to send me away. With him. And I just thought, well . . ." She looked back to the floor. "God, how can you stand to look at me?"

A chair leg scraped on the linoleum. His voice came from right in front of her.

"I'm very sorry you felt you had to do that." He took her hand and gave it a gentle squeeze. "Look at me. Please."

It took everything she had to meet his gaze. To her surprise, he didn't look angry. Sad, maybe, but not angry.

"There have never, ever been terms or conditions on you staying here. There never have been, there never will be. I wouldn't give you to him or to anyone. And as much as I want Mrs. Barton back, I won't turn you out to make that happen. Never. Understand?"

The truth was plain on his face. She nodded.

"As far as I'm concerned, this"—he made a twirling motion with his finger—"never happened. Okay?"

She sniffed again, wiped her eyes, nodded.

He gave her hand another squeeze then rose from the table. "I've got to finish up here. Why don't you check on the garden?"

When she got up, the world grayed at the edges and her knees wobbled a little. After a second, the room brightened, and her legs steadied. Water sloshed in the sink. Plates and silverware clinked. When she was certain her legs would keep her upright, she went to the door, paused, and looked back over her shoulder.

"Thank you, Mr. B."

He held up a dripping hand and waved without turning around. She went out into the warm evening.

———

The screen door clicked quietly into place. Kevin listened to her footsteps fade, then waited anxiously for her to come into view in the window over the sink. It took her longer than normal, and he worried that she might just take off. When she appeared, he let out a long, shuddery breath. She didn't weed or pick bugs off the tomatoes, she just sat on one of the chairs. She drew her legs up, wrapped her arms around her knees, and laid her head down. From the way her sides hitched, he knew she was crying again and he wished he could comfort her, assure her that everything would be okay—but he needed time.

Cold sweat slicked his forehead. A cramp gripped his stomach. He clutched the edge of the sink, squeezing his throat tight against the rising nausea. He didn't want to puke in the sink, but he didn't trust his ability to get to the toilet. He hung on until the wave passed. When it did, he again looked out the window. Dina was still in the chair and that was good. He dried his hands, went upstairs, and sat on the edge of his bed.

A minute passed. Another. He punched himself on the thigh. The meaty thunk of his fist echoed in the silent room.

"Asshole!"

He had seen it coming. They had spent a lot of time together since the blackout, more since Monica and Kelly left. But over the last few days she'd been putting herself in his path more than usual. He had attributed it initially to loneliness or her need for assurance but he'd seen it coming, he'd seen it edging toward something else. Monica's words rang sharply in his head, and she was right: he *had* enjoyed Dina's clumsy flirtations. It was cute but harmless.

"Bullshit!" He socked his thigh again. A deep ache spread through the muscle. "You saw. You *knew*. And you didn't stop it. You wanted it, you sick bastard."

Bullshit, indeed. He *had* seen it coming and he hadn't stopped it. Sure, he had backed away this afternoon at the pond, but when he heard her behind him in the kitchen? When he turned and found her right there, right behind him? What was coming was plain in her eyes, on her lips. He had seen, he had understood, and he hadn't tried to stop it, hadn't deflected her with some joke or quip. When her lips found his, something nasty happened. A hungry voice whispered in his head, low and insistent, the voice of lust and desire, responding to her warm lips and the press of her body.

Go with it, the voice said. *Let her take it as far as she wants. If she leads, it won't be your fault.*

The voice was seductive, whispering of the pleasures of young, desirable flesh, the pleasure of a long, lean body so different from his wife's, the only body he had known for more than twenty years.

There was no denying the movement of his lips in response to hers, or the movement of other parts of him. His hands had risen on their own, and he wasn't sure at first where they were going or what they would do when they got there.

The voice had cautioned him. *Just respond. Follow her lead. Don't force anything.*

The voice was his own, but the idea was eerily similar to someone else: Eli Sobchuk. "I'm not going to force anything," Sobchuk had said. "But if she were to be amenable—"

"Jesus, I'm no better than him."

He shuddered and gritted his teeth against a fresh wave of nausea. He wanted to stop thinking but he couldn't.

It was his greatest failure, worse than standing by while his wife ran kids off of Curtis Pinkney's car or shot at Maybe-George Morris from the porch or extracted wood from the town supplies and extra patrols from Sobchuk in the aftermath. It was worse than handing over his bag with their food and water to Dougie Austin and his band of pirates. He had almost given in to his basest instinct, had almost violated the sacred trust in the worst possible way, had almost done what Sobchuk and Monica said he wanted to do.

Almost.

Kevin sat up a little straighter.

"Almost," he said aloud. "Almost. It doesn't matter how close you came because you didn't. *You* stopped it. And you won't let it happen again."

A warm feeling spread through his chest. It had been close, yes. Part of him *had* wanted to let it happen, but in the end, he had come to his senses. He, Kevin Barton, had been strong. He had not broken. Goldie Barton would have gone along, would have let things happen, because Goldie always went with what others wanted. But Goldie had been replaced. The patina had been worn away, revealing something—someone—else beneath.

"I am strong."

Strong was not a word he had applied to himself before. He said it again, "I am strong." It felt right, it felt good.

Kevin stood and grabbed a light sweatshirt from the pile of clothes, then grabbed a second one for Dina. The mosquitoes had been bad all week. They needed a cover-up if they were going to work outside at this hour. He strode from the room, feeling better than he had since Monica had left.

CHAPTER 25

JAKE WATCHED MONICA move about the kitchen in quick, jerky movements. She banged a cupboard door open. Clanged a pan on the counter. Threw clean silverware back into a drawer. Her pretty face was drawn, her mouth turned down at the corners. Jake watched her the way he watched the big snapper turtles that sometimes laid eggs in the sandy slope behind the barn: carefully. Snappers were quick and ornery. He gave them a wide berth. He wanted to give Monica Barton a wide berth, too, but he could feel the weight of Alma's pale-blue eyes on his back, could feel her urging him on. More so, he felt the weight of winter bearing down on them.

Time to get on with it. They were hanging in there for now, but they needed all six of them working all together, at the same time, to get through this. The real work was ahead of them, and summers were short. There was a lot to get done.

Alma apparently decided it was time to push things along. "Jake, maybe you can help Monica bring in some more water?"

"I don't need any help." Monica's voice was gutting knife sharp.

Jake could take a hint. His knees creaked as he pushed himself up from the table.

"It's okay, those're heavy buckets."

Monica looked from one Hillman to the other, eyes narrowed. *She's quick on the uptake,* he thought. She grabbed two pairs of five-gallon buckets from the counter and was out the door. By the time he caught up to her, she had one half full. She glared at the sparkling water streaming out of the faucet as if she could speed it up with a look.

"Whew, these old legs ain't what they used to be." Jake mopped his forehead with his bandanna and eyed the clouds, trying to read the weather. He didn't need to look at Monica to know *her* forecast.

"I can handle this myself."

"Well, why make two trips when you can make one? Water's heavy."

The creek water smelled of cold metal. Monica shifted one bucket out of the way, put the empty one beneath the spigot. Maybe she could speed up the water after all—it seemed to be flowing faster than normal.

He cleared his throat.

"Save it, Jake." She took a deep breath and released it, sending some of the hardness to the sky with it. When she resumed, her voice was like river stones—hard, but with some of the edge worn off. "I know you're trying to help, but there's nothing to say. He's made his decision, and I've made mine."

Jake kicked at the ground. It was one thing doling out unsolicited advice about fertilizer or chopping corn or pasture rotation on Thandie's front porch—that stuff was public in a small town, and the sort of thing you could talk about anywhere. What happened behind the closed doors of a marriage was something else entirely. You kept out of it unless asked. And even then, you went on light feet.

"Whatever happened is between you and him. But I've gotten to know the two of you pretty well these last couple months, and I know you love each other—"

"Don't talk about love." She traded bucket number two for number three. A little water spilled. It spattered on the ground between them. "Don't talk about love. He's shown what love is worth to him."

Her voice was brittle, like skim ice, and he thought for a second she might cry. Alma always said men died younger than women because they bottled everything up; Monica Barton was bottled and under pressure. Maybe that was what she really needed.

She pushed her hair back from her face. "I know you're trying to help. But he put that girl above his own family. He put her safety above his daughter's, or mine. What does that tell you?"

Jake felt like he was back in 'Nam, walking point. He could practically hear the whop-whop-whop of Hueys. Walking point was terrifying, especially on those warm, lazy days when it felt like nothing bad could happen. Men got lazy on those days, careless. Then someone would step on a mine or a punji stick and all hell would break loose, and they'd spend the next twenty minutes firing blind into the jungle while rifle rounds sizzled past their ears, wounded buddies screamed for help, and mortars whistled down into their midst. And it always started with that one step. Jake was about to take that step.

"I think he's trying to protect all of you."

"Protect, hell. The only thing he's trying to protect is his cheap—I don't even know the right word for it. He says she's like a daughter to him." She laughed, a short, bitter bark. "I've seen him look at her, Jake. He doesn't look at Kelly that way, and you don't look at either of them that way."

So it was true, what she thought. He couldn't believe it was true, but stranger things had happened. He put a hand on the back of his neck, rubbed at a knot of muscle. "Maybe you're seeing what you want to see."

She put her hands on her hips. Water overflowed the bucket. It carved a path through the mud and disappeared in the grass.

"Why would I want to see that?"

"Wait, wait, wait."

He took off his hat and ran his arm across his brow, wishing for all the world he was riding his tractor around in the sun, bringing a load of hay out to the herd, or cutting a tree, raking hay, shoveling manure, even. Anywhere but here. Why wasn't Alma the one having this conversation?

"I don't mean you wanted to see it. Who would? I'm just not so good with words, Monica. Give me a second here."

He looked up at the big maple shading the yard. A large gray hornet's nest was tucked in the branches about twenty feet up. He frowned. Bad winter coming.

"I don't think you're going to find the answer up there, Jake."

For the first time since she arrived, he heard the hint of a smile in her voice. He laughed.

"You sound like Alma. I don't mean you'd *want* to see it." He scratched his chin, though it wasn't itchy. "You ever take one of those blot tests the shrinks use?"

"A Rorschach test?"

"Yeah, Rorschach test, that's it. I had to take one when I went in th'Army. They show you a blob and say, 'What do you see?' and you say, 'A butterfly' and they say, 'Mmhm' and then they show you another and another, and you see what you see and tell them. But if someone holds up the blot and says, 'This is a bat', you're gonna see a bat."

"Nobody told me what I . . ." Plow lines appeared across her forehead. "What is it?"

"Nothing."

She was still frowning, but it looked different than the scowl she'd been wearing since her arrival. Jake thought he'd better lay off for now, which was just as well. When you reached the end of your patrol line, you didn't keep going just to see what was around the bend, you turned round and beat feet for base.

"Here, let me get those buckets." Jake grimaced and lifted the two full buckets. Carrying these pails was killing him. He'd been meaning to extend the line clear into the house, but he needed Kevin for that. Monica slid the last empty bucket under the spigot with her foot.

"I'll bring in these two when they're full. Do you . . . do you need me for anything here? I think we need some meat."

There were a million things he needed her for, but maybe a little time now would yield a happier, more productive Monica later. And they would all benefit from that.

"Sure. I've got a hankering for some grouse. Think you can get one?"

"I'll see what I can do."

He was at the door when she caught up to him with her two full buckets, and he marveled at how strong she was for such a little woman. He put one of his buckets down and held the door open for her. She'd be shed of the water soon enough; maybe she could get rid of her other burden in the woods. He grunted his way up the steps and into the kitchen and set his buckets down. Alma planted a kiss on his cheek and patted him on the chest. That was a nice reward too.

—

Eli woke in an especially fine mood. He put on clean clothes, culled from the massive pile in town hall. First choice on supplies was one of the benefits of leadership. He hummed a power ballad from one of the hard rock groups he listened to in high school as he went downstairs.

It was going to be a good day. The Pinkney kid had paid off in spades. It was amazing how a little buttering up about all the fine work he'd been doing in town could loosen a boy's tongue. A few minutes of that, a casual turn of the conversation, and the kid had spilled his girlfriend's dirty little family secrets all over the table. Just Barton and the girl, all alone in that big house. Easy pickings. It cost him nothing but time, unlike George Morris, whose price had been a little steeper.

Even the sight of his messy house couldn't put a damper on his day, not today, because in a few hours, he was going to have his own little housemaid to take care of things.

"Yes, indeed," he said on his way out the door. "Taking care of a *lot* of things."

He walked down Main Street, surveying the town—his town—as he went. The Four Corners, where his *career* had been launched with one simple decision, one single act of faith; faith that one man in the road was more formidable than a crowd. No one had followed him into the road, not until the Army stopped, but they followed him now. He had won far more than a few boxes of food that day.

And he would win today. He had been surprised that Barton hadn't delivered the girl. The man didn't seem like the refusing type. He was a follower, a sheep, a man eager to please, but even sheep had lines they wouldn't cross. Barton's line was the girl. Well, that's what sheepdogs were for. With a sheepdog or two nipping at his heels, Barton would cave.

As for the girl, he'd be nice to her, and no matter how horny he got, he wouldn't force anything. He was no rapist. It might take some time; it might take more effort than the girls in Oneonta, but she'd give it up. Every no was one step closer to a yes.

He smiled and exchanged greetings with people on his way to town hall. *His* people. If it came to it, he could turn the whole damn town against Barton. He'd already turned the man's wife against him, this would be easy. All he needed was some kind of evidence against him, some kind of charge that he was stealing wood or vegetables or eggs. It wouldn't take much; Hitler stirred up the Germans against Poland with a series of phony provocations in the weeks leading up to the invasion. It had been easy enough to get George Morris to steal wood from the Bartons. In times like these, you could get anyone to do just about anything for a little bit of food or wood.

Uncle Henry was handing out work assignments when Eli arrived. After some glad-handing and a few inspirational words in the parking lot, Eli went inside. He picked a box of Pop-Tarts off the pantry pile and took his seat behind the judge's bench, relishing the frosted strawberry breakfast pastry. He would need to find something to occupy Uncle Henry this morning. Something on the other side of town. His uncle would not approve of his plans.

A knock sounded on the door. Roger came in with the night patrol's report. "Had a group of five trying to set up in the old Bucek place." He grinned and showed Eli some fresh scrapes on his knuckles. "We reached an agreement with them." His cousin was well suited indeed to security.

"Go see Gail and make sure that's cleaned up, you don't need to get an infection," Eli said. "Then grab a couple hours of shut-eye, get Troy—no, wait a minute. Get that new guy, Big Red. You know who I mean?" Roger nodded. "Yeah, he's big and he's got a mean streak in him. Get him and meet me here at lunchtime. We're going to pay a little visit to our friend up the hill this morning."

"Who, Jake?"

"No, Barton."

Eli slid a second packet out of the Pop-Tarts box and tossed it over. Roger caught it and tore it open greedily.

"Bring something along to keep the peace, just in case. I don't think we'll have any trouble though."

Roger stopped, mid-chew, a glimmer in his eye. "Peacekeeper? What kind?"

"Something quiet. I want finesse, not force, but we might need a judicious application of the latter." Eli pointed at the Pop-Tart in his cousin's hand. "Don't go outside till you finish that. When you go, send Uncle Henry in. I've got a job for him."

Roger wolfed down the first Pop-Tart and started on the second.

Henry, he decided, was needed to help shore up the barricade on the state road north of town. That would keep him occupied while Eli attended to his business up the hill.

Yes, it's going to be a good day, indeed.

———

Since Dina's attempted seduction, they had skittered around each other like mice, avoiding eye contact, leaving absurdly large space between them, and having short, awkward conversations. Despite her insistence that she was okay, he worried that she might take off after all.

They worked at opposite ends of the garden, pulling weeds and picking bugs. Even with twenty feet of corn, beans, tomatoes, and other plants between them, he could feel her back there. *Maybe I should go fishing instead.* He straightened to stretch his aching back, looking out over the hamlet below, and froze.

Three figures approached along the county road. It was closing on noon, the sun was high and the air hot, but Kevin grew cold. There was no mistaking the short, barrel shape of Eli Sobchuk. Flanking him were two taller figures. Kevin could tell by the slouch that one of them was Roger Fields. He was twirling something around as he walked, something that was too short to be a walking stick, too wide at the end to be a golf club.

Keep going, keep going. The words repeated in his head like a prayer, as he silently urged them to follow the county road. They didn't. They turned onto Harpur's Hill Road, and the cold Kevin felt turned to ice as he recognized the third person. He had lost weight, replaced flab with lean muscle, but he still had that red hair. Dougie Austin. Kevin was frozen solid, unable to move, unable to make a sound as they came up the hill. Sobchuk, with Roger Fields and Dougie Austin, come to collect. They were halfway to the driveway when his jaw unstuck.

"Dina," he said, through a dry mouth. "You need to get out of here."

"What?" The hurt was palpable in her voice.

"I didn't mean it that way," he said. "Sobchuk. Sobchuk's coming. Go!"

"What? Sob—oh. Oh! Where? Where am I supposed to go?"

They hadn't planned for this. Thoughts zigged and zagged. Run. Hide. He didn't want to send her into the woods because anyone could be out there. Jake's? They'd see her run across the road, and he didn't know if anyone was home.

"Inside. I don't know. Quick, they're almost here!"

She dropped her basket and ran for the house, disappearing through the back-front door. Kevin wiped his sweaty palms on his jeans. A cold rock seemed to have settled in the pit of his stomach. The deep, steady breaths he took did nothing to quiet the hammer blows in his chest.

"You can do this," he said to himself. "You are strong. You can do this."

Swallowing his fear, he went to meet them at the end of the driveway.

—

Jake had asked for grouse, but Monica hadn't exactly been thinking clearly when she left the house—she'd grabbed the rifle instead of the shotgun. Maybe she was good enough to plunk a grouse in the eye with a rifle; more likely she'd just be wasting ammunition. Jake. He had gotten into her head and muddied her mind; she needed the woods to clear it.

Emotion had been running roughshod over intellect lately, a problem of hers that went back as far as she could remember. She was making everyone miserable as a result. She knew it and she was powerless to stop it. Worse, since leaving Kevin, she'd been little more than a passenger at the Hillman house, and that, she knew, wouldn't cut it. She was eating food, drinking water, taking up space, and sapping everyone else's energy in the process. In short, she was becoming the very thing she had feared about Dina in the early days of the blackout, and Dina had never been a passenger. The girl had always worked hard, had contributed.

A light breeze shushed through the soft hemlock needles. Small birds made small sounds high overhead, small feet crept in the litter of twigs and last year's leaves carpeting the spongy forest floor. The hemlock's trunk was wide and solid against her back. She closed her eyes and inhaled deeply, cleansing herself with the piney scent of the tree and the damp smell of leaf mold, the clean smell of the forest.

She sat with the rifle laid across her lap, placed her hands flat on the ground on either side of her and dug her fingers into the duff. Grit wedged beneath her nails. Her fingertips scraped against chunks of rock. Last year's dried needles crackled in her grip. A brown spider scuttled away. She didn't recoil from it. Spiders, ants, worms, bugs of all kinds were fine outside. She thought of Dina, who took such care to wash all the weird greens and roots and mushrooms she brought in to keep the bugs out, how she took care to never let the screen door slam, how she always seemed to be tuned in to Monica's moods and phobias, and her eyes filled with tears.

She had been unfair to Dina. Crushes were crushes, they couldn't be helped, and she'd had her own share as a teen. While her girlfriends all liked the young, athletic gym teacher in their school, Monica had fallen hard for Mr. Fitzsimmons, the slightly graying, paunchy trigonometry teacher. Why? Who knew?

Kevin, however, should have known better. Instead, he seemed to encourage her, egging her on, as if he were excited by her attention. It just wasn't right. And she had left them together.

"Maybe you're seeing what you want to see," Jake had said, and his words had struck a particular chord. Why, she didn't know. No woman wants to see her husband flirting with anyone, let alone a teenage girl. Before the blackout, they had been living in the age of trade-ins and cheap upgrades. New software and operating system, new car, new wife or girlfriend. Men were always trading in their women, looking for someone younger, someone prettier, someone with bigger tits and a tighter ass, someone who was either more interested in sex or more willing to put up with it on demand. Sooner or later, the younger wives would be saddled with the same problems as the older ones though. What then?

A chipmunk squeaked. Monica looked around, but she was alone, just her and her thoughts; thoughts she didn't want to entertain but needed to. There were so many things, so many little signs. Kevin's sex drive had increased quite a bit since the blackout—did he think of *her* when they made love? There was the way he always seemed to be talking to her. "She misses her family," he had said. "I'm just trying to make her feel a part of things." And that had rankled, because the implication was that *she* wasn't doing enough to make Dina feel welcome. Well, the truth hurt, didn't it?

And that was another part of it too. He was so sensitive to Dina's moods and her needs, yet he had done his best to keep Kelly away from Curtis and avoided serious conversation about him or Kelly's feelings for him.

But the clincher was that he fought for her. That was what she kept coming back to.

The only thing Kevin had ever fought for was love. *Her* love. He had done it when they were still in college and had been dating a while. They weren't exclusive. She had started dating another boy, and Kevin had responded. Not with violence, not with fists, but action. He had pursued her with what Grandmother Willsey called, "Good old-fashioned courtin'!" and he had won. Now he was fighting for her, and, if his story was to be believed, against a man who had all the power of the town behind him. He was fighting for a girl who wasn't even part of his family. He had kept things from Monica and put them all at risk. It wasn't like him, it wasn't part of his nature, and that was why she was sure he must be carrying on.

A whining mosquito raised the hairs on the back of her neck. Kevin tossed aside his family for Dina. But what did it mean to be family? He had quit his job and moved three hundred miles upstate when Monica's mother got sick. For three years he ran errands and did chores for her mother, cleaning gutters, patching the roof, painting bedrooms and hallways, hauling crap down from the attic and up from the cellar to take to the dump. He burned sick days and personal time to drive Mom to her appointments and sat with her for hours in hospice at the end, and he never complained. On more than one occasion, she had asked him why he was so nice to her, and he had said, "She's family. You've got to take care of family."

Deep down, she thought he *really* wanted to tell her, "She's your mother, take care of her yourself." Part of her almost *wanted* him to say that because it would have assuaged her own guilt. Were the shoe on the other foot, she wasn't sure she'd be willing to do the same for Kevin's parents, even though she loved them. She certainly wouldn't have been so cheerful about it.

Family. Kelly listed Dina as her sister on her Facebook page. When friends or relatives visited and Dina was there—which was most of the time—Kevin introduced her as "our second daughter." He greeted her with things like, "How's my girl today?" And, as Kevin had maddeningly pointed out, Monica herself had been the one to suggest taking Dina in when the Duchess was threatening to move in the middle of the school year. Why?

"She's family."

Family. Her words, her logic. *She* had been the first to declare Dina McCray family, but it was Kevin who lived it. She talked the talk; Kevin walked the walk.

"Family doesn't flirt with family. I know what I'm seeing." The chipmunk squeaked a sharp rebuke and dived into a hole beneath a log.

Jake's talk of inkblots and imaginary butterflies and bats called it all into question. Her problem with Dina had started with food. No, not with food, with fear. Everything rose out of that. She was afraid, afraid of dying, afraid of seeing her daughter and her husband starve. She had been looking for a reason to push Dina out. Of course, she had found one. Or, more correctly, someone had planted the reason in her mind. Someone told her the butterfly was a bat. Someone who had no stake in their life, but maybe wanted something from it nonetheless. And who was that?

"Sobchuk. That bastard."

Sobchuk interpreted the inkblot for her. Sobchuk had twisted her emotions and concerns over food and supplies into fear of something worse. He had projected his own image onto her husband, and she had let him, even though she knew what he was all about and had known it for a long time.

For the first three years they lived here, Sobchuk was the technician Schuyler sent to do the yearly maintenance on their furnace. While she found his country-folksy manner phony, he knew his way around a furnace, and there were no problems with him. Until the last time.

Monica had drawn the short straw and stayed home to wait. After Kelly and Kevin left for school and work, she checked up on emails and the day's news. It would have been fine, except Sobchuk did something no service person had done before or since: he arrived early. And she was still in her nightgown.

It was a filmy, sexy thing, high on her thighs and low on her chest, held up with spaghetti straps, a holdover from the night before, when she had used it to seduce Kevin. Her robe, carefully cinched while Kelly was home, had come undone. Monica breezed into the kitchen for one last cup of coffee, her open robe billowing wide, and there he was, his hand raised to knock on the kitchen door.

His dull eyes popped wide. Monica felt a momentary jolt of excitement. Here she was, on the downhill slope to forty, giving an obvious thrill to a man who was at least ten years younger.

He made no effort to look away. A wolfish grin split his face. The brief thrill became a creeping chill from her scalp all the way down her neck. She had a brief urge to run upstairs and cover up, but this was her house; she wasn't going to run away from anyone, damn it. She pulled her robe tight, belted it even tighter, crossed her arms even tighter than that, and opened the door.

His small, even teeth gleamed. He wasn't much taller than she, but he was big with powerful-looking hands and a deep chest.

"Good morning, Missus Barton!"

He took a big step inside the door. His eyes cut down her front, tracing the V formed by the folds of her robe. They lingered on the bare flesh visible at her throat, following the contours of her breasts, running down the curve of her calves to her naked feet.

"You're letting cold air in."

He took another step in. She had to reach around him to close the door, putting her far closer than she wanted to be. He smelled of stale coffee and oil.

"I'm here to service your furnace," he said.

Oh my God, I'm in some '70s porno film. It almost made her laugh, but he seemed bigger than when he'd stepped into the house, like the spongy bath toys Kelly played with, the ones that expanded two or three times in the water. She stepped back, doing everything possible not to touch him, and pointed at the basement door, one arm wrapped securely around herself.

"Downstairs," she said in a flat voice. "Same as always."

He tipped his head forward in acknowledgment and passed by, his heavy boots clomping down the stairs into the basement. As soon as he was out of sight, she ran upstairs and put on the loosest, frumpiest clothes she could find: baggy pants, turtleneck, oversized sweater, anything to hide her shape and put an extra barrier between his eyes and her body. The sort of clothes she'd worn in middle school in a vain attempt to stop kids from noticing her early developing chest and taunting her with names like "Moo-nica."

For the next half hour, bangs, clanks, and clicks filtered up through the floorboards as he worked. Monica wore out a track on the first floor, kitchen to dining room to den to living room, unable to concentrate on anything, all too aware of the empty house and the stranger in the basement. Finally, his feet pounded back up the stairs. She met him in the kitchen. The odor of oil hung around him like a cloud.

"Everything looks fine, Missus Barton. Real fine."

He handed her a sheet of paper and walked her through a laundry list of things she didn't care much about—filters and nozzles, flue gasses and internal pressure, temperature settings and check valves. She "uh huh'd" and "I see'd" and "ok'd" in the proper places, while trying to keep at least two feet of space between them.

"Are all your registers working?" he said. "You getting proper heat through the house? You getting enough upstairs?"

"We're fine."

"You may have some air in the pipes. I can bleed that off for you if you want."

"It's fine. We can take care of it ourselves, thank you."

Five seconds that felt like fifty passed.

"Okay. If you have any problems, just give us a call. Have a nice day."

The blast of cold air as he opened the door couldn't blow out the smell of oil that lingered behind. She watched him load his gear into his van, then sit in it for several minutes, filling out paperwork and drinking from a thermos. Finally, he backed out of the driveway and rolled down the hill on his way to the next job. She let out a breath she didn't know she'd been holding.

She would have let it go.

She told herself she imagined the whole thing, that it was a coincidence of situation and professional jargon that relied on potentially double-edged words like *nozzle* and *injector* and *nipple valve*. Hell, she might have been insulted if he *hadn't* reacted the way he did, and she wondered if the guys at Schuyler dreamed about walking into something like this. From that perspective, he would have been a fool *not* to have gone on his little fishing expedition.

She would have let it go, but he was back fifteen minutes later.

"Sorry," he said, though he didn't look at all sorry. "I left my pliers downstairs. Can't do the job without the right tool."

What was almost funny before was no longer close to being funny now, and it wasn't flattering. It scared her, and Monica Barton didn't like being scared, especially not in her own house.

"Get them and go."

Back to the basement he went. She went straight to the phone and called Kevin. She didn't tell him what Sobchuk was up to, but she wanted Sobchuk to know she was in contact with the outside world, just in case he got any other funny ideas while he was downstairs.

He came back up and stopped in the doorway. "Got them," he said, holding up a grimy tool.

She covered the mouthpiece with her hand. "Great. Goodbye." Then she uncovered the phone. "No, not you, honey. Schuyler's here, just finishing up the furnace. Yep. Everything's fine. Yep."

She stayed on the phone until he was gone. Twenty minutes later, she had dumped Schuyler in favor of Murray Oil & Gas.

Monica put her head back and looked at the canopy high above. Spots of sunlight fell on her face. Sobchuk had played on her jealousies and her insecurities. Why? Maybe he hoped she'd turn Dina out on the street and he could scoop her up like some old-style truant officer. To her great shame, that was exactly what she tried to do. If Kevin hadn't stuck to his guns, if he hadn't decided to fight, Dina might be at Sobchuk's house right now. She *knew* what Sobchuk was all about and had played right into his hands. Kevin, blinded as he was by his hero worship of Sobchuk, had still managed to say no to him. And now they were in that big house alone, defenseless.

"Shit, Kevin. What have I done?"

She sprang to her feet and dusted bits and pieces of the forest floor off her damp bottom. Hunting could wait. She owed two people—no, five people, really—an apology. Everyone had been affected by her anger and stupidity. It wouldn't be easy but it had to be done. She would start with Kevin.

CHAPTER 26

KEVIN STOOD AT the edge of his driveway, hoping Sobchuk and his crew would say hello and keep on going. They didn't. They stopped directly in front of him, Sobchuk huffing a little, his face red from the exertion of walking up the hill. Roger and Dougie flanked their leader, hanging back a few steps. The object Roger had been twirling around was a baseball bat. Dougie's eyes widened in recognition, then grinned, the grin of a snake about to devour its prey.

"Good afternoon," Kevin said with a nod. Polite, not friendly.

"You disappoint me, Barton," Sobchuk said. "I asked nice, you didn't deliver, so I'm here to collect."

No folksy good humor here. No grins, no winks, no backslapping, just cold, hard business. Kevin glanced at Roger, at the baseball bat that rested on his shoulder. It looked just like the one leaning uselessly against the wall next to Kevin's bed.

Keep them in front of you. Maybe you can fake your way out of this. You are strong. You can do this.

"Don't do this, Eli. You've done great things. Don't ruin it."

Sobchuk's big chest grew a size or two. Kevin pushed on. Maybe he could flatter him to reason.

"You could be remembered as a great man, Eli. Right up there with Roosevelt, with . . . with . . . Giuliani after 9/11. You put your life on the line for this town. But if you do this, Eli, then you're no different from every other fat cat with his hand in the barrel. Only instead of money for yourself or sweetheart deals for your pals, you'll be throwing it all away for sex. With a sixteen-year-old." Kevin swiped his tongue across his dry lips, threw a quick glance up the street. Jake's dooryard seemed impossibly far away now, and if anyone was out there looking this way, they might not see anything due to the scrub that had grown up at the road's edge all summer. "I can't do anything about Albany or Washington. For all I know, there is no Albany or Washington anymore. But I can do something about you."

Sobchuk laughed. It started deep in his gut, rolled up his chest and out into the calm late summer air. Behind him, Dougie and Roger exchanged smirks.

Sobchuk pinched his thumb and forefinger into the inner corner of each eye.

"Hoo, that's good. I don't get near enough laughs in a day. 'I can do something about you.' What are you going to do about me? Not vote for me? Run against me? That's a laugh." His good humor evaporated. "You sit up here in your fancy house and look down on us like you're better than us, but you don't know shit about shit, Barton. You don't know what it takes to run this thing or how this town works."

"Dina's a *person*, not a thing. She doesn't want to go with you. Don't tarnish your legacy, Eli. What will you gain? A few days, a few weeks of"—he curled his lip—"pleasure? And how much pleasure will you get by raping her?"

Sobchuk looked genuinely offended.

"That's just—that's just—I'm no rapist, Barton. Like I said, I'll be nice, and if she happens to take a liking to me, well, we'll see what happens. And don't get me started on age of consent." Sobchuk smirked. "It wasn't that long ago that the age of consent in this great state of ours was ten, believe it or not. People used to get married right at twelve or thirteen."

"In the Middle Ages," Kevin said. "People had to start young then. They were lucky to reach thirty."

"Look around you, Barton. We're a third-world country now. This is the new Middle Ages. I'm thirty-three, that makes me an old man. And you?" He snorted. "You're ancient. When this thing started, we had sixty-five able-bodied adults. We've picked up a few and we've lost a few, but what do you think is going to happen come winter?"

"I'm no pimp. She's a child, Eli. A child."

Sobchuk laughed, his breath hot on Kevin's face. "She's no child. Hell, she's probably not even a virgin. You know how kids are. Even if she hasn't gotten her cherry popped, she's probably given a hummer or two. From what I hear, high school girls give out BJs like they're candy. Stand aside, Barton."

Sobchuk took a step to his left.

Kevin shadowed him, blocked his path to the house. "No. I won't let you take her." An idea came to him then. *Please, let this work.* "We won't let you take her."

"We?" Sobchuk laughed. "Where's the 'we', Barton? I just see you."

Kevin raised his right arm, pointed up and back toward the second-floor window that overlooked the road. Sunlight reflected off the glass, bright as a spotlight, dazzling the eye.

"Monica is up there. Right now, she's got her rifle pointed at your head." He struggled to keep his voice level. "When I drop my arm, she shoots. She really doesn't like you, Eli. She might even shoot you on general principle."

Roger and Dougie backed off a few steps. Kevin kept his arm up, hoping it looked steadier than it felt.

Sobchuk squinted against the glare. "She's a good shot, is she?"

"Yes. She hunted all the time as a kid. She's got—"

"Yeah, yeah, I know. She's got the county big buck record for a woman, she won the target competition three times over at the county fair, blah blah blah. Shooting a man's a lot different than plunkin' a paper target. Or a deer."

"If it hadn't been dark, George Morris would be in the ground right now. What did you give him to steal our wood?"

It had been Dina's idea, and by the slight twitch, Kevin saw it was true. A few weeks ago, the idea that Sobchuk had engineered the theft of his wood had seemed preposterous.

"Here's how this is going to work," Kevin said. "Go back to town, Eli. You forget this whole thing, and I will too."

"And if I don't?"

"Your cousins will be wearing your brains home. Unless she shoots them too." Roger and Dougie took another step back. "She's got a bit of a temper, my wife."

"So I've noticed." Sobchuk stopped smiling. "Now I'll tell *you* how it's going to work: the girl comes out, or we go in and get her."

Kevin twitched his hand.

Sobchuk didn't flinch. He planted his feet, spread his arms out wide, and lifted his face toward the window. "Go ahead and take your shot, Missus Barton," he called out. "This is your best chance!"

No one moved. One minute passed, then another. Kevin's fingers tingled, then began to go numb. Sobchuk turned back to Kevin, his face rock hard.

"This town is smaller than it used to be, Barton. No phones, no email, no text messages, but word gets around." He stepped up and pressed his chest against Kevin's, and though Kevin had the height advantage, Sobchuk seemed to loom over him. "And the word around town is your woman and your kid up and flew off like the tourists in the fall. So, go ahead, put your arm down. The game's over."

Kevin lowered his gaze and his arm. No shot rang out. No brains spattered. The only sound was a distinct whoosh of breath from Dougie or Roger.

"You've got more balls than I thought, Barton. Now quit jerking me off. Send the girl out, I'll let you keep your house. Of course, with only one person living here, you won't need near as much wood as you've got nor most of those things in the garden. We'll be happy to have your excess." He grinned. "Hell, if you bring the stuff down yourself, maybe I'll even let you see her once in a while. But no more nookie for you."

Kevin set his feet. He folded his arms across his chest and thrust out his jaw.

"Fuck you."

"Jesus Holy Christ, enough already." Sobchuk turned away and jerked a thumb over his shoulder at Kevin. "Guys."

They came forward, fanning out to box Kevin in. Roger hefted his baseball bat. Dougie cracked his knuckles like a movie villain. Both looked like they were going to enjoy this.

"Guys, come on," Kevin said. "This is nuts."

He backed up, eyes darting from Roger to Dougie and back again. His only play was to make a break for the house. It was a longshot.

Not only would he have to outrun them both to the door, he'd have to barricade every door in the house and the windows. Too many. Maybe he could make it all the way up to the bedroom, where he could get his own bat and use it to smash in the head of Roger or Dougie, whichever one came through the door first. Or he and Dina could go out the bedroom window, onto the porch roof, jump down and make a run for it. Dina. He realized he had no idea where Dina was hiding. Shit. It was a terrible plan. It was also the best plan because it was the only one he had.

Just as he was about to stop backing up and flee, he ran out of room, bumped into Rex. The lifeless car stopped him cold. He was boxed in. Resistance was pointless, but he wasn't going to let them walk in and take her without a fight.

Dougie angled to Kevin's right. Though Roger had the weapon, Kevin couldn't take his eyes off Dougie, the boy who had tortured his dreams for months. Roger came straight on, wiggling the bat like he was waiting on a pitch. Kevin's bowels squirmed. *I will not shit myself. I will not give them the satisfaction.*

What had he been thinking? Dina was the runner. He should have sent her to the woods or straight to Jake's house as soon as he saw them coming up the street. Now it was too late.

"Come on, guys," he said around a tongue made of cotton. He half-crouched, trying for some sort of defensive position. "You're taking orders from him? A guy who can't even get a woman on his own?"

Dougie lunged. Kevin spun to meet him. Roger stepped in, the bat a brown streak in the air. Kevin's left thigh exploded in white-hot pain. His leg collapsed, and he fell to the weed-choked driveway. His leg. Holy God, his leg; he'd never felt such pain before. He clutched his thigh. A foot connected with his stomach, driving all the air out of him. He writhed on the ground, curling up to protect his head, his stomach, his balls as they kicked at him, at his ribs, his legs, his ass.

"Okay, okay, that's enough," Sobchuk said. One last foot connected with Kevin's shoulder, and then the beating was done.

Kevin lay there, gasping, trying to get his breath back. Dust coated his lips and his tongue. His stomach and back ached from the kicks, but it was nothing compared to his thigh. It felt like someone had cut it open, stuck a roadside flare in it, and lit it.

"That's going to keep you off your feet a couple-three days, I'm guessing." Sobchuk's voice came from far away, through a pain that rang like gongs in Kevin's ears. "It would be a shame if it was broke. We'd probably have to shoot you, like a horse."

"Pussy," Roger said. "That was just a check swing."

That was no check swing. Kevin rolled into a sitting position. He scooted to the side, away from Roger and his bat. Pins and needles spiked everything below his left knee.

"If you take her," he managed, between harsh gasps of breath, "you better kill me now, because I'll come for you."

"That's not very neighborly of you, now is it?" Sobchuk nodded at Roger, who raised the bat. Kevin threw his arms up to ward off the blow, but it never came.

"Stop it, please!" Dina's panicked voice rang from behind him.

Kevin twisted around. "Dina, get out of here. Run!"

"No." She knelt next to Kevin, her face paper white. She looked up at Sobchuk. "I'll go. Just leave him alone. Please."

Kevin's swelling thigh pushed tight against his jeans. He crawled up the side of his car to something resembling a standing position. Every movement set off a fresh burst of heat in his thigh.

"Dina, no. Get out of here. Run."

"Run where? I can't live out there on my own. I can't watch you get hurt for me. I've already caused so much trouble. Just let me get my things and I'll go."

"At last, someone's talking sense here." Sobchuk nodded at Dougie. "Make sure she doesn't try to sneak out the back or something."

Kevin hung onto the side of the car. He flexed his wounded leg. It moved in slow motion, the muscle throbbing like a second heart. Feeling was coming back to his toes, his foot, but the leg wouldn't support his weight. Sweat dripped off his face into the dust at his feet.

"I'll send up an ice pack, we still got a few of those lying around." Sobchuk put a hand on Kevin's shoulder, magnanimous in victory. "Don't you worry, Barton. I'll take good care of her."

Kevin gathered his good leg and launched himself into Sobchuk. The unexpected attack knocked the heavier man back into the high grass. Kevin landed on top. He jammed his hand under Sobchuk's chin, pushing his head back.

"Hey," screeched Roger. "Get off him! Get off him!"

Sobchuk bucked beneath him. Kevin clamped one hand on his now-exposed neck and squeezed. He sensed a movement and rolled to his right, his hands not leaving Sobchuk's thick neck. Roger's bat whistled just past his head. Then Sobchuk was on top of him, punching him in the face and head, his little Chiclet teeth bared in rage.

Kevin ignored the blows. He got both hands on Sobchuk's neck and put every ounce of strength and energy he had into his fingers, sank them into the soft, thick flesh. Sobchuk stopped punching. He raked at Kevin's fingers and hands. Kevin pressed his thumbs into the hard ridges of his windpipe. Months of sod busting, woodcutting, digging, chopping, and hauling had paid off. The paper pusher had toughened up, while the common laborer had gotten soft.

Sobchuk's face went through multiple shades of red. Tears trickled from the corners of his eyes. His mouth twisted and worked, but no sounds came out of his closed-off throat. Kevin pulled him down so they were face-to-face like lovers, leaving Roger no easy target for his bat. Heavy-toed boots thudded against his sides, but Kevin held on. It was his only chance.

Red shaded toward purple. Sobchuk's tongue stuck out from between his little white teeth. Blood trickled down from where he had bitten it. His eyes bulged like a frog's. Harder and harder Kevin squeezed. Arteries and veins thrummed against his fingers and still he squeezed.

Jesus, how long does it take to strangle a man? It felt like he'd been latched onto Sobchuk's throat for hours, yet he was still alive.

Golden stars burst in his vision as a new blow struck his battered thigh. Kevin screamed. His whole body spasmed. It was just enough. Sobchuk ripped Kevin's fingers off his throat and fell away. Roger hit him again on the thigh. The world went gray. The bat slammed into his back, then his arm, then his thigh again before it stopped. He lay in the matted grass, groaning and shaking, his fingers still hooked into claws. From nearby, Sobchuk gagged and coughed.

"Not . . . yet," Sobchuk hacked the words out of his damaged throat. "Not . . . yet."

A moment later, a hand grabbed the back of Kevin's shirt, turned him over roughly. Sobchuk's face eclipsed the sky. Pieces of dried grass clung to his hair and beard. Exploded veins bloomed on his nose and across his cheeks, making him look like a career drunk. Bright red blood filled the white of his right eye. Sweat rolled down his face, dripped off his nose onto Kevin like rain.

"I was . . . going to . . . leave . . . you alone." He sounded like a tracheotomy gone bad. "Now? Fuck . . . you."

Kevin's muscles screamed as he pushed himself to a sitting position. Every time he moved his head, it took the world half a second or so to catch up. He felt like the marble on one of the labyrinth games, where you have to guide the marble through the maze by tilting the board this way and that. Roger stood with the bat cocked, ready to use, but Kevin had no fight left.

"Once . . . we're gone—" Sobchuk gagged and spat a bloody gob into the grass. Breath whistled in and out of his damaged throat. He swung a trembling hand in Kevin's direction. "Kill him. The woods."

Color drained from Roger's face. "What?"

Sobchuk grimaced and massaged his throat. "You . . . heard me. Take him . . . up the woods." He nodded. "Do it."

Roger looked at Kevin with wide, shocked eyes. Kevin crawled to the driveway and again pulled himself up using his car. Black and gray beads swirled at the edges of his vision. The ground rolled beneath his feet like he was at sea. He swiped his shaky hand across his wet lips. It came away sticky with blood. A knob had risen on his left cheek. His hands were hooked into claws, hard to open. He looked around, looked for help from somewhere, but there was no one. Across the road there was nothing but the dense shrubs and small trees growing out of the ditch that separated Jake's pasture from the road.

Dina and Dougie came out of the house.

"It's . . . about . . . time." Sobchuk's voice sounded like a rusty tailpipe being dragged down the road by a car. "Let's . . . go."

Kevin couldn't look directly at Dina; he had failed. Again.

Dina gasped when she saw him. She threw her bag to the ground and rushed forward. Roger lowered the bat like a tollgate. She shoved him away and peered at Kevin's face. He looked away. Looking at her hurt worse than his injuries.

"What did you do to him? You said you wouldn't hurt him."

"Self . . . defense. He tried to . . . kill me."

"I'm sorry, Dina. I'm so, so sorry."

She hugged him. He felt her shudder and tremble in his arms, but she did not cry. She clung to him the way Kelly used to when she woke from a nightmare, but the nightmare was just beginning for her. He patted her back and mumbled apologies into her shoulder. She didn't beg him to help her, didn't ask him for something impossible.

"I'm sorry," she whispered. "It's all my fault."

"It's not your fault. It's not your fault. It's his fault for being the way he is, and it's my fault for not being able to stop him. I tried, Dina. I tried."

He felt like crying. Or throwing up. He rested his head on her shoulder, his face turned toward the street which tilted left and right before finally settling in its accustomed place. Pain was doing strange things to his eyesight: the middle was too bright, the edges were too fuzzy. He shifted his head a little, tried to focus on the dark shape in the thicket, but it was gone, he must have imagined it.

"Break it up," Sobchuk rasped. Roger poked Kevin in the side with the tip of the bat.

Dina slapped at the bat, and Roger fell back, holding it across his chest and looking decidedly pale. Kevin couldn't hope to overpower him, not in his current condition, but maybe, just maybe, he could convince him to let him go. Then he could figure out a way to rescue Dina.

Dougie snickered. "You're going to have your hands full with her, Mr. Sobchuk. Maybe you should do a full body search, make sure she's not packing a knife."

"Enough," Sobchuk said, and Dougie's laughter cut off. "Let's go."

They started down the driveway, Dina between Sobchuk and Dougie. She looked back, then stopped.

"Why isn't he coming?" She pointed at Roger.

"Keeping an eye . . . on him." Sobchuk's voice was barely above a whisper, but he was getting his wind back. "Make sure he doesn't do anything crazy. Come on."

Kevin chanced another peek at the ditch. His vision was blurry; the world wouldn't hold steady, but there was almost certainly someone over there, hiding in the shrubs.

Sobchuk, Dina, and Dougie were near the end of the driveway. Roger stood several feet to Kevin's left, the bat still held across his chest. Dina was in the middle of them all, too close for comfort. Even if that *was* an expert marksman—or woman—on the other side of the road, she was too close. Too much could go wrong.

"Wait," he said. "One more thing. Dina, come here."

Sobchuk looked skyward but made a shooing motion. Dina came. Dougie followed close.

"Can you give us a little space, please?" Kevin said.

Dougie looked to Sobchuk, who shrugged. Dougie said, "If you run, we beat the shit out of him. Again." He backed off.

Kevin put his hands on Dina's shoulders, moved his lips close to her ear.

"It's going to be okay," he whispered, hoping for all the world he wasn't seeing things. "Get ready to run." *Please, now. Now!*

It wasn't like the movies. In the movies, you always heard the rifle shot, followed by the ka-ping of the ricochet. Not in real life. Not this close.

A divot of gravel exploded up from the driveway about two inches to the right of Sobchuk's foot at almost exactly the same time as the rifle report reached his ears. Sobchuk yelped and did a little skip dance, like a character in an old Western. Dougie and Roger turned in small circles, trying to look everywhere at once.

Kevin shoved Dina toward the house. She took off. He tried to follow but his leg buckled and he hit the dirt. In desperation, he crawled through the weedy gravel around the front edge of the car, dragging his leg behind. Once safe, he peered around the car.

A blue cloud of gun smoke floated up in the air. Below it, Monica pushed her way through the shrubs. The rifle was trained on Sobchuk.

"You two," she called out to Dougie and Roger. "Get the hell out of here. Don't charge me, I've got a man in the road with a shotgun who will shred you if you try. And drop that bat."

The bat clattered to the ground. Roger and Dougie raised their hands and sidestepped across the lawn. When they reached the street, they took off at a run down the hill.

Monica advanced across the road. Jake came into view from the left, his shotgun at hip level, pointed at the ground.

Monica said, "The only thing you're walking away from here with is your life, and you should be thankful for that. If you ever set foot on this hill again, I will kill you. You don't fuck with my family, you miserable piece of shit."

"Hey, now." Sobchuk held his hands out in a placating gesture. "I'm just trying . . . to do you a favor. Unless you don't mind your husband screwing around. Or maybe you'll join them."

Monica resettled the rifle butt against her shoulder. Her finger curled around the trigger, tight, tighter.

Oh God, don't do it.

He was afraid to call out to her. She was on the edge, and any attempt at pulling her back might just push her over instead, the way the smallest noise, a rolling pebble, a cough, a whisper, can send an avalanche roaring down a mountainside.

Sobchuk saw it too. His knees began to quiver.

Monica took a deep breath and held it. She set her feet. For one horrible second, Kevin was sure she was going to do it. Then her breath came out in a steady hiss, and her finger straightened and rested along the trigger guard. She kept the barrel trained on Sobchuk's chest though.

"You can dream about that while you jerk off. That's as close as you'll get to any of us. Now, I want you to walk real slow out of this driveway and back down the hill. Don't come back. We'll be watching. *I'll* be watching."

Sobchuk cast one last glare at Kevin but did as she said. Monica followed, twenty paces behind, the rifle trained on his back.

Jake came into the driveway, his shotgun cradled over his arm. He grunted as he bent over Kevin. "You okay?" the big man asked.

"I've been better." He sat up, slowly, then once more used the car to get to his feet. "I am so glad to see you. Where's Kelly?"

"She's acrost the way with Alma. I'll go and tell her you're okay."

Kevin nodded. He was about to thank Jake, but his arms and legs started to tremble. The world grayed again. His legs ceased to function, and he was on the ground, eye-to-toe with Jake's work boots.

"Kevin? Kevin?" Jake's voice, from far away. "Dina, get him a blanket. Quick. Kevin? Stay with us." Thick-fingered hands gripped his arms, rolled him onto his back. He was looking at the sky, blue and clear, but it was wrong, it was too far away, like he was looking at it through the wrong end of a telescope. He was going to ask Jake if he saw it, too, and then everything disappeared.

—

The voices came back, first tinny and distant, as if they came through a cheap radio two rooms away. A face blotted out the sun, and he panicked. Sobchuk. Sobchuk was back. Kevin tried to punch, but his hands were pinned, he couldn't move, and then his vision cleared, and he wasn't looking at Sobchuk at all. He was looking at Monica's beautiful, worried face, and Kelly, pale and frightened, looming over Monica's shoulder. He tried to reach up again, this time to touch them, but something kept him from moving. He looked down and saw a green blanket tucked tight around him.

The blanket was comforting weight, the sight of his wife and daughter even more of a comfort. He fell back. Someone had put something soft beneath his head. But someone was missing.

"Dina!" he cried, struggling to get up. "He's got Dina! We've got to get her!" He kicked at the blanket, and the pain shot through him then.

Monica put gentle hands on his chest, pressed him back against the gravel driveway that bit into his back. "It's okay, it's okay. She's here. She's right here."

She shifted over and Dina slid in next to her. "It's okay, Mr. B. He's gone."

Relief washed over him. He lowered his head. The sky was so bright it was nearly white, though it didn't look far away this time. It all started coming back to him—the bat, his fight with Sobchuk, Monica with the rifle.

"Can I get up?"

"Can you?" Monica said.

"I think so."

She loosened the blanket and helped him to a sitting position. The world tilted and spun, but he didn't pass out. His whole body hurt like hell, especially his thigh. After a few seconds, everything steadied.

"Water?"

Monica held a cup to his lips. The water was warm and metallic and possibly the best he'd ever had.

Once he'd drunk his fill, they helped him up, and he was stable enough to stand. Monica, Kelly, and Dina watched, ready to catch him if he fell. He took a deep breath and smiled. Dried blood cracked and flaked off his lips.

He reached for Monica's hand. It felt hot in his still chilly fingers. They fell together. Kevin buried his face in Monica's thick hair, drank up her smell, absorbed the heat from her body, used her strength for himself.

"Oh God, Kevin, I'm so sorry. If I had just listened to you . . . I'm sorry, Kevin. I let that bastard get into my head. I don't know how you can forgive me."

"I don't know how I can't forgive you," he said. "You saved my life. But I'm sorry too. I should have told you right from the beginning what he was after. I don't know why I didn't."

Kelly clamped herself onto the two of them. He reached around with one arm and hugged her. They formed a little triangle on the gravelly driveway, hugging and crying in the hot afternoon. Kevin felt Monica pull away.

"Dina," she said. Kevin watched his wife's face work. She tried, but she couldn't seem to find the words she wanted. Instead, she opened up the triangle and held out her arm. "Get in here. You're part of this family too."

Dina joined them. They stayed that way until Kevin's leg became too painful to stand on.

———

Walking was hard. His thigh burned and throbbed. It felt like the only thing keeping it from breaking open and spilling hot red blood and mushed muscle was his jeans. His knee buckled when he tried to put his full weight on it. Dina supported his weight on that side since the others were too short. She had her arm looped around his waist. He leaned on her shoulder. Monica had his right.

"How did you know?" Kevin's breath came in short gasps, but talking helped divert his attention from his leg. Sweat poured off his face and spattered the road.

"I didn't," she said. "I got lucky. I had put the rifle away. I—I was coming to apologize. I saw them from up the road. Saw you standing there with your hand in the air. What was that all about?"

"Tell you later." He took short little breaths through clenched teeth, like Monica had in Lamaze class. It helped him about as much as Monica said it helped her. In other words, not much.

"When I saw that little shit with his bat, I almost charged right down the road. But I knew I needed a weapon and went back for the rifle. Jake was coming in for lunch. If it weren't for him, I might have just gone out and shot them all. It was his idea to flank them."

"Thank God for Jake," Kevin said. In more ways than one. An image of bodies strewn about the street filled Kevin's head.

"I would have stopped him sooner," Monica said, referring to Sobchuk, "but I was afraid I was going to hit you or Dina. I had to get a good line on him."

A walk that normally took thirty seconds took ten minutes at least. Tall trees overshadowed the end of Jake's driveway, bringing blessed coolness. Kevin's shirt was drenched. Up near the house, he saw chairs, a picnic table, old milk cartons, steps leading to the kitchen door, everywhere, surfaces to sit on. That's all he wanted to do right now, sit, but he was so far away. His good knee started wobbling. The world went wavery and panic fluttered around inside.

"I'm going down," he said.

Dina tightened her arm around him. "Just a little further."

"No, I need to sit."

He almost went down, but Monica and Dina half-carried, half-dragged him to the picnic table.

Alma Hillman brought more water and a plastic baggie full of cold creek water to serve as an *ersatz* ice pack. She pressed the baggie against his thigh as a compress. Once the cold penetrated the denim, it felt heavenly. His heart rate settled, and he felt calmer.

Monica stood before him, eyes brimming with tears. Kevin could never remember her crying so much in a day.

"I'm so proud of you, Kevin."

"Don't be. I couldn't"—his voice caught—"I couldn't stop them. If you hadn't come along—"

"You shouldn't have had to face them alone. You stood up to him. You didn't give in. Like me. I'm so ashamed of myself." She swallowed and turned to Dina. "I'm so sorry, Dina. I was ready to believe the most horrible things. I was ready to kick you out. I'm just . . . I'm just so sorry."

Dina grabbed Monica and pulled her close. They held each other, rocking back and forth, apologizing for sins real and imagined, both forgiving the other. Kevin didn't know how long it went on for as a wave of exhaustion caught him and knocked him into a heavy sleep.

———

Hours after the beating, his leg still throbbed. Monica cut his pants up the seam so they could examine his thigh. It was swollen and purple from knee to hip. Whether the steady stream of cold compresses helped or not, he didn't know. They forced him to take two pills from their dwindling supply of aspirin. His body was bruised all over—both arms, his side, his face. Kevin imagined a boot print on the side of his head under his hair. Jake did a rudimentary examination, probing and flexing his limbs. Nothing seemed broken. Kevin was still dizzy. Jake checked his pupils.

"Same size," he said. "I don't think you've got a concussion."

The six of them shared dinner at the Hillmans' picnic table. Kevin was ravenous, though his split lip and sore jaw made it difficult to eat. After the meal, they sat, empty plates scattered in front of them.

"So," Jake said. "I guess you'll be moving in with us, right?"

"If you don't mind all our drama," Kevin said.

"We've needed some excitement in our lives," Alma said.

It hurt like hell to laugh but felt good too. Kelly clutched his arm. Every so often, she looked up at him, as if assuring herself that he was still there and alive. It had been a close call. Despite the worries, and the physical beating he had taken, he felt good. They were together again and safe. At least for the moment.

"Do you think Sobchuk is going to make more trouble?" he asked. "He's already tried to split up my marriage, kidnap Dina, and kill me."

Jake rubbed his chin.

"Well, here's the thing," he said after a moment. "He's getting a lot out of us: milk, and I promised him some beef a little later. I'd say it's in his best interests to keep us happy up here . . . and safe."

"I think we should cut him off, plain and simple," Monica said.

"We can't do that," Kevin said. "There's forty, fifty people down there who haven't done anything wrong. We can't punish them for him."

Monica sighed and dropped a hand to the table. "I knew you'd say that. If we cut him off, maybe the people down there would get angry and put someone else in charge, and then our problem is solved."

"Or he'd turn people against us, form an army, and come up here and take what he wants."

"Do you think people would do that?" Monica said. "If they knew what he tried to do?"

"They love him down there," Kevin said. "He gets them food, gives them work and security. People are willing to overlook a lot for something like that. Look at how many excuses I made for him," he added.

"You know," Jake mused, "maybe we've done enough already. He's stubborn like his old man but he's a lot smarter. Monica already told him everything there is to say: 'stay off the hill. Leave us alone.' Maybe we just go down there and say that. 'Leave us alone, and you'll keep getting what you need, period.' They got plenty of wood, good hunting and fishing all around without having to come up here."

"And who's going to take this proposal down to him?" Monica said. "What's to stop him from arresting us or shooting us or something?"

"Like I said, he's smart. Ammunition's too valuable to waste in a shootin' match. And people are too important to waste—he needs every person he's got. *We* need everyone we've got. As for who goes? I'll do it. He won't do anything to me. He needs me too much."

"No," Kevin said. "I'll go. As soon as my leg is better."

"Daddy, you can't go," Kelly protested. "He'll kill you!"

"No, it has to be me." As soon as he said it, he knew it was true. "I'm the one he has the problem with. I'm not going to put any of you at risk for me. It's not right.

"And there's something else. Even if he agrees to leave us alone, it's not good enough. We have to get him out of power." He looked around at them, his gaze finally coming to rest on Dina. "There are other girls in town, other women. What if he tries this with one of them? We can't let him do that. If he's not in charge, he's got no power."

"Won't he just grab someone and rape them?" Kelly asked.

Kevin ran his fingers along his swollen, split lip and thought about it. "I don't think so. He was offended when I called him a rapist. He doesn't see coercion as rape." He held up a hand to forestall Monica's protest. "*I* know it is. That's not my point. He thinks it's only rape if you're using a weapon or physical force.

"We have to take away his power. But we can't do it with an act of war. We need to get people on our side." He tapped his fork against his plate, thinking. Thinking of who had come with Sobchuk on his trip up the hill. And who had not. "And I think I know how we can do it."

CHAPTER 27

THREE DAYS LATER, Kevin's limping shadow led him down the dusty road to town. The swelling in his thigh had gone down substantially, though it felt like someone had sewn a rock up in it. The angry purple had gone green and was now turning a puke yellow. Best of all, the dizziness was mostly gone, except for if he turned his head really fast.

"I can't believe you're doing this," Monica said when he prepared to set out. "Don't leave me a widow, or I'll track you down in the afterlife and kill you again."

She hugged him.

"Ow, ow, ow."

"Sorry."

"Standing up to Sobchuk was the easy part," he said, and kissed her. "Standing up to *you*, that was hard."

"I'm glad you did."

"I'd better get going. It's going to take me all day to get there," he joked.

Weeds grew shoulder high out of the ditch, a chaotic tangle of purple, white, and yellow flowers. There were no road crews coming to cut them back with weed whackers. Jake's cows stared at him from the other side of the fence in placid curiosity. He stepped over the flattened remains of a mummified turtle, likely a fatality from last summer. *There was one good thing about this*, he thought. *No more roadkill.*

Curtis Pinkney's car sat at the foot of the hill on flattening tires, a relic of a lost life. He didn't know for sure that it was Curtis who had supplied Sobchuk with the information that had emboldened him to come up the hill, but you didn't need to be a Mensa member to solve that equation. There was no reason to believe the affable young man had done it out of any malice. Whatever. Curtis was not his concern, not right now. This was all about Sobchuk and bringing him down.

He hurried past the turn-in to town hall as quickly as his stiff leg would allow, heart pounding at the thought of encountering Sobchuk before he was ready. The urge to run back home and hide under the covers was strong, but he was stronger. He swallowed and hobbled on, knowing he'd be back soon enough.

———

George Morris lived in a small house on a small lot just north of the Four Corners. Luck was with Kevin: George sat in the deep shade of his front porch.

Kevin hailed him from the sidewalk. "You mind if I come up?"

George, a thin man with wiry gray hair and heavy black glasses, frowned. "You're not s'pposed t'be here," he said. "Sobchuk said."

"I just want to talk." Kevin held up his hands to show they were empty. "Privately."

Kevin thought the man was going to tell him to peddle his papers somewhere else, but after a long pause, George waved him up.

By the time he climbed the steps to the porch, Kevin was exhausted. George gasped at the sight of Kevin's battered face, indicated an empty chair. Kevin lowered himself gratefully, though he feared he might not be able to get back up again.

"You should have seen me three days ago," Kevin said, touching his face. The swelling was mostly gone, but the colors remained.

"Maybe you folks should move into one of the empty houses in town. Safer. Lots of folks likely to be on the move soon before winter comes."

Kevin had only passed words with George a few times here and there over the years. He could not at all be certain that this was the voice he'd heard on his porch that night that seemed so long ago. The heavy black revolver that sat on the small table before them, however, was certainly the type that would make the sort of click and boom he'd heard that night.

A crumpled pack of cigarettes sat beside the revolver. George reached for the pack and shook one out. With a hand that wasn't quite steady, he put the cigarette in his mouth, but made no move to light it.

"I hear there's been lots of dustups between the night patrols and stragglers lately," George said.

"This happened in the daytime, George. And it wasn't stragglers that did it."

George said nothing. He stared straight ahead at the straight road running past his house. Kevin leaned forward a little and played his hunch. "George, the person who did this to me is the same one who sent you to steal my wood."

George looked up sharply, his face as gray as his hair.

"I didn't—"

"George."

The older man blinked twice, then his shoulders drooped. He sat for a moment, head bowed, then fished in his pocket for a match. He lit the cigarette, took a deep drag and held the smoke in his lungs a long time, like he was smoking pot, then let it out in a long stream. He took a second puff, took the cigarette out of his mouth and held it in the air between them, his hand trembling slightly.

"You smoke?"

"No."

"Started when I was thirteen, maybe fourteen. Pack a day, going on near forty years now. Tried to quit a couple-three times. Made it six weeks once, cold turkey. Always went back."

One more puff, then he pulled a ceramic ashtray printed with a casino logo toward him. He snuffed out the cigarette, taking great care not to bend or break it. Once satisfied it was out, he placed it on the table next to the ashtray.

"I'm quitting again. Trying to make them last."

Kevin understood. "How many did he give you?"

"A carton. I was out. Couldn't sleep. Couldn't eat. I was miserable." He took off his glasses and thumbed the corner of his eye. "A carton. And a couple extra MREs."

He picked up the cigarette again with his nicotine-stained fingers. "I'm sorry," he said. "I've been tore up over it ever since. I wasn't trying to kill your wife. I knew her when she was little. She played with my kid sister. You know that, right? I shot high on purpose. I would never . . . I was just trying to get away without getting killed."

"I know."

Kevin wasn't even angry anymore, not at George, anyway. He explained what Sobchuk had done to him, to his family, what he had wanted to do to Dina. When he was finished, he pushed himself up out of the chair. His leg straightened grudgingly.

"Will you help me bring him down?"

There was a long pause. Finally, George said, "Yes."

"Good. Now I just need more people."

"Henry Chambers."

"Sorry?"

"Henry Chambers," George said. He lit the cigarette again. "He's probably the only one who can influence Eli. Talk to Henry. He'll do the right thing. He's a good man."

———

It was very late in the afternoon by the time Kevin was ready to face Sobchuk. Lunch was over and cleaned up, the afternoon crews were gone, town hall looked deserted. Kevin stood in front of the building, his mouth dry, his heart pounding. Sobchuk was in there. Henry had told him so, had told him that Sobchuk had been largely holed up inside for the last three days or so. Kevin was confident. He was strong. He was about to be alone in a room with the man who had casually ordered his death three days ago. He was terrified. His hand trembled as he reached for the door and pulled it open.

"Anyone home?"

No answer. Kevin stepped into the foyer, stood with his back against the door, keeping it propped open, allowing a shaft of light, of safety, to fall across the floor. Finally, summoning his newfound strength, he let the door shut and made his way painfully to the public meeting room, Sobchuk's lair.

The blinds were down, the room almost nighttime dark.

"Well, well, well."

Despite the three days, Sobchuk's voice was still raspy. Kevin squinted through the gloom, picked out the Sobchuk shape at the front of the room, in the supervisor's seat. The gloom helped. Not being able to see the man clearly in the dark made him less threatening, but the voice—the voice stopped him, made the sweat spring out cold on his neck.

"Well, well, well. You've got a lot of nerve, showing up here."

Kevin swallowed hard and forced himself forward, step by step, deeper into the room, closer to the man who had tried to kill him. "I thought we should talk," he said.

Sobchuk spun in little half circles, back and forth, back and forth. The chair squeaked with each turn.

"I don't know that we have more to say."

"I think there's a lot to say, Eli. Mainly about what happens next."

The squeaking stopped. Sobchuk's voice was low and full of menace. "You know, Barton. I've got a man who will swear to the fact that you tried to kill me, and I've got the marks on my throat to prove it. I can lock you up, even shoot you if I wanted. No one would bat an eye."

"Are you sure about that, Eli? Really sure? Because I've been talking to people today."

It was quiet for so long Kevin almost thought Eli had fallen asleep or dematerialized from the room.

"You've got a bigger set of balls than I thought, Barton. Or a lot less brains."

"Eli, I think we need to work something out here so that we all get what we want."

"You know what I want."

"Dina is not a part of this discussion."

Sobchuk commenced his idle spinning in the chair again. Squeak, squeak. Slumped down in the chair, now facing the wall, not Kevin.

"Then maybe you'd better leave."

The man was like a dog trying to pull the last shred of meat off a bone, and Kevin had had enough. His weary leg groaned as he surged around the desk. He grabbed the chair and spun it around, slammed his hands on the arms and leaned in, his body screaming its protest at the sudden rush of activity, his mind screaming its protest at suddenly finding himself face-to-face with the man who had stopped the Army, the man who had overseen his beating, the man who had casually ordered his murder. The shock Kevin felt was mirrored in Sobchuk's wide eyes. Three days ago, Kevin had stood with his palms out, begging for reason. Now, Sobchuk shrank back in the big chair, his quaking hands palms out in front of his throat. It lasted just two seconds, maybe three, but also forever, because time had no meaning in the blackout. The sight of Sobchuk cringing before him was a salve for all his wounds—body and mind.

"Listen, you asshole. Forget Dina. You're either going to have to find a woman who wants you or pay someone to do it. I'm talking about beef, I'm talking about milk, I'm talking about keeping people alive."

The whites of Sobchuk's eyes glimmered in the dark. His breath whistled in and out through his damaged throat. Kevin released the chair and took a step back but stood as tall as his aching body would allow.

"We both want the same thing," he said. "We want to come through this alive, with as many people surviving as possible. Neighbors helping neighbors, right?"

"What's your point?"

"We've become very tight with the Hillmans. Jake and Alma were really unhappy with what happened the other day. They've grown quite fond of Dina."

Sobchuk tapped his fingers on the desk. Kevin pushed on.

"They're talking about cutting off the milk supply. And forget about meat. The people in this town love you now because you got them food. You think they'll feel the same way when there's nothing to eat? They'll toss you out like a sack of rotten potatoes."

It was an empty threat, but Kevin was banking on the man being smart enough to know that the hunting parties, the big garden, the smokehouse, would only get him so far. Winters were long and cold in Harpursville, and they would need more than a few of Jake's cows to get past it.

The chair groaned under Sobchuk's weight as he leaned back in it and stared up at the ceiling, considering. After a long moment, he leaned forward again.

"Fine," he said. "What do you want?"

"Three things. First, just like Monica said the other day, nobody comes up the hill unless we ask. Harpur's Hill Road is off limits.

"Second, if any of us—any of us—comes to town for any reason, we get the same rights and protection and respect as everyone else. No funny business." He searched the wording carefully, looking for any loopholes he could close, found none. Well, except for the meaning of "funny business"—that covered everything and nothing. He took the edge out of his voice. "We don't need to be at each other's throats over this. It's not going to help you, me, or anyone in this town."

"So far, so good," Sobchuk said. "What's number three?"

"Number three, you're out. You can stay in town, but you have to step down."

Sobchuk rose. He went chest to chest with Kevin, but Kevin wasn't afraid, not anymore. Sobchuk was just a short man with a big chest who had once done something great but had let it go to his head.

"And why the hell would I do that?"

"Because George Morris has a conscience, that's why. So does your uncle. And your cousin."

Sobchuk's breathing came hard and fast, like a bull ready to charge. He glared up at Kevin, his fists opening and closing, his jaw clenched.

Kevin said, "We'll form a council, rule by committee. And until we get that set up, you're done. Resign, effective immediately. You'll step down, turn it over."

Sobchuk snorted. "To who? You? You can't even run your household, how you gonna run this town?"

Kevin limped over to the front window and pulled up the blinds. Light flooded the room. He turned back to Sobchuk.

"It's funny," Kevin said. "You told me I didn't understand the people of this town, but you're the one who doesn't understand. Folks here value hard work, integrity, honesty. I saw that from the first day I moved in. It's one of the things I've always liked about Harpursville. Folks were willing to follow you as long as you stuck to those values."

The door opened. Henry Chambers, reedy and somber faced, entered. Behind him came his wife, Brenda. And Cassie Magglio. George Morris. Even Roger Fields. Henry nodded at Kevin, then looked his nephew up and down, his lip twitching in distaste.

"You really cocked it up, Eli," he said.

CHAPTER 28

JAKE SAID IT was mid-October, which would make it just about six months since the lights went out. Kevin didn't know for sure, but if Jake said it was October, it probably was. What he did know was the morning was cold and crisp, and the slanted sun edged every leaf in gold.

Faint wisps of breath trailed out behind him as he approached his house. What used to be his lawn was a straw-colored mass of tangled grasses and nodding brown seedheads. Ranks of goldenrod topped with gray fluff lined the road. Dried up milkweed with pods exploding, many other plants he didn't recognize, brown and dying, bent under the weight of the morning dew. From his place at the end of his driveway he saw no sign of intruders, nothing but a beaten-down deer track leading to the remnants of his used-up garden. Everything looked undisturbed. The doors and windows on this side of the house were shut tight.

Chilly air bit the tip of his nose; his ears and chin were safe, covered by the shaggy hair that flowed down to his shoulders, and the beard he tried to keep respectably trimmed. His stomach growled. Back across the road, Alma was making omelets with some green peppers. Eggs, always eggs: scrambled, fried, over easy, hard-boiled, poached. His doctor would have a cow if he knew how many eggs Kevin ate, yet Kevin felt healthier than he had in years. Ted was a distant memory. He wondered if his doctor was even alive, then quickly pushed away all thoughts of anyone not currently living in their very small world. It was just easier that way.

The cars sat side by side in the driveway on sagging tires. He peered in the windows, made sure no one was sleeping in there. They had already drained the gas from both tanks because Jake would find a way to use it safely at some point. He trailed his hand along the windshield. The dew had a thick, almost sludgy quality to it. Cold, but not quite cold enough for frost. Soon though.

He circled the house once, eyeing the grass for pathways, studying the house for obvious signs of intruders. Weaponless, he wanted to be certain there was no one inside before he entered. They came over at least once a week to check on things, and he and Monica spent the odd night or two here when they needed more privacy than Jake's house provided. Monica also believed a vacant house broke down faster than an occupied one, the way the tires on their cars had gone flat with no one to drive them. It was like exercise to a human body, she said, insisting that exercise to a house was doors opening and closing, floors being walked on—and a bed being bounced in. He wasn't going to argue with her on that one.

The doorknob was cold in his hand. He turned the key, pushed the door open, entered the kitchen. Silence. He stood still, not breathing, waiting for a creak, the whisper of fabric or voices, a suppressed cough or sneeze. There was nothing, so he began his patrol.

The pantry was empty, the shelves filmed with dust. Cobwebs clung to the corners of the ceiling, draped over the window frame. He thought about running a dust rag over the counters, the shelves, the windowsill, but for what purpose? As much as it pained him to see the house this way, cleaning would imply that things were going to go back to normal, and Kevin didn't think that was going to happen for a long time, if ever. They were looking at a long, cold winter, and he couldn't spend his energy on such a useless task.

Sobchuk was gone. He stepped down with a gracious and inspiring speech, and the world had not ended. If anything, his legend in town had grown, which rankled Monica to no end. Kevin didn't care anymore. The Army had returned in late July—not Major Pettit, however. They announced a resettlement option, refugee camps somewhere in the south, Georgia or West Virginia, and no real answers on what had happened or when it was going to be fixed. A handful of Harpurites opted to leave with them, Sobchuk among them. He did not bother to say goodbye to Kevin. Harpursville's population had dwindled. The initial round of deaths had struck the elderly and those whose lives depended on serious medication. There had been some accidents and one double suicide. They'd also added a few people, stragglers who were intercepted by patrols and opted to stay. Still no doctors, though.

Ten fifteen according to the wall clock, the time the world ended half a year ago. Yet an end of one thing was the beginning of something else, and the new world wasn't so bad. Hard, yes, but good. It brought him closer with his family, had even expanded it. He was in better shape than at any time in his adult life, had learned new skills, and had found a whole new side of himself. No, it wasn't all bad.

No time for sentiment, he had a job to do. It was autumn, the weather was turning, and autumns were even shorter than summers in this part of the world. The air had a winter smell, the foliage was well past peak, and they needed more blankets. He passed through the silent downstairs like a ghost, peeking in rooms just to be sure they were empty, and made his way upstairs.

It smelled faintly of mildew. He found an open window in the bathroom. The sill and curtains were damp from a recent rain. The sash stuck in its swollen frame. He pushed, but the sash didn't budge. Just before his next shove, he paused. Shouts came from Jake's house. Kevin tensed, ready to run to defend his new home, but the shrieks were joyful, Kelly and Dina whooping it up like contestants on a game show who had just won a new car or a luxury vacation to Spain or something. He smiled at the happy sound of his girls. Circumstance had forced them to grow up in so many ways, but they were still such kids.

He leaned hard on the sash and slammed it shut, cutting off the sound. Kelly's room and the guest bedroom were clear and secure. In the master bedroom, he went straight to the walk-in closet. Just as he still checked his useless watch and still looked both ways before crossing the street, he yanked the pull chain on the overhead fixture. Chuckling at his foolishness, he pulled the chain again. The closet went dark.

Kevin pulled the three thickest quilts off the shelf and left the closet, intending to set them on his bed and return for more. Struck by the sense that something was off, he looked over his shoulder at the dark closet, but nothing was out of the ordinary. With a shake of his head, he moved toward the bed. Flickering movement caught his eye. He turned, expecting to see a mouse scuttering across the night table, but there was no mouse, just a rhythmic flash of green.

Quilts tumbled from his arms to the floor. He stumbled forward, clutched the bedpost for support. A shiver ran up his spine; it was like déjà vu, recognition, but not quite understanding.

Downstairs, the kitchen door blasted open. The girls—*his* girls—thundered into the house. Laughing, crying, shouting, they pounded through the downstairs, calling for him, but he couldn't answer. Not with his mouth hanging open.

Kevin's knees gave out. He collapsed on the edge of the bed, mouth hanging open, staring at the alien-green numbers flashing on his clock radio.

12:02. 12:02. 12:02.

12:03.

DISCUSSION QUESTIONS

1. In POWERLESS, the reader never knows more than the characters do in terms of what caused the power outage; the state of the world outside the town; or how long it will continue. When the Army rolls through town, we are given more information, however, many questions are still left unanswered. How did this narrative approach influence or affect your reading experience?

2. How well prepared do you think you are for the sort of widespread power outage described in this book?

3. Do you believe the events in the book would have unfolded differently if the Bartons lived in an urban environment? How so?

4. Kevin and Kelly decide to walk Dina home. It is seven miles to Dina's house which makes it a fourteen-mile round trip for Kevin and Kelly. Along the way, the three of them are accosted by several teenage boys on bikes who steal Kevin's backpack as a sort of "toll" for passing through. They make it clear their parents have sent them out in search of food. After what happens, Kevin chooses to take the girls home and keep Dina with them. No more attempts are made to walk Dina home after this incident. Do you think Kevin did the right thing? Do you believe that had it been Monica with them, the

outcome would have been different? During the encounter, Kevin keeps the hunting knife Monica insisted he take hidden, fearing it would make the situation worse. Was this the right decision? What would you have done in this scenario?

5.   Early in the novel, Dina refers to the Bartons as "my beloved second family" and is clearly quite comfortable in their home. How does the power outage impact her relationships with each of the family members? What does she do to try to secure her place? Should she have run off on her own to try to go home? Should she have been more insistent about asking the Bartons to make more attempts to reunite her with her family? What alternatives do you believe were available to Dina?

6.   Once Eli is informally chosen to lead the town through the power outage crisis, he proposes sweeping all vacant homes for supplies that can be distributed throughout the community. Many residents are uncomfortable with this plan. What do you think? Do you think Sobchuk's idea was reasonable? Do you believe that breaking into vacant homes and taking supplies to support the community in a time of crisis is acceptable? Or should the residents of Harpursville have simply managed with what was available to them?

7.   Initially, Kevin is relieved when Sobchuk takes charge of the town and imposes some semblance of order on Harpursville, putting people to work so that all members of the community are provided for in some way. Do you think Sobchuk's plans were beneficial to the town? Or do you believe everyone should have remained responsible for their own houses?

8.   Kevin finds a great deal of food at the home of the Silvas, who are not in residence. As he is taking it to town hall, Monica stops him. She wants to keep the food for their own household whereas Kevin wants to take it to the town hall to be pooled for the benefit of the community. Monica doesn't believe that the food will be used for everyone, but Kevin does. Monica says, "Our priority has to be here,

this house, this family, first and foremost." Kevin wants to stick with Sobchuk's plan for the community at large but ultimately, he gives in to Monica and they split the food he found at the Silva home. Who do you believe is right in this situation? Monica or Kevin? Should the families of Harpursville prioritize their own households over the larger community? Do you believe that Monica is being cynical and Kevin being overly trusting? Or do you believe that Monica is correct: that their household will not benefit from the pooled community resources? Did later events prove either of them right? Which would you prioritize if you were in this situation? Household or community?

9. Eli Sobchuk attempts to make a sickening deal with Kevin concerning Dina. Kevin chooses to keep this information from Monica. For her part, Monica chooses not to divulge to Kevin why, precisely, Sobchuk makes her uncomfortable and angry. Do you think the spouses did the right thing by not communicating these things to one another? Do you think the events of the novel would have transpired differently if one or both of them had been more forthcoming with one another? Why do you think each of them chose not to tell their spouse what happened with Sobchuk?

10. Throughout the novel, Monica is more inclined than Kevin to threaten or use violence in various situations. Ultimately, she prevails, keeping both Dina and Kevin from harm. Do you think Monica is justified? Do you think Kevin was not aggressive enough? Whose approach do you agree with? In the situation in the novel where there is no longer anyone to enforce laws, which approach do you think is most effective?

ACKNOWLEDGMENTS

IF YOU'RE READING THIS I figure it's either because you know me and are curious about what I'll say (and if you're in it) or because you're *like* me: the kind of reader who reads *all* of a book because it's all part of the book. Regardless of who you are, I hope you've enjoyed reading this, and I hope you'll give a nod or a cheer for each person mentioned here, for this book wouldn't be in your hands without them.

The biggest thanks goes to the most important person in my life, my wife, Susan, who has offered her unwavering support and encouragement at every stage of this journey. Once she found out about it, that is. You see, I was a "Secret Writer" for some time, afraid to share my writing with her because of my own fears and doubt, afraid she'd think I was a nutjob or worse, a hack. My fears were groundless. She's my biggest cheerleader, but also an enthusiastic and insightful first reader, and (shameless plug) an excellent website designer. Thank you, love. I am also forever grateful to my daughters, Meg and Kate. They have grown from incredible children into incredible adults, who changed and challenged my world view every day. I guess you can read this now!

I cannot understate the influence Lisa L. Regan and Nancy S. Thompson have had on me as a writer. We became blogging buddies way back in the days when everyone had to have a blog and then we took turns swapping manuscripts back and forth. Their constructive comments have helped this become a better book and me become a better writer. They made me feel like maybe I could actually do this thing. Lisa believes in me enough to offer me a slot in her fledgling Breaking Night Press. I only hope this works out for both of us!

Pen first went to paper on this book on a wintry Sunday afternoon at a meeting of the Cooperstown Writers' Circle at the Smithy. Thank you to Circle members Kristin Brower Walker, Beladee Griffiths, and Angelika Rashkow, who read various parts of this manuscript, as well as Danielle Newell Henrici, Seth Cagle, Ed Garbarino, Dan Gregory, Balasz Selendy and John Vriesma. I miss our Sunday afternoons; we had a lot of fun and I know I learned a lot from all of you. You always wanted to know how this turned out, now you do! Other early readers include Kate Newton, and Mara Rutherford provided great advice on the query letter that landed me my first agent, Carrie Pestritto. Thank you, Carrie, for taking me on and helping me shape this book further—and for giving it a much better name than the one I was working under! Things did not work out in the long term but I enjoyed working with you and learned quite a bit.

In terms of some of the "final sculpting," I can't say enough about the work of editor extraordinaire, David Downing. I thought I had given this manuscript my all. David challenged me to find more, to give more. While reading his editorial letter and copious margin notes I had so many "Ah, hah!" and "Why didn't I see that?" moments. It was an eye-opening experience, and it turned out to be a lot of fun. Thank you, David.

Tajare Taylor and Cindy Doty provided copyediting and proofreading and did a great job. Any errors in this book are the result of me declaring "Authorial Style" or "Intent" or just plain pigheadedness and ignorance and do not reflect on their sharp eyes and knowledge. Randal Schaffer and the team from Findaway Voices did a fantastic job bringing life to the audiobook.

And finally, I guess thanks are also in order to Mother Nature. It was while driving in a hurricane that I found the seed that has grown into this book.

ABOUT THE AUTHOR

Jeff O'Handley has been a science and technical writer as part of his job since the late 1980's, but fiction is his passion. This talented and insightful author provides depth to his characters and explores their stories in a way that can be related to on a very personal level. Jeff can often be found 'butt-deep in a swamp' removing invasive species, leading a nature walk in the woods, or promoting recycling as part of his work for a boots-on-the-ground conservation organization. Jeff is a die-hard Boston Bruins fan who loves the outdoors and has a resistance to tech, but grudgingly admits to the usefulness of smartphones and computers. Jeff grew up on Long Island, NY but has embraced the rural life of central New York, where he lives with his wife and two daughters.

Find out more about Jeff and his work at www.jeffohandley.com